The Original
Bulldog Drummond: 3

The Original
Bulldog Drummond: 3

The Female of the Species

★

Temple Tower

★

The Oriental Mind

'Sapper'
(H. C. McNeile)

The Original Bulldog Drummond: 3
The Female of the Species, Temple Tower & The Oriental Mind
by 'Sapper' (H. C. McNeile)

Leonaur is an imprint of Oakpast Ltd

Material original to this edition and
presentation of text in this form
copyright © 2010 Oakpast Ltd

ISBN: 978-0-85706-030-3 (hardcover)
ISBN: 978-0-85706-029-7 (softcover)

http://www.leonaur.com

Publisher's Notes

The views expressed in this book are not necessarily
those of the publisher.

Contents

The Female of the Species   7
Temple Tower   197
The Oriental Mind   381

The Female of the Species

Chapter 1

In Which I Make Drummond's Acquaintance

Even now, after three months' calm thought, I sometimes feel that I must have dreamed the whole thing. I say to myself that this is England: that I am sitting at lunch in my club hoping that that gluttonous lawyer Seybourne will not take all the best part of the Stilton: that unless I get a move on I shall be very late at Lord's. I say all that just as I always used to say it—particularly about Seybourne. And then it suddenly comes over me—the events of those amazing days.

I don't suppose anybody will believe me: I wouldn't believe the story myself if somebody else told it to me. As I say, I sometimes think it must be a dream. And then I turn back my left sleeve nearly to the elbow and look at a three-inch scar, still red and angry, though it's healing nicely now. And I know it was no dream.

Was it a joke? If so, it was the grimmest and most desperate jest that has ever been cracked, and one wherein the humour was difficult to find. Moreover, it was a joke that would have brought the propounder of it to the gallows—had we but been able to catch her. For there was a woman at the bottom of it, and women can suffer the death penalty in England for murder.

No it was no dream: no jest. It was grim, stern reality played for a stake sufficient to crack the nerve of the principal player on our side had he been possessed of nerves to crack. A game played against time: a game where one mistake might have proved fatal.

Personally I am a peace-loving individual of mild appearance: I like my rubber of bridge at the club and my round of golf: I am not averse to letting people know that I was wounded in the leg in France. Moreover, I fail to see why I should gratuitously add the information that I was in the horse lines at the time, and Heaven alone knows where the bullet came from. I mention these points merely to show that I am just a very ordinary sort of person, and not at all of the type which seems to attract adventure. In fact, until that amazing Whitsun, the only thing in any way out of the ordinary which had ever happened to me was when I, on one occasion, tried to stop a runaway horse. And the annoying thing then was that the driver assured me he had the horse under control. Three weeks had elapsed, and I was still in hospital, so I didn't argue the point.

The truth is that I am not one of those enviable men who are at their best when in a tight corner, or when confronted with the need for immediate action. If, as I read somewhere once, men consist of two classes—those who can stop a dog fight and those who can't—honesty compels me to admit that I belong to the latter. In fact, put in a nutshell, I am a rabbit.

And yet I wouldn't have missed that adventure for anything. I can't flatter myself that I did very much: indeed, there were times when I fear I was merely in the way. For all that, never once did a single member of the extraordinary bunch of men who were playing on our side say any word of reproach or irritation. They never let me feel that I was a passenger even when the strain was greatest.

However, enough of this preamble. I will start at the beginning. For many years it has been my custom to spend a few days round Whitsuntide with some old friends of mine called Tracey. They have a charming house not far from Pangbourne—Elizabethan, and standing in delightful grounds. There is generally a small party—perhaps a dozen in all—and I may say that the keyword to the atmosphere of the house is peace. It may be that I am a little old-fashioned, but the pleasure to be derived from what is sometimes described as an evening's jolly seems to me to be overrated.

As usual I went to them this year, arriving on the Thursday before Whitsuntide. The motor met me at the station, and, having shaken Jenkins, the chauffeur, by the hand, I got in. Somewhat to my surprise, he did not at once drive off: he appeared to be waiting for someone else.

"Captain Drummond, sir," he said to me, "who is stopping at the house, came down to get a paper."

"Captain Drummond, Jenkins," I mused. "Do I know him?"

"I think not, sir," he answered, and it seemed to me that a very faint smile twitched round his lips. In fact, there was a sort of air of expectancy about Jenkins—excitement almost—that was most unusual. Jenkins I have always regarded as a model servant.

"Five to one, my trusty lad. That's better than breaking your false teeth on a plum stone."

I turned at this somewhat astounding utterance and regarded the speaker. He was still immersed in the paper, and for the moment I couldn't see his face.

"Put anything on Moongazer?"

"'Alf a dollar each way, sir," said Jenkins, so far forgetting himself as to suck his teeth in his excitement.

"You'll get your money back. Second at fours. That's not so bad for the old firm."

"Pity about cook, sir," said Jenkins earnestly. "She don't 'old with backing both ways. Moongazer—win only—she was." He consulted a small notebook, apparently to verify the statement.

"That sheds a bit of gloom over the afternoon, Jenkins."

Captain Drummond lowered the paper, and seemed to become aware of my existence for the first time. "Hullo! hullo! hullo!" he exclaimed. "The new arrival. Home, Jenkins—and for God's sake don't break it to the cook till after dinner."

He got into the car, and it struck me that I had seldom seen a larger individual.

"Do you think it is quite wise to encourage the servants to bet?" I inquired a little pointedly as we started.

"Encourage, old lad?" he boomed. "They don't want any encouragement. You have to keep 'em off it with a field gun."

He waved a friendly hand at an extremely pretty girl on the pavement, and I took off my hat.

"Who was that?" he said, turning to me.

"I don't know," I answered. "I thought you waved at her."

"But you took off your hat."

"Because you waved at her."

He pondered deeply.

"I follow your reasoning," he conceded at length. "The false premise, if I may say so, is your conclusion that a friendly gesture of the right hand betokens previous acquaintance. I regret to say I do not know the lady: I probably never shall. Still, we have doubtless planted hope in her virginal bosom."

He relapsed into silence, while I glanced at him out of the corner of my eye. A strange individual, I reflected: one, somehow, I could hardly place at the Traceys'. Now that he was sitting beside me he seemed larger than ever—evidently a very powerful man. Moreover, his face was rather of the type that one associates with pugilism. He certainly had no claims to good looks, and yet there was something very attractive about his expression.

"The Cat and Custard Pot," he remarked suddenly, and Jenkins touched his hat.

"It's nearly an hour," he said, turning to me, "since I lowered any ale. And I don't really know Bill Tracey well enough to reason with him about his. The damned stuff isn't fit to drink."

The car pulled up outside a pub, and my companion descended. I refused his invitation to join him—ale is not a favourite beverage of mine—and remained sitting in the car. The afternoon was warm, the air heavy with the scent of flowers from a neighbouring garden. And in the distance one got a glimpse of the peaceful Thames. Peaceful—the *mot juste*: everything was peaceful in that charming corner of England. And with a feeling of drowsy contentment I lay back and half closed my eyes.

I don't know what drew my attention to them first—the two men who were sitting at one of the little tables under a tree. Perhaps it was that they didn't seem quite to fit in with their surroundings. Foreigners, I decided, and yet it was more from the cut of their clothes than from their actual faces that I came to the conclusion. They weren't talking, but every now and then they stole a glance at the door by which Drummond had gone in. And then one of them turned suddenly and stared long and earnestly at me.

"Who are those two men, Jenkins?" I said, leaning forward.

"Never seen 'em before today, sir," he answered. "But they was 'ere when the Captain stopped for his pint on the way down. Lumme—look there."

I looked, and I must admit that for a moment or too I began to have doubts as to Drummond's sanity. He had evidently come out by some other door, and he was now standing behind the trunk of the tree under which the men were sitting. They were obviously quite unaware of his presence, and if such a thing hadn't been inconceivable I should have said he was deliberately eavesdropping. Anyway, the fact remains that for nearly half a minute he stood there absolutely motionless, whilst I watched the scene in frank amazement. Then one of the two men happened to glance at me, and I suppose my face must have given something away. He nudged his companion, and the two of them rose to their feet just as Drummond stepped out from behind the tree.

"Good afternoon, my pretties," he burbled genially. "Are we staying long in Pangbourne's happy clime—or are we not?"

"Who the devil are you, sir?" said one of the men, speaking perfect English, except for a slightly guttural accent.

Drummond took out his case and selected a cigarette with care.

"Surely," he remarked pleasantly, "your incompetence cannot be as astounding as all that. *Tush! tush!*—;" he lifted a hand like a leg of mutton as the man who had spoken started forward angrily. "I will push your face in later, if necessary, but just at the moment I would like a little chat. And since the appearance of you both is sufficient to shake any man to the foundations, let us not waste time over unnecessary questions."

"Look here," snarled the other angrily, "do you want a rough house, young man?"

"Rough house?" said Drummond mildly. "What is a rough house? Surely you cannot imagine for one minute that I would so far demean myself as to lift my hand in anger against my neighbour."

And then the most extraordinary thing happened. I was watching the strange scene very closely, wondering really whether I ought not to interfere—yet even so I didn't see how it was done. It was so incredibly quick, and as far as I could tell, Drummond never moved.

The two men seemed to close in on him suddenly with the idea obviously of hustling him out of the garden. And they didn't hustle him out of the garden. Far from it. There came a noise as of two hard bodies impinging together, and the gentleman who had not yet spoken recoiled a pace, holding his nose and cursing.

I sympathized with him: it is a singularly painful thing to hit one's nose hard on somebody else's head. In fact, the only completely unmoved person was Drummond himself.

"You shouldn't kiss in public places, laddies," he remarked sadly. "It might make the barmaid jealous. And I do declare his little nosey-posey is beginning to bleed. If you ask the chauffeur nicely he might lend you a spanner to put down your back."

The two men stood there glaring at him, and they were not a prepossessing pair. And then the one who had done the talking drew his friend of the damaged nose on one side, and spoke to him in a low tone. He seemed to be urging some course on the other which the latter was unwilling to accept.

"My God, sir," muttered Jenkins to me, "the bloke with the bleeding nose has got a knife."

"Look out. Captain Drummond," I called out. "That man has a knife."

"I know, old lad," he answered. "He's been playing at pirates. Not going, surely? Why, we've never had our little chat."

But without a backward glance, the two men passed through the gate and started walking rapidly down the road in the direction of the station. And after a time Drummond sauntered over to the car and got in.

"After which breezy little interlude," he murmured, "the powerful car again swung forward, devouring mile after mile."

"Would you very much mind explaining?" I remarked dazedly.

"Explaining?" he said. "What is there to explain?"

"Do you usually go about the country molesting perfect strangers? Who are those men?"

"I dunno," he answered. "But they knew me all right." He was staring at the road ahead and frowning. "It's impossible," he muttered at length. "And yet—"

He relapsed into silence, while I still gazed at him in amazement. "But," I cried, "it's astounding. If I hadn't seen it with my own eyes, I couldn't have believed it possible."

He grinned suddenly. "I suppose it was a bit disconcerting," he answered. "But we're moving in deep waters, laddie—or, rather, I am. And I tell you frankly I don't quite know where I am. Why should those two blokes have followed me down here?"

"Then you have seen them before?"

He shook his head. "No. At least, I saw them when I stopped for some ale on the way down to the station. And they aren't very clever at it."

"Clever at what?"

"The little game of observing without being observed. Apart from their appearance, which made them stick out a mile when seen in an English country inn, the man whose nose suffered slightly positively hissed into the other's ear when he first saw me. In fact, I very nearly dealt with them then and there, only I was afraid I'd be late for your train."

"But why should they follow you?" I persisted. "What's the idea?"

"I wish to God I knew," he answered gravely. "I don't think I'm losing my nerve, or anything of that sort—but I'm absolutely in the dark. Almost as much as you are, in fact. I loathe this waiting game."

"Of course," I remarked resignedly, "I suppose I am not insane. I suppose there is some sense in all this, though at the moment I'm damned if I can see it."

"Presumably you read Kipling?" he said suddenly. I stared at him in silence—speech was beyond me. "A month ago," he continued calmly, "I received this."

From his breast pocket he took a slip of paper, and handed it to me. On it some lines were written in an obviously feminine hand.

'When the Himalayan peasant meets the he-bear in his pride, He shouts to scare the monster, who will often turn aside. But the she-bear, thus accosted, rends the peasant tooth and nail And the point, I warn you, Drummond, is discovered in the tail.'

I handed the paper back to him.

"What do you make of it?" he asked.

"It looks like a stupid joke," I said. "Do you know the writing?" He shook his head.

"No; I don't. So you think it's a joke, do you?"

"My dear sir," I cried, "what else can it be? I confess that at the moment I forget the poem, but the first three lines are obviously Kipling. Equally obviously the fourth is not."

"Precisely," he agreed with a faint smile. "I got as far as that myself. And so it was the fourth line that attracted my attention. It seemed to me that the message, if any, would be found in it. It was."

"What is the fourth line?" I asked curiously.

"'For the female of the species is more deadly than the male'" he answered.

"But, surely," I cried in amazement, "you can't take a thing like that seriously. It's probably a foolish hoax sent you by some girl you cut at a night club."

I laughed a little irritably: for a man to take such a message in earnest struck me as being childish to a degree. A stupid jest played by some silly girl, with a penchant for being mysterious. Undoubtedly, I reflected, the man was a fool. And, anyway, what had it got to do with the two men at the Cat and Custard Pot?

"'The female of the species is more deadly than the male,'" he repeated, as if he hadn't heard my remark. "No hoax about it, old lad; no jest, believe you me. Just a plain and simple warning. And now the game has begun."

For a moment or two I wondered if he was pulling my leg; but he was so deadly serious that I realized that he, at any rate, believed it was genuine. And my feeling of irritation grew. What an ass the man must be! "What game?" I asked sarcastically. "Playing peep-bo behind the trees?"

He let out a sudden roar of laughter.

"You probably think I'm bughouse, don't you?" he cried. "Doesn't matter. The only real tragedy of the day is that the cook didn't back Moongazer each way."

Once again he relapsed into silence as the car rolled through the gates of the Traceys' house.

"Good intelligence work," he said thoughtfully. "We only decided to come down here yesterday. But I wish to the Lord you'd learn to control your face. If you hadn't given a lifelike representation of a gargoyle in pain I might have heard something of interest from those two blighters."

"Confound you!" I spluttered angrily.

"You couldn't help it." He waved a vast hand, and beat me on the back. "I ought to have warned you. Must have looked a bit odd. But it's a pity—"

The car pulled up at the door, and he got out.

"Little Willie wants a drink," he remarked to Tracey, who came out to greet us. "His nervous system has had a shock. By the way, where's Phyllis?"

"Playing tennis," said our host, and Drummond strolled off in the direction of the lawn.

"Look here. Bill," I cried when he was out of earshot, "is that man all there?"

"Hugh Drummond all there?" he laughed. "Very few men in England more so. Why?"

"Well, if he hits me on the back again I shan't be. He's rammed my braces through my spine. But, honestly, I thought the man was mad. He's been talking the most appalling hot air on the way up, and he assaulted two complete strangers at the Cat and Custard Pot."

Bill Tracey stared at me in surprise. "Assaulted two strangers at the Cat and Custard Pot!" he repeated. "What on earth did he do that for?"

"Ask me another," I said irritably. "Two foreign-looking men."

"That's funny," he remarked thoughtfully. "Rodgers—the gardener—was telling me only a few minutes ago that he had seen two foreign-looking men hanging round the house this morning, and had told them to clear off. I wonder if they were the same."

"Probably," I said. "But the fact that they were hanging round here hardly seems an adequate reason for Captain Drummond's behaviour. In fact, my dear Bill—What's the matter?"

He was staring over my shoulder in the direction of the lawn, and I swung round. Drummond was running towards us over the grass, and there was a peculiar strained look on his face. He passed us without a word, and went up the stairs two at a time. We heard a door flung open, and then we saw him leaning out of his bedroom window.

"I don't like it, Algy," he said. "Not one little bit."

A somewhat vacuous-looking individual with an eyeglass had joined us, whom the remark was obviously addressed to.

"Ain't she there, old bean?" he remarked.

"Not a trace," answered the other, disappearing from view.

"Can't understand old Hugh," remarked the newcomer plaintively. "I've never seen him in this condition before. If I didn't think it was impossible I should say he'd got the wind up."

"What's stung you all?" said Bill Tracey. "Isn't Mrs Drummond playing tennis?"

"She was—after lunch," answered Algy. "Then she got a note. Your butler *wallah* brought it out to her on the court. It seemed to upset her a bit, for she stopped at once and came into the house."

"Where," remarked Drummond, who had joined us, "she changed her clothes. It was a note, was it, Algy: not a letter? I mean, did you happen to notice if there was a stamp on the envelope?"

"As a matter of fact, old lad, I particularly noticed there was not. I was sitting next her when she took it."

The butler passed us at that moment, carrying the tea things.

"Parker," said Drummond quietly, "you gave a note to Mrs Drummond this afternoon, I understand."

"I did, sir," answered the butler.

"Did you take it yourself at the front door?"

"I did, sir."

"Who delivered it?"

"A man, sir, who I did not know. A stranger to the neighbourhood, I gathered."

"Why?" snapped Drummond.

"Because, sir, he asked me the nearest way to the station."

"Thank you, Parker," said Drummond quietly. "Algy, it's quicker than I expected. Hullo! Jenkins, do you want me?"

The chauffeur touched his cap.

"Well, sir, you know you asked me to adjust your carburettor for you. I was just wondering if you could tell me when the car will be back."

"Be back?" said Drummond. "What do you mean?"

"Why, sir, the Bentley ain't in the garage. I thought as 'ow Mrs Drummond had probably taken it out."

And if anything had been needed to confirm my opinion that this vast individual was a little peculiar, I got it then. He lifted his two enormous fists above his head and shook them at the sky. I could see the great muscles rippling under his sleeves, and instinctively I recoiled a step.

The man looked positively dangerous.

"Thrice and unutterably damned fool that I am," he muttered. "But how could I tell it would come so soon?"

"My dear fellow," said Bill Tracey, gazing at him apprehensively, "surely there is nothing to get excited about. Mrs Drummond is a very good driver."

"Driver be jiggered," cried Drummond. "If it was only a question of driving I wouldn't mind. I'm afraid they've got her. For the Lord's sake, give me a pint of ale. Yours is pretty bad—but it's better than nothing."

And then he suddenly turned on me of all people.

"If only you could have kept your face in its place, little man, I might have heard something. Still, it can't be helped. God made you like it."

"Really," I protested angrily, but this extraordinary individual had gone indoors again. "The man is positively insulting."

"Nothing to what he can be if he dislikes you," said the being called Algy placidly. "He'll be all right after he's had his beer."

Chapter 2
In Which I Find a Deserted Motor Car

Now, in view of the fact that this is my first essay in literature, I realize that many of my relatives may feel it their bounden duty to buy the result. Several, I know, will borrow a copy from one another, or else will endeavour to touch me for one of the six free copies which, I am given to understand, the author receives on publication. But most of them, in one way or another, will read it. And I am particularly anxious, bearing in mind the really astounding situations in which I found myself later, that no misconception should exist in their minds as to my mood at the beginning.

Particularly Uncle Percy—the Dean of Wolverhampton. He is, I am glad to say, a man of advanced years and considerable wealth. He is also unmarried, a fact which has never occasioned me great surprise. But few women exist who would be capable of dealing with his intellect or digestion, and so far he does not seem to have met one of them. For his benefit, then, and that of others who know me personally, I may state that when I saw Captain Drummond engaged in the operation, as he called it, of 'golluping his beer with zest', I was extremely angry. He, on the contrary, seemed to have recovered his spirits. No longer did he shake his fists in the air; on the contrary, a most depressing noise issued from his mouth as he put down the empty tankard on the table. He appeared to be singing, and, incredible though it may seem, to derive some pleasure from the operation. The words of his dirge seemed to imply that the more we were together the merrier we would be—a statement to which I took the gravest exception.

I was to learn afterwards the amazing way in which this amazing individual could throw off a serious mood and become positively hilarious. For instance—on this occasion—having delivered himself of this deplorable sentiment, he advanced towards me. Fearing another blow on the back, I retreated rapidly, but he no longer meditated assault. He desired apparently to examine my cuff-links, a thing which did not strike me as being in the best of taste.

"You approve, I trust?" I said sarcastically.

He shook his head sadly.

"I feared as much," he remarked. "Or have you left 'em at home?" he added hopefully.

I turned to Bill Tracey.

"Have you turned this place into a private lunatic asylum?" I demanded.

And all Bill did was to shout with laughter. "Cheer up, Joe," he said. "You'll learn our little ways soon."

"Doubtless," I remarked stiffly. "In the meantime I think I'll go and have some tea."

I crossed the lawn to find several people I knew assembled in the summerhouse. And, having paid my respects to my hostess, and been introduced to two or three strangers, I sat down with a feeling of relief beside Tomkinson, a dear old friend of mine.

"Really," I said to him under cover of the general conversation, "there seem to be some very extraordinary people in this party. Who and what is that enormous man who calls himself Drummond?"

He laughed, and lit a cigarette. "He does strike one as a bit odd at first, doesn't he? But as a matter of fact, your adjective was right. He is an extraordinary man. He did some feats of strength for us last night that wouldn't have disgraced a professional strong man."

"He nearly smashed my spine," I said grimly, "giving it a playful tap."

"He is not communicative about himself," went on Tomkinson. "And what little I know about him I have learned from that fellow with the eyeglass—Algy Longworth—who incidentally regards him as only one degree lower than the Almighty. He has got a very charming wife."

He glanced round the party.

"You won't see her here," I remarked. "She has apparently taken his Bentley and gone out in it alone. Having discovered this fact, he first of all announces 'They've got her!' in blood-curdling tones, and then proceeds to lower inordinate quantities of ale. And his behaviour coming up from the station—"

"What's that you said?"

A man whose face was vaguely familiar turned and stared at me.

"Why, surely you're Mr Darrell!" I cried. "You play for Middlesex?"

He nodded.

"I do—sometimes. But what's that you were saying about Drummond having said 'They've got her?'"

"Just that—and nothing more," I answered. "As I was telling Tomkinson, Mrs Drummond has apparently gone out in his Bentley alone, and when he heard of it he said, 'They've got her.' But who 'they' are I can't tell you."

"Good God!" His face had suddenly become grave. "There must be a mistake. And yet Hugh doesn't make mistakes."

He made the last remark under his breath.

"It all seems a little hard to follow," I murmured with mild sarcasm. But he paid no attention: he had glanced up quickly, and was staring over my shoulder.

"What's this I hear about Phyllis, old boy?" he said.

"The Lord knows, Peter." Drummond was standing there with a queer look on his face. "She got a note delivered here by a stranger. It came while I was at the station. And Algy said it seemed to upset her. Anyway, she went indoors and changed, and then went out alone in the Bentley."

A silence had fallen on the party which was broken by our hostess. "But why should that worry you. Captain Drummond? Your wife often drives, she tells me."

"She knows no one in this neighbourhood. Mrs Tracey, except your good selves," answered Drummond quietly. "So who could have sent a note here to be delivered by hand?"

"Well, evidently somebody did," I remarked. "And when Mrs Drummond returns you'll find out who it was."

I spoke somewhat coldly: the man was becoming a bore.

"If she ever does return," he answered.

I regret to state that I laughed.

"My dear sir," I cried, "don't be absurd. You surely can't believe, or expect us to believe, that some evilly-disposed persons are abducting your wife in broad daylight and in the middle of England?"

But he still stood there with that queer look on his face. "Peter," he said, "I want to have a bit of a talk with you."

Darrell rose instantly, and the two of them strolled away together.

"Really," I remarked irritably, when they were out of earshot, "the thing is perfectly preposterous. Is he doing it as a joke, or what?" Algy Longworth had joined them, and the three of them were standing in the middle of the lawn talking earnestly.

"I must say it does all seem very funny," agreed our hostess. "And yet Captain Drummond isn't the sort of man to make stupid jokes of that sort."

"You mean," I said incredulously, "that he really believes that someone may be abducting his wife? My dear Mary, don't be so ridiculous. Why should anyone abduct his wife?"

"He's led a very strange life since the War," she answered. "I confess I don't know much about it myself—neither he nor his friends are very communicative. But I know he got mixed up with a gang of criminals."

"I am not surprised," I murmured under my breath.

"I'm not very clear about what happened," went on Mary Tracey. "But finally Captain Drummond was responsible somehow or other for the death of the leader of the gang. And a woman, who had been this man's mistress, was left behind."

I stared at her: absurd, of course, but that bit of doggerel at the end of Kipling's verse came back to me. And then common-sense reasserted itself. This was England, not a country where secret societies nourished and strange vendettas took place. The whole thing was a mere coincidence. What connection could there possibly be between the two men at the Cat and Custard Pot and the fact that Mrs Drummond had gone out alone in a motor car?

"It seems," Mary Tracey was speaking again, "from what Bill tells me, that this woman vowed vengeance on Captain Drummond. I know it sounds very fantastic, and I expect we shall all laugh about it when Phyllis gets back. And yet—" she hesitated for a moment. "Oh! I don't want to be silly, but I do wish she'd come back soon."

"But, Mrs Tracey," said someone reassuringly, "there can be no danger. What could happen to her?"

"I quite agree," I remarked. "If on every occasion a woman went out alone in a motor car her friends and relations panicked about her being abducted, life would become a hideous affair."

And then by tacit consent the subject dropped, and we dispersed about our lawful occasions. I didn't see Drummond, but Darrell and Longworth were practising putting on the other side of the lawn. I strolled over and joined them.

"Your large friend," I laughed, "seems to have put the wind up most of the ladies in the party fairly successfully."

But they neither of them seemed to regard it as a subject for mirth.

"Let us hope it will end at that," said Darrell gravely. "I confess that I have rarely been so uneasy in my life."

And that, mark you, from a man who played for Middlesex! Really, I reflected, the thing was ceasing to be funny. And I was just getting a suitable remark ready, when Longworth suddenly straightened up and stared across the lawn. Bill Tracey was coming towards us, and at his side was a police sergeant. And Bill Tracey's face was serious.

"Where's Drummond?" he called out.

"He said he was going to stroll down to the river," said Darrell.

He cupped his mouth with his hands and let out a shout that startled the rooks for miles around. And very faintly from the distance came an answering cry.

"What's happened?" he said curtly.

"I don't know," answered Bill uneasily. "Quite possibly it's capable of some simple explanation. Apparently the Bentley has been found empty. However, we'd better wait till Drummond comes, and then the sergeant can tell his story."

I noticed Darrell glance significantly at Longworth; then he calmly resumed the study of a long putt. With a bang the ball went into the hole, and he straightened himself up.

"My game, Algy. So Hugh was right: I was afraid of it. Here he comes."

We watched him breasting the hill that led down to the river, running with the long, easy stride of the born athlete. And it's curious how little things strike one at times. I remember noticing as he came up that his breathing was as normal as my own, though he must have run the best part of a quarter of a mile.

"What's up?" he said curtly, his eyes fixed on the sergeant.

"Are you Captain Drummond?" remarked the officer, producing a notebook.

"I am."

"Of 5a, Upper Brook Street?" He was reading these details from the book in his hand.

Drummond nodded. "Yes."

"You have a red Bentley car numbered ZZ 103?"

"I have," said Drummond.

With maddening deliberation the worthy sergeant replaced his notebook in his breast pocket. And another curious little thing struck me: though Drummond must have been on edge with suspense, no sign of impatience showed in his face.

"Have you been out in that car today, sir?"

"I have not," said Drummond. "But my wife has."

"Was she alone, sir?"

"To the best of my belief she was," answered Drummond. "She left here when I was down at the station in Mr Tracey's car meeting this gentleman."

The sergeant nodded his head portentously. "Well, sir, I have to report to you that your car has been found empty standing by the side of the road not far from the village of Tidmarsh."

"How did you know I was here?" said Drummond quietly.

"The constable who found the car, sir, saw your name and address printed on a plate on the instrument board. So he went to the nearest telephone and rang up your house in London. And your servant told him you was stopping down here. So he rang up at the station in Pangbourne."

"But why take all the trouble?" said Drummond even more quietly. "Surely there's nothing very extraordinary about an empty car beside the road?"

"No, sir," agreed the sergeant. "There ain't. That's true. But the constable further reported"—his voice was grave—"that he didn't like the look of the car. He said it struck him that there had been some sort of struggle."

"I see," said Drummond. Quite calmly he turned to Darrell.

"Peter—your Sunbeam, and hump yourself. Algy—ring up Ted and Toby, and tell 'em they're wanted. Put up at the hotel. Sergeant—you come with me. Tracey, ring up the railway station and find out if two foreign-looking men have been seen there this afternoon. If so, did they take tickets, and for what destination? Let's move."

And we moved. Gone in a flash was the large and apparently brainless ass; in his place was a man accustomed to lead, and accustomed to instant obedience. Heaven knows why I got into the Sunbeam: presumably because I was the only person who had received no definite instructions. And Drummond evinced no surprise when he found me sitting beside him in the back seat. The sergeant, a little dazed at such rapidity of action, was in front with Darrell, and except for him none of us even had a hat.

"Tell us the way. Sergeant," said Drummond, as we swung through the gates. "And let her out, Peter."

And Peter let her out. The worthy policeman gasped feebly once or twice concerning speed limits, but no one took the faintest notice, so that after a time he resigned himself to the inevitable and concentrated on holding on his hat. And I, having no hat to hold on, concentrated on the man beside me.

He seemed almost unaware of my existence. He sat there, motionless save for the swaying of the car, staring in front of him. His face was set and grave, and every now and then he shook his head as if he had arrived at an unpleasant conclusion in his train of thought.

My own thoughts were frankly incoherent. Somehow or other I still couldn't believe that the matter was serious—certainly not as serious as Drummond seemed to think. And yet my former scepticism was shaken, I confess. If what the sergeant said was right: if there were signs of a struggle in the car, it was undoubtedly sufficiently serious to make it very unpleasant. But I still refused to believe that the whole thing was not capable of some simple solution. A tramp, perhaps, seeing that an approaching car contained a woman alone had stopped it by the simple expedient of standing in the middle of the road. Then he had attacked Mrs Drummond with the idea of getting her money.

Unpleasant, as I say—very unpleasant. But quite ordinary. A very different matter to all this absurd twaddle about gangs of criminals and dead men's mistresses. Moreover, I reflected, with a certain amount of satisfaction, there was another thing that proved my theory. On Drummond's own showing he attached considerable importance to the two foreign-looking men at the Cat and Custard Pot. Now it was utterly impossible that they could have had anything to do with it since they were sitting there in the garden at the very time that Mrs Drummond must have left Tracey's house in the car. Which completely knocked Drummond's conclusion on the head. The whole thing was simply a coincidence, and I said as much to the man beside me. He listened in silence.

"Ever been ratting?" he asked when I'd finished.

Once more did I stare at this extraordinary individual in amazement. What on earth had that got to do with it?

"Well—have you?" he repeated when I didn't answer.

"In the days of my youth I believe I did," I answered. "Though the exact bearing of a boyish pastime on the point at issue is a little obscure."

"Then it oughtn't to be," he remarked curtly. "It's only obscure because your grey matter is torpid. When a party of you go ratting, you put a bloke at every hole you know of before you start to bolt your rats."

He relapsed again into silence, and so did I. The confounded fellow seemed to have an answer for everything. And then just ahead of us we saw the deserted car.

A constable was standing beside it, and a group of four or five children were looking on curiously. It stood some three or four feet from the left-hand side of the road, so that there was only just room for another car to pass. And the road itself at this point ran through a small wood—barely more than a copse.

"You've moved nothing. Constable?" said the sergeant.

"Just as I found it. Sergeant."

We crowded round the car and looked inside. It was an ordinary open touring model, and it was obvious at once that there were signs which indicated a struggle. The rug, for instance, instead of being folded, was half over the front seat and half in the back of the car. A lady's handkerchief, crumpled up, was lying just behind the steering-wheel, and one of the covers which was fastened to the upholstery by means of press studs, was partially wrenched off. It was the cover for of the side doors, and underneath it was a pocket for maps and papers.

"This is your car, sir?" asked the sergeant formally.

"It is," said Drummond, and once more we fell silent.

There was something sinister about that deserted car. One felt an insane longing that the rug could speak, that a thrush singing in the drowsy heat on a tree dose by could tell us what had happened. Its head, of course, was pointed away from Pangbourne, and suddenly Drummond gave an exclamation. He was looking at the road some fifteen yards in front of the bonnet.

At first I noticed nothing, though my sight is as good as most men's. And it wasn't until I got close to the place that I could see what had attracted his attention. Covered with dust was a pool of black lubricating oil—and covered so well that only the sharpest eye would have detected it.

"That accounts for one thing, anyway," said Drummond quietly.

"What is that, sir?" remarked the sergeant, with considerable respect in his voice. I was evidently not the only one who had been impressed with the keenness of Drummond's sight.

"I know my wife's driving better than anybody else," he answered, "and, under normal circumstances, if she pulled up, she would instinctively get into the side of the road. So the first question I asked myself was why she had stopped with the car where it is. She was either following another car which pulled up in front of her, or she came round the corner and found it stationary in the middle of the road, not leaving her room to pass. And the owners of the car that did not leave her room to pass wanted to conceal the fact that they had been here, if possible. So, finding they had leaked oil, they tried to cover it up. God! if only the Bentley could talk."

It was over in a moment—that sudden, natural spasm of feeling, and he was the same cool, imperturbable man again. And I felt my admiration for him growing. Criminal gangs or no criminal gangs, it's a damnable thing to stand on the spot where an hour or two earlier your wife has been the victim of some dastardly outrage, and feel utterly impotent to do anything.

"Do you think it's possible to track that car?" said Darrell. We walked along the road for a considerable distance, but it was soon obvious that the idea was impossible. Far too much traffic had been along previously, and since there had been no rain the chance of following some distinctive tyre marking had gone. "Hopeless," said Drummond heavily. "Absolutely hopeless. Hullo! one of those kids has found something."

They were running towards us in a body led by a little boy who was waving some object in his hand.

"Found this, governor, in the grass beside the road," he piped out.

"My God!" said Drummond, staring at it with dilated eyes.

For "this" was a large spanner, and one end was stained a dull red. Moreover, the red was still damp, and when he touched it, it came off on his finger. Blood. And the question which rose in all of our minds, and the question which none of us dared to answer was—Whose? I say, none of us dared to answer it out loud. I think we all of us had answered it to ourselves.

"You don't recognize the spanner, I suppose, sir?" said the sergeant. "Is it one from your car or not?"

"I do recognize it," answered Drummond. "It's the regular set spanner I keep in the pocket with the maps and papers and not in the toolbox, because it fits the nut of the petrol tank."

"The pocket that was wrenched open," I put in, and he nodded.

"Show us just where you found it, nipper," said the sergeant, and we all trooped back to the Bentley.

"Here, sir," said the urchin. "Behind that there stone." He was pointing to a place just about level with the bonnet, and it required no keenness of vision such as had been necessary to spot the dust-covered pool of oil to see the next clue. From the stone where the spanner had been found to a point in the grass opposite where the other car must have stood, there stretched a continuous trail of ominous red spots. Some were big, and some were small, but the line was unbroken. Blood once again—and once again the same unspoken question.

"Well, sir," said the sergeant gravely, "it's obvious that there has been foul play. I think the best thing I can do is to get back to the station and phone Scotland Yard. We want a lookout kept all over the country for a motorcar containing a wounded lady."

Drummond gave a short laugh.

"Don't be too sure of that, sergeant," he remarked. "It was only my wife who knew where that spanner was kept. I should be more inclined, if I were you, to keep a lookout for a motor containing a wounded man. Though I tell you candidly if this thing is what I think it is—or, rather, what I know it is—you're wasting your time."

And not another word would he say.

Chapter 3

In Which I Get it in the Neck

It was hopeless, of course, as I think we all realized from the beginning. But it was impossible to sit still and do nothing. And for the rest of that afternoon, until long past the time for dinner, we scoured the country. Drummond drove the Bentley alone—he was in no mood for talking—and I went with Darrell.

It was in the course of that wearisome and fruitless search that I began to understand things a little more clearly. My companion amplified Mary Tracey's vague remarks, until I began to ask myself if I was dreaming. That this affair was the work of no ordinary person was obvious, but for a long time I believed that he must be exaggerating. Some of the things he told me sounded too incredible.

They concerned a man called Carl Peterson, who, it appeared, had been the head of the gang our hostess had alluded to. This man was none other than Wilmot, of airship fame. I, naturally, remembered the name perfectly—just as I remembered the destruction of his airship, mercifully after all the passengers had disembarked. Wilmot himself was killed—burned to death, as were the rest of the crew.

And here was Darrell, in the most calm and matter-of-fact way, stating something completely different.

"I was one of the passengers that night," he said. "I know. Wilmot—or, rather Peterson, as we prefer to call him—was not burned to death. He was killed by Drummond."

"Killed!" I gasped. "Good God! what for?"

Darrell smiled grimly.

"It was long overdue," he answered. "But that was the first opportunity there had been of actually doing it."

"And this woman knows that he killed him?" I said.

"No—and yes," he said. "She was not there at the time, but four days later she met Drummond by the wreckage of the airship. And she told him the exact hour when Peterson had died. I don't know how to account for it. Some form of telepathy, I suppose. She also told him that they would meet again. And this is the beginning of the meeting."

"So that verse was sent by her, was it?"

He nodded.

"But it seems rather an extraordinary thing to do," I persisted. "Why go out of your way to warn a person?"

"She is rather an extraordinary woman," he answered. "She is also a most terribly dangerous one. Like all women who have a kink, they are more extreme than men. And I don't mind telling you, Dixon, that I'm positively sick with anxiety over this show. An eye for an eye, and a tooth for a tooth—you know the old tag? I'm afraid it's going to be a life for a life."

"You mean they may kill Mrs Drummond?" I cried in horror.

"Just that and nothing more," he said gravely. "Drummond killed her lover: she will kill his wife. She would have no more scruples over so doing than you would have over treading on a wasp. The only thing is—does it suit her book? Is she going to try and get Drummond into her power by using his wife as a lever? And only time will tell us that."

"What sort of a woman is she?" I said curiously.

"To look at she is tall, dark, and very *soignee*. She's handsome rather than pretty, and I should think has some Southern blood in her." He smiled slightly. "But don't run away with the impression that she'd be likely to look like that if you met her. Far more probably would she be a wizened-up crone covered with spectacles, or a portly dame with creaking corsets. So much for her appearance. Her character is a thing to stand aghast at. She has the criminal instinct developed to its highest degree: she is absolutely without mercy: she is singularly able. How much, of course, was her and how much Carl Peterson in the old days is a thing I don't know. But even if it was him principally, to start with, she must have profited considerably by seeing him at work. And a final point which is just as important if not more so than those I've already given, she must be a very wealthy woman. Peterson's life was not a wasted one as far as other people's money was concerned."

"It sounds a tough proposition," I murmured.

"It is," he agreed gravely. "A damned tough proposition. In fact, Dixon, there is only one ray of sunshine that I can see in the whole business. To do them both justice, in the past they have never been crude in their methods. In their own peculiar way they had a sense of art. If that sense of art is stronger now with her than her primitive desire for revenge, there's hope."

"I don't quite follow," I said.

"She will play the fish—the fish being us. To kill Mrs Drummond offhand would be crude."

"I fail to see much comfort," I remarked, "in being played if the result is going to be the same. It's only prolonging the agony."

"Quite so," he said quietly, "but is the result going to be the same?"

A peculiar smile flickered for a moment round his lip.

"You probably think I'm talking rot," he went on. "At least, that I'm exaggerating grossly."

"Well," I admitted, "it's all a little hard to follow."

"Naturally. You've never struck any of these people before. We have. We met them quite by accident at first, and since then we've almost become old friends. We know their ways: they know ours. Sometimes we've fought with the police on our side: sometimes we've fought a lone hand. And up to date on balance we have won hands down. That is why I cannot help feeling—at any rate hoping—that this woman would not regard the slate as being dean if she merely killed Mrs Drummond. It has been our wits against theirs up till now. She wants much fuller revenge than such a crude action as that would afford her."

"I am glad you feel optimistic over the prospect," I murmured. *"Chacun a son gout."*

"Of course," he went on thoughtfully, "I may be wrong. If so—it's hopeless from the start. They've got Drummond's wife: if they want to they can kill her right away. But somehow or other—"

He broke off, staring at the road ahead. The light was of that half-and-half description when headlamps are useless and driving is most difficult.

"Anyway, I'm afraid this is a pretty hopeless quest," I said. "We don't even know what sort of a car we are looking for—"

He touched the accelerator with his foot.

"What's that dark thing there beside the road?" he said. "It's a car right enough, and you never can tell."

We drew up beside it, and the first thing I noticed was a pool of lubricating oil in the road, under the back axle. Only a coincidence, of course, I reflected, but I felt a sudden tingle of excitement. Could it possibly be the car we were looking for?

We got out and walked up to it. The car was empty—the blinds of the back windows drawn down.

"We'd better be careful," I said a little nervously, "the owner may be in the field."

"On the other hand, he may not," said Darrell coolly, and opened the door.

It was an ordinary standard limousine, and at first sight there seemed nothing out of the normal to be seen. There was no sign of disorder, as there had been in the Bentley: the rug on the seat was carefully folded. And it was almost mechanically that I opened one of the back doors, to stand nearly frozen with horror at what I saw. The covering of the front bucket seat beside the driver's was saturated with blood from the top right down to the floorboards.

"Good God!" I muttered, "look here."

Darrell came and looked over my shoulder, and I heard him catch his breath sharply.

"This evidently," he remarked, "is the car we are after. There's a torch in the pocket of the Sunbeam: get it, like a good fellow."

By its light we examined the stain more closely. The average width was about six inches, though it narrowed off towards the bottom. But one very peculiar point about it was that near the top were a number of strange loops and smears, stretching away out of the main stream. They were the sort of smears that a child might make who had dipped its fingers in the blood, and had then started to draw patterns.

"The person who sat in this seat must have bled like a pig," said Darrell gravely. "From a wound in the head obviously."

Whose head? Who was it who had sat in the seat? Once again the same ghastly question, unasked and unanswered, save in our own minds. But I remember that to me all his hopes and ideas about crudeness and art suddenly became rather pitiful. To me there seemed no doubt who it was who had sat in that seat. And I felt thankful that Drummond wasn't there with us.

One could picture the poor girl sitting there, probably unconscious, with the blood welling out from some terrible wound in her head, while the devil beside her drove remorselessly on. A hideous thought, but what alternative was there?

"What do you make of it, Dixon?"

Darrell's voice cut into my thoughts.

"I'm afraid it's pretty obvious," I said. "And I'm afraid it rather disposes of your hopes as to crudity and art. This is the crudest and most brutal attack on a woman, that's all."

"You think so?" he said thoughtfully, "And yet it's all a little difficult to understand. Why did they stop here? What has become of them?"

"It's a road without much traffic," I answered. "Probably they changed into another car to put people still more off the scent. Don't forget that if they had garaged this car anywhere for the night they would have had some pretty awkward questions to answer."

"That's true," he agreed. "And yet it presupposes that the thing had been arranged beforehand."

"It probably was," I pointed out. "They were anyway going to change cars, and the fact that the poor girl was so terribly wounded did not make them alter their plans."

"But why mess up two cars?" he argued. "That's what I can't get at."

He once more switched the torch on to the stained cover.

"You know," he said, "those loops and smears puzzle me. What on earth can have caused them? What possible agency can have made that stream of blood divert itself like that? Hold the torch a moment, will you? I'm going to copy them into a notebook."

"My dear fellow," I remarked, "what on earth is the use? Do it if you like, but I should say that the best thing we can do is to make tracks for the nearest police station and give them the number of this car. We want to find the owner."

"It won't take a moment," he said, "and then we'll push off. There— is that about right?"

He handed me his rough sketch: a copy of it is before me, as I write.

[The book here includes a picture of a scrawled message]

"Yes," I remarked, "that's pretty well how it looks. But I'm afraid it's not going to help us much."

"You never can tell," he answered. "Those marks didn't come there accidentally—that I swear. It's a message of sorts: I'm certain of it."

"It may be a message, but it's absolute gibberish," I retorted. "Now don't you think we'd better push on to a police station. I've got the number of this car—ZW 3214."

He looked at me thoughtfully.

"Can you drive my Sunbeam?" he said.

"I blush to admit it," I answered, "but I'm one of those extraordinary people who have never driven a car in my life."

"That's a pity," he remarked. "Because I was going to propose that I stopped here while you went. I think one of us ought to remain in case anything happens."

"Good God!" I said, "hasn't enough happened already? However, I don't mind staying. Only get a move on: I'm beginning to feel like dinner."

"Stout fellow," he cried. "I'll be as quick as I possibly can."

He got into his car, and in half a minute was out of sight.

Now as I have already explained I am not one of those fortunate individuals to whom battle, murder, and sudden death come as the zest of life. And honesty compels me to admit that at no period of my career have I more bitterly regretted not having had lessons in driving. Moreover, I am essentially a town man: the country always seems to me to be so full of strange noises. Especially at night—and it was dark by now.

I lit a cigarette—quite unaware of the horror with which Drummond would have viewed such a proceeding. To see and not be seen, to hear and not be heard, was a dictum of his I was to learn later.

All sorts of weird whispering sounds came to my ears as I stood there beside the car. And once I gave a terrific start as a shrill scream came from the field close by.

"An animal," I reflected angrily. "A rabbit caught by a stoat. Don't be such a fool."

I began pacing up and down the middle of the road, conscious of an absurd desire for someone to speak to, even if it was only an inebriated farm labourer. And then by way of forcing discipline on my mind, I made myself go over the whole amazing business from the beginning.

What was the letter that had made Mrs Drummond leave the house? Where did the two men at the Cat and Custard Pot come in? Why had this car stopped here and what had happened after? And finally those strange smears. Were they indeed some message, and if so who had written it? Was it that poor girl trying to write some final communication as she felt her life slipping away from her?

My thoughts turned to Drummond, and I felt most bitterly sorry for my earlier sarcasm. Still, there had been some excuse: I defy any ordinary person to have viewed his behaviour without feeling some doubts as to his sanity. The fact remained, however, that I owed him the most abject apology. Not that my apology would be much use to the poor devil in exchange for his wife.

I ground my cigarette out with my heel, and stared down the road. Surely it was about time for Darrell to get back. And as I stood there leaning against the bonnet, a bird got up with a sharp cry from a point in the hedge some hundred yards away. It was the cry of sudden alarm from which a poacher might have read much, but I read nothing.

And then a twig cracked: I heard it distinctly and stiffened. Another—and yet another, whilst I stood there motionless peering into the darkness. Did my eyes deceive me, or was there something dark moving cautiously along the grass beside the road, in the shadow of the hedge? I recalled times in France when strange things took shape in No-Man's-Land: when men became as bushes and bushes as men. And putting my hand to my forehead I found it was wet with sweat.

I listened again: all was silent. The stealthy mover, if there was a mover, was moving no more. My imagination probably, and with a shaking hand I extracted my cigarette case. Damn it! what was there to be frightened at?

"Lawks sakes—look at this 'ere!"

The voice came from the hedge not ten yards away, and in my fright I dropped my case in the road. Then with an effort I pulled myself together: to be frightened at my time of life by a mere yokel was not good for one's pride.

"Look 'e 'ere, mister."

"Where are you?" I said. "I can't see you."

The fellow gave a cackling laugh which made me think he was not quite right in his head. And then came another remark which caused me to start forward in horror.

"A dead 'un."

"Where?" I cried, moving towards him slowly. My mouth felt suddenly dry. It required all my will power to force myself to go. I knew what I was going to see: I knew that there in the darkness just ahead of me I would find some half-witted yokel staring inquisitively at the body of the unfortunate girl. There would be a terrible wound in her head, and at each step I took my reluctance increased. I loathed the thought of having definite proof: up to date there had been a doubt, however shadowy.

"Where?" I said thickly, once again, and then I saw him just in front. His back was towards me, and he was bending over something that lay in the ditch close to the hedge. He was chuckling to himself in an idiotic way, and I heard a voice croak at him: "Shut up!" It was my own.

I reached his side, and bent over, too. And for a moment or two I stood there staring, hardly able to believe my eyes. True, a body was there, lying in that peculiar twisted position which tells its own tale. True, there was a terrible wound in the head, clearly visible even in the darkness. But it was not a woman; it was a man. And the feeling of relief was stupendous.

I turned to the yokel foolishly: turned and froze into immobility. The idiotic chuckling had ceased, and the face that was thrust near mine wore a sarcastic smile.

"Too easy," he remarked.

A pair of hands fastened on my throat, and I began to struggle desperately. Dimly I realized that it was a trap: that the man had been acting a part so as to draw me into an advantageous position in which to attack me. And then all other thoughts were blotted out by the appalling knowledge that as far as strength went I was a child in his hands. There was a roaring in my ears, a ghastly tightness in my throat. And I remember that my last coherent thought before I became unconscious was that if Drummond had been in my place the result would have been very different.

It was fitting, therefore, that the first man I should see when I opened my eyes was Drummond himself. For a moment or two I couldn't remember what had happened, and I stared foolishly around. I was lying on the grass beside the road, and my head and coat were sopping wet. Drummond with Darrell and another man were standing close to me in the light of the headlamps of a car.

"Hullo!" I said feebly.

They swung round.

"Hullo! little man," said Drummond. "You gave us a nasty shock. What fun and laughter have you been engaged in?"

"Where's the dead man?" I cried, sitting up.

They all stared at me.

"What's that?" said Drummond slowly. "A dead man, you say?"

I struggled to my feet, and stood swaying dizzily.

"Steady, old man," said Drummond. "Easy does it."

"There was a dead man," I repeated, and then I stared round. "Where's the other car?"

"Precisely," agreed Drummond. "Where is it? It wasn't here when we arrived."

"Not here," I repeated stupidly, "I don't understand. What's happened?"

"That's easily told," said Drummond. "By mere chance I ran into Peter at the police station, and when I heard what you'd found I came along with him and this officer. We must have gone half a mile beyond here before he knew we'd gone too far. So we turned and came back. And the pool of oil told us where the car had been. Peter knew you couldn't drive, so we thought you must have been abducted in the car. And then quite by chance the officer found you in the ditch. You looked like a goner at first, but we sluiced you with cold water, and you'll be as fit as a trivet in a minute or two. When you do let's hear what happened to you."

"I'm all right now," I said. "A bit dizzy, that's all. Let me sit down in the car for a little."

It was quite true. My head was quite clear, and, except for a most infernally stiff neck, I felt none the worse for my experience. And I told them exactly what had taken place. They listened in silence, and it was only when I hesitated a little over saying who it was I had expected to find in the ditch that Drummond spoke.

"I understand," he said curtly. "Go on."

I finished my story, and then he spoke again.

"If any confirmation is needed," he remarked, "the ditch should supply it. Where was the body lying?"

I got out of the car and led them to the spot. As he had said, the ditch did supply it. A great pool of blood showed up red and sinister in the light of Darrell's torch, but of the body of the man whose blood it was there was no trace.

"So what happened," said Drummond thoughtfully, "is fairly easy to spot. But the reason for it is a little more obscure. The gentleman who caressed your windpipe had evidently been sent back to retrieve car and corpse. Finding you here he gave you the necessary medicine. Then he removed corpse in car. But if that was the great idea, why were car and corpse left here in the first place?"

"Would you recognize the man who attacked you, sir?" said the police officer, speaking for the first time.

"I think I'd recognise him," I said, "but I couldn't give you a description of him that would be the slightest help."

"Well, there doesn't seem much use our standing here any more," remarked Drummond at length, and his voice was weary. "We know the number of the car, so the owner can be traced. But I shall be very much surprised if we find that helps us much."

He sighed, and lit a cigarette. "Come on, Peter, we'd better be getting back. My stomach is flapping against my backbone for want of food, and we can't do any more good here."

And I, for one, agreed with him fervently.

CHAPTER 4

In Which We Get the Semblance of a Clue

Looking back on it now after the lapse of time, I find it hard to recall my exact state of mind that night. I remember that amongst certain members of the house party I found myself in the position of a popular hero. To have been assaulted and left for dead conferred an air of distinction on me which I found rather grateful and comforting. The tacit assumption seemed to be that only abnormal strength of constitution on my part had saved my life.

I also remember experiencing a distinct feeling of pique that amongst other members of the party my adventure seemed to cut no ice at all. They appeared to regard it as the most ordinary thing in the world. Two new arrivals had come—the two whom Longworth had been told to summon under the names of Ted and Toby. Their surnames were respectively Jerningham and Sinclair, and Tracey had managed to squeeze them into the house. And it was in describing the events of the afternoon and evening to these two that the point of view of this second section of the party became obvious. Not, I mean, that I wished it to be exaggerated in any way: at the same time I admit that I felt, when all was said and done, that whilst Drummond and Darrel had been in perfect safety at a police-station, I had had a murderous assault made on my life. And to have it described by Darrell as getting a clip over the earhole struck me as somewhat inadequate. The replies of the audience also left, I thought, a certain amount to be desired.

Jerningham said: "Pity you didn't ladle the bloke one back."

Sinclair said: "Splendid! So we know one of them by sight, anyway."

Then they all dismissed the matter as trifling, and resumed the interminable discussion. Not that I minded, you understand—but it struck me that it showed a slight lack of a proper sense of proportion.

However, I waived the matter: it was not my wife who had been forcibly dragged from her car in broad daylight. Had it been I should have been insane with worry. And that was the extraordinary thing about Drummond. Outwardly he seemed the most self-possessed of us all, and only the strained look in his eyes showed the mental condition he was in.

Bill Tracey was absolutely beside himself. That such a thing should have happened in his house made him almost incoherent. And it was characteristic of Drummond that, in spite of his own agonising suspense, he should have gone out of his way to ease things for Bill.

"My dear fellow," he said more than once, "please don't blame yourself. The fact that it happened to take place here is nothing whatever to do with you. They waited till they were ready and then they struck. That they happened to become ready when we were staying with you is just pure chance."

Which, though perfectly true, did but little to alleviate his feelings of responsibility. It was his house, and the bald fact remained that one of his guests, and a woman at that, had been decoyed away from it and been made the victim of foul play. And apart from his natural grief at such a thing happening, the prospect of the notoriety involved concerned him, of course, more than any of us save Drummond himself. It was Jerningham who summarized the situation after a while.

"Let's just see," he said, "that we've got this thing clear. Whilst playing tennis this afternoon Phyllis got a note delivered by hand of such importance that she stops playing and goes out alone in the Bentley. At that time Hugh was having a bit of back chat with the two foreign-looking blokes—"

"Who have not been traced at the railway station," put in Tracey.

"Who have since disappeared," went on Jerningham. "But it is generally agreed that they had something to do with it, though what we don't know. Shortly after, the Bentley is found deserted, showing every sign of having been the scene of a struggle."

"She dotted him one, Ted," said Drummond with certainty. "She dotted him good and hard with that spanner. In fact she killed him— glory be to Allah!"

They pondered this point in silence for a while.

"It stands to reason, old boy," went on Drummond, "that the man Dixon saw lying in the ditch is the same man whose trail we followed on the grass beside the Bentley."

"Very well then," said Jerningham, "make it so. She dotted him one. Finding herself suddenly attacked she out with the spanner and slogged him good and hard. So then the other bloke—there must have been at least one more—bunged Phyllis into the back of the other car, stuffed his pal into the seat beside him, and pushed off."

"It don't sound right to me, Ted," said Drummond slowly.

"What's wrong?" demanded Jerningham.

"All the last part. If you were driving a motorcar in broad daylight, and had to take with you a fellow who was bleeding like a pig from a wound in the head, would you put him on the seat beside you? Especially if you did not want to draw attention to yourself."

He took a long gulp of beer.

"Not so, old lad: you'd bung him on the floor at the back. And from Peter's description of the blood in the car that's what happened. If he'd been sitting in the seat beside the driver, the front of it would have been stained, too. It wasn't—only the back."

"I don't see that it matters much, anyway," I remarked. "Back or front the result is the same. Perhaps Mrs Drummond was beside the driver."

"Good Lord!" said Drummond, sitting up and staring at me. "I hadn't thought of that. Perhaps she was."

"What's stung you?" said Darrell, surprised, and we all looked at him curiously. He seemed strangely excited.

"Supposing Phyllis was sitting in that seat," he remarked. "Supposing the man was bleeding to death behind. Supposing she managed to get her hand over the back of the seat, with the idea of getting some message through by dipping her finger in the blood and writing on the cover."

His excitement infected us all though, for the life of me, I couldn't see what he was getting at.

"Well—get on with it," said Darrell.

"Don't you see that the writing would be upside down?" cried Drummond. "Where's your notebook, Peter? Turn the page the other way round."

We crowded over his shoulder and stared at the rough sketch.

"It is," shouted Drummond. "Smeared letters, or I'll eat my hat. There's a *K* there: two *K*s. And *L*: and *E*. What's that first word? Something *KE*.... *LUKE* is it?"

"Like," I hazarded. "That first letter might be L."

"Then it's *LIKE LAK*," said Drummond, and we stared at one another a little blankly. If that was the solution it didn't seem to advance us much. *Like Lak*. It was meaningless. Probably not realizing that it was useless the message had continued into the stream of blood where it had been obliterated. But that was no help.

"Anyway," said Drummond quietly, "it proves one thing. She wasn't unconscious."

He got up and went to the open window, where he stood with his back to us, staring out into the darkness. His shoulders were a little bowed: his hands were in his pockets. And, by Jove! I felt for the poor chap. Somewhere out under those same stars—perhaps twenty miles away, perhaps a hundred—his wife was in the hands of this infamous gang. Up-to-date, action had kept him going, even if it had only consisted of futile motoring up and down roads. Now the time of forced inaction had come. There was nothing to distract his thoughts, nothing to take his mind off the ghastly possibilities of the situation.

There was no use sympathizing with him: the matter had passed beyond words. Besides, it struck me that he was of the brand that is apt to shy away from sympathy like a frightened colt. And so we sat on in silence, hardly daring to meet one another's eyes, with the same fear clutching at all our hearts. It didn't seem to matter very much whether or not Mrs Drummond had been conscious in the car. Was she conscious now? Was she even alive? It seemed too incredible to be sitting there in that peaceful room contemplating such an appalling thought. And yet what was there to be done? That was the maddening part of it. Literally the only clue in our possession was the number of the car—ZW 3214. It was true that I might recognize the man who had nearly throttled me, but even on that point I felt doubtful. And that wasn't going to be much use unless I saw him again.

The same applied to the two men at the Cat and Custard Pot. Both Drummond and I would recognize them again—but where were they? And even if they were found they would probably prove to be only very minor characters in the caste. The telephone on Tracey's desk rang suddenly, sounding unnaturally loud in the silence, and we looked at it almost apprehensively. Was it some further complication, or was it news?

"Hullo!" said Tracey, picking up the receiver. "Yes—speaking."

Drummond had swung round, his hands still in his pockets. And he stood there, his face expressionless, while the metallic voice from the machine, punctuated by occasional grunts from our host, droned on. At last Tracey replaced the receiver, and shook his head gloomily.

"Nothing, I'm afraid," he said. "It was the police. They've traced the car, and it belongs to a man called Allbright in Reading. He's a retired grocer, and absolutely above suspicion. He is away from home at the moment, and the car must have been coolly stolen from his garage this morning. He has a deaf housekeeper, who is also above suspicion, and who was in complete ignorance that the car had gone until visited by the police this evening."

Once more silence fell on the room, and Drummond, with the faintest perceptible shrug of his shoulders, again turned his back on us and stared into the darkness. Our only positive clue gone—or at any rate valueless, the outlook blacker, if possible, than before. The butler brought in a tray of drinks and Tracey waved his hand at it mechanically.

"Help yourselves," he remarked, but nobody moved.

And then at last Drummond spoke. His back was still towards us: his voice was perfectly quiet. "This situation is too impossible to continue," he said. "Something is bound to happen soon."

And as if in answer to his remark the telephone bell jangled a second time.

"I told you so," he said calmly. "This is news."

Tracey had again taken the receiver: and again we watched him with a kind of feverish anxiety. Was Drummond right? Or was it some further futile communication from the police?

"A lady wishes to speak to you, Drummond," said Tracey, and the tension suddenly became acute. "She won't give her name."

Drummond went to the instrument, and we waited breathlessly. And if there is a more maddening proceeding during a time of suspense than having to listen to one end of a telephone conversation I have yet to experience it. We heard the metallic voice of the other speaker; we saw Drummond give an uncontrollable start, and then freeze into absolute immobility.

"So it is you," he said in a low voice. "Where is Phyllis?"

Again that metallic voice, and then quite clearly a laugh.

"Damn you," said Drummond, still in the same quiet tone. "What have you done with her?"

This time the voice went on for nearly a minute, and all we could do was to watch the changing expressions on his face and try to imagine what was causing them. Anger, bewilderment, and finally blank surprise were all registered, and it was the latter which remained when the voice ceased.

"But look here!" he cried. "Are you there? Damn it—she's gone!"

He rang the bell furiously for the Exchange.

"Where did that last call come from?" he asked. "London. Can you possible get me the number?"

We waited eagerly, only to see him lay down the receiver wearily.

"The public callbox at Piccadilly Circus," he said.

"It was Irma?" almost shouted Darrell.

"Yes—it was."

He stood there frowning, and we waited eagerly.

"It was that she-cat right enough. I'd know her voice anywhere. And she's got some dirty game up her sleeve."

"What did she say?" asked someone.

"She first of all said that she was charmed to renew her acquaintance with Phyllis, and that it seemed quite like old times. She went on to say that so far she had only been able to have a very brief chat with her, but that she hoped for many more in the near future. She was sure I would like to know that she was unhurt, but how long that condition of affairs lasted depended on me entirely. That I should have a letter from her in the morning making things quite clear, and that all she could advise me to do for the present was to have a good night in. Then she rang off."

"Well—that's something," said Darrell. "We know she's unhurt."

"Yes—I don't think she would lie," agreed Drummond. "But what's she getting at? How can it depend on me?"

"That seems fairly obvious," said Jerningham gravely. "You're going to be put through it, old man, and if you don't play nicely Phyllis is going to suffer. There's no good not facing facts, and she's got you by the short hairs."

Drummond sat down heavily.

"I suppose you're right," he said slowly. "I'll do anything—anything. I wanted to ask her tonight if she would take me instead of Phyllis, but she'd rung off."

Darrell laughed shortly.

"I don't think the answer would have been very satisfactory even if she hadn't," he said. "You're not a very comfortable person to have about the house, old boy."

"Hell!" said Drummond tersely.

Then he stood up, and the expression on his face made me feel profoundly thankful that I was never likely to come up against him.

"I'm going to take one of your boats, Tracey," he remarked. "Don't wait up for me: I shan't go to bed tonight."

The next moment he had vanished through the open window.

"Poor devil," said Bill. "I'm sorry for him. But I don't see that there's anything to be done."

"There isn't," said Darrell. "We can only wait for this letter tomorrow morning."

He helped himself to a whiskey and soda, and I followed his example. That was all we could do—wait for the letter. But it was impossible to prevent oneself speculating on the contents. What test was Drummond going to be put to? Was he going to be told to commit some crime? Some robbery possibly with his wife's safety depending on his success? What a ghastly predicament to be in! To have to run the risk of a long term of imprisonment, or else to know that he was putting his wife in danger. And even if he ran the risk how could he be sure that the others would stick to their side of the bargain? Avowedly they were criminals of the worst type, so what reliance could possible be put on their word?

The others had gone off to the billiard room, leaving Tracey and me alone. And suddenly the utter incredibility of the whole situation came over me in a wave. Not twelve hours ago had I been sitting peacefully in my club, earnestly discussing with the secretary whether the new brandy was as good as the last lot. He had said yes: I had disagreed. And it had seemed a very important matter.

I laughed: and he looked up at me quickly. "I don't see anything very humorous in the situation," he remarked.

I laughed again. "No more do I, Bill, not really. But it had just occurred to me that if I was suddenly transported to the smoking-room of the club, and I told the occupants that since I last saw them a lady had been kidnapped from your house, I had found a dead man in a ditch, and finally had been nearly murdered for my pains—they might not believe me."

He grunted. "You're right," he said. "They might not. At times I hardly believe it myself. Damn this accursed woman Irma—or whatever she calls herself!" He mixed himself a drink savagely. "We're going to have hordes of newspaper men round the place, poking their confounded noses into everything. And, being Whitsuntide, they'll probably run special steamers to view the scene of the crime. I tell you, Joe, I wouldn't have had it happen for worlds. Of course I'm very sorry for Drummond—but I wish it had taken place somewhere else."

"Naturally," I agreed. "At the same time, Bill, don't forget that everything that happened did take place somewhere else. The dead man I found was twelve miles from here—and he has since disappeared. The car has disappeared, too. In fact there's nothing to connect the matter with this house."

"What do you mean?" he said. "Nothing to connect it with this house! What about Mrs. Drummond? Wasn't she staying here?"

"She was—undoubtedly. But hasn't it occurred to you—mind you,

I only put it forward as a possibility—that Drummond may be compelled by the gang who have got her to keep the fact of her disappearance quiet?"

"But the police know it already," he cried.

"They know she went out in a car, and that the car was found empty. That does not necessarily mean that she has disappeared. We know she has, but that's a very different matter. And if, as I surmise, Drummond is going to be ordered to commit a crime as the price for his wife's life—or at any rate safety—the first essential is that he should keep the police out of it as much as possible."

"Commit a crime!" He stared at me for a moment or two and then put down his glass on the table. "You really think that that is going to be the next move?"

"I don't know any more than you do," I said. "The whole thing is so absolutely amazing that no ordinary rules seem to apply. If they had murdered the poor girl outright as an act of revenge it would at any rate have been understandable. But this new development can only mean that they are going to put pressure on him through his wife."

"Well, I must frankly admit," he said at length, "that the less that is known about this affair the better I shall be pleased. At the same time I'd hate to know that Drummond was running round the country robbing churches or something of that sort."

He paused, struck by a sudden thought.

"It might be a case, not of blackmail exactly, but of ransom. On the payment of a sum of money she will be returned."

"Is he a wealthy man?" I asked.

"Quite well off. Do you think that's the solution, Joe?"

"My dear old man," I cried, "ask me another. I don't think I've ever been so hopelessly at sea in my life. I shall put a cold compress round my neck, and go to bed. Presumably all our questions will be answered tomorrow morning."

And to bed I went—but not to sleep. Try as I would I could not stop thinking about the affair. That last idea of Bill Tracey's had a good deal to be said for it. And what would happen if Drummond wouldn't pay—or couldn't? People of the type we were up against were not likely to ask a small sum.

Would they go on keeping her a prisoner until he had scraped together the money? Or would they murder her? I shuddered at the thought: this was England, not a bandit-infested desert. They would never dare to run such an appalling risk. They might threaten, of course, but at that it would stop. And then as if to mock me I saw once

45

again that evil face with its cynical smile, heard that voice: "Too easy," felt those vicelike hands on my throat. Would they stop at that?

At last I could bear it no longer. I got up and lit a cigarette: then I went and sat down by the open window. A very faint breeze was stirring in the trees: from the other end of the lawn came the mournful cry of an owl. And somewhere out there in the darkness was that poor devil Drummond, on the rack with anxiety and worry.

Suddenly the moon came out from behind a cloud, throwing fantastic shadows across the lawn—the clear-cut black and white shadows of the night. And after a while I began to imagine things, to see movement where there was no movement, to hear noises when there was no noise. Every board that creaked in the house seemed like the footsteps of a man, and once I started violently as a bat flitted past close to. In fact I came quite definitely to the conclusion that during the hours of darkness Piccadilly was good enough for me. With which profound reflection I got back into bed, and promptly fell asleep. But what the footman thought, I don't know. Because when a motor car with blood spouting from the radiator is on the point of knocking you down, and you see that it isn't really a radiator, but the face of a man with a cynical smile who continually says "Too easy," it is only natural that you should push that face. I did—and it was the footman's stomach. The only comfort was that he had already put down the tea.

Chapter 5

In Which the Letter Arrives

And now I come to the beginning proper of the amazing adventure which was to occupy us for the next few days. The happenings of the preceding day were only the necessary preliminaries without which the adventure could not have started.

As I have said, the two alternatives which I had in my mind as I went downstairs the next morning could be summed up in the two words—ransom or crime. And it was with a queer feeling of excitement that I saw Drummond standing in the hall holding a bulky letter in his hand. *The* letter.

"How's the neck?" he remarked.

"So so," I said. "You've heard from that woman?"

He nodded his head thoughtfully.

"I have. And I'll be damned if I can make out if I'm mad or if she is. Go and hit a sausage, and then we'll have a council of war."

I went into the dining-room, to find that the rest of his pals had nearly finished. None of the women were down yet, so conversation was non-existent. And ten minutes later we all duly assembled in Tracey's study.

"I've read this letter twice," said Drummond, coming straight to the point, "and as I said to Dixon I don't know whether I'm mad or she is. He looked a bit fine-drawn, I thought, but much less worried than he had done the previous night.

"I should think the best thing to do is for me to read it aloud to you," he went on. "The postmark on the envelope is of no assistance. It was posted in London, and that doesn't help. Somewhat naturally also there is no address."

He spread out the sheets and began.

"'*Mon Ami*,

"'In case you have forgotten, I wish to recall to your memory the circumstances of our last meeting. A little more than six months ago you may remember we met beside the wreckage of the airship. And I told you then that I knew you had killed Carl. It matters not how I knew: some things are incapable of ordinary explanation. But if it is of any interest to you, I did, as a matter of fact, make further inquiries from people who had been on that last voyage. And from them I learned that I was right, and that you did kill him.

"'Six months ago, Drummond, and during those six months you have never been out of my thoughts for long. There was no hurry, and during a winter spent in Egypt I have been indulging in the luxury of anticipation. They say it is better than realization: the next few days should decide that point as far as this particular case is concerned. There was another reason also which necessitated a little delay. Various arrangements had to be made in England—arrangements which took time. These have now been made, and I trust that in the near future you will find them satisfactory.

"'However, I go too fast. The first thing I had to decide was what method I should adopt for punishing you adequately. My revenge, if I was to enjoy it to the full, had to be carefully thought out. I wanted nothing crude;' (I caught Darrell's eye at that moment) 'I wanted something artistic. And above all I wanted something long drawn out.

"'And so your brilliant intellect will at once perceive that no mere death coming suddenly out of the blue could fit into my ideas. You smile, perhaps: you recall that in the past you were frequently threatened with death and that you are very much alive today. Agreed, *mon ami*; but do not forget the little verse I sent you. Doubtless you have inspected the message contained in it, and it is up to me to prove that that message is no empty boast.

"'For example, it would have been the easiest thing in the world to have killed your dear Phyllis yesterday afternoon. And her positively murderous assault on one of my most trusted assistants really made me very angry for a while. The poor man is quite dead.

"'In parenthesis, *mon cher*, who on earth is the funny little man you left to guard the car when you found it? From the description I've heard he's a new one on me.'"

"Damn the woman!" I spluttered, and even Drummond grinned suddenly. Then he went on.

"'To return, however. It would have been very easy to have killed her, but so far from doing so the dear girl is sitting with me as I write. Not only easy—but just. We should have been all square. But I want more satisfaction than that, Drummond, much more. And so I will come down to my little scheme.

"'In the past your physical strength has always excited my warmest admiration. But I have never been quite so certain about your mental ability. Luck, I think, has entered a good deal into the matter, and though I should be the last person to belittle luck, yet it is apt to affect the issue somewhat unfairly.

"'And so on this occasion I propose to test your brain. Not unduly, I trust, but enough to afford me a certain amount of amusement. Do not be alarmed—your physical strength will be tested also. If you emerge triumphant your dear Phyllis will be restored to your bosom. If on the other hand you fail, then I shall claim my pound of flesh. In other words, what might have so easily been done yesterday afternoon will merely have been postponed.

"'The test is expressed simply by two words: Find Phyllis. You raise your eyebrows: that, you say, is somewhat naturally the test. But wait, *mon ami*, and I will explain a little further. You have doubtless heard of hidden treasure hunts: perhaps joined in one yourself. This is going to be run on the same rules. You will receive clues which you will interpret to the best of your ability. These clues will lead you to various places where further clues will await you. They will also lead you to various places where you may or may not enjoy yourself. Things will happen which you may or may not like. In fact, my dear Drummond, to put the matter in a nutshell, you may or may not pull through. As I said, I have made my arrangements with some care.

"'One further word. This little matter is between you and me. I have no objection to your roping in your friends—in fact, the more the merrier. But I don't want the police butting in. You could not avoid it yesterday afternoon, I know, so you are forgiven for that. But get them out of it now—quickly. Another thing, too. I don't want Uncle Percival or whatever he calls himself asking absurd questions from any of the Broadcasting centres. If that should happen our little game would cease abruptly. So bear those two points in mind: no police, no broadcasting. And that, I think, is all. You will get your first clue today.'"

Drummond laid down the letter, and lit a cigarette.

"What do you think of it?" he said.

"The thing is a fantastic leg pull," cried Tracey.

But Drummond shook his head doubtfully. "I wonder," he said. "What do you think, Peter?"

"That she means every word of it, old boy," answered Darrell, positively. "That's no leg pull: it's damned grim earnest."

"Hear, hear," said Jerningham. "We're for the trail again."

"You mean to tell me," spluttered Tracey, "that this woman has hidden your wife, and now expects you to go chasing round the country till you find her! Dash it—it's absurd."

"Absurd or not absurd," said Drummond gravely, "that is exactly what this woman has done. And from what I know of her it's going to be some chase." He got up, and suddenly, to my amazement, an almost ecstatic grin spread over his face.

"Gosh! boys," he said, "if it wasn't that it was Phyllis, what a glorious time we should have. Why did we never think of it before with Carl? We might have had two or three games in our spare time."

Then he became serious again.

"Look here, Tracey," he said: "and you, too, Dixon, may I rely on you not to say a word of this even to the ladies? The fewer people who know about it the better. If this came to the ears of a newspaper man we'd have the whole of Fleet Street on our heels. So—not a word to a soul."

"A police sergeant to see you, sir."

The butler was holding the door open.

"Mind," said Drummond urgently, "not a word."

The officer who had gone with us to the deserted Bentley the previous afternoon entered the room.

"Good morning. Sergeant," said Drummond quietly. "Found Mr Allbright's car yet?"

The policeman shook his head.

"I'm afraid not, sir," he said. "May I ask if you have any news of your wife?"

Drummond frowned suddenly: then he gave a short laugh. "Yes—I have. Look here. Sergeant—you're a man of discretion."

I looked at him covertly: what tale was he going to tell?

"Well, sir," said the officer, with a slightly gratified smile, "they don't make you a sergeant for nothing."

"Precisely," said Drummond. "Well—the fact of the matter is this. My wife has run away—bolted. With another man." He lit a cigarette with a sort of savage resignation. "I didn't say so yesterday, but I feared even then that that note that was brought her was from the swine who—"

He broke off abruptly—words had failed him—and strode to the window.

"Poor old Hugh," said Sinclair sadly. "It's a devilish business. That dirty little sweep of all people, too."

Drummond invoked the Deity twice, while the sergeant stared at him blankly.

"But look here, sir," he said, "what about all that blood?"

"That, Sergeant," remarked Drummond, "is the staggering part of the whole business. When my wife rang me up last night to tell me that she had—she had left me, she said 'I suppose you've found the Bentley by now.' I said to her, 'But what about the blood on the grass?' She said 'What on earth are you talking about? If it's a riddle I haven't got time to buy it now.' Then she rang off. She knew nothing about it, sergeant—absolutely nothing."

The officer's face was blanker than before.

"Since then," went on Drummond, "we've been trying to reconstruct what happened. And the only possible conclusion we can come to is this. The car belonging to Mr Allbright was stolen by two or three men. Driving along the road they came on the deserted Bentley. Well, if they'd steal one car, they'd steal another. So they decided to steal that too. And then they fell out—why. Heaven alone knows. Probably one of them was already at the wheel of the Bentley—and there was a struggle in which somebody got hit over the head with the spanner. Much harder than was intended. They all became frightened, and bundled the wounded man into the closed car. Of course," he continued modestly, "it's only crude amateur deduction: there are doubtless many objections to our theory—"

"Many," agreed Darrell, staring out of the window.

"Which your trained brain will spot," went on Drummond. "But the great point as far as we are concerned is this. As far as I am concerned, I should say. The whole thing is merely an amazing coincidence. The blood we saw on the road, the blood in Mr Allbright's car, has nothing to do with my wife's disappearance. And since I still have hopes that she will realize the error of her way and come back to me, the last thing I want is to run any risk of hardening her heart by worrying her with police inquiries."

"You know my views, Hugh," said Jerningham.

"And I damned well don't want to hear them again," snapped Drummond.

"A lounge lizard like that!" cried Jerningham scornfully. "How you can dream of forgiving her I don't know."

"Lounge lizard, gentlemen?" said the bewildered policeman.

"That's right, sergeant," Jerningham pointed an outraged finger at space. "A lounge lizard. A ballroom snake. What matter that his Black Bottom is the best in London."

"My Gawd! sir," gasped the other. "His 'ow much?"

"What matter, I say?" swept on Jerningham. "Is that a thing which should commend itself to reasonable decent men?"

"I should 'ardly say so myself, sir," agreed the sergeant fervently.

Jerningham paused to recover his breath.

"What is the gent's name, sir," said the sergeant, producing his pencil and notebook.

"Albert. Albert Prodnut," said Jerningham, and Drummond sat down abruptly.

"And his address?"

"I wish we knew," answered Jerningham. "If we did, doubtless by this time Captain Drummond would have removed his liver with a rusty penknife. I speak metaphorically."

"So you don't know where he is, sir?"

"Somewhere on the Continent," said Drummond in a hollow voice.

"And your wife, too?"

Drummond groaned and hid his face in his hands, while Jerningham rose and took the sergeant by the arm.

"No more now, sergeant," he whispered confidentially. "He is strung up to breaking point. In a week or two, perhaps. Or a month. And in the meantime you will treat what we have told you as absolutely confidential, won't you?"

He propelled him gently towards the door.

"It's all very strange, sir," he said in a worried voice.

"If you knew Albert Prodnut you'd think it was a damned sight stranger," said Jerningham feelingly. "One of those strange cases of mental aberration. Sergeant—almost I might say of psycho-sclerosis—which baffle the cleverest doctor. Leave him to us now."

The door closed behind the harassed officer, and Jerningham held up his two thumbs.

"Prodnut," said Drummond weakly. "Why Prodnut?"

"Why not? It's very difficult to think of a name when you're suddenly asked for one. There is a ring of sincerity about Albert Prodnut that carries entire conviction."

"Look here, you fellows," said Tracey seriously, "this is getting beyond a joke. You can't expect any man out of a lunatic asylum to believe that absurd rigmarole."

"We had to say something," remarked Drummond. "Personally I think we told the tale rather well."

"Yes—but what about me?" said Tracey. "It's a tissue of lies from beginning to end."

"We can't tell the truth," answered Drummond gravely. "Look here, Tracey. I'm very sorry about this, and I quite appreciate the difficulties of your position. In the bottom of your mind you probably think that that woman's letter is a bluff. I know it isn't. We've got to keep the police out of this if we possibly can. And I really couldn't think of anything better on the spur of the moment."

"You still mean," said Tracey amazed, "to take that woman at her word! To go hunting about all over England on clues she sends you which will probably lead you nowhere nearer your wife than you are at present!"

"What else can I do?" cried Drummond. "She's in the position of being able to dictate terms."

Once again the door opened and Parker came in, this time with a telegram on a salver. "For you, sir," he said, handing it to Drummond.

He tore open the yellow envelope, and as he read the message a look of complete bewilderment spread over his face. "Well, I'm damned!" he muttered. "No answer, thank you, Parker. Listen here, you fellows," he went on as the butler left the room, "what in the name of fortune do you make of this?

"My first a horse may draw or even two the rest is found at York and aids the view and when you've solved that bit by dint of trying an inn you'll find where fishermen are lying"

"It's the first clue," said Jerningham excitedly. "She said you'd get it this morning."

"But it's hopeless," cried Drummond in despair. "The simplest crossword reduces me to a jibbering wreck. If I've got to try and solve these damned things I'm done before I start."

"There are half a dozen perfectly good people to help you, old boy," said Darrell. "Sling the paper over. Let's put it down as it's meant to be—in the form of a verse."

He scribbled the words on a piece of paper while we leaned over his shoulder. And even Tracey seemed impressed by this sudden new development.

"Now then," said Darrell, "does that make it any better?"

My first a horse may draw, or even two; The rest is found at York, and aids the view. And when you've solved that bit by dint of trying, An inn you'll find where fishermen are lying.

"If line three is right," I said, "the first two are a complete clue in themselves."

"That's so," agreed Tracey. "But what sort of a clue? Is it the name of a man or a town or what?"

"Let's assume it's a town to start with," said Jerningham. "There's an inn mentioned in the last line."

"What's found at York?" demanded Drummond gloomily.

"Ham, dear old boy," burbled Algy Longworth.

"And Archbishops," said Sinclair hopefully.

"I don't know that it can be truthfully maintained," said Tracey mildly, "that either ham or Archbishops aid the view."

"Hold hard a bit," remarked Darrell. "Let's start at the beginning. 'My first a horse may draw, or even two.' Presumably that means two horses. So it's a horse-drawn vehicle suitable for one or two horses."

"By Jove! Peter, you're a bunking marvel," cried Drummond. "Cart, cab, wagon."

"You don't have a two-horse cab," objected Jerningham.

"Wagon sounds possible," said Darrell. "There must be places beginning with Wagon. Got a map Tracey?"

"Here's the Times Gazetteer," he answered. "By Jove! Wagonmound."

"Got it!" shouted Drummond. "There's bound to be a mound at York."

But Tracey was shaking his head.

"Sorry. I spoke too soon. The darned place is in New Mexico. And that's the only place beginning with Wagon that's mentioned."

"Hell!" said Drummond, and relapsed into silence.

"What about Dray," I remarked. "You speak of a one-horse dray and a two-horse dray."

"Stout fellow," cried Drummond. "Look up Dray, Tracey."

"There are about forty Draytons," he said. "Lots of Draycotts: Drayminster, Drayney."

"Drayminster!" I yelled. "Minster, York Minster."

"I believe you've got it," said Darrell. "It fits at any rate as far as the first two lines are concerned."

"By Jove! you fellows," cried Jerningham. "Listen here. This is the AA handbook. Drayminster. Population 2231, Sussex. 55 miles to London. Now brace yourselves for it. Hotel—the Angler's Rest. We have got it."

For a while we all stared at one another too excited to speak. Was there a mistake? Fishermen lying; Anglers' Rest. No one could say that York Minster was not an aid to the view: a dray could certainly be drawn by one or two horses. It fitted, every clue fitted.

"Get packed, boys," cried Drummond. "We lunch at the Angler's Rest. Gosh! I feel better. We've started. Beer, Tracey old lad, pints of beer! And you and Dixon shall wish us good hunting."

The beer arrived, and then Drummond raised his hand as for some solemn rite. Slowly he waved it to and fro, and once more did the words of his favourite refrain burst forth with vigour:

"The more we are together—together—together: the more we are together the merrier we shall be."

"A new music-hall song?" I inquired politely.

And all they did was to roar with laughter.

"When we start hunting, boys," he said, "that shall be the war-cry. Don't forget—once for the rally, twice for danger."

I suppose it was foolish of me, but I really couldn't help it. There was something contagious about the spirits of this extraordinary gang which must have infected me.

"I must learn the tune," I said. "For if you'll allow me I should very much like to join you in whatever is coming."

They all stared at me, then, a little doubtfully, at one another.

"Of course," I said stiffly, "if you'd prefer I didn't."

"It isn't that," interrupted Drummond. "Look here, Dixon, if you're going to come in on this thing you'd better be under no delusions. You got a taste last night of the sort of people we're going to be up against. And believe you me that's nothing to what we shall strike. I want you to understand quite clearly that if you do join us you'll be taking your life in your hands at most hours of the day and night. I mean it—quite literally. It's not going to be a question of merely solving little puzzles."

"I'll chance it," I answered. "As a matter of fact I dislike most strongly the implication behind the phrase funny little man."

Once more the whole lot burst out laughing. "Right," said Drummond. "That settles it. But don't say you weren't warned if you get your ear bitten badly."

Chapter 6

In Which I Get the Second Clue

The village of Drayminster is one of the beauty spots of England. Somewhat out of the beaten track, it is as yet unspoiled by motor coaches and hordes of trippers.

The river Dray meanders on its peaceful way parallel to the main street, and in the very centre of the village stands the Angler's Rest. A strip of grass separates it from the water's edge, and moored to two stakes a punt stretches out into the stream from the end of which the energetic may fish for the wily roach and perch. A backwater—but what a pleasant backwater.

"Your lady friend," I said to Drummond, "has undoubtedly an artistic eye." We were sitting on the lawn after lunch, and he grunted thoughtfully. The others had departed on a tour of exploration, and save for the motionless figure of the landlord's son at the end of the punt, we were alone.

"If only I could be absolutely certain that we were right," he remarked. "That we aren't wasting our time sitting here."

"Unless the whole thing is a stupid hoax," I said reassuringly, "I'm certain our solution was correct."

It was the inaction that chafed him, I could see. I think he had expected to find another clue waiting for us on our arrival. But there had been nothing, and gradually his mood A of elation had left him. He had kept his eyes fixed so searchingly on an elderly parson and his daughter during lunch that the poor man had become quite hot and bothered. In fact, it wasn't until our host had assured him that the reverend gentleman had come to the hotel regularly for the last twenty years that he desisted.

"It's not a hoax," he said doggedly. "So why the devil, if we're right, haven't we heard something more?"

"Quite possibly that's all part of the game," I answered. "They may know that that is a method of rattling you."

"By Jove!" he cried, "I hadn't thought of that."

He looked quite relieved at the suggestion.

"There's one thing we might do," I went on. "It may not be any good, but it can't do any harm. Let's find out if there are any houses in the neighbourhood that have recently changed hands. If they are hiding your wife a house is the most likely place to do it in."

"Dixon," he said, "you're the bright boy all right. My brain at the moment is refusing to function altogether. Hi! John—or whatever your name is—cease tormenting fish and come here a moment."

Obediently the boy put down his rod and approached.

"Now, you know all the big houses in the neighbourhood, don't you?"

The boy nodded his head.

"That's right, mister. There be the Old Manor—that be Squire Foley's. And there be Park House. That do belong to Sir James—but he be away now."

"Has there been any house sold round about here recently," I put in.

The boy scratched his head.

"There be Widow Maybury's," he said. "She did sell her little cottage, and be gone to live with her darter near Lewes."

"Who bought it," I cried.

"They do say he be a writer from Lunnon, or sommat fulish like that. He just comes occasional like."

"Is he here now," asked Drummond.

"Ay," said the boy. "He come last night. There was a young leddy with him."

I caught Drummond's eye, and it was blazing with excitement.

"They come in a motor car," went on the boy.

"Where is the cottage?" said Drummond.

"End o' village," he replied. "'Lily Cottage,' it do be called."

Drummond had already risen to his feet, and the boy looked at him doubtfully.

"He be a terrible funny-tempered gentleman," he said. "He set about Luke Gurney with a stick, he did—two or three weeks ago. Had to pay Luke five pounds, he did, or old Gaffer Gurney would have had him up afore the beak."

"My lad," said Drummond, "there is half a crown. You may now resume your occupation of catching fish."

He turned to me. "Are you coming," he said.

"Well," I said a little doubtfully, "we'd better be careful, hadn't we? This fellow may be a perfectly harmless individual."

"In which case we will withdraw gracefully," he cried. "Damn it, man, I believe we're on the scent. Why—Good God! Phyllis may be actually there now."

"All right—I'll come," I said. "Only—cautious does it." But for the moment Drummond was beyond caution. The thought that possibly his wife was within half a mile of him had sent him completely crazy, and it was only with the greatest difficulty that I restrained him from bursting straight into the house when we got there. "You can't, my dear fellow," I cried. "We must have some sort of excuse."

It was a small cottage standing back a little from the road. A tiny patch of garden in front was bright with flowers, and two pigeons regarded us thoughtfully from a dovecot. "We'll ask if it's for sale," he said, and then suddenly he gripped my arm like a vice.

"Look up at the top left-hand window," he muttered. I did so, and got a momentary glimpse of the saturnine, furious face of a man glaring at us. Then like a flash it was gone.

"Dixon," he said hoarsely, "we've done it. She's in there. And I'm going through that house with a fine comb."

A little dubiously I followed him up the path. Nothing that I could have done would have stopped him, but even before he knocked on the door I had a shrewd suspicion that he was making a blazing error. It seemed impossible that, after all the chat and bother there had been, the solution should prove so simple. And a blazing error it proved. The door was flung open and the man we had seen peering at us through the window appeared. And to put it mildly he was not amused.

"What the—" he began.

"Laddie," interrupted Drummond firmly, "something tells me that you and I will never be friends. Nevertheless I am going to honour your charming cottage with a call." He extended a vast hand and the other man disappeared into the hat-rack—an unstable structure. Drummond disappeared upstairs. And the scene that followed beggared description. The hat-rack, in falling, had pinned the owner underneath. Moreover, as far as I could see, one of the metal pegs was running straight into the small of his back. Then came a shrill feminine scream from above, and Drummond appeared at the top of the stairs looking pensive. He was still looking pensive when he joined me.

"I fear," he murmured, "that someone has blundered."

A rending crash from behind announced that the hat-rack was still in the picture, and we faded rapidly down the street.

"A complete stranger," he remarked. "With very little on. Most embarrassing."

I began to shake helplessly.

"But I maintain," he went on, "that no man has a right to possess a face like that. It's enough to make anyone suspicious."

A howl of rage from behind us announced that the battle of the hat-rack was over.

"Pretend," said Drummond, "that I'm not all there."

"Hi, you, sir," came a shout, and we paused.

"You are addressing me, sir?" remarked Drummond majestically as the other approached.

"You scoundrel," he spluttered. "How dare you force your way into my house?"

"My Prime Minister will raise the point at the next meeting of Parliament," said Drummond. "Do you ever hit yourself hard on the head with a heavy spanner? Hard and often. You must try it. It's so wonderful when you stop. The audience is terminated."

He turned on his heel, and strode off down the street, whilst I touched my head significantly.

"Good God!" said the other. "Is he mad?"

"Touched," I murmured. "Result of shell shock. He'll probably be quite all right in an hour or two when he'll have completely forgotten the whole incident."

"But the cursed fellow ought to be locked up," he cried angrily.

"His relatives don't want it to come to that if it can be avoided," I said. "I much regret the incident, sir—but. . . ."

"Bring me a mushroom omelette without. . . ." Drummond had suddenly returned, and was staring fixedly at his late victim.

"Without?" stammered the other nervously. "Without what?"

"Without mushrooms, you fool. Damn it—the man's not right in his head. What else could it be without? Come, fellow, I would fain sleep."

He seized me by the arm, and stalked off in the direction of the Angler's Rest, leaving the other standing speechless in the road.

"Did we put it across him?" he said when we were out of hearing.

"More or less," I answered. "He said you ought to be locked up."

"I really don't blame him," he conceded. "She was a pretty girl, too," he continued irrelevantly as we arrived at the hotel. "Very pretty."

Darrell and Jerningham were both on the lawn, but the others had evidently not yet returned.

"Any luck?" they asked as we pulled up a couple of chairs.

"Damn all," said Drummond moodily. "I pushed a bloke's face into a hat-rack, and contemplated a charming lady with very little on, but we never got the trace of a clue. What's worrying me, chaps, is whether we ought to sit still and wait, or run round in small circles and look."

"After your recent entertainment," I remarked mildly, "I should suggest the former. At any rate for a time."

"Perhaps you're right," he agreed resignedly. "All I hope is that it won't be for long."

"But you don't imagine, do you, old boy," remarked Jerningham, "that Phyllis is likely to be round about here? Because I don't."

"What's that?" said Drummond blankly.

"This is but the beginning of the chase. And I don't think Mademoiselle Irma would have run the risk of bringing her to the place where all of us would certainly be, granted we solved the first clue. All we're going to get here is the second clue."

"And probably have a darned sticky time getting it," said Darrell.

He stretched out his legs and closed his eyes, and after a while I followed his example. The afternoon was drowsy, and if we were going to have a sticky time, sleep seemed as good a preparation for it as anything. And it seemed only a moment afterwards that a hand was laid on my shoulder, and I sat up with a start.

The shadows had lengthened, and at first I saw no one. The landlord's son had ceased to fish: the chairs that the others had occupied were empty.

"You will, I am sure, excuse me," came a pleasant voice from over my shoulder, "but your snores are a little disconcerting to the sensitive ear."

"I beg your pardon," I said stiffly as I rose. "Falling asleep when sitting up is always dangerous."

He regarded me affably—a pleasant-faced little white-haired man.

"Don't mention it," he said. "I do to others as I would they should do to me. And I feared you might collect a crowd, who would misconstrue the reason of the uproar in view of the proximity of the Angler's Rest."

He sat down in the seat recently occupied by Drummond.

"You are staying long?" he inquired pleasantly.

"That largely depends," I answered.

"A charming village," he remarked. "A bit of old-world England, the like of which I regret to say is becoming all too rare. They tell me it was fifth—or was it sixth—in the competition for the most beautiful village."

He frowned. "How annoying. Was it fifth or sixth?"

"Does it," I murmured, "make very much difference?"

For a moment or two he stared at me fixedly.

"It might," he said gravely, "make a lot."

Then he looked away, and I felt a sudden pricking feeling of excitement. Was he implying something? Was there a hidden meaning in his apparently harmless remark? Was he one of those people who really are worried by failing to remember some small, insignificant detail such as that—or was it the beginning of a new clue?

"Only, I should imagine, to the lucky inhabitants," I said lightly. "For my own part I am content with it whatever place it occupied in the list of honour."

He nodded. "Perhaps so. It is certainly very lovely. And the inn is most comfortable. I always feel that in such a setting as this the old-time English beverage of ale tastes doubly good—a point of view which was shared, I think, by a very large individual who was sitting in this chair half an hour or so ago."

"I know the man you mean," I answered. "He is a very capacious beer drinker."

"He crooned some incantation which seemed to assist his digestion," he went on with an amused smile. "You are all one party, I suppose?"

"As a matter of fact we are," I said politely, restraining a desire to ask what business it was of his. If there was anything to be got—I'd get it. "We are here," I added on the spur of the moment, "on a quest."

"Indeed," he murmured. "How interesting! And how mysterious! Would it be indiscreet to inquire the nature of the quest?"

"That I fear is a secret," I remarked. "But it concerns principally the large individual of whom you spoke."

"My curiosity is aroused," he said. "It sounds as if a lady should be at the bottom of it."

"A lady is at the bottom of it," I answered.

He shook his head with a whimsical smile.

"What it is to be young! I, alas! can only say with the poet 'Sole-sitting by the shores of old romance.'" Once again did he give me a peculiar direct stare before looking away.

"At the moment," I remarked, "the quotation eludes me."

"It may perhaps return in time," he smiled. "And prove of assistance."

"In what possible way can it prove of assistance?" I said quickly.

"It is always an assistance to the mind when a forgotten tag is recalled," he remarked easily.

I said nothing: was I imagining things, or was I not? He seemed such a harmless old buffer, and yet. . . .

"As one grows older," he went on after a while, "one turns more and more to the solace of books. And yet what in reality are words worth? *'Si jeunesse savait: si vieillesse pouvait.'* The doctrine of life in a nutshell, my friend."

Still I said nothing: why I know not, but the conviction was growing on me that there was a message underlying his remarks.

"Words may be worth a lot," I said at length, "if one fully understands their meaning."

For the third time he gave me a quick, penetrating stare.

"To do that it is necessary to use one's brain," he murmured. "You will join me in a little gin and vermouth?"

"Delighted," I said perfunctorily. Then—"May I ask you a perfectly straight question, sir?"

He returned to his seat from ringing the bell.

"But certainly," he said. "Whether I give you a perfectly straight answer, however, is a different matter."

"Naturally," I agreed. "Do you know why we are here or do you not?"

"You have already told me that you are in quest of a lady."

He raised his glass to his lips.

"Votre sante, m'sieur—and also to the success of your search. If any stray words of mine have assisted you I shall be doubly rewarded for having roused you from your slumbers."

He replaced his glass on the table.

"Exquisite, is it not—the gold and black of the colour scheme? But alas! the air grows a little chilly *pour la vieillesse.* You will pardon me, I trust—if I leave you. And once again—good hunting."

He went indoors and I sat on, thinking. More and more strongly was the conviction growing on me that the second due lay in our conversation: less and less, could I see a ray of light. Was it contained in that quotation: *'Sole-sitting by the shores of old romance?'* He had said it might prove of assistance—and then had passed off his remark.

Who had written it, anyway? It came back to me as a dimly remembered tag, but as to the author my mind was a blank. Had the well-known old French proverb any bearing on the case?

His voice from a window above me cut into my reverie.

"I feel sure that you are tormenting yourself over the author of my little quotation," he chuckled. "It has suddenly occurred to me that his name was actually mentioned in our conversation."

The window closed, leaving me staring blankly at it. Mentioned in our conversation! No author's name had been mentioned: to that

I could swear. And yet would he have said so if it was not the case? It seemed stupid and unnecessary.

Once more I ran over it, trying to recall it word by word. It was maddening to think that I was now possibly in actual possession of the information we wanted, and yet that I couldn't get it.

I ordered another gin and vermouth: perhaps, after all, I had been mistaken. An old gentleman in all probability with an impish delight in the mysterious who was deliberately playing a little joke on me. And then the window above me opened again.

"Goodbye, my friend. I am sorry to say that I have to leave this charming spot. And I trust for all your sakes that your brain will prove equal to my little problem."

I got up quickly: surely that remark clinched the matter. He was one of the others, and I'd make him tell me more. A Ford was standing by the door, and a minute or two later I saw him getting into it. "Look here, sir," I said, "I must insist on your being more explicit. You do know why we are here; you have been giving me the second clue."

He raised his eyebrows.

"You have told me why you are here," he answered. "And as for the second clue, the phrase sounds most exciting. And as for me I have a train to catch. To the station, driver."

The car started, leaving me standing there blankly. And then he put his head out of the window.

"Good hunting."

I suppose Drummond would have pulled him out of the car by the scruff of the neck: I wasn't Drummond. I watched the car disappear up the road, then I went back to my neglected gin and vermouth, swearing under my breath.

"Who," I said to the landlord who came out at that moment, "is the old gentleman who had just driven off?"

"He entered himself in the book, sir, as Mr Johnson of London. More than that I can't tell you."

Evidently disposed for a chat he rambled on, whilst I pretended to listen. And suddenly—I don't know what the worthy man was talking about at the moment—I fired a question at him.

"Have you got any books of poetry in the hotel?"

It must have been a bit disconcerting, for he stared at me as if I had taken leave of my senses.

"I believe the missus has," he said in an offended voice. "I don't hold with the stuff myself. I'll ask her."

He went indoors to return in a few moments with the information that she had Longfellow, Shelley, Wordsworth, Keats. I cut short the catalogue with a yell, and this time the poor man looked really alarmed.

"Wordsworth," I said. "Please ask her to lend me Wordsworth."

He again went indoors, and I sat there marvelling at my denseness. "And yet what in reality are words worth?"

At the time the phrasing had struck me as peculiar, a little pedantic. And there it had been sticking out right under my nose. Now there was nothing for it but to go clean through until I found the quotation, and then if my reasoning was right we should find the clue in the context.

Mine host handed me the book with an air of hurt dignity, and retired once more indoors whilst I started on my lengthy task. In couples the others came back looking moody and disconsolate, and disinclined for conversation. They took no notice of me, and I, for fear I might raise false hopes, said nothing. Plenty of time to talk if I proved right.

Dinner came, and over the steak and kidney pie, I found it.

Lady of the Mere,
Sole-sitting by the shores of old romance.

I stared at the page blankly. Lady of the Mere. What earthly good was that? Had all my time been wasted? Was the old man a harmless jester after all?

"Everything to your satisfaction, gentlemen?" The landlord came up to our table, and a I drew a bow at a venture. "Tell me, landlord," I said, "is there in this neighbourhood any place called the Mere?"

He stared at me for a moment or two without speaking. "There is," he answered at length, and his jovial expression had vanished. "May I ask why you want to know, sir?"

"Curiosity," I said, hardly able to keep the excitement out of my voice. "Is it a pond—or what?"

"It's a house," he said. "An old house. About three miles from here."

"Who is the owner?" I cried.

"Owner!" he gave a short laugh. "There ain't been no owner, sir, for nigh on ten years. And there ain't never likely to be."

"What's the matter with the place?"

"I bain't a superstitious man, gentlemen," he said gravely, "but it would take more'n a bag of gold to get me across the threshold of the Mere—even by day. And by night, I wouldn't go—not for all the money in the Bank of England."

"Haunted, is it?" I prompted.

"Maybe—maybe not," he answered. "There be grim things, sir, black things go on in that house. Ten years ago the owner, old Farmer Jesson, were murdered there. A fierce man he was: used to keep the most awful savage dogs. And they do say that he found his young wife with a lad—a powerful-tempered boy. And they had a terrible quarrel. The lad, so the story goes—'e struck the old man and killed him after an awful struggle. And as he died he cursed the lad and his young wife. He cursed the house: he cursed everything he could think of. Certain it is that the lad and the lass disappeared: folks do say they died where they stood and then were mysteriously removed. As I say, I bain't superstitious, and I don't rightly hold with that story. But what I do know is that since then there be strange lights and noises that come from the old place—for I've seen 'em and heard 'em myself. And I do know that there come a young gentleman from London who heard the tales and didn't believe them. He went there one night, and they found him next day on the ground outside, lying on his back and staring at the sky—as mad as a hatter. No, no, gentlemen—take my advice and give the Mere a wide berth, or you'll regret it."

He bustled off to attend to a new arrival.

"How fearfully jolly," I remarked.

The others were staring at me curiously.

"Why this incursion into local superstition?" asked Darrell.

"No particular reason," I answered on the spur of the moment. "As I said, just idle curiosity."

Chapter 7

In Which We Come to the Mere

I really don't know why I didn't tell them at once. Somehow or other the whole thing seemed so terribly thin as I ran over it in my mind. And told secondhand it would have sounded even thinner. A tag from Wordsworth: the coincidence of a name. And that was positively all.

I felt that something more definite was wanted, and there seemed only one way of getting it. I would go there myself and reconnoitre. I admit that I didn't like the idea particularly: that bit about the man who was found on the ground outside, as mad as a hatter, was so wonderfully reassuring. At the same time I'd had three cocktails, and I was now having my second glass of port. And the suspicion that this cheery band regarded me as a rabbit rankled. Their opinion would change pretty rapidly if I came back with the next clue in my pocket.

After all it was I who had solved the first one and spotted Drayminster, and though I might not be their equal in mere physical strength it was brain that was needed on a show like this. And in that department I ventured to think the boot was on the other leg.

I ordered another glass of port. Just local superstition, of course: good enough for inebriated yokels wandering home at night. They would hear noises and see lights anywhere. But for an educated man to be put off by such an absurd story was nothing short of ridiculous. I'd borrow a bicycle after dinner, and have a look round the place. Only three miles mine host had said: I'd be back comfortably by eleven o'clock. And if I'd found nothing I would not mention my conversation of before dinner.

The others had drifted away from the table, and were sitting in the lounge outside as I went through. They seemed bored and depressed, and with difficulty I repressed a smile as I thought of the change that would occur when I came back with the goods. I should have to solve it for them too in all probability: in fact it had been a very fortunate moment for them when I had decided to help them.

The first thing to do was to get hold of a bicycle, and in that I was successful at once. The landlord's son would be only too pleased to lend me his, and after a few minutes it was brought round to the front door.

"Be you going far, mister," he said, "because there bain't too much oil in the lamp."

"I'm going to the Mere," I answered as casually as possible. "Which is the way?"

The boy's jaw dropped, and he stared at me speechlessly.

"To the Mere," he stammered at length. "But you can't go to the Mere at night. It bain't safe."

I smiled a little pityingly.

"Rot, my good boy," I said. "Anyway, I'll chance it. Now, which is the way?"

"Straight along the road," he answered, pointing up the street. "And when you get about two mile out of Drayminster, you'll find a turning going down to the right. Take that, and in about another half mile or so you'll see the house in front of you."

He hesitated for a moment: then he burst out with a further warning.

"It ain't safe, sir: it be a terrible place at night."

"Light the lamp, my lad," I said. "Your bicycle will be quite safe, anyway."

He fumbled with a match, and I glanced in through the open door. The others were still in the lounge, and just for a moment or two I hesitated. Should I tell them after all? When all was said and done it was their show more than mine, and the thought of Drummond beside me had much to commend it. And then I dismissed it: was I, a grown man, going to admit that I was frightened of a stupid story?

"The lamp be lit, sir," said the boy. "But you be terribly foolish to go."

He turned away and slouched in at the back door, while I got ready to mount. Foolish or not, I was going, and the sooner I started the sooner I'd be back.

It was a beautiful night, warm and without a breath of wind, and I was soon clear of the village. The moon had not yet risen, but there was no mistake about the road which ran for the first mile beside the river. Then it swung away to the left over some high ground. I found the turning the boy had spoken of without difficulty—one that evidently would lead back towards the river. The surface was poor—it was scarcely more than a lane, and little used at that—and very soon some high trees made the darkness so intense that the going was hard. In fact, after a short time I dismounted and pushed on on foot.

Now I make no bones about it, but the fact remains that with every step I took I found myself wishing more heartily that I had listened to the boy's advice. Whether it was due to the effects of the port wearing off or whether the reality was worse than what I had anticipated is immaterial. But after I'd walked about fifty yards it was only by the greatest effort of will that I prevented myself turning and fleeing incontinently.

There was a sort of dank feeling about that lane which got on my nerves, and the feeble little circle of light from the lamp dancing about in front of me as the bicycle jolted only seemed to make the surrounding darkness more impenetrable. And at last, acting on a sudden impulse, I blew it out, and left the bicycle standing against the hedge. If the landlord's three miles was right I must be very near my destination.

Came a sudden jink in the lane, and there within fifty yards of me stood the house. I stopped instinctively: what a fearsome-looking place it was. Trees were all round it except on one side where a large pool of water lay stagnant and unruffled—doubtless the pool that had given the place its name. The house itself was a big one, and gave an impression of indescribable gloom. It seemed to squat there in its setting of trees like a dead thing. No gleam of light came from any window: no sound broke the absolute silence.

I sat down on the bank beside the lane: some plan of action had to be decided on. Up till now I hadn't really thought what I was going to do when I got there: now it had to be faced. Obviously there was no use in sitting down and looking at the place: the clue, if my supposing was right, was not likely to be obtained that way. It would be inside the house, and if I wanted to get it that is where I should have to go. And the more I thought of it the less did I relish it.

I tried to find excuse for myself. How, for instance, could I get in? The answer to that was obvious—I certainly couldn't tell unless I tried. Was it wise for a man to attempt such a thing single-handed? The answer to that consisted of one word—coward. Had I come all this way—made all this song and dance in my own mind—merely to run away when I arrived. I forced myself to view the matter from a common-sense point of view.

"Here," I said out loud, "is an old untenanted house—set, it is true, in gloomy surroundings which look all the more gloomy because it happens to be dark. But it is merely a house consisting of bricks and mortar. You are a man of the world. Are you going to admit to yourself that you are afraid of exploring those bricks and mortar? Are you going to allow yourself to be influenced by an ancient story of something that happened ten years ago? At any rate go a bit closer and have a look."

At that I compromised to start with. I would go a bit closer and have a look. Very likely I should find everything shut and barred: if so I should have no alternative but to go home. Skirting along the undergrowth I approached the house. Stone steps covered with weeds led up to the front door, which was overhung with trailing creepers and ivy. For a moment I hesitated: then I went up the steps and cautiously tried the handle of the door. To my great relief it was locked, and the feeling that honour was satisfied was very strong. I could now go back to the Angler's Rest in order to get something to open the door with. And even as I so decided I seemed to hear Drummond's voice saying— "What about the ground floor windows? Didn't you try them?"

Right! I would. And then there would be no possibility of any back chat. Keeping close into the wall I skirted round the house. And I hadn't gone twenty yards before I was brought up standing. There in front of me was a wide-open window. All I had to do was to put my leg over the sill and I should be inside the house.

I peered in doubtfully: dimly I saw a table, some chairs, and, on the other side of the room, an open door. The musty smell of long disuse was overpowering, and I knew that if I hesitated for long I should hesitate for good. I flung a leg over, and stepped on to the floor.

The dust was thick everywhere. It rose in choking clouds, and deadened the sound of my feet as I crept towards the open door. It was almost like walking on a carpet, and it struck me that whatever might have happened in the past no one, could have been in the house for months, if not years. So what was the good of going on? I paused in the doorway to consider that new point. If no one had been in, the clue could not be in the house: it must, if I was on the right track, be in the garden outside.

In front of me was the hall. I could just see the staircase to my right, and opposite me was a piece of furniture that looked like a hat-rack. I peered across at it: was it my imagination, or was there something white that was hanging on one of the pegs—something that might be a piece of paper? Was it possible that here was the actual clue I was searching for?

I tiptoed across the hall: and almost trembling with excitement I struck a match. One word was written on it—Excelsior.

The match burned out, and I did not light another. No need to rack one's brain to interpret that message. True, it proved I was on the right track, which was gratifying to my pride as a solver of conundrums, but it also indicated with painful clearness the next move. There was only one way to Excelsior in that house, and that was to go upstairs. And the thought of going upstairs left me chilled to the marrow.

I stood staring at the dim outline of the staircase fading into utter blackness at the top. Where I was, a faint light did come from the open door by which I had entered. Above, the darkness was absolute. Should I, or should I not? And though I say it myself, I consider that a certain amount of credit was due to me for deciding in the affirmative. I'd go and have a look at the top of the stairs.

Still on tiptoe I crossed the hall to the foot of them. A mouldering carpet existed in patches, and I began to ascend cautiously for fear of tripping up. But no care on my part could prevent the stairs creaking abominably, and in the silence of the house each step I took sounded like a pistol shot.

At last I reached the top. Now that I was there the darkness was not quite so intense: a little of the light from the open door below managed to filter up. To my right and left ran a passage, and putting my hand in my pocket I counted the coins. Odd to the left: even to the right. There were seven, and I started feeling my way towards the left. And I can't have taken more than half a dozen steps when a strange creaking noise came from the hall, and at the same moment I realized it was getting darker. I stopped abruptly, and peered below. And what I saw froze me stiff with fright. The door by which I had entered was closing, and even as I looked at it, it shut with a bang. Then once more absolute silence.

For a moment or two I gave way to blind panic. I rushed as I thought in the direction of the stairs, and hit a wall. I turned round and rushed another way, and hit another wall. Then I forced myself to stand still: I'd lost my bearings completely: I hadn't an idea where the stairs were. Like a fool that I was I had walked straight into the trap, and the trap had shut behind me.

My first instinctive thought was to light a match—anything seemed better than this impenetrable blackness. And then prudence won. If there were people round me all I should do would be to give myself away. I was safer in the dark. At any rate we were on equal terms.

I crouched against the wall with my heart going in sickening thumps, and listened. Not a sound. The silence was as complete as the darkness. And I began to wonder if there was anyone in the house—any human that is. Was it a material agency that had shut that door—or was it something supernatural? Would some ghastly thing suddenly hurl itself on me: something against which even Drummond with all his strength would be powerless? Every ghost story I'd ever heard of came back to me along with the comforting reflection that I had always ridiculed the idea that there were such things. But it is one thing to be sceptical in the smoking-room of your club, and quite another when you are crouching in inky darkness in a deserted house from which your line of escape has been cut off.

Suddenly I started violently: an odd slithering noise had begun. It was rather as if a sack full of corn was being bumped on the floor, and it seemed to come from my left. I peered in what I thought was the right direction while the sweat ran off me in streams. Was it my imagination, or was there a faint luminosity in the darkness about three feet from the ground? I stared at it and it moved. With each bump it moved, and it was coming closer. Step by step I backed away from it: step by step it kept pace with me. And for the first time in my life I knew the meaning of the word terror. Frightened I had been many times: this was stark, raving horror. I was stiff and paralysed with fear. Was this the thing that had sent the other man mad?

Then, as if a veil had suddenly been torn away, came the change. One instant there had been merely a faint lessening of the darkness: the next I found myself staring into a shining yellow face of such inconceivable malignity that I almost screamed. It was not two feet away, and about on a level with my chest. I hit at it blindly, and found my wrist caught in a grip of steel. Then I felt a hand creeping up my coat until it reached my throat, and I began to struggle wildly.

I kicked into the darkness, and my foot hit something solid. There was a grunt of pain, and the grip on my throat tightened savagely. The face drew nearer, and there came a roaring in my ears. And I had just given myself up as finished when a thing happened so staggering that I could scarcely believe my eyes.

Out of the darkness from behind the shining face there came a pair of hands. I could see them clearly—just the hands and nothing more, as if they were disembodied. There was a curious red scar on the middle finger of the right hand, and the left thumbnail was distorted. With the utmost deliberation they fastened on the throat of my assailant, and began to drag him backwards. For a while he resisted: then quite suddenly the grip on my throat relaxed. Half insensible

I sank down on the floor and lay there watching. For the moment my only coherent thought was relief that I could breathe again, that the yellow face was going. Writhing furiously, its mouth twisted into a snarl of rage, it seemed to be borne backwards by those two detached hands. And even as I tried foolishly to understand what it all meant, there came from down below a well-known voice—"The more we are together." The relief was too much: I did another thing for the first time in my life. I fainted.

I came to, to find the whole bunch regarding me by the light of half a dozen candles.

"Look here, little man," said Drummond, "what merry jaunt have you been up to this time?"

"How did you know I was here," I asked feebly.

"The landlord's son told us you'd borrowed his bicycle," he answered. "And since they all seemed very alarmed at the pub we thought we'd come along and see. We found your machine outside, and then we found you here unconscious. What's the worry? have you seen a ghost?"

"Seen and felt it," I said grimly. "A ghastly shining yellow face, with fingers like steel bars that got me by the throat. And he'd have killed me but for a pair of hands that came out of the darkness and got him by the throat as well."

They looked at me suspiciously until Jerningham suddenly peered at my neck.

"Good God!" he said, "look at the marks on his throat."

They crowded round, and I laughed irritably.

"You don't imagine I dreamed it, do you. The thing that attacked me had a grip like a mantrap."

"Tell us again exactly what happened," said Drummond quietly.

I told them, starting with my conversation with the old gentleman that afternoon. And when I'd finished he whistled softly.

"Well done, Dixon: well done! It was a damned sporting thing to come here alone. But, laddie don't do it again I beg of you. For unless I'm greatly mistaken, but for our happening to arrive when we did your only interest by this time would have been the site for your grave."

He lit a cigarette thoughtfully.

"Phosphorous evidently on the man's face who attacked you. An old trick. Probably our headlights alarmed them, and the owner of the hands dragged him off. So that there are at least two unpleasing persons in this house beside us."

He rubbed his hands gently together.

"Splendid! At last we come to grips. Blow out those candles, boys: there's no good advertising our position too clearly. And then I think a little exploration of the old family mansion."

Once more we were in darkness save for the beam of Drummond's torch. He had it focused on the floor, and after a while he stooped down and examined the marks in the dust.

"What an extraordinary track," he remarked. "There doesn't seem to be any sign of footmarks. It's one broad smear."

We crowded round, and it certainly was a most peculiar trail. In width about eighteen inches to two feet, it stretched down the middle of the passage as far as we could see. And suddenly Drummond turned to me with a queer look in his eyes. "You say this face seemed to be about on a level with your chest," he said.

"Just about," I answered. "Why?"

"Because it strikes me that you've had even a narrower escape that we thought," he remarked. "The thing that attacked you hadn't got any legs. It was a monstrosity: some ghastly abnormality. The owner of the pair of hands dragged it after him, and that's the trail it left."

"It is a jolly house," murmured Darrell. "What does A. do now?"

"What the devil do you think," grunted Drummond. "A. follows the trail, and for the love of Mike don't get behind the light."

Now I don't suppose I should ever have thought of that. I could see Drummond in front, his right arm fully extended, holding the torch, while he kept over to the left of the passage. Behind him, in single file, we all of us followed, and, once when I drifted over to the right, Sinclair, who was just behind me, pulled me back.

"If anyone shoots," he muttered, "they shoot at the torch. Keep in line."

And the words had hardly left his mouth when there came an angry *phut* from in front of us, and a splintering of wood from behind. Simultaneously Drummond switched off the light. Silence, save for our heavy breathing—and then once again did I hear that ominous slithering noise.

"Look out," I cried. "That's the thing moving."

Then came Drummond's voice, sharp and insistent. "Light. Give me light. My God! what is it?"

And never to my dying day shall I forget the spectacle we saw when Darrell's torch focused and steadied on Drummond. The thing was on him—clawing at him: a thing that looked like a black sack. Its hands were fastened on his throat, and it was by his throat that it was supporting itself. Because it had no legs—only two stumps. It was mouthing and gibbering, and altogether dreadful. Some faint luminosity still remained on its face, but in the light of the torch it was hardly noticeable. And then I forgot everything in watching that ghastly struggle.

The dust was rising in little eddies as Drummond moved, carrying the thing with him. Of its almost superhuman strength no one knew better than I, and in a few seconds the veins were standing out on Drummond's forehead. Then he braced himself against the wall, and gripped its wrists with his hands. I could see the muscles taut and bulging under the sleeves of his coat as he tried to wrench the thing's hands away from his throat. But in spite of his enormous strength, he told me afterwards that but for the knowledge of a certain ju-jitsu grip by which a man's fingers can be forced open, the thing would have throttled him unless we had helped. As it was, help was unnecessary: the murderous hold relaxed, and, with a heave, Drummond flung the thing away from him. It landed on the floor with a thud, and for a space it stood there balancing itself on its hands and glaring at us. Then, like some great misshapen ape, it disappeared up the passage, moving on its hands and stumps.

"Good Lord!" grunted Drummond, "what a little pet."

"Where's the gun, Hugh," said Darrell curtly. His torch was flashing on the empty passage. "Put it out, Peter," snapped Drummond. "I'm thinking that gun belonged to the other bloke. We'll follow up in darkness."

And then, before we had gone two steps, there came from in front of us a loud crash, followed by a terrible scream. The scream was not repeated: only a low moaning noise could be heard, and after a while that also ceased. Once again the silence was absolute.

"For the love of Heaven," came Drummond's hoarse whisper. "Keep your eyes skinned. Who is the last man?"

"I am," said Jerningham. "Don't worry about this end." We crept forward, guided by momentary flashes of Drummond's torch. The trail was easy to follow. It led along the passage for about fifteen yards, and then turned to the right through an open door.

"Stop here," said Drummond quietly. "I'm going in alone."

And just as little details about him had struck me before, so on this occasion did the almost incredible swiftness and silence of his movements impress my mind. One instant he was there: the next he was not, but no sound had marked his going.

We clustered round the open door waiting. Once a board creaked inside, and then suddenly we heard a startled exclamation, and Drummond rejoined us.

"There's something pretty grim happened," he muttered. "Stand well away from the door. I'm going to switch on the torch."

The beam flashed on, and outlined against it was the ominous silhouette of a revolver held in his other hand. And for a space the two remained motionless: then the revolver fell to his side.

"Great Scott!" he muttered. "Poor brute!"

The crash and the scream were accounted for: also the silence that had followed. Lying motionless on the floor close to the further wall was the thing that had attacked him. And it needed no second glance to see that it was dead. There was a dreadful wound in the head; in fact, it was split completely open. And further details are unnecessary.

For a while we stared at it stupidly—the same thought in all our minds. How had it happened? Because save for the motionless figure on the floor the room was empty. What was it that had struck the poor brute this ghastly blow in the darkness. Nothing had come out of the door, and the only window was boarded up.

It was a peculiar room with stone walls and a stone ceiling, and what it could have been used for in the past completely defeated me. Let into the wall near which the body was lying were six iron rings: except for them, the walls were absolutely bare. They were fixed in a straight line about a yard from the floor, and were three or four feet apart. And below each ring the boarding was worn away as if it had been gnawed by rats. "Didn't the landlord say that the farmer who was murdered kept savage dogs?" said Darrell. "He probably used those staples to chain them up."

"Maybe he did," said Drummond grimly. "But there ain't any dogs here now, Peter, and what I want to know is what killed that poor brute."

Once again we fell silent staring at the twisted body.

"He looks as if he had been bashed over the head with a steam-hammer," said Jerningham at length. "That crash we heard was it."

"Yes, damn it!" cried Drummond. "But what caused the crash."

He took a step or two towards the body, and even as he did so there came to me, out of the blue so to speak, an idea. What made me think of it I don't know: what made me suddenly remember my conversation with the old gentleman that afternoon, I can't say. But the fact remains that mercifully I did. It was the remark he had made to me that had first caused me to suspect him. I could see him, even as I stood there, giving me that strange, penetrating stare and saying "Was it fifth or sixth? It might make a lot of difference." And the dead thing was lying between the fifth and sixth ring.

"I think I've got it," I said slowly. "It's part of the clue I was given this afternoon, and up till now I'd forgotten it."

They listened while I told them, and when I'd finished Drummond nodded his head thoughtfully.

"You're probably right," he said. "Let's work on the assumption, at any rate."

"That's all very fine and large," grunted Darrell. "But we don't want the same result, old boy. And it strikes me that if you make a mistake you won't make a second."

"I've got to chance it, Peter," answered Drummond doggedly. "If Dixon is right, we're on the track of the next clue. And nothing matters except getting that. Let's think for a moment. What's the natural thing to do when you see a ring in a wall? Pull the blamed thing, isn't it?"

"Probably what that poor brute was doing when he was killed," said Sinclair.

"Then I will pull it, too," announced Drummond calmly.

"For Heaven's sake, man," cried Jerningham, "What's the use?"

"That remains to be seen," said Drummond. "But we're going to pull those rings—and we're going to pull 'em now. Toby, go back to the car with Algy. Keep close together going through the house. In the toolbox you'll find my towrope. Bring it. And don't forget that there is at least one unconsidered little trifle loose in the house."

"If I'm right," he went on as they left the room, "the danger must lie close to the wall. That thing never moved with a wound like that in his head: he died on the spot where he was hit. Anyway, one must take a chance."

And his hand as he lit a cigarette was as steady as a rock.

Chapter 8

In Which We Explore the Mere

It is nervy work waiting. I know that my feelings were strongly reminiscent of those that I had experienced in France when the latest reports from the seats of the mighty indicated that enemy mining was proceeding underneath one's trench. To dangers seen and heard one can get tolerably used, but the unseen, silent horror of this room was making me jumpy. I felt I almost preferred my fight in the darkness with the thing that now lay dead. At last, after what seemed an interminable time, Sinclair and Longworth returned with the rope.

"See anyone?" said Drummond casually.

"Not a soul. But I thought I saw a gleam of light from one of the top rooms," said Sinclair.

"Probably our friend of the gun. Give me the rope, and let's get on with it."

"Look here, old man," said Darrell, "let's toss."

"Go to hell," remarked Drummond tersely. "It's good of you, Peter, old lad, but this is my show. The only point is that in case anything happens I rely on you to carry on the good work."

He walked across to the fifth ring and slipped the rope through it. Then he stepped back, and we breathed again. Nothing had happened so far.

"Stand clear," he said. "I'm going to pull."

He gave a tug on the rope, and the next instant it was wrenched out of his hand. Some huge object had flashed downwards through the beam of his torch and landed with a sickening thud on the dead man, tearing the rope out of his grasp as it fell. Instinctively he turned the light upwards. In the ceiling was a square, black hole, and we had a momentary glimpse of a face peering at us through it. Then it was gone, and we were left staring upwards foolishly.

It was Drummond who recovered himself first.

"A booby-trap that I like not the smell of," he said savagely. "Keep that hole in the ceiling covered, Ted, and shoot on sight."

It must have weighed a couple of hundredweight—the slab that had come out of the ceiling. There was a staple let into the centre of it, with a wire rope attached, by which it had evidently been hoisted back into position the first time. One could see the faint outline of some sort of winding gear above the opening, but of the man who had operated it there was no sign.

"No—I like not the smell of it," he repeated grimly. "It's murder—pure and simple. But if the swine think they're going to stop us they're wrong."

"What's the next move?" said someone shakily.

"See what happens when we pull the sixth ring," he said. "If what Dixon said is right, that's the other important one."

"Probably the floor will give way this time." remarked Algy Longworth gloomily. "I feel I should like a mother's soothing comfort."

We waited tensely while Drummond again adjusted the rope. He began to pull, and suddenly he gave a triumphant exclamation.

"It's moving."

It was: a crack was appearing in the wall. And then with a faint creak the whole block of stone swung round on a pivot, leaving an opening about three feet wide and six feet high.

"The poor brute was looking for that, I suppose," said Drummond, "and in the darkness pulled the wrong ring."

He crossed the room, and then stopped abruptly. He was staring at a piece of paper fastened to the back of the part that had moved.

"Well done, little man," he read slowly. "Any casualties yet? But you've still got a long way to go, and I've got some far better jests for you before you've finished. Incidentally the charming gentleman without any legs is an impromptu turn as far as I am concerned. I found him on the premises when I arrived, and he struck me as being quite in keeping with the general character of the house. I rather think he must be the so-called ghost, and I do hope he's behaved himself. But if he hasn't don't blame me. His predilections seem quite delightfully murderous, and he resents any intrusion terribly. But doubtless somebody loves him. Phyllis is still quite well, though just a *leetle* bit off her food. Isn't this fun?"

"Damn the woman," said Drummond angrily. Then he began to laugh. "Though, 'pon my soul," he went on, "if it wasn't for Phyllis, I think I should agree with her."

"Time enough for that, old boy, when we're through," said Jerningham. "Hasn't it struck you that at the moment we're in a rather bad strategical position? It's a sitting shot either from the ceiling or through that opening."

"You've said a mouthful, Ted," agreed Drummond, "Back into the passage, and we'll have a council of war."

The moon had risen, and an eerie half light was filtering through the dirty windows, making the place seem, if possible, more ghostly than before.

"Now then," said Drummond, "let's get down to the meat juice. I should think that what our one and only Irma says is right, and that the poor devil dead in there has been responsible for all the stories about this place. Probably used that phosphorous trick to frighten people. Anyway, he's out."

"Next man in is the bloke with the hands who let drive with his *bundook*," said Darrell thoughtfully.

"And any other little pals of his who may be lying about," went on Drummond. "But the thing to decide is where is the next clue?"

"The betting is a pony to a dried pea that it's down that secret passage," said Jerningham.

"Then down the passage we go, old son. But not all of us. If this was an ordinary house I wouldn't mind. But that booby-trap in there was specially prepared, and there are probably others. The question is how many of us go. I think three are enough. That leaves three to guard this end. You five do fingers out for it: two of you to come."

"Let's all come in," said Sinclair. "You too, Hugh."

"No," said Drummond decisively. "I'm going, anyway. Get a move on."

"What are fingers out?" I asked mildly.

"Laddie," said Drummond, "you may be a whale at conundrums, and I take off my hat to you over this evening's show. But your education is a bit deficient. At the word go, extend as many fingers as you like in front of you. One hand only: thumbs don't count. Go."

I extended two: a complicated mathematical proceeding took place, and the winner appeared to be Sinclair. "Once again," said Drummond. "Only the four of you. Go."

This time I extended three, and hoped for the best.

"Thirteen in all, and we start with Dixon."

"Splendid," I murmured: I didn't mind who he started with. The passage, in spite of the dust, was comfortable: and, as far as I could see, the ceiling was ordinary lath and plaster.

"Come on then," said Drummond. "I'll go first, then Dixon, then Toby."

I opened my eyes abruptly. I suppose I'm not very clever at that game. I appeared to have won, anyway, which was frightfully jolly and all that.

"Just guard this end, you three," said Drummond. "And you'd better give us a couple of hours at least."

He stepped back into the room, and flashed his torch up at the hole in the ceiling. No sign of anyone, and he led the way across the floor to the opening in the wall.

"Don't forget," he whispered urgently, "that anything may happen."

"I won't," I assured him, and wondered if a ton of masonry on one's head was a comparatively painless death.

The passage led downwards, and the walls and ceiling gradually grew damper and damper, until large drops of water splashed on my head at each step I took forward. Drummond was in front with his torch, and progress was slow as he tested every foothold he took before advancing. At length he paused, and waited for us to come up with him.

"I believe we're under the mere," he announced.

"Hooray!" I cried enthusiastically. "I've always wanted to drown."

And suddenly he began to shake with laughter. "You priceless bird," he remarked. "Look here—you go back—you've done your fair share for tonight—and Toby and I will go on."

"Be blowed for a yarn," I said. "Let's get on with it." Once more we crept forward, and at length the passage started to rise again. It seemed to be bending right-handed the whole time, and was getting drier and drier. Suddenly Drummond paused; we had come to a fork. To the right a flight of stone steps led upwards: to the left it continued on the level.

"Shall we try the steps first," whispered Drummond, and the next instant he switched off his torch. For quite distinctly and from close to had come the sound of a woman's voice.

"It can't be possible that we've found her," he breathed.

"What—your wife?" I muttered.

"No—the other," he answered. "Supposing she didn't expect us to track her so quickly, and as a result we've caught her up."

Once again came the voice, and this time a man spoke too.

"It's up the steps," said Drummond. "Toby—you wait here: we may be putting our heads straight into it. If anything happens, sprint back to the others and tell them. Dixon—you come half way up as far as the bend."

I crept up behind him, feeling with my fingers on the walls. And suddenly I found Drummond's hand on my arm.

"Stay there," he whispered. "I'm going on alone."

Not two yards in front of us a beam of light shone out from under a closed door.

I waited tensely, crouched against the wall: could it be possible that we had run this woman to earth—that she was on the other side of the door? And, if so, how many men were likely to be with her? True, we had only heard one voice, but that meant nothing.

With a crash Drummond flung open the door and stepped into the room. A man and a woman were sitting at a table on which the remains of a meal were lying. Two candles guttered in the sudden draught, and with a cry of fear the woman rose to her feet.

"Keep your hands on the table—both of you," snapped Drummond.

"Who are you?" said the man in a surly voice, his eyes fixed on the revolver. "And what d'you want?"

"A little conversation, my friend," said Drummond. "In the first place—who are you? And who is the lady?"

He flashed his torch on her face, and stared at her intently. She was a haggard, unkempt woman. Her face was lined and wrinkled, her hair streaked with grey. And she looked most desperately ill.

"Never you mind who we are," said the man angrily. "It ain't no blasted business of yours, is it? What are you doing in this house, anyway?"

"I admit," answered Drummond pleasantly, "that under normal circumstances you would have a certain amount of justification for your question. But you can hardly call this house normal, can you?"

"Are you the police, mister?" said the woman, speaking for the first time.

"I am not," said Drummond. "I've got nothing to do with them."

"Well, what do you want," said the man again. "Are you one of the bunch who have been fooling round this house for the last few weeks."

"We get warm," remarked Drummond. "No—I am not one of the bunch. At the same time, though not of them I am after them, if you get me. But for them I should not be here. Am I to take it, then, that you disown them also."

The man cursed foully. "Disown them," he snarled. "For two pins I'd have murdered the lot."

"Then it was not you who rigged up that pleasant little booby-trap?"

"What booby-trap? Look here, mister, I'm getting fair sick of this. For God's sake clear out."

The woman put a restraining hand on his arm, and whispered

something in his ear. She seemed to be trying to pacify him, and after a time he shrugged his shoulders and stood up. "Sorry, sir, if I lost my temper. But if you ain't the police, and you ain't one of that bunch, then what do you want?"

"One moment," said Drummond. "Dixon," he called over his shoulder.

"Look here," he whispered as I joined him, "would you recognize the hands of the man who dragged that thing away from you?"

"I certainly should," I answered. "And it's not this bloke."

He nodded. "Good. That's one thing settled, anyway. Now," he resumed. "I'll tell you what we want. Hidden somewhere in this charming country mansion is a piece of paper or a letter or a message of some sort which I am looking for. Do you know where it is?"

The man looked at the woman, and she looked at him. "I reckon I do," he said. "And it's in a place you'd never find if you looked for ten years."

Drummond's eyes never left his face. "How do you know where it is?" he said quietly.

"Because I saw one of them people put it there," answered the man.

"Will you show me where it is?" continued Drummond.

Once again the woman bent and whispered to him.

"All right," he said. "Look here, sir, I'll show you where it is if you'll give me your word that you won't tell a living soul you've seen us here."

And suddenly the truth dawned on me.

"I believe," I whispered to Drummond, "that this is the man who murdered the farmer ten years ago. They've been hiding here ever since."

"Are you the man who murdered Farmer Jesson?" shot out Drummond abruptly.

The woman gave a little scream, and clutched his shoulders.

"Never you mind who I am," he said angrily. "You've forced your way in here, and I've got to trust you. But unless you give me your word to say nothing, you can damned well look for that envelope yourself."

"I give you my word," said Drummond quietly.

"What about your friend?"

"I speak for all of us," said Drummond. "Now lead on. But you'd better understand one thing, my friend. Any monkey tricks, and you'll be for it good and strong."

The man looked straight at him.

"Why should there be any monkey tricks?" he remarked quietly. "All I want is to see the last of you as soon as possible. Follow me."

He took a lantern off a nail in the wall and lit the candle inside. Then he led the way down the stairs.

"Who's this?" He stopped suspiciously as the light showed up Toby Sinclair still waiting in the passage.

"A friend of mine," said Drummond. "My promise covers him."

"There's someone else about here, Hugh," said Toby in a low voice. "While you've been up there I've seen a gleam of light along the passage to the left, and I'm almost certain I heard movement."

Drummond turned to the man.

"Do you hear that?" he said curtly. "Who is it?"

The man shrugged his shoulders.

"Ask me another. This place has been like a rabbit warren lately."

"Which way do we go?"

"Along there," he pointed, "where your friend says he saw the light. Don't you want to go? It doesn't matter to me."

He stood there swinging his lantern. By its light I could see Drummond staring at him intently: was it or was it not a trap? The man's face was expressionless: he seemed completely indifferent as to whether we went or whether we didn't. And at last Drummond made up his mind.

"Lead on," he ordered. "But don't forget I'm just behind you, and there will be no soft music to herald the hitting."

Certainly there was no further gleam of light from in front, and the feeble flicker of the candle only seemed to intensify the surrounding darkness. The passage itself was opening out a little, and the roof was higher, so that walking was easy. And we must have gone about thirty yards when we came to a heavy wooden door. It was open, and our guide passed through without any hesitation.

"The note is in this room," he said, holding the lantern above his head. By its light we could see it was of a similar type to the one we had just left. There was a table and a couple of chairs, and the whole place smelt of disuse, and reeked of damp. Water dripped from the ceiling and the walls, and it struck me that wherever we had been before, we were now most certainly under the mere.

"Well, get it," snapped Drummond. "This place stinks worse than a seaside boarding-house."

"It isn't quite so easy to get it," said the man, and, even as he spoke, I knew we were trapped. A sudden look in his eyes; a scowl that was half a sneer—and then darkness. He had blown out the candle.

"Hell!" roared Drummond, and from the door the man toughed.

"You poor boobs," came his mocking voice. "You don't know enough to come in out of the wet."

Well—perhaps that remark was worth it to him: perhaps it was not. It just gave Drummond time to switch on his torch. By its light we saw the door closing, and the fingers of the man's hand round it. And the next instant a shot rang out. For quickness of shooting combined with accuracy I would never have believed it possible. Drummond had plugged him through the fingers. A torrent of blasphemy came from the other side of the door as we sprang towards it: but we were just too late. The bolt clanged home as we got there: we were shut in. And from the other side of the door the blasphemy continued.

At last it ceased, and Drummond bent and picked something off the floor.

"I have here," he said, "the top joint of one of your fingers. The next time I see you, my friend, you shall have it served up as a savoury."

We listened to the retreating footsteps, and he gave a short laugh.

"On balance I think we win," he remarked. "Peter and Co. are bound to find us, and until they do we can think out a few choice methods of cooking fingers."

He lit a cigarette thoughtfully, and then he laughed.

"Damn the fellow! And that fish-faced woman was in it, too, I suppose. They certainly fooled us all right."

He flashed his torch round the room. There was no trace of a window, but of one thing there was more than a trace. It stared us straight in the face—a sheet of notepaper pinned in the centre of the wall opposite the door. We crowded round it, and in silence we read the message written in the handwriting we were getting to know so well.

"Will you walk into my parlour said the spider to the fly? My dear friend, I grieve for you. This is not the old form at all. But then I always thought, little one, that your resemblance to a bull in a china shop was just a little too pronounced. And this time you've done it. Honestly I never thought the chase would end quite yet. In some ways I'm sorry: I had one or two beauties left for you. In fact the next clue is in tomorrow's Times, which I now fear you will never see.

"How many of you are there in here, I wonder? That will be reported to me naturally in due course, but my woman's curiosity prompts me to put down the question now. Because I have taken steps to cover all tracks, and I fear your bodies will never be recovered.

"Goodbye, *mon ami*. What I shall do with Phyllis remains to be seen. Play with her a little longer, anyway, I think."

We stared at one another speechlessly. What on earth did the woman mean—"bodies never recovered."

"That's where she's made her blooming error," grunted Drummond. But his voice didn't carry much conviction. "Let's have a look at that door," he went on. "There must be some way out."

But there wasn't; the door was as solid as the wall. And it was while we were examining the bolt that a faint hissing noise became audible. Drummond straightened up and stood listening.

"What the deuce is that?" he muttered. "And where does it come from?"

Once again his torch flashed round the room. The noise was increasing till it was almost a shrill whistle and we located it at once. It came from a small circular metal pipe that stuck out about three inches from the wall close by the door. I put my finger over it: the pressure was too great too keep it there. Some gas was being pumped into the room, and the same thought struck us all. There was no ventilation.

"She would seem," said Drummond calmly, "to have won. Unless Peter arrives in time. Sorry, you chaps."

"What's the gas," cried Toby Sinclair. "I used to know something about chemistry."

"Well, I didn't," said Drummond. "And whatever it is it's not likely to be for the benefit of our health."

"Keep the torch on the pipe, Hugh," said Toby quietly. He, too, put his finger on the end, then he tasted it and smelt it.

"I wonder," he muttered, and his voice was shaking a little. "No smell: practically no taste. Do you fellows mind if I take a chance."

"We mind strongly if you don't," said Drummond calmly. "And do it darned quickly."

Sinclair struck a match: came a sudden little pop and from the end of the pipe there shot out a long blue flame.

"I was right," he said, wiping his forehead. "It's carbon monoxide. Another five minutes and she would have won. As it is if we take turns at breathing through the keyhole we ought to escape with only a head like the morning after."

"Mother's bright boy," said Drummond lightly, but I saw his hand rest for a moment on Sinclair's shoulder. "Explain."

"Carbon monoxide, old boy. Don't taste, or smell, and you can't see it. One of the most deadly poisonous gases known to science. If you light it it forms carbon dioxide which isn't poisonous, but only suffocates. So if as I say we breathe through the keyhole in turn, and Peter isn't too long, we ought to get away with it."

It was a weird scene—almost fantastic. I remember thinking at the time that it simply couldn't be true; that it was some incredible nightmare from which I should shortly wake up. In turn we solemnly stooped down, put our mouths to the keyhole and sucked in the pure air from the other side of the door. One, two, three; one, two, three—for all the world like performing marionettes.

It was Sinclair who noticed it first, and nudged us both to draw our attention because speaking was ill-advised. The flame was decreasing in size. Now it was burning fitfully. At times it shot out to its original length. At others it almost died away. And then suddenly it went out altogether.

He took a piece of paper from his pocket and a pencil.

"Go on at the keyhole," he wrote. "Don't speak unless it's essential. Room full of carbon dioxide, but no more coming now."

One, two, three—suck; one, two, three—suck; till my back was aching and I cursed Darrell and the others for not coming. Surely to Heaven it must be at least three hours by now since we had left them. And then another ghastly thought struck me. Even when they did come how were they going to open the door without a key? And there was no key in the keyhole.

One, two, three—suck: damn this confounded woman and all her works. I felt that I would willingly have given the whole of my extremely modest fortune and then some to have had the privilege of putting her in the room, and laughing at her from the other side of the door.

One, two, three—suck; t was becoming utterly intolerable. Once I chanced it and took a breath in the room, and it felt as if an eiderdown had been pressed over my mouth. Carbon dioxide—used-up air. Old tags of chemistry came back to me in the intervals of one, two, three—suck.

Suddenly we all of us paused instinctively: a key had been put in the keyhole. The bolt was turning, and with our heads feeling as if iron bands were fastened round them we stood and watched. Trying not to breathe, and with our lungs bursting for air we watched the door open. A hand came round the edge—a hand with a curious red scar on the middle finger. It was the man who had dragged the thing away from me earlier in the evening.

I signed furiously to Drummond, but as he said afterwards it was a matter of complete indifference to him whose hand it was. All he wanted was air, and a grip on somebody's throat. He got both, and he was not feeling amused.

He was a big man, the owner of the hand, and he was wearing some form of respirator. He was also a powerful man, but as I have said Drummond was not feeling amused. He shot across the room, did the owner of the hand, as if he'd been kicked from close quarters by a mule—whilst we shot into the passage. Then having locked the door and removed the key we sat down and just breathed. And if anybody is ever in doubt as to what is the most marvellous sensation in the world, they may take it from me that it consists of just breathing—under certain circumstances.

From the other side of the door came the sound of furious blows. He seemed to be hurling himself against it with the whole weight of his body.

"What about it, Hugh," said Toby. "The respirator he has on is only of use against carbon monoxide."

"Then let him have a whack at breathing through the keyhole," said Drummond grimly. "Gosh! I wouldn't go through that last half hour again for twenty thousand quid. Besides I want my other little pal, and if I can find him he'll eat his finger here and now."

But of neither the woman nor him was there any trace. The room was empty; the birds had flown. And as we stood in the passage at the foot of the stairs that led to the room they had been in, the only sound that broke the silence was the hoarse shouting of the man who was caught in the trap that had been laid for us.

"I think we'll let the swab out," remarked Drummond thoughtfully. "We might get something out of him."

And it is possible we might have, had not the last little effort in that pleasing country mansion taken place. It was purely accidental, and I was responsible for it. About a yard along the passage beyond the fork a steel bar was sticking out from the wall. It looked strong: it looked quite capable of bearing my weight. So I sat on it, and found it was not capable of bearing my weight. It collapsed under me, and I found myself on the floor. And even as I picked myself up there came from the room we had left a frenzied scream of fear, and a strange rushing noise.

Stupidly we stared at the door, focusing our torches on it. From underneath it water was pouring through. From each side, getting higher and higher, it came trickling out, until it shot like a jet from a fountain through the keyhole.

"Run," roared Drummond. "Run like hell. If that door gives we're done. We've let the lake in."

It was true: the meaning of the phrase about the bodies not being recovered was clear at last. We raced wildly along the passage back towards the house. Would the door hold long enough? And it did—by about five seconds. We heard the crash as it gave when we were in the lowest part, and we pounded on up the rise. Behind us came the swish of the water now pouring unchecked through the open doorway. It came in a wall six feet high along the passage, and like a huge wave breaking on the shore it hurled itself after us two feet above the level of the mere, and then, angry and swirling, receded to its proper height.

In front of us we could see the opening into the house: behind us, black and evil-looking, the water still eddied and heaved. A chair which had been swept along by the torrent bobbed up and down on the surface and then gradually became still. But of the man who had been in the room there was no trace. Hidden somewhere in that underground labyrinth his body still remains, and the waters of the mere have sealed his tomb.

Slowly we climbed the last bit of the passage and stepped into the room.

"Thank the Lord," said Jerningham, "you're all right. We were just coming to find you, when the most extraordinary upheaval took place in the lake."

Dawn had come, and we followed him to the window outside.

"It's almost died away now," he went on. "But about five minutes ago, right out there in the centre, the water began to heave. Almost like a whirlpool. What's happened?"

"An airy nothing," remarked Drummond. "They've tried to gas us, and they've tried to drown us, and—" He broke off suddenly staring across the mere. "It's a difficult light to see in," he said, "but isn't there someone moving over there in the undergrowth?" Personally I could see nothing, but after a moment or two he nodded. "There is. I see 'em. Two. Back from the window, boys: this matter requires thought. No one has come out this way, I take it?"

"Not a soul," said Darrell.

"Then," said Drummond to Sinclair and me, "those two on the other side are fish-faced Lizzie and her gentleman friend."

"Shall we round 'em up?" remarked Toby.

Drummond lit a cigarette thoughtfully.

"I think not," he said at length. "Look here—let us consider this matter because it seems to me that we have come to the parting of the ways. I suppose nobody has a bottle of Bass? Bad staff work. However, let us pull ourselves together, and get the grey matter to function."

He sighed profoundly.

"A ghastly hour to do so, but I have the glimmerings of an idea. Now, first of all there were in this house four individuals that we know of. First, the legless bird who got a brick on his head. Now it's possible that what she said in her note was right, and that he wasn't one of the party, but just went with the house. Anyway it doesn't matter, he is out of it."

He held out an enormous finger.

"That's one. Secondly, there's the bloke who pulled him off Dixon, and whose face we saw through the hole in the ceiling. He, dear little chap, is very dead down below there. He's drowned."

Another finger joined the first.

"And short of sending down a diver his body can never be recovered. Nor any other body that might be down there. Do you get me?"

"Not the slightest," said Jerningham cheerfully. "Are there any more down below?"

"No—and at the same time, yes," remarked Drummond.

"Lucid as ever," murmured Peter Darrell. "Hasn't anybody got any beer to give him?"

Drummond grinned gently.

"It does sound a bit involved," he agreed. "But it isn't really. The passage we went down runs under the mere. Moreover, since the good-looking lady and gentleman on whom we called did not come out this way they must either still be below, or they got out some other. If they are below they also are drowned: if, on the other hand, they got out...."

"Then they're not," said Algy brightly.

"Sit on his head," remarked Darrell.

"There were two people moving on the other side of the mere," pursued Drummond. "So let us assume that the passage continues under the water and comes out in the undergrowth opposite. Further, that those two escaped. What then, my brave hearts—what then? What message of fun and laughter are they going to give to our little Irma?"

He paused triumphantly, and Algy scratched his head.

"Dashed if I know," he burbled.

"Sit on his head," repeated Darrell morosely.

"The last thing they saw of us," went on Drummond, "was when we were locked in that confounded room with carbon something or other pouring into it. And if old Toby hadn't had a brain storm that is the last that anyone would ever have seen of us. Do you get me now? For the purposes of this little affair that is the last that anyone will see of us."

We sat staring at him, realizing at length what he was driving at.

"But look here," said Toby doubtfully, "if we're going on with the chase they're bound to find out."

"Why?" demanded Drummond. "We've disguised ourselves pretty often before. Peter, Ted and Algy will carry on as before: you, Dixon, and I are dead. Drowned, laddie, in the cold, dark waters of the mere."

"By Jove! Hugh," said Darrell thoughtfully, "I believe that is a thundering good idea."

"I'm certain it is," said Drummond. "Look here," he went on gravely, "we've seen enough tonight to realize that this isn't a game of kiss-in-the-ring. I confess that I hadn't thought that she would go to quite the lengths she has done. It is by a sheer piece of luck only that one or all of us are not dead now. Don't let there be any mistake about that. She meant to kill us—or some of us. And that gives us a foretaste of what is to come. If she has gone to these lengths in the earlier stages of the hunt, we're going to have the devil's own time later. Well—what's she going to say to herself? She knows us of old. She knows that if we three had been killed, you three would not give up. She'll expect you after her."

Darrell nodded. "Quite right."

"So we'll have the hunter hunted," went on Drummond cheerfully. "You'll be chasing clues: they'll be chasing you and we'll be chasing them."

"There's one small flaw in your otherwise excellent scheme," I put in. "How are they to know that the next clue is contained in this morning's Times? Only we three saw her message to that effect, and we're dead."

"Damn the man," said Drummond. "He's quite right."

"Let's wait until we see the message," remarked Jerningham. "It may be obviously intended for you, in which case we should naturally spot it. Or it may prove necessary for us all six to cover our traces. Let's leave that for a bit. The thing that must be done at once is for you three to go to ground here somewhere, and for us three to register alarm and despondency. We'll go and search the grounds, and if by any chance we run into your two pals, we'll pretend we're looking for you. Ask them to help, or if they've seen you."

"You're right, Ted," said Drummond. "Go to it. We'll lie up here."

Chapter 9

In Which We Get the Second Clue

And so began the second phase in this strange game. I know that I was feeling most infernally tired and yet sleep would not come. My brain was too busy with the amazing happenings of the previous night. Once again I saw that luminous face being dragged away from me through the darkness, and I fell to wondering what the poor brute had really been. Was the woman right in what she had written? Had this hideous, demented creature been the sole occupant of the house for years, and thus given it its bad reputation? Living by day in the secret passage under the mere, and coming out at night if it thought intruders were about. With a shudder I glanced through the open door where it still lay with the stone on top of it; anyway, death had been quick.

And then my thoughts turned to the amazing brain that had planned it all. What manner of woman could this be who dealt out flippant notes and death alternately? The labour of preparing the mechanism for dropping that heavy stone and then pulling it up again must have been enormous.

And suddenly Drummond spoke half to himself and half to me.

"She means to get us all: nab the whole bunch. She won't rest till she does." Then he smiled a little grimly. "And you thought it was a joke."

"Guilty," I acknowledged. "You must admit though that it's a little unusual."

He laughed shortly, and then he began to frown. "I can stand anything on two legs or on four," he grunted, "but these mechanical devices don't give a fellow a chance. And I'm uneasy about those other three. Seems to me we're letting them bear the brunt from now on. She'll concentrate on them."

He relapsed into a moody silence, and I said nothing. There seemed to be nothing to say. What he feared was quite correct, or so it appeared to me. Only the merest luck had saved several of our lives that night, and luck could not be expected to continue indefinitely. Any one of us might have pulled that fifth bolt instead of the wretched creature who now lay dead underneath it. And then, had there been time to wind it up, another might have been bagged as well.

That was the devil of it all: we weren't confronting ordinary dangers and risks, but specially and cunningly prepared ones. It was a case of the German booby-traps over again, where the most harmless-looking objects hid delay-action mines.

"What the dickens are we going to do with that body?" said Drummond suddenly.

"Why not put it into the water," said Sinclair, "and then close the passage up?"

"Not a bad idea. Stoop as you pass the window, in case those two are still outside."

And so we lifted the stone sufficiently to extricate it, and carried it down the passage to the water's edge. More wreckage had appeared to join the chair: the place smelt and felt like a charnel-house. We toppled the poor brute in, and beat it for the house: anything was better than that dank death-trap. And then we pushed on the sixth ring and the secret door slipped back into position.

"Thank the Lord that's over," said Toby with a sigh of relief. "And all I can say is that I hope in future she confines her activities to the open air."

Footsteps on the stairs made us step back hurriedly, but it proved to be only the other three returning.

"What luck?" cried Drummond.

"I think we've done the trick, old boy," said Darrell. "We ran into them on the other side—a woman of repulsive aspect and a man with his hand bound up. We were running round in small circles pretending to look for you. Incidentally, what you thought was right: that passage comes out near a broken-down old ruin on the other side. There was a rusty iron door which they had presumably opened. And when we saw them we told 'em the tale. Asked them if they'd noticed the extraordinary upheaval in the lake, and inquired with the utmost agitation if they'd seen three men anywhere about. Said we'd been ghost-hunting. I don't know if they believed us or not, but I don't see that it matters very much if they did. We never let on by the quiver of an eyelid that we suspected them."

"What did they say?" said Drummond.

"'If your friends have been ghost-hunting,' the man said, 'I fear they've found a very substantial one. My wife and I were out for an early morning stroll, when we suddenly saw the upheaval in the lake. And if you will look down that passage'—he pointed through the opening—'you will see the water. I fear that your friends must have inadvertently found a most dangerous piece of mechanism, which I have heard of often but never believed to be really existent. Nothing more nor less, in fact, than a diabolical arrangement for flooding the whole of this underwater passage which comes out into the house on the other side. Doubtless you found the opening there.'

"We did," I said, registering horror and despondency.

"'Then if your friends have not come out that end, I very much fear they must all be drowned. For they certainly haven't come out this.'

"'How dreadful!' said the woman, and Algy made hoarse noises presumably meant to indicate grief."

"They were damned good," said Algy plaintively.

"My dear man, you sounded like a cow with an alcoholic stomach cough," said Jerningham.

"But what happened finally?" demanded Drummond.

"They drifted off, and it seemed to us they were still on the lookout for something. And then it suddenly struck us what it was. It's the other bloke: the one who is drowned down below. So we sprinted back here in order to prevent them coming at any rate yet. As there seem to be only the two openings they're almost bound to come and examine this end as soon as we are gone. And it was going to mess things up a bit if they found all you three here. So what I suggest is this. You three must go to ground in real earnest somewhere. And you must wait until we give you the all clear—in a day or two or perhaps a week."

"Go to blazes," said Drummond.

"We in the meanwhile will go and drown our sorrows in beer, and later on we'll bring you the corks to smell. We'll also get a copy of The Times, and then will come the problem of smuggling you out of this house unseen. We'll have to discuss that later."

"Right you are, Peter," said Drummond. "You've about hit it. Incidentally, where shall we go to ground?"

He glanced round, and finally stared at the ceiling.

"That seems to me to be the best spot," he remarked thoughtfully. "We know it can be inhabited because that bird was up there. And if those two come we might be able to hear something. Only how the deuce do we get up there? A chair on the top of the table and I might reach."

He could—just—and in an instant he had swung himself through the hole and disappeared from view.

"Splendid," His face reappeared through the hole. "Plenty of room for all three of us. Come along, Dixon—I'll pull you up."

He got me by the wrists, and heaved me up beside him as easily as I would lift a child. And then Toby Sinclair followed.

"Take away the chair and the table, Peter," he said. "And for the love of Allah bring back a dozen with you in your pockets. My mouth is like an asbestos washer."

"We'll come back, old boy, as soon as we possibly can," said Darrell. "I'll drive your car and take Dixon's bicycle. And we shall say that you have been suddenly summoned to London for failing to pay the poor girl her weekly postal order if any questions are asked."

"Say what you like," said Drummond resignedly. "But bring me beer."

And so commenced a weary vigil. A passage, evidently communicating with the rest of the network, led out of our hiding-place, but there was no longer any incentive to explore. All we could do was to sit and wait until the others came back and told us the coast was clear. And that might not be for hours. In fact it seemed to me that anyway it would be unsafe to go before night if we were to succeed in getting away unseen. Which left us with the joyful prospect of spending fourteen or fifteen hours in the most acute discomfort.

Suddenly Drummond sat up and put a finger to his lips. I had heard nothing myself, but as I had already discovered all his senses seemed twice as keenly developed as my own. And after a while I too heard a creak on the stairs outside, and then another.

"Not a sound," he breathed. "But if they find us we've got to sock 'em. Keep back from the opening or they may see us."

We drew back so that we could only just see the doorway, and waited. There was someone coming along the passage now, and a moment or two later our friend of the damaged hand put his head cautiously round the corner. Then he spoke to someone behind him.

"All right," he called out. "Come on."

The woman joined him.

"What's the use?" she said peevishly. "You're not going to find him here."

"Cut it out," he snarled. "If Jim was in the passage when the door gave with the water he may have escaped up this end and be waiting inside."

He tugged on the sixth ring, and the secret door swung open once more. Then he disappeared down the passage while the woman leaned against the wall.

"Not a sign." He came back into the room and dosed the door. "But those three guys have bunged that madman's body into the water."

He stood in the centre of the room gnawing his fingers.

"I wonder how much they knew," he muttered.

"What does it matter what they knew," said the woman. "Let's get out of this—I'm fed up."

"You'll get a clip under the jaw in a minute," he remarked. "We're getting a couple of hundred of the best for this job, and you ain't likely ever to earn a couple of hundred pence with a face like yours."

"Well, what is it you want to know?" cried the woman irritably.

"Whether those other three guys—the ones that came down to us—are really below there."

"Heaven save the man, where else can they be?" She stamped her foot. "You got 'em in the room, didn't you? And you locked 'em in the room, didn't you? And you turned on the gas, didn't you? And they were still in the room twenty minutes after. Where else can they be now?"

"I'd like to have seen 'em," he muttered.

"Well, since you ain't a ruddy fish, you can't," she remarked. "I'm going. I want some sleep."

She paused in the doorway.

"Come on, Bill," she said in a milder voice. "It's clear enough what happened. When Jim pulled the lever he didn't get out quick enough. He got caught by the water, poor old stiff—and he's down there himself now. And so are the other three."

"I suppose you're right," he answered. "We'll push off."

And then he glanced up towards the ceiling.

"What about putting that stone back?"

"Leave it," said the woman. "If anyone gets into trouble it's going to be those three who were fooling around outside. Nobody knows we've been here, and nobody ever will if you'll only get a move on instead of standing there like a dummy. Besides, you ought to have that hand of yours looked at."

"Blast that big fellow," said the man venomously. "I'd give something to have a once over with him."

The woman laughed shortly.

"You would," she said. "From what I saw of him you'd give up every hope of ever being recognized again. He'd eat you—with one hand. Come on—or I'll fall asleep where I stand. The telegraph office won't be open till nine, and there's nothing to be done till then. You've got her address, haven't you?"

"I've got the usual one," he answered, following her from the room.

Their voices died away as they went along the passage, and I thought the unfortunate Drummond was going to have an apoplectic fit. "Just as we were getting something useful," he groaned. "An address. The address."

"Probably only an accommodation one," said Toby sleepily. "Wake me if I snore, chaps, but I must have a bit of shut eye."

And still sleep would not come to me. I got into every conceivable position I could think of: I counted innumerable sheep going through a gate: but at the end of an hour I was wider awake than ever. The other two were peacefully unconscious, and at last I gave up trying. It was as well, in any case, that one of us should remain on guard, and so I settled myself as comfortably as I could and waited for the time to pass. From below came the occasional crack of a board as the sun's warmth began to penetrate into the house, but except for that no sound broke the silence. Seven o'clock came—eight: in my imagination I could smell the smell of hot coffee and bacon and eggs. I could see racks of toast and marmalade disappearing down the throats of the other three thugs at the Angler's Rest. And I wondered why Heaven was treating me so. To the best of my belief I was no worse than other men. Within reasonable limits I had paid my just whack of Income Tax: I had, only recently, registered enjoyment over the acidulated beverage which my Aunt Jane fondly imagined to be port. And as a reward I found myself sitting in an attic, several inches of dust and a bad smell on a beautiful summer's morning. Moreover when I gazed into the vista of the future all I could see was myself disguised as a German tourist or the hind legs of a cow having fun and games in even more damnable spots than the one in which I was at present. Emphatically not what the doctor had ordered. . . .

I shifted my position so as to distribute the cramp more evenly throughout my anatomy, and in doing so I saw into the room below. Just the same except that the shadow thrown by the open door had moved as the sun got higher. A simple little problem in trigonometry, I reflected. If the door was eight feet high and the shadow was nine feet long what was the height of the sun above the horizon? Door over shadow was tangent of the angle. Or was it cosine? Anyway one would want a book of logarithms. . . . One would want. . . .

My tongue grew suddenly dry. The height of the sun above the horizon had nothing to do with the sudden eddy of dust that swirled up in the passage outside. Nor had it anything to do with another shadow that had just appeared—the shadow of a human being. Someone was outside: someone whom I could not see—yet.

I glanced round at the other two. They were six or seven feet away: to wake them up would cause noise. Moreover they were sleeping silently, so it was best to leave them as they were.

Once more I turned back to the room: the shadow had materialized. Standing in the doorway was a woman—one of the most beautiful women I have ever seen in my life. I put her age at about thirty, though it may have been two or three years more. She was, as far as my masculine eye could judge, perfectly dressed—but it was her face, or rather her expression, that held me spellbound. There was contempt in it, and hatred—and yet, mingled with them, a sort of pity and regret. Once her eyes travelled to the bolts in the wall, and she smiled—a lazy, almost Oriental smile. And then she did an extraordinary thing. Still standing motionless she glanced upwards. Not at me, not at the hole in the ceiling, but as a woman looks up in prayer. The whole expression of her face had changed: there was in it now a wonderful triumph. Her eyes were half-closed: her whole body seemed to relax into utter surrender. And suddenly she spoke:

"I would have kept him till last, my loved one—but it was not to be. But there are still the other three—and her. After, I will come to you."

And then it seemed to me that she took in her arms a head I could not see—and kissed lips that to her were real. Lingeringly, passionately as a woman kisses her lover. Gradually her arms fell to her side, and for a while she stood with her face transfigured and her eyes closed. Then she drew herself up: the vision had vanished. She gave one more glance round the room and was gone, leaving no trace of her visit save a faint, elusive scent. Jasmine, and yet not quite jasmine—something I had never smelt before, something I could never mistake in the future. Something unique, something in keeping with the woman herself. For she had seemed to me in that moment of self-revelation, when she spoke to the unseen, to be of the type for whom men will sacrifice their honour and even their lives.

Stiffly, like a man waking from a dream, I moved over to Drummond and shook him by the shoulder.

"What is it?" he said, instantly awake.

"Your friend Irma has been here," I answered quietly.

"What!" he almost shouted. "Then why in hell. . . ."

He was standing up in his excitement, but with an effort he pulled himself together. "How do you know it was her? Tell me about it."

He listened in perfect silence whilst I told him what I had seen.

"I couldn't wake you without making a noise," I said when I had finished. "And I don't know," I added candidly, "that I could have wakened you anyway. I watched that woman almost as if I had been in a trance. But one thing is certain—she thinks you are dead. Another thing is certain—she is going for the other three. And your wife. And then she will commit suicide."

"You think she's mad," said Drummond.

"No, I don't think that she's mad. I think she's more dangerous even than that. She's a woman with an obsession—a mission in life. That man she spoke to was real to her—as real as you are to me. He is still her lover though he is dead. And her mission is to revenge his death. She's got foreign blood in her, and if I wanted any more proof than I have had already as to the seriousness of this show I've got it now. This is a vendetta—and only your deaths will finish it."

"Perhaps it's as well he didn't wake you up, Hugh," said Toby thoughtfully. "You can bet she's covered her traces pretty effectually, and what could you have done if you had caught her? It wouldn't have helped you to find Phyllis. In addition you'd have given away the fact that you're not dead."

"You may be right," agreed Drummond at length. "But, by Jove! I'd like to have seen her. You'd recognize her again, Dixon?"

"In a million," I said. "And I'd recognize that scent."

"Which is less likely to change than her appearance," he remarked shortly. And then he frowned suddenly. "You're quite certain, aren't you, that it was genuine—this performance of hers? I mean you don't think that she knew we were here and did it to bluff us."

"If that show wasn't genuine," I said, "she is the most marvellous actress the world has ever seen. No: I'm certain it was *pukka*."

He grunted thoughtfully and sat down again. "Perhaps so," he said after a while.

"Besides," I went on, "what could be her object in doing it if she knew we were here?"

"When you know the lady as well as I do," he answered, "you'll realize that she doesn't conform to ordinary rules."

He relapsed into silence, his chin sunk on his chest, and for the first time the full realization of what we were engaged in came to me. Before, this woman had been a legendary figure, a writer of would-be flippant letters, a maker of skilfully devised death-traps. Dangerous certainly—more than dangerous—but with at any rate some idea of making a sporting game of it. I had believed that if we did pull through, if we did follow the clues successfully, she intended to play the game and restore Drummond's wife to him. And I had believed that she proposed to give us a sporting chance of so doing. Now I believed it no longer.

However much Drummond might doubt it I knew that what I had seen was genuine. The woman had ceased to be a legend and had become a reality—a reality ten times more dangerous than any legend. Gone was any hope of a sporting chance: she meant and always had meant to kill the lot of us. What strange jink in her brain had made her decide on this particular method of doing so was beside the point—probably the same jink that makes a cat play with a mouse before finishing it off. The cruelty that lies latent in the female. And she was gratifying that whilst pursuing her inexorable purpose. Letting us think we were playing a game, whilst all the time she had no intention of playing herself. Letting us think we had a chance of success, whilst all the time we had none.

For what chance had we? True by the most marvellous fluke we had escaped the night before—but flukes cannot continue indefinitely. Sooner or later she would have us, as she had always meant to have us. And the cellar below showed exactly the amount of mercy we should receive.

What chance had Drummond against such an antagonist? I glanced at him, sunk in thought, his great fists clenched by his side. Let him get his hands on anything on two legs—well and good. God help the thing! But this wasn't a question of brute strength: this was a question of cunning and brain. This wasn't man to man: this was a human being against mechanical traps. Strength was of no avail against poison gas and specially prepared devices.

I wondered if he was even now thinking out some plan of-campaign. To meet guile with guile was our only hope, and somehow he didn't strike me as being the right man for that. Something to hit hard and often and he won in a canter: but first find the thing to hit. "Gosh! I hope they've brought the beer."

I sighed a little wearily: such was our leader's mentality. "Doubtless they will when they come," I assured him.

"When they come!" he grunted. "You wouldn't hear a howitzer going off in the next room, laddie. They have come. That flat-footed blighter Algy has fallen over his own feet twice already. Cultivate the old ears, Dixon: in the dark they're worth more to you than your eyes."

"Damn the man," I reflected, but a suitable reply eluded me. For

I could hear absolutely nothing even then. "I wonder if they butted into little Pansy?" He got up and yawned prodigiously, and as he did so I heard cautious footsteps coming along the passage. The next moment Peter Darrell appeared in the door followed by the other two. "All right, Hugh?"

"Thirsty, Peter—darned thirsty. Where's the ale?" He lowered himself though the hole and dropped to the floor.

"We've got a dozen, old boy. Is that enough?"

"Do you drink beer, Dixon?" asked Drummond, looking up.

"Not usually at this hour of the morning," I answered. "Thank God for that," he said in a relieved voice. "It's a most deplorable habit, and I'm glad you don't suffer from it. Incidentally, chaps, you haven't run into Irma by any chance, have you?"

"Well I'm damned!" Jerningham glanced at Darrell. "Why do you ask, Hugh?"

"Because according to Dixon the poppet has been here, holding spiritual converse with our late lamented Carl. Of course he doesn't know the darling by sight, and Toby and I were both asleep. But from his account of the interview it must have been her." He paused with his glass half way to his mouth. "Have you seen her?"

"As we were leaving the village, old boy," said Jerningham, "a closed car, going fast, met us. And as we passed it a woman looked out of the window. Peter was driving, and Algy was in his usual condition of comatose imbecility, so it was only I who saw her. I just got a fleeting glimpse, but I thought it was Irma myself. I wasn't sure; but from what you say it must have been. I tried to get the number of the car, but the road is dusty and I couldn't see it. And then just as I was telling Peter, we went and punctured. Otherwise we could have followed. What did she come here for?"

"To gloat over my corpse, Ted, and to assure Carl that you three weren't forgotten," said Drummond. "She's out for the lot of us."

"Bless her little heart," remarked Peter. "But she'll have to be a bit more explicit as far as I'm concerned."

He produced a copy of The Times from his pocket.

"Here's the invitation to the party: but Allah alone knows what it means."

He pointed to two verses in the Personal Column. They were headed—To dear Hugh.

A lily with the plural put before A thing of beauty, but in this case, more Like the fair lady whom you met last night. When found, at any rate, you'll start quite right. Dipped in the river Styx one part alone stayed dry. Leave out the next, but take the cry Of every schoolboy. That should give a man. And now, you poor fish, find it if you can.

"Does anyone know the story of the girl who went to a fancy dress ball dressed as a lily," said Algy hopefully.

"Sit on his head," groaned Peter. "What the hell does it mean?"

Chapter 10

In Which the Third Clue is Solved

I have said earlier that this is my first essay in writing, but I should imagine that one of the rules must be to refrain as far as possible from boring the misguided optimists who are endeavouring to wade through the completed effort. And, therefore, I will refrain from giving any description of the rest of that day. It had been unanimously decided that it would be unsafe for Drummond, Sinclair and me to leave before nightfall if we were to avoid any risk of being spotted. And so beyond mentioning that the beer expired shortly after midday, that Toby Sinclair revoked twice at bridge and was soundly beaten by Drummond for his pains, and that I got an acute attack of the hiccoughs due to ale on an empty stomach, I will draw a veil over our doings. Quiet reigned on the Western Front, broken only by the curses of the particular individual who was, at the moment, wrestling with the doggerel in The Times.

Drummond from the outset gave it up. With a graceful movement of the hand he waved it from him, as a child might wave a plate of prunes and semolina pudding, Algy Longworth having at last got his story about the lily off his chest was found guilty of telling the world's hoariest chestnut, and having been thrown into the passage refused to play any more. So it was left to the rest of us to try and solve it. And honesty compels me to admit that we failed—utterly. It seemed completely meaningless.

'A lily with the plural put before.'

That seemed to give Slily. Toby Sinclair insisted that there was a loch of that name somewhere in the Hebrides, but on being pressed was not quite sure it wasn't an island off the coast of Cork. And that was about as far as we got. Except for Achilles: I got that.

'Dipped in the river Styx one part alone stayed dry.'

That seemed to point to the Achilles Statue, an unsuitable spot, as Drummond pointed out moodily, for erecting a booby-trap. And we were all somewhat moody when we left at ten that night for his house in London. Concealment was necessary and personally I was hidden under a rug at the back of the first car. Before that I had always felt a certain contempt for individuals who endeavour to evade paying for a railway ticket by travelling under the seat. Now I regard them with nothing short of admiration. To walk is a far, far better thing.

But we arrived at length, and having got Algy Longworth's shoe out of my mouth we crept through two dustbins to the back door. It was a risk coming to his house at all but it had to be run, since all his props for makeup were there. And after a short pause the door was opened by a manservant, who evinced not the slightest surprise at the sight of the procession.

"Have you seen any one loitering about the house, Denny?" said Drummond as the door closed behind us.

"No, sir. But a man called this afternoon and asked for you."

"What sort of a man?"

"A stranger, sir. And I am inclined to think, not an Englishman."

"What did you say?"

"The truth, sir. I said you were away from home."

Drummond looked thoughtful.

"Look here, Peter—we've got to try and ride them off. I'm tolerably certain we weren't spotted coming in here, but it looks as if they were watching the front. Go with Ted and drive up openly to the house. Ring the bell. When Denny comes—tell him the news in a voice broken with grief. Tell him I'm dead. Tell him twice if you think the blighter outside hasn't heard. Denny—you will clutch the door, turn pale with anguish and sob out—'No man had ever a better master.' And for God's sake don't breathe port all over the street. After that, Peter, you three go off to your rooms and wait for further orders. Somehow or other we've got to solve this confounded thing."

"Right-ho, old boy, I'll pitch Denny the tale. And then we'll wait to hear further from you."

And it was while we were waiting for them to come that I had an idea. Old Tom Jenkinson. If any man in London could solve it he could. A former schoolmaster of mine now retired, and a member of my club. He still appeared to regard me as a dirty and ink stained schoolboy. But over acrostics, riddles or crosswords he was a perfect genius. I said as much to Drummond.

"Splendid," he remarked. "Is he likely to be at the club now?"

"Never leaves it before midnight."

"Then go and scribble a line to him, old boy, explaining what we want—and I'll send it round by Denny. You'll find paper in that room up there, but see that the curtains are pulled tight before you switch on the light."

Dear Mr Jenkinson, (I wrote)
I would be deeply obliged to you if you would send me the solution of the enclosed rhyme. It represents a town or locality or place of some sort, presumably in the British Isles. It is a matter of urgent importance that I should get the answer as soon as possible. Knowing you I feel sure that you can solve it at once, and the bearer of this note will wait for a reply. I hope Mrs Jenkinson is in the best of health.
Yours sincerely,
Joe Dixon

"Splendid," said Drummond. "Peter has been, and according to Denny there was a man loitering by the railings who overheard what was said. Moreover, he's gone now, so it may have done some good. Anyway we'll send Denny round with that note at once."

"Go out by the back door," he said as his servant came in, "and take this to the Junior Reform. Wait for an answer. And don't forget—if anyone asks you—I'm dead."

"Very good, sir," said the man impassively. "There is a new cask, sir, behind the door."

"A good fellow," remarked Drummond. "And improved considerably since the death of his wife. She was a muscular woman and a martyr to indigestion, and the result left much to be desired."

He lit a cigarette, and began pacing up and down the room.

"Lord! but I hope this old buster of yours solves it," he said once or twice.

"If he doesn't, it's insolvable," I assured him. "But there's just a chance, of course, that he may not be in London."

And the instant I'd said it I regretted having spoken. His face fell, and he stared at me blankly.

"If so," I hastened to add, "we can always get him through, the club. Letters will be forwarded."

"But it means delay," he muttered. "More hanging about."

An hour passed, and two, and suddenly he lifted his head listening.

"Denny's back," he said. "Now we shall know."

His voice was quiet, but there was a strained look in his eyes as he watched the door. Should we have the answer, or did it mean further waiting? And mercifully it was the former, his servant had brought an answer. I opened it, and the others listened breathlessly.

Dear Dixon, (it ran)
Before giving you the solution of your ridiculous little problem there are one or two points to which I would draw your attention. In days gone by, when you went, if memory serves me aright, by the name of Stinkhound, I endeavoured, for my sins, to teach you the rudiments of English composition. Why then do you offend my eyes, and give me further proof, if such were needed, of my complete failure, by using the word 'would' twice in the first sentence. 'I should be,' not 'I would be,' is the correct opening to your ill-written missive. Again, if the matter is of urgent importance, obviously you require the answer as soon as possible—a clear case of tautology. Lastly, your interest in Mrs Jenkinson's health, though doubtless well meant, is a little tardy. She died some five years ago.

However—to your problem. My opinion of your intellect was always microscopic: even so, it is incredible that any one out of an asylum could have failed to solve it at sight—knowing that it was meant to represent a place. Let us take the first stanza. Clearly the last line has nothing to do with it: it is put in to cheer you on when you have interpreted the other three. Now, of course, I do not know the nature of the lady you met last night: your repellent habits are, I am glad to say, a closed book to me. But in this case she was obviously not a thing of beauty. *Ergo*—she was ugly or plain. But few places contain the letters *UGLY*: whereas there are many Plains in the British Isles. One in particular leaps to the mind—Salisbury Plain.

You may at this point ask what relation Salisbury has to a lily with the plural put before. Knowing your abysmal ignorance of everything remotely approaching to culture you probably will. The ancient name for Salisbury, my dear Dixon, was Sarum. To this day you will see the word written on many of the milestones around the town. Well, I suppose even you have heard of an Arum Lily. And therefore the first stanza is solved and gives us—Salisbury Plain, a large area—comprising as it does a considerable portion of the County of Wiltshire.

The second stanza is clearly designed to narrow our field. It does—to a remarkable degree. The first line could, of course, be solved by a child of six. But as *Ruff's Guide to the Turf* is doubtless more familiar to you than Homer's *Iliad* I shall assume that your mind has not even reached that infantile standard. Achilles was the son of Peleus by Thetis, one of the Nereids. And ancient mythology tells us that to make him invulnerable she dipped him in the Styx, holding him by the heel. Hence the phrase, the heel of Achilles which was the only part that remained dry. The first line therefore gives us Heel.

The cry of every schoolboy.'

What the repulsive little horrors call it now I do not know—but when you were one of them, what word rose most often to your lips? What was your moan—your everlasting bleat? Tuck. You gorged your bellies on tuck, and slept, as a result, in school—making disgusting noises. Tuck, Stinkhound—tuck.

That should give a man.

Have you never read *Ivanhoe*? Have you never heard of Robin Hood, and the fat and jovial Friar Tuck, his constant companion and father confessor? And so we have Heel, Tuck and Friar. A glance at the verse will show us that Tuck is to be left out—and that reduces us to Heel and Friar.

On Salisbury Plain is an ancient Druidical temple known as Stonehenge. Outside the main circle is a great stone—the sun-stone. This is the point where a spectator, centrally placed within the temple, would see the sun rise on Midsummer Day. And the common name for the sun-stone is the Friar's Heel.

Wherefore, the solution of your childish effusion is the monolith known as the Friar's Heel at Stonehenge on Salisbury Plain. And in conclusion I can only endorse most wholeheartedly the terse and apt description of you given in the middle of the last line.

Faithfully yours,

Thomas Jenkinson

PS—I have often wanted to know one thing. Were you or were you not the miserable little boy who first nicknamed me Wart Hog and the late Mrs Jenkinson Slab Face? A nickname—like a caricature—should bear some relation to the truth, Dixon, if it is to be considered clever. And to call me a Wart Hog is positively stupid.

"I got Achilles at any rate, confound the old ass," I remarked, as I put the letter down. "Well—there you are. Now we know."

"Stonehenge," said Drummond. "Close to Amesbury."

"With cantonments all round it," put in Toby Sinclair. "I motored past it last summer."

"How far away?" Drummond looked at him thoughtfully. "I haven't been there since I was a kid, and there was nothing built then."

"I suppose about a mile to the nearest," said Sinclair. "Perhaps less. And there's another thing, too. By day there are hordes of trippers all over the place—guides and all that sort of stunt. You've got to pay to go in."

"So nothing can happen by day. And by night—with troops as close as that—they will have to be careful."

He went to the telephone, and gave a number.

"Peter," he said as soon as he got through, "come round at once—all of you. Back door, as before."

He sat down and stared at me.

"I wonder what is the best rig for you," he pondered. "In a way, you're the least important as only the man and the woman of last night know you."

"And our venerable friend of the Angler's Rest," I reminded him.

"True. I'd forgotten him. Still a moustache, a pair of spectacles and the earnest air of a tourist should meet the case. And if you see any of those three, efface yourself. Toby—I've got a very good line in elderly professors for you. Butterflies, I think. You can gambol lightly over Salisbury Plain making a noise like a killing-bottle."

"Thanks, dear old boy," said Sinclair. "What are you going to be?"

"That remains to be seen," answered Drummond with an enigmatic smile. "I've got two or three half formed ideas."

The smile faded slowly from his face.

"But whatever it is, I'm thinking that the sooner we begin to put the fear of God into this bunch the better."

And I realized suddenly how he had earned the sobriquet of Bulldog.

A minute or so later Peter Darrell and the other two came in.

"You've solved it?" asked Jerningham eagerly.

"A pal of Dixon's has," said Drummond. "A stone called the Friar's Heel at Stonehenge. You can read the letter later."

"And you can read this one now," said Darrell. "Delivered by hand."

It consisted of one line.

Read today's Times. Personal column.

"So she really does think we're dead, Peter." Drummond rubbed his hands together. "Excellent. However, let's get down to it. In the first place, from now on you three have got to run this show alone. Officially, that's to say. And, dash it all, I don't like it."

"Cut it out, you ass," laughed Jerningham.

"It's all very fine and large, Ted—but they mean business. And I don't want any casualties. I believe that what Dixon said is absolutely right. Whether she is insane or not is beside the point: there's not much sign of insanity about her plans up to date. But from what he heard her say this morning we are all for it, and Phyllis as well, before she goes to join Peterson. She was never remarkable, was she, for the quality of mercy. And now that she's obsessed with this idea, she will be utterly merciless. It's revenge run mad. So for the love of Heaven be careful. I'd never forgive myself if one of you took it in the neck."

"We'll be careful all right, old boy," said Darrell quietly. "But Phyllis has got to be found, hasn't she?"

"I know that. But I'm wondering if it wouldn't be better for you three to chuck it and leave it to me."

"We have but little desire for a rough house," said Jerningham, "but there's going to be one in a moment unless you cease talking tripe."

"Well, well; so be it," grinned Drummond. "But I thought I'd just mention it. So as I said before—let's get down to it. From what Toby says, the place is stiff with people all the day. So by day there can't be any risk. Now, it's possible that all we are going to get there is another clue—in fact, it's probable. I really don't see how they can rig up anything in a public place like that which can be dangerous—even at night. And so as I see it—there's just one thing to fear, and that can only happen at night."

"What's that?" said Darrell.

"Common or garden murder, Peter," said Drummond gravely. "There may be a clue; on the other hand, it may be a trap."

"Murder," I said doubtfully. "In a place like that."

"Why not?" said Drummond coolly. "What leads in nine cases out of ten to the discovery of a murder? Motive. And what possible known motive is there for killing any of them. We know the motive: who else does? If we told this story to the police we'd be laughed out of court."

"And Phyllis would pay the price," said Jerningham gravely.

"We know they are utterly unscrupulous: we know that they intend to kill them. What more likely than that they'll have a dip at it at the Friar's Heel. And that is a thing I do not propose to risk unless it is absolutely essential. No, Peter, my mind is made up, old boy—so there's no use your looking like that. I promise you that when it is necessary, I'll send for you."

"What is your suggestion, Hugh?" said Jerningham after a whale.

"This, Ted. From what Dixon overheard Irma say, this little show will not be concluded until they've got you—all three. I may be wrong, but I don't think they will try for you in London: in her own distorted way she is going to play this game through to the end in the way she intended. And, therefore, nothing further will take place until you come to the Friar's Heel. Now my proposal is this. But for this freak pal of Dixon's, Heaven alone knows when we should have solved that last clue. So there will be nothing surprising about it if you take at least a couple of days over finding the answer. And during those two days—or until I wire for you—you will remain in London, ready to leave the instant you hear from me."

"And you three?" asked Darrell.

"We'll go down in disguise and spy out the land. Maybe we shall find nothing; maybe the clue, if there is one at the Friar's Heel, will only be given to one of you. If so, I'll wire you. But it's possible that we shall find the clue, and get a short cut to what we want."

"I don't like it, Hugh," said Jerningham.

"Ted, old boy, it's best from every point of view. I don't want one of you killed—or the lot. And, my dear old lad, they mean business. Supposing you were all killed, from another point of view altogether—where should we be? Ignorant of where Phyllis is, with the game over as far as they are concerned. The whole bunch of us wiped out. The only person left then to finish off is Phyllis. There are such things as silencers for guns, laddie, as we know only too well. No, no: it's absolutely obvious. We will go first and see what we can find out. If we find out nothing—then you come in. If, on the contrary, we get on their tracks—then you still come in, but in a far sounder strategical position than if you went down now. Because when you arrive they will think the Friar's Heel is your objective, whereas in reality it won't be. They will lie up for you there, and you will short-circuit them."

"He's right, Ted; perfectly right," said Darrell unwillingly. "I wish he wasn't; but he is."

"So I shall rig up Toby and Dixon tomorrow, and they will go to some pub in Amesbury."

"What's your own game, Hugh," said Algy.

"That, old boy, you will know in due course. For the time being I think it's best that none of you should know. It's going to be touch and go—this show—and I'd sooner have an absolutely free hand. And finally, don't forget the old Froth Blower's dirge. Twice for danger."

"Froth Blower's?" I asked. "Is that the thing I've heard you singing?"

"Laddie," laughed Drummond, "you can't be real. When peace comes your education shall be taken in hand. Now is all clear?"

"Absolutely," said Darrell.

"Then a long night in, chaps. We'll want all we can get in the sleep line. And one other thing. If you want to get me, drop a line to John Bright at the Post Office, Amesbury."

They went casually with a nod and a grin—did the other three; demonstrativeness was not a characteristic of this crowd. But when they'd gone, Drummond sat for some time staring in front of him with his beer untasted on the table at his side. And at last he rose with a grunt. "Come on; bed. I hope to Heaven they'll be all right in London."

He showed me to my room, where a pair of his pyjamas had been laid out.

"Hope they won't be too small," he said with a grin. Then he paused by the door. "Deuced good of you and all that, Dixon, to mix yourself up in this show. Though, 'pon my soul, I don't know what we'd have done without you."

And, astounding though it may seem, I can recall no remark made to me in my life that has occasioned me greater pleasure. Whether it had anything to do with it, I don't know, but certain it is that no sooner had my head touched the pillow than I was asleep. And the next thing I knew was his servant shaking me by the shoulder the next morning.

"Nine o'clock, sir," he said. "And the Captain would like you to come along to the music-room as soon as you've had your bath."

The music-room appeared to be so-called because there was no trace of any musical instrument in it. It resembled nothing so much as an old clothes shop. Suits of all sorts and descriptions littered the floor; wigs, false hair and the usual makeup appliances were on the table. Drummond was standing in the middle with two complete strangers by him. One of them was obviously of the hairdresser type; the other was an elderly man of scholastic appearance.

"Morning, Dixon," said Drummond. "Now, Albert, there you are. What are we to do with him? A minimum on his face, because he's not used to it."

The hairdresser man eyed me critically.

"I thought a moustache," went on Drummond. "And glasses. For Mr Seymour. Don't forget, Dixon—Fred Seymour."

"Can't we dispense with the moustache?" I said. "It's certain to fall off at the wrong moment."

"Not as I shall fix it, sir," said the hairdresser in a pained voice. "Will you kindly take a seat here?"

"Who is the old bloke?" I whispered to Drummond as I passed him.

"My dear fellow," he cried, "excuse me. I quite forgot. This is a very old friend of mine—Professor Stanton—Mr Dixon. He's come to give Toby some advice on butterflies."

"A fascinating hobby, Mr Dixon," remarked the Professor, and I stared at him in amazement. Surely I knew that voice.

"Great Scott," I muttered. "It's you, Sinclair."

They all laughed.

"What an amazing disguise," I cried. "But for your voice I'd never have known you."

"And under the ministrations of the excellent Albert the result will be the same in your case," remarked Drummond. "The whole essence of disguise, Dixon, is to make it as simple as possible, and therefore as unnoticeable."

He was watching Albert's efforts as he spoke.

"Most people are extraordinarily unobservant," he went on. "If you wear different clothes to usual, alter your walk a little, and put on a pair of dark spectacles, you'll pass nine people out often that you know in the street without being recognized. Whereas if you wear a large red nose and fungus all over your face you may not be recognized, but you'll certainly be noticed. And once you're noticed the danger begins. Albert, I think a respectable bank clerk of about thirty-five is what we want."

He began rummaging in the pile of clothes.

"We'll give you a rather badly cut suit of plus fours, and a cap. Horn rimmed spectacles, Albert. Now let's have a look at him."

The three of them stared at me critically.

"Get into these clothes," said Drummond. "I can't be sure till you're out of that dressing-gown."

I contemplated the garments with distaste. "I suppose there are people who wear things like that," I remarked, "or nobody would make them."

"It's a misfit," he said. "I bought a dozen of 'em once, and that's about the last. Don't mind if your stockings come down a bit; it helps the effect. Yes, Albert: that will do."

"I think so, sir," said Albert complacently, and at that moment I saw myself in the glass.

The shock was ghastly, but at the same time I was forced to admit that the result was amazing. I do not look at my face more often than necessary as a general rule, it shakes me too badly to see it. But the reflection that confronted me as I stood there was that of a complete stranger. Moreover, it was true to type. I had seen hundreds of similar examples at the seaside during August, or on char-a-banc trips.

"Then that's finished," said Drummond. "Now the only pub, as far as I can make out, is the Amesbury Castle. I think you'd better arrive separately, and you can strike up an acquaintance afterwards."

He smiled suddenly and held out his hand.

"Thank you, Dixon; I'll take charge of that."

"Charge of what?" I said blankly.

"Blokes dressed like you, old boy, do not use expensive gold and platinum cigarette cases with Asprey written all over 'em. We'll put that in my safe, and here is a tasty little thing in leather. Nor, laddie, do most bank clerks smoke Balkan Sobranies. I suggest the perfectly good yellow packet. . . ."

"I loathe Virginian cigarettes," I groaned.

"Well," he conceded, "you may smoke cheap Turkish if you like. But a Balkan Sobranie would shout aloud to heaven. Anything more, Toby?"

"Nothing, I think, Hugh. We aren't to know you, are we?"

Drummond smiled. "You won't know me, Toby," he said quietly. "All you've got to do is to keep your mouths shut, and your eyes open—and if you want me, John Bright at the Post Office finds me. If I want you I'll let you know."

He grinned again. "So long, boys. Leave the house by the back door separately, and for Heaven's sake, Dixon, try not to appear self-conscious. Be a city clerk: don't only look it."

Which was a policy of excellence, but not quite so easy as it sounded. As I walked along Berkeley Street I felt that everybody was looking at me. And when I ran straight into a woman I knew opposite the Ritz, I instinctively lifted my cap. She stared at me in blank surprise, and I dodged down Arlington Street to recover. Ass that I was—giving myself away at the very first moment. But after a while confidence began to return. I realized that though Joe Dixon would have caused a mild sensation garbed as I was—Fred Seymour caused none at all. And I further realized that if I as Joe Dixon had met me as Fred Seymour, I should have paid no attention to me. Fred Seymour was just one of a numerous type—no more conspicuous than any other individual of that type. The truth of Drummond's remark about the red nose was obvious. I was just an inconspicuous unit amongst thousands of others.

And so, as I say, gradually my confidence returned. I walked normally, and to test myself I determined to pass the commissionaire outside my club. I looked him straight in the face: he returned the look without a sign of recognition. And he on an average must see me five hundred times a year.

A sudden thought struck me: I had no baggage. For a while I debated between the rival merits of a rucksack and a handbag, deciding finally on the former. Then I bought a couple of shirts and some socks, and thus equipped, I made my way to Paddington. The last phase of the game, though I little knew it, had begun.

CHAPTER 11

In Which I go to Friar's Heel by Day

Up to this point the telling of my story has been easy, even if the manner of the telling has been crude and poor. But from now on it becomes more difficult. Things happened quickly, and we were all of us scattered in a way we had not been before. In fact, for the greater part of the time, the only member of the bunch who I was able to talk to was Toby Sinclair. But I will do my best to make clear the happenings that led up to that last astounding denouement, which even now seems like some fantastic nightmare to me. And if some of those happenings are boring I can only crave pardon, and assure my readers that it is necessary to write of them for the proper understanding of what is to follow.

I arrived then, at the Amesbury Castle in time for a late lunch. It was a typical hotel of the English country town, relying more, I should imagine, on lunches and dinners to pay its way than on people taking a bed. The food was of that grim nature which one associates with hotels of the type—plain and tough. An aged waiter, with most of yesterday's ration on his shirt front, presided over the dining-room, and looked at me in a pained way as I came in.

"Very late, sir," he remarked.

"And I am very hungry," I answered cheerfully. He polished a menu card morosely on his trousers.

"Mutton hoff," he said. "Beef, 'am, tongue—and pertaters. Been a run on the mutton today," he added confidentially.

I gazed at the flies making a run on the beef and decided on ham and tongue.

"Many people staying here?" I asked.

"Full up for lunch," he said. "And the hotel be fairly full, too. A bunch of people came last night. Lumme! 'ere's another."

I glanced at the doer to see Toby Sinclair coming in.

"Splendid," he cried, in a high voice that nearly made me laugh. "Food, waiter, for the inner man, and then to resume my search. Tell me, have you seen a *Bragmatobia fuliginosa?*"

The waiter recoiled a step.

"A 'ow much," he demanded. "There's beef, 'am, tongue and pertaters."

"And only this morning," went on Toby, "I am convinced I perceived a *Psecadia pusiella*. Members, my dear sir," he said to me, "of the great family of *lepidoptera*. In other words butterflies."

"Beef, 'am or tongue," said the waiter resignedly. "The mutton's hoff."

"Ham, waiter, with a fragment of chutney. You are, sir," he turned again to me, "on a walking tour perhaps?"

"That is my idea," I said. "But I propose to make this hotel my headquarters."

"You may possibly care to come out with me once or twice. My name is Stanton—Professor Stanton."

"Mine is Seymour," I told him.

"Well, Mr Seymour—" He broke off suddenly. "Waiter, I asked for ham and chutney, not the mummified sole of a shoe covered with glue."

"The tongue is worse," said the waiter drearily. "And that there chutney has been here two years to my certain knowledge."

"As far as I am concerned it will remain for another two years. Give me some bread and cheese. Dixon," he said to me urgently, as the waiter left the room, "there's a man in the lounge outside I want you to have a look at. I only got a glimpse of him that night at the Mere, but I believe it's the bloke who was with the woman. Anyway he's got his hand bandaged up. No Mr Seymour, a lifetime is all too short for my entrancing hobby. Bless me! waiter, I think this cheese must have been here for two years also. Get me a pint of ale, will you? Yes, sir—a lifetime is too short. Nevertheless I hope to capture the *Cyligramma fluctuosa* before I die. Are you doing anything this afternoon?"

"I thought of going over to Stonehenge," I remarked.

He nodded. "We'll go over to Stonehenge. I wonder if one can hire a car."

And at that moment a man passed through the lounge. He looked in at the door, gave us both a casual glance and then disappeared.

"It is certainly our friend of the Mere," I said. "I'd know him anywhere. Now what the devil is he doing here?"

"Why shouldn't he be here?" said Toby. "This is the centre of activity at the moment."

"It may be," I agreed. "But don't forget that Darrell and Co. know him just as well as we do, and they might come at any moment as far as the enemy knows."

"That's true," he said. "Still, their intelligence work is probably good. We've got to watch him, Dixon. Waiter," he called out, "is it possible to hire a motor car? Mr Seymour and I were thinking of visiting Stonehenge."

"There be a Ford down at the garage," answered the waiter. "You might be able to get 'old of that if no one eke ain't already. Be you staying 'ere or do you want the bill?"

"Staying," said Toby. "Room 23. Well, Mr Seymour, shall we go and see about this Ford? I have an idea that I might perhaps see a *Cerostoma asperella* if my luck is in. Ah! pardon, sir—pardon."

He had bumped into a man just outside the door—the man we had both recognized.

"I trust I have not hurt your hand at all," he went on earnestly. "So clumsy of me."

The man muttered something and sheered off, whilst I followed Sinclair into the street.

"The gentleman was suspiciously close to the door, Dixon," he said quietly.

"Still, I don't think he suspected us," I answered.

"Not as us, perhaps. But I think the whole bunch of them suspect everybody. When you boil down to it, they're tackling a pretty dangerous proposition. If the police did get hold of them, abduction and attempted murder form a nasty charge."

"That is the very point that has occurred once or twice to me," I said. "One can understand the lady risking it: she has the best of motives—revenge. But I'm blowed if I see where these other fellows come in. There's no question of revenge with them. So what the devil are they doing it for?"

He shrugged his shoulders.

"Money. I'm told that in Chicago you can hire a gunman for a dollar. And I haven't the very smallest doubt that you can do the same in England if you know where to look. We heard that bloke at the Mere mention two hundred pounds. And there are scores of swine who would murder their mothers for that. Good Lord!"

His voice changed suddenly to that of the Professor.

"And so, my dear Seymour, if we can get this car I will try and show you some of those beauties of nature which I feel sure are as yet quite unsuspected by you."

A man brushed past, favouring us both with a penetrating stare.

"What's the matter?" I said, when he was out of earshot.

"Just for a moment I thought the dead had come to life," said Sinclair. "You saw that man who passed us?"

"That thin-lipped blighter who stared? Yes: I saw him. Is he one of them?"

"I haven't a notion," he remarked. "Look here, I'm just going to drop a line to Hugh, and I'll tell you the rest when we get in the car. Here's the garage."

The Ford turned out to be available, and I got in and waited for Sinclair, who was scribbling a note in the office.

"We'll post it in some pillar-box as we go out," he said as he joined me. "Better than leaving it at the main post office. Stonehenge, please, driver."

"What did you say," I asked, when we'd started.

"I told him about the man at the pub," he answered. "And also about that other bloke. Of course there may be nothing in it, but the likeness is really so astounding to a man we once had dealings with and who was one of the leaders of this very gang, that for a moment I thought it was him."

"Is there any reason why it shouldn't be?"

"Every reason. He died most substantially three or four years ago. Hugh killed him."

He grinned suddenly.

"Of course this is all Greek to you, so I'll tell you about it. When we first bumped into Carl Peterson—now defunct—and the lady you saw at the Mere, it was at the instigation of Mrs Drummond—before she was Mrs Drummond. It's altogether too long a story to tell you the whole thing; but in a nutshell, they were engaged in a foul criminal plot. Assisting them was one of the biggest swine it has ever been my misfortune to run into—a man called Henry Lakington. He was a mixture of chemist, doctor, thief, murderer and utter blackguard. But clever—damned clever. He wasn't as big a man as Peterson because he hadn't got the vision—but he was a far more ineffable swab. Peterson, at any rate, at times had the saving sense of humour: this man had none. And in the course of our little contest Drummond fought him and killed him. It was one or the other, and that's a bit dangerous for the other, if the one is Hugh. Now that man who passed us is the living spit of Henry Lakington; he might be—

and for all I know is—his twin brother. And the coincidence struck me as so peculiar that I thought I'd mention it to Hugh. Of course, there's probably nothing in it."

"You are convinced," I said, "that this man Lakington was killed."

"Absolutely certain of it," he answered. "On that point there's not a shadow of doubt. But if there's anything in the theory that certain types of mentality have certain types of faces that man would steal the bird seed from a pet canary's beak. Hullo! here we are."

It was years since I had been to Stonehenge, and emphatically the impressiveness of the ruin had not been increased by the military buildings that had sprung up around it. Equally emphatically the difficulty of playing any monkey tricks there either by day or night had considerably increased.

At the time we arrived several empty char-a-bancs were standing on the road, and crowds of trippers were wandering round the huge stones escorted by guides. And having paid our modest entrance fee we joined a group.

"There, ladies and gentlemen, you have the slaughter stone on which the victim was sacrificed as the first rays of the sun, rising over the Friar's Heel, touched his body. Inside you perceive the altar stone...."

The guide droned on, but I paid scant attention. My thoughts were concerned with the present, and not with the past. Was Drummond right in his surmise, was this place—the scene of so much death in the dawn of history—to be the setting for murder as merciless as anything of old? What he had said was correct in one respect certainly; if Darrell, or any of them, were done to death it would be, to the world at large, a crime without motive. And the instant those three were disposed of, the end would come for Mrs Drummond.

It had been sound generalship on his part, leaving them in London. But the crux of the whole matter was whether, if there really was a clue to be obtained, we should get it. True, that we saved them the risk of being murdered, but did we not also prevent any possibility of getting information? Granted that our disguises held, what reason was there for us being told anything? To get a short cut to our goal, as Drummond hoped, presupposed our obtaining the necessary clue. And as far as I could see at the moment, the only connecting link we possessed was the man with the wounded hand.

To the other who, Toby Sinclair said, was like this dead man Lakington, I attached no importance whatever. Chance likenesses are frequent, and the mere fact that he bore a striking resemblance to a dead criminal was no proof that he was a criminal himself. No, the man with the damaged finger was our only link, and I began to wonder if we hadn't been foolish in losing sight of him.

I glanced round: Toby Sinclair had wandered off and joined another group. And it suddenly occurred to me that it could do no harm to make a closer inspection of the Friar's Heel. It was a perfectly ordinary and normal thing to do, and would not cause any suspicion even if our opponents had spies in the crowd. And there was always the bare possibility of finding a clue.

I wandered over to it, to find a big man in rough seafaring clothes staring at it curiously.

"Rum old pile this, guv'nor, ain't it? I've seen the same sort of thing at Stornoway up in Lewis. Though I reckons the stones there ain't as big. This Friar's Heel as they call it is a big 'un all right."

"You've been to the Hebrides," I said casually.

"Been there! Lor' bless you, there's not many parts of this little old globe that I ain't been to. And with it all I guess there are as curious things and as beautiful things in England as anywhere else. Only people don't know it, or else they're too lazy to go and look."

I looked at him curiously out of the corner of my eye. Could this be another clue? If it was it meant we had been spotted. And then I took a pull at myself: I was beginning to suspect everybody and everything.

"Stopping in these parts?" he went on.

"For a few days," I said.

"Funny sort of country," he remarked. "Good for the soldiers, I suppose, but it's a bit too bare for me. I like it with a few more woods and trees. Still—it's fine, especially at night. I reckon that these pebbles would look grand with the moonlight shining on them."

Once again I stared at him thoughtfully.

"Yes, one could imagine all sorts of terrible things happening here at night," I said quietly. "Ghosts of old Britons who had been sacrificed: and violent deaths, and—murder."

He laughed. "You ain't half got an imagination, guv'nor, have you? But I take it you're one of the town bred lot—meaning no offence. Put you down in the country at night and you begin to see things that ain't there and hear things that ain't real. Murder! Who's going to murder anyone here?" He laughed again. "I don't suppose anyone ever comes to a place like this at night," he went on. "And yet it's a rum thing. I was bicycling along that road late last night—been seeing some friends of mine—and it seemed to me as if there was something moving about the place. Round this very stone.

Of course it was dark and I may have been mistaken, but there ain't generally much wrong with my sight."

Last night, I reflected. Had the clue been guessed at once, Darrell and the other two could have been at the Friar's Heel by then. Had there been someone here in readiness? To give them a further clue, or to deal with them—otherwise?

"You didn't investigate?" I asked casually. "See if you were right?"

"Not me, guv'nor. None o' my business. And one of Ben Harker's rules in life has always been to mind his own business."

He produced a well-used old briar from his pocket, and proceeded to fill it from a weather-beaten leather pouch.

"Have a fill?" he said. "Ship's tobacco; the best in the world."

"A bit strong for me, I'm afraid, Mr Harker," I thanked him. "We miserable city clerks are hardly used to that sort of smoke."

"You prefer them damned fags, I suppose," he grunted. "Ah! well, everyone to his own taste. Personally...."

He paused, and I glanced at him. His fingers had ceased filling his pipe, and he was standing absolutely motionless staring over my shoulder. Only for the briefest fraction of time did it last, and then he continued his interrupted sentence.

"Personally, I can't ever get any taste out of a cigarette."

As I say the pause was only for a fraction of a second—a pause which I might quite easily have missed had I not happened to have been watching his hands. But I hadn't missed it, and I knew that he had seen somebody or something behind me that had caused it.

"A match at any rate, I can offer you," I said, and as I spoke I turned round casually. Coming slowly towards us was the thin-lipped man who resembled Lakington.

"Thanks," he answered, lighting his pipe in the unmistakable method of a man used to the wind. Then he handed me back the box. "Well, good day to you," he said. "Maybe if you're staying in these parts we shall meet again."

He strolled off with the slight roll of the seaman, and I lit a cigarette. Certainly nothing he had done or said connected him in the slightest degree with the game, and yet I wasn't quite sure. Why that sudden pause in the middle of a sentence? And then it struck me that there was nothing to connect the man who had caused it with the game either except a resemblance to a dead criminal.

I sat down on the ground, and proceeded to study the huge stone, acutely conscious that the thin-lipped man was standing just behind me.

"You are interested in this sort of thing?" he remarked politely.

"As much as a bank clerk who knows nothing about it can be," I answered.

"It has always been a hobby of mine," he said. "The past is so infinitely more interesting than the present. One admits of imagination; the other is bare and brutal fact. These motor cars; this crowd of terrible people peering in their asinine way at the scene of age-old mysteries. Doing the place at high pressure, instead of steeping themselves in the romance of it."

He talked on, and there was no denying that he could talk. His voice was pleasant and well modulated, and after a while I began to listen entranced. Evidently a widely travelled and well-read man, with the rare gift of imparting information without becoming a bore. And after a while I began to keep up my end of the conversation.

It was when he happened to mention the Zimbabwe Ruins in Mashonaland, ruins that I had broken my journey at Fort Victoria in order to see; rams, as many believe, of a vanished civilization, which had fascinated me at the time, that I became really interested.

He, too, knew them, and we started an argument. I maintained that they were an ancient legacy from some civilized people dating back, perhaps, to before the days of Solomon: he inclined to the theory that they were only the work of local natives and, at most, mediaeval.

"Evidently," he said at length, "you have studied the matter more closely than I have. Did you spend long there?"

"I was actually in South Africa for about six months," I told him. "And I used to collect opinions from those qualified to express them."

"A fascinating country. Though perhaps for any big scheme of emigration which would cover all classes of our countrymen Australia is more suitable."

"I've never been there," I said. "As a matter of fact I'm thinking of going next year. And to New Zealand."

"By the way," he said affably, after we had chatted for another ten minutes or so, "if you are staying in this neighbourhood you might care to have a look at my collection of curios. Though I say it myself I think I may say there are few finer in the country. And a man of taste like yourself would appreciate them."

"It is very good of you," I remarked, "and I should greatly like to see them."

He had risen, and I stood up also.

"Where is your house?"

He glanced at his watch thoughtfully.

"I have my car here," he said, "and if you can spare an hour I could run you over and show them to you. Then my car can take you back to your hotel."

"There is only one small difficulty," I said, "I came over from Amesbury with a gentleman I happened to meet at lunch. I see him over there—Professor Stanton. An enthusiast on butterflies."

"Professor Stanton," he cried. "Not *the* Professor Stanton."

"I really don't know," I murmured. "I met him quite by chance at lunch today."

"But," he exclaimed excitedly, "if it's Professor John Stanton his reputation is worldwide."

I suppressed a slight smile; whatever Toby Sinclair's reputation might be in certain purlieus of London, it could hardly be described as worldwide.

"He's coming to join us," I remarked, "and you can ask him."

"But it is him," he cried, as Toby approached. "What stupendous luck. My dear Professor," he advanced with outstretched hand, "you remember me. What a fool I was not to recognize you in Amesbury when I passed you."

Sinclair stared at him blankly.

"I fear you have the advantage of me, sir," he remarked.

The other waved a deprecating hand. "Ah! but, of course, you would not recall me. I am merely one of the thousands who have sat at your feet. It was presumption on my part to imagine that my face would be familiar to you. But how entranced I was at that lecture you gave on the habits of *Pieris Rapae*."

"You must be making some mistake, sir," said Toby coldly. "I am not the gentleman you think."

"Modesty, Professor, modesty. Tell me have you discovered a specimen of it yet? You told us, if you remember, that it was to be your life work."

"Though you are making a mistake, sir, as to my identity—yet I can well imagine that it would have been the life work of the man I resemble. The rarest of all the species, perhaps. But I have seen today a marvellous specimen of the *Opsiphanes syme*."

"Stupendous," said the other admiringly. "What eyesight: what wonderful eyesight. Well, I mustn't detain a public character. Good day sir, good day. And if you care to join your friend in a little visit he has promised to make to my humble abode, I shall be delighted to show you my amateur collection."

He bowed courteously and walked off, leaving Sinclair and me staring at one another.

"I say, old boy," said Sinclair, "I hope this is all right. I wonder who the hell Professor Stanton really is. Hugh's made a bit of a bloomer there. He oughtn't to have given me the name of a *pukka* character. Anyway, I think I pulled the jargon on him all right. I must consult my list of names again."

And it was as he was pulling it out of his pocket that a strange noise close by drew our attention. It appeared to come from a little man of astonishing aspect, whose fake teeth were clicking together in his excitement. He also seemed to be trying to speak. We waited. By this time I was prepared for anything.

"Are you acting for the films," he spluttered at length. "Or are you being more stupid than you look for some purpose?"

"Explain yourself, little man," said Toby with interest.

"Lying, sir—lying offensively on a subject which is sacred to some of us." His teeth nearly fell out, but he pushed them back with the care of long practice. "Using words, sir, which betray you as an impostor. How, sir, did you see a specimen of *Opsiphanes syme*?"

"With the jolly old peepers, laddie," said Toby soothingly.

"Bah!" cried the little man. "Are you so profoundly ignorant of the subject you desecrate that you do not know that only in the swamps of Brazil is that beautiful butterfly found?"

"No wonder he said my eyesight was good," said Toby thoughtfully.

"And further, sir—do you see that?" He pointed a shaking finger at two Cabbage Whites chasing one another nearby. "The rarest of all the species, you called them. *Pieris Rapae*, sir. Bah! you make me sick. You should be prosecuted, sir; you should be prosecuted."

"Look here, you'll swallow your teeth in a minute," said Toby, but the astounding little creature had already departed, waving his fists in the air.

"Takes all sorts to make a world, gents," came a laughing voice from behind us. "But you do certainly seem to have said the wrong thing." We swung round: the man who looked like a sailor was standing there. "Don't you know anything about butterflies—or is he talking through his hat?" He gave Toby a penetrating stare. "Dangerous thing, sir, pretending to know more than you do. Or be what you ain't."

He strolled away, and once again we looked at one another. "He's one of 'em," I said. "For a certainty. That's torn it."

"Hell," he remarked. "And again, hell. What about Lakington the second? Is he one, too?"

CHAPTER 12

In Which I Write My Mind to Drummond

Toby Sinclair was thoroughly despondent. "I looked up a bunch of Latin names in an encyclopaedia," he said morosely. "How the dickens was I to know that the damned thing only lived in Brazil?" We were sitting in his room at the hotel. "And the devil of it is, Dixon," he went on, "that if Lakington is not one of them we've still given the show away to that sailor bloke. You could see his suspicions sticking out a yard."

"Hold hard a moment," I said. "You say we've given it away."

"Well then—I have, if you like that better," he said sulkily.

"Don't get huffy, old man," I laughed. "I'm not trying to pretend that I should have done any better than you if I'd been the Professor. But as luck would have it I was only a clerk."

"What are you driving at?" He looked at me curiously.

"Simply this. Up to date I have not given myself away—either to the sailor or to the man you call Lakington. I think I may say that I have been the bank clerk on holiday to the life."

"Yes—but they know you know me," he objected.

"They know—and if they choose to take the trouble to ask it will be corroborated—that you and I met casually in the coffee room at lunch today. If you are an impostor, which unfortunately they must know by now, there is still no reason whatever why I should have known it earlier."

"But you know it now as well as they do."

"Now—yes," I agreed. "But the fact that I went to Stonehenge with you throws no suspicion on me. I didn't know it then."

"I'm hanged if I get you," he said.

"You've got to clear out," I remarked. "Vamoose. Hop it. Disappear from this place for good."

"I'm blowed if I do," he said.

"My dear fellow—you must. If we're to do any good and help Drummond in any way, it's impossible that you should stay on. They know you're an impostor; they know I know you're an impostor. Well, how can we both stop on here? Am I to cut you dead? Or am I to continue talking to you realizing that you are an impostor? Don't you see that it's sufficient to bring suspicion on me at once? Besides—I'm going to speak quite frankly. Your value to the side at the moment is nil. In fact, old man, you're a positive source of weakness."

"I suppose you're right," he agreed reluctantly. "Well—what do you suggest?"

"That you tell them downstairs that you've changed your mind and will not require your room. Then you hop it, and I'm sorry to say, as far as I can see, you fade out of the picture. I shall stay on, and without being blatant about it, I shall drop an occasional remark about your extraordinary idea of a holiday. The strange sort of kink that makes a man pretend to be what he isn't—that line of gup. Form of conceit—you know. I can easily cough it up. And by doing that I shall remove any small half-formed suspicion they may have about me. I am just an ordinary bank clerk taken in by you, as anyone else might have been."

He grunted and rose to his feet. "You're right. I'll go. Drop a note to Hugh explaining things—and tell him I'm eating mud." And then he suddenly paused. "But, good Lord! Dixon—it's no good. The damage is done. If they've got a line on me they'll know Hugh and you and I aren't dead."

"They haven't got a line on you as yourself," I said. "You might be somebody else rigged out like that—Algy Longworth for instance. Clear out and clear out quick. For unless you do, if I'm not greatly mistaken you'll be for it. They will think you're just another member of Drummond's bunch, and as such require to be exterminated. I'm going down now into the bar; if I happen to see you before you go I shall be pretty terse in my remarks."

"What sickening luck," he muttered. "Damn that blinking butterfly."

"It's bad luck," I said, "but I'm sure it's the only thing to do. Look out into the passage and see if there's anyone about. Then I'll make a bolt for it."

He opened his door, and gave me the all clear. And a few moments later I strolled into the bar. A little to my surprise the seafaring man was there, seated in a corner. He was talking earnestly to someone, and as I saw who his companion was, my pulse beat a little quicker. It was our friend of the Mere, the man with the damaged hand. Proof—absolute and definite.

I ordered a pint of ale and sat down near them. And the instant he saw me the sailor leaned across and beckoned me to join them. "Draw up, mate," he cried. "You know it's none o' my business, but what was your friend's great idea this afternoon. I've just been telling this gentleman about it. Your butterfly pal, I mean, who knew nothing about butterflies."

"I assure you," I said a little stiffly, "he's no friend of mine. He's the most casual acquaintance. He happened to be lunching late at the same time as I was, and I gathered that he was a Professor Stanton, and an authority on butterflies. And he suggested we should go to Stonehenge together."

"Can't understand it," said the sailor man. "Now, if one of you started to talk to me about seafaring matters, I guess I'd spot in two shakes how much you know about the sea. And what's the good, anyway, of pretending you know what you don't know? You look such a blazing fool when you're found out."

"I think the explanation is very simple," I remarked. "It's merely a peculiar form of conceit. That man probably knows a smattering about butterflies, and for some reason or other likes to pose as an expert. He got it in the neck all right from that little man with the false teeth."

The sailor slapped his thigh with a blow like a pistol shot and roared with laughter. "Got it in the neck! Not half he didn't. Well, it will teach him a lesson. And butterflies—of all things. Look out—here he is."

Tony Sinclair came fussing in, and as soon as he saw me he crossed to our table.

"Ah! Mr Seymour," he said, "our little trip tomorrow must be cancelled, I fear. I have been unexpectedly called back to London, to my annoyance."

"I am sorry to hear that—er—Professor," I said a little stiffly.

"Going to catch *Opsi*—whatever it was—in Trafalgar Square," chuckled the sailor.

"I quite fail to understand you, sir," said Toby, drawing himself up. "Well—goodbye." He turned to me and held out his hand. "I trust you will enjoy the remainder of your holiday."

He went out into the lounge, and I watched him paying his bill.

"Really an extraordinary case," I said thoughtfully. "He's the last man in the world I should have thought would do anything so foolish. Even now I can't help thinking there must be some explanation. Though I suppose it's really a very unimportant matter."

"You never can tell," said the sailor darkly. "It may be that you're well clear of him, mate. Blokes don't masquerade like that unless they've got to. And they haven't got to unless there's something wrong somewhere."

"I quite agree," said the man with the damaged finger, speaking for the first time. "And as I happen to be a member of the police, I think I'll just keep an eye on the gentleman."

He finished his drink and left the room, and the sailor whistled under his breath.

"I wonder what the bloke has done," he said. "Or whether it's what you said—just a form of conceit. Anyway—have another."

For a moment or two I sat there undecided. Only too well did I know that the man with the damaged hand was not a member of the police, only too well did I know what he was a member of.

"Thanks," I said perfunctorily. "The same again, please." Should I, too, follow and tell Toby? But if I did, the sailor would in all probability begin to suspect me. He was a member of the gang, too, and it was vital that I should be thought genuine. At the same time, how could I possibly let Sinclair run into some trap? He'd been a fool to come over and speak to me, seeing who I was with. Still, I couldn't let him down. He must be warned.

"I think, after all, I won't have another at the moment," I said. "I shall go out for a bit of a stroll. I'll go on up and get my hat."

"Right ho! mate. You might see the Professor getting more butterflies."

I left the bar and went upstairs to my room. Was I doing the right thing or was I not? After all, nothing much could happen in Amesbury in the middle of the afternoon, and Toby was quite capable of tackling the man with the damaged finger single-handed. If he knew about him—that was the point.

I went down slowly into the lounge, trying to decide. The sailor was still sitting in his corner of the bar: he evidently regarded the rest of the half-section as preferable to a walk.

"A note for you, sir." The girl called to me out of the office.

"For me?" I said, staring at her.

She was holding it out, and I glanced at it. It was addressed to F. Seymour, and the unfamiliar name almost caught me napping.

"That's not—" I began, and then I remembered and took it. "Thank you," I said. "Who left it?"

"I really don't know, sir," she said. "I've been out of the office for a few minutes and I found it lying here when I got back."

Who on earth could it be from? No one knew me: and then, of course, I got it. Toby had left it on his way out. I slit open the envelope, and for a moment I stared at the contents uncomprehendingly.

Do not follow Toby—H. D.

H. D. Drummond! but where was he? How on earth did he know I had intended to follow Toby? And even as I racked my brains for an answer, a thickset man in plus-fours crossed the lounge and entered the bar. He had a short, clipped beard, flecked with grey, and his hair was thinning a little over the temples.

With an immense feeling of relief I followed him. Thank Heaven! He had arrived on the scene. Naturally I was not going to pretend to know him, but I couldn't resist throwing him a casual glance as I passed. By the mere fact that I was there he would know that I had carried out his orders so that it was unnecessary for me to do more. And I had the satisfaction of getting a quick look of approval.

"Changed your mind, mate, after all," called out the sailor. "However, better late than never, and good beer tastes none the worse for the waiting."

"It looked so infernally hot in the street," I said. "And even the chance of seeing our butterfly expert arrested for bigamy wasn't a sufficient inducement to go out."

I purposely spoke in a loud voice so that Drummond should hear.

"Bigamy; that's good," chuckled the sailor. "With a face like his I should think he'd be lucky to get one. Say"—he lowered his voice confidentially—"what do you make of the bloke in the corner. The one with the grouse moor on his face?"

"Nothing much," I said. "Why? You don't think he's another criminal, do you? Seems a perfectly ordinary sort of bird."

And then it suddenly occurred to me that it would be a good thing to let Drummond know that this man I was talking to was one of the enemy.

"By the way," I said casually, "seeing that you're a beer drinker, I suppose you're a Froth Blower."

The sailor shook his head. "I've heard of it," he remarked. "But I ain't a member. What's the idea?"

"Well, they've got a sort of anthem," I said, conscious that Drummond was looking in our direction, "by which they recognize one another. It goes something like this."

"Great Scott!" said the sailor after I'd finished. "Does it? You've got a funny sort of voice, haven't you, mate? Or is that really the tune?"

"It should under certain circumstances be sung twice," I remarked. "This is one of them."

"I'll take your word for it," he said urgently. "I don't want to be rude, guv'nor, but your voice is one of them things when a little goes a long way. Have another gargle?"

I declined his offer, and a little later I made my way into the lounge. Drummond had left the hotel, and it was fairly obvious that the only interest that the seafaring gentleman could have in me was one of curiosity. Though we had done our best to allay suspicion, Toby Sinclair's mistake had greatly increased my difficulties. To be associated, however innocently, with a man who has been found out as a fraud is bound to make one conspicuous. And that is exactly what I had no desire to be.

The saving point in the situation up to date had been—though I said it myself—my own acting. And as I sat in the lounge, idly scanning a local paper, I confess I felt a little amused. Drummond's absolute assurance that we should not recognize him struck me as being distinctly funny. Seldom had I seen a more obvious disguise than the one he had adopted. Of course, I realized that he had definitely given himself away to me by writing the note, but even without that I should have known him anywhere. The beard was so very obviously false. In fact, I made up my mind that when I dropped him a line to tell him exactly what had happened over Toby Sinclair I would warn him about that beard. It looked the sort that might fall off in the soup. And one thing was certain. If any of the enemy who had known him in days gone by—the woman herself, for instance—should chance to see him, he would be spotted for a certainty.

It surprised me, I confess. In one way and another I had heard so much of his resource and daring that it seemed all the more amazing that he should be so crude. To do him justice, the results he had obtained with Sinclair and myself were extremely good. Why, then, did he fail so dismally over himself? Could it be that he was so self-confident that he had become careless? Or was it merely that he was relying absolutely on the fact that the other side thought we were dead?

A very strong asset, doubtless—immensely strong—for just so long as they continued to think so. And that was where the great danger of Toby Sinclair's mistake lay. Supposing they got him and stripped off his disguise. He had been a member of Drummond's gang all through: he would be recognized at once by the woman. And the instant he was recognized it would be obvious to the meanest capacity that we had not been drowned. If he had escaped we must all have escaped.

And once that fact was known, suspicion would be bound to fall on me in spite of anything I might do. As for Drummond with his beard, a child would spot him at the other end of the street. Had not the sailor himself been suspicious the instant he saw him? And did it not prove, if further proof was necessary, that up to date I was entirely unsuspected? Otherwise would he have spoken as he did to me?

It certainly gave me a feeling of confidence, but just as certainly it increased my responsibility. As far as I could make out, I was the only person who with any degree of safety could carry on. Sinclair was out of it; and I found myself hoping to Heaven that Drummond would stop out too. Of course, I knew he wouldn't, but with his extremely conspicuous appearance he would do far mere harm than good. In fact, as I continued to think over it I began to feel thoroughly irritable. This wasn't a game of Hunt the Slipper, or Kiss in the Ring, It was a game in which, as we knew to our cost, any false step might prove fatal. And it wasn't playing fair to any of us to come into the thick of it with an appearance that called to high heaven—this is a disguise. Toby Sinclair's mistake had been foolish, perhaps, but that I had managed to rectify by acting promptly. But nothing I could do would rectify Drummond's. He, once he was seen, was beyond hope.

I crossed to a writing-table: something must be done. He might be our leader and all that, but I failed to see the slightest reason why I should run a considerably increased risk of getting it in the neck.

> Surely, *I began*, it is nothing short of insane to come here with such a blatantly false beard on. The thing shrieks at one. The man who looks like a sailor, and who, as I told you by signal in the bar, is one of them, suspected you at once. I rode him off, of course—but if the woman should see you, you're done for. We all are. Would it not be wiser, in view especially of Sinclair's bad mistake this afternoon, for you to leave this thing in my hands for the moment. I am the only one who is unknown to the other side. I obeyed your instructions, and did not go after him when he left the hotel, but are you aware that he was followed by the man whose finger you shot off. What is going to happen if they catch him? Don't you see that the whole show is up? They will realize at once that none of us were drowned. And what then? Once that occurs, you will forgive my blunt speaking, but you won't last a minute. You will be spotted immediately. And because of my association with Sinclair they will even suspect me.

Would it not, therefore, be better if, as I said before, you lie low for a bit? I will keep my eyes open, and find out what I can—notifying you at once of any developments. My principal hope lies in the sailor, and in the man with the damaged hand. The latter we know is one of them: the former I am equally certain is one also. Not, of course, absolutely so: but his whole demeanour at Stonehenge this afternoon was most suspicious. In fact, only the certainty of my perfect disguise prevents me from thinking that he was giving me the next clue. And if he was, it is Stornoway, in the island of Lewis. But of this I am not sure. Why should he waste a clue on an inoffensive bank clerk? Let us hope, at any rate, that I am wrong. Our difficulties in crossing undiscovered to such a sparsely populated locality as the Hebrides will be great.

Then there is another man about whom I think Sinclair wrote to you. He resembles apparently a man you killed some years ago called Lakington. We met him in the street here before starting for Stonehenge; and we again met him at the Friar's Heel itself. I had a long talk with him first, and found him a most delightful and cultivated individual. In fact, I cannot believe that he is one of the enemy. Then Sinclair joined us, and committed his terrible gaffe. He told him he had actually seen a butterfly which, as we subsequently gathered, only grows in Brazil! Now whether this man, who for purposes of reference I will call Lakington, actually spotted this mistake, or whether he didn't, I cannot say with any degree of certainty. But the point is really immaterial. Because the man who looks like a sailor most certainly did. After Lakington had left us, an odd little man, who obviously knew what he was talking about, though he acted as if he wasn't all there, told Sinclair to his face that he was an impostor. And the sailor, who was close by, heard. Now do you see the danger we are in? Sinclair is spotted: you, I'm afraid, are spotted also, so that only I am left. And if by any chance they begin to suspect me—which is not likely, but at the same time is a possibility we must reckon with—the coincidence would be too marked to escape their notice. One newcomer in disguise might be anybody: three—one of whom is a big man—tapes us unerringly. We shall have lost the priceless asset of secrecy.

Wherefore I beg of you lie low. Hide, if necessary, in whatever room you may have taken, and wait for information from me. I am repeating myself, I know, but frankly, my dear fellow, it never even dawned on me that you would appear quite as you are. I venture to think it would almost have been better if you had come as yourself. However, the mischief is done now—and all that we can try to do is to rectify it.

You may rely implicitly on me; but please do not make my task any harder than it is already.

I read through what I had written. Strong, perhaps—but not one whit too strong. He must be made to understand the enormity of his offence. And if he didn't: if he persisted in going about the place as he was, I should have to consider very seriously whether or not I would throw the thing up. Where would they have been without me up to date? I had more than half solved the first clue: I had completely solved the second: and, through old Jenkinson, I had given them the answer to the third. Which entitled me to express my opinion pretty tersely. And if Drummond didn't like it, he could damned well lump it.

I addressed an envelope to John Bright, and called for a stamp. And it was while I was waiting for it to be brought that a trick of memory brought to my mind an incident in some detective story I had read years ago. A man had given himself away by leaving behind him a piece of blotting-paper which he had just used. And the blotting-paper, when held up to a looking-glass, revealed exactly what he had written.

Just one of those little things, I reflected, where brain counts. One of those small details where the blundering type of fellow is apt to get caught. So I took the blotting-paper, tore it into small pieces, and dropped them in the paper-basket. "Bit extravagant, aren't you, mate?" With a feeling of annoyance, I turned round in my chair. Standing by the door of the bar was the sailor, and with him was the man with the damaged hand. And they were both staring at me.

For a moment I was tempted to ask him angrily what the devil it had to do with him, but I instantly suppressed the impulse. After all, it was a very harmless remark—one, moreover, which I was quick enough to see gave me an excellent opportunity of consolidating my position.

"A habit we clerks get into in a bank," I said. "Clean blotting-paper always after finishing a job."

"Is that so?" he remarked. "What a good idea." I rose and crossed to the front door—I had no wish to post the letter in the hotel. And it was as I was actually stepping on to the pavement that a sudden awful thought struck me. Supposing—what was to prevent them, as soon as I was gone, from getting the torn-up pieces out of the basket and fitting them together.

At all costs I must prevent that, and the question was how. The sailor was still by the door, though the other man had disappeared. There was only one thing to be done: get back to the table, write another letter, and in some way or other retrieve those incriminating pieces.

I wrote another letter, and still he stood there. But at last he went, and I made a dive for the basket. The bits were all together, but mixed up to a certain extent with old cigarette ends and two used pipe-cleaners. However, there was no time to worry over trifles: it was imperative that I should get that blotting-paper. I grabbed the lot, including the pipe-cleaners, and some soft, wet object, and crammed everything into my pocket. Then, breathing freely, I once more stood up, only to see that confounded sailor pop out again like a jack-in-the-box from the bar.

"Lumme, mate!" he cried, "what have you got on your coat? It looks like something out of a dustbin."

I glanced down, just as the soft, wet object fell with a flop on the carpet.

"Why," he said with interest, "that's the rotten plum I threw away an hour ago. You don't half have funny habits at your bank, old man, do you?"

The situation was undeniably difficult, and the only thing to do was to carry it off lightly.

"I threw away an important paper by mistake," I laughed.

"Well, you must have had St Vitus's dance in your fingers when you picked it up again," he said. "You've got an old bootlace and two toothpicks on your coat, sticking in the plum juice."

He retired into the bar again leaving me fuming inwardly. The man was absolutely ubiquitous: it seemed impossible to get rid of him. Moreover, it was one of those stupid little things that have the power of irritating one profoundly. To be seen by anybody grabbing rotten plums out of a wastepaper basket is annoying: in this case it might have been worse but for the cool way I had ridden him off.

However, there was only one thing to be done—dismiss the matter as unimportant. I had retrieved the blotting-paper which was the main point: the next item on the programme was to post my letter to Drummond. And then the real business would begin.

I strolled along the street, thinking out the best means of tackling the problem. The whole thing boiled down to a question of subtlety and brain: of meeting cunning with cunning. Once I had obtained the next clue, or located our opponents' main even if only temporary headquarters—strength would doubtless be required. And then

Drummond could shed his ridiculous beard and emerge from seclusion. But until then—well, my letter was concise on that point.

My eyes suddenly narrowed: surely there was Drummond himself—beard and all—going into the Post Office. I quickened my steps. I felt that my letter was so vitally important that it would be worth while running some small risk to obtain immediate delivery. Every additional moment that he was at large in that absurd and obvious get-up increased our danger.

He was leaning over the counter as I entered, and I went and stood next to him.

"Are there any letters here for Bright?" he asked the girl "John Bright."

She turned round to look, and I nudged his arm gently, showing him at the same time the letter I held in my hand. Then I dropped it on the floor.

"One just come," said the girl handing over Toby Sinclair's note.

Drummond took it, and then, as she attended to me, he stooped down and picked up mine. I bought some stamps, and stayed chatting with the girl for a few moments to give him time to get away. Then with a feeling of relief that my warning had reached him safely I followed at a reasonable distance. That vital matter was settled anyway.

Once more I returned to the problem. Two main lines of action presented themselves, so it seemed to me. The first lay in shadowing the sailor, or the man with the damaged finger, or possibly both: the second entailed a further visit or visits to the Friar's Heel, and both courses involved certain obvious difficulties.

It was true that up till now I had successfully avoided suspicion, but if I proceeded to attach myself permanently to either of the two men, how long should I continue avoiding it? If I tried to stalk them at a distance I was at once confronted with the fact that Salisbury Plain is not a very populous spot, and that I was almost certain to be discovered. On the other hand, if I went to the Friar's Heel, what chance should I have of obtaining any clue? Why should anything be said to an inoffensive bank clerk?

The best course I decided would probably be a mixture of the two. I could cultivate the sailor's acquaintance, and if I kept my ears open I might learn something of value either from him or the man with the damaged hand. But I would confine my dealings with them to the bar, or at any rate the hotel, unless some opportunity presented itself to accompany them anywhere outside. In addition I would pay a further visit to the Friar's Heel, and see if I could pick up anything there.

And that was the conclusion I had reached as I turned into the lounge. Prudent, and at the same time calculated to give the maximum of result. The sailor was in his usual corner of the bar, and he waved a cheerful hand at me as I entered.

"Been picking up any more plums?" he inquired. "Anyway, what about that gargle you wouldn't have before?"

"My shout this time," I said genially as I sat down. "Just been having a stroll through the town. What is it?"

He was leaning towards me, and signing me to put my head close. "I believe," he said in a hoarse whisper, "that that man's beard is false."

"What man?" I asked bewildered.

And then, to my rage and fury I saw that Drummond had just entered the bar. For a moment or two I could scarcely speak, so angry did I feel. After my urgent letter, after my imperative warning, for the triple distilled fool to parade himself again in the hotel of all places was too maddening.

"I don't think so," I managed to get out after a while. "Why should a man wear a false beard?"

"Why should a man pretend to know about butterflies when he doesn't?" he remarked. "Why should a man pick rotten plums and toothpicks out of a wastepaper basket?"

"I trust," I said stiffly, "that you don't think there is anything mysterious about me."

"Lumme! no, mate," he laughed. "There ain't nothing mysterious about you." He was staring covertly at Drummond all the time. "It is false," he affirmed. "It waggles."

"Confound him and his beard," I cried. "Let's have that drink."

And even as I beckoned to the waiter, what little self-control that I still had after Drummond's colossal idiocy very nearly left me. Who should be crossing the lounge and heading straight for the bar but Algy Longworth?

He came drifting in and I stared at him speechlessly. Had everybody gone mad I wondered. That he should come here at all must be due to Drummond. And that Drummond should have sent him knowing that the man with the damaged hand was in the hotel could only be explained by the fact that our much vaunted leader's brain had failed.

True they took no notice of one another, and after a time, Longworth came over and sat down at the next table to ours. He, of course, did not know me, and I therefore judged it safe to address a casual remark to him. It might perhaps enable him to clear out.

"Motoring through?" I said casually.

He nodded.

"Jolly place, isn't it?" he remarked. "I always love dear old Salisbury Plain, ever since I spent six months on it at the beginning of the war. But I don't know this end very well: I was up Ludgershall way. Is it far from here to Stonehenge?"

"Stonehenge," repeated the sailor. "About three miles, I suppose. This gentleman and I were there this afternoon."

"I thought of going tonight," said Algy, and I felt I could have cheerfully murdered him.

"Did you?" remarked the sailor, staring at him thoughtfully. "Well, it's an interesting place, ain't it, mate?"

He turned to me.

"What did they call that stone where we were talking? The Friar's Heel, wasn't it?" And as he said it he deliberately raised his voice. I had a momentary glimpse of the man with the damaged hand standing in the door staring at Algy. Then he disappeared, and I saw him leave the hotel quickly. The damage was done: the message had been given.

CHAPTER 13

In Which I go to Friar's Heel by Night

I don't mind confessing that I very nearly chucked in my hand. The whole thing was too disheartening. It was worse than disheartening—it was suicidal. I realized, of course, that my letter had not reached Drummond in time for him to warn Longworth that the sailor was one of the other side, but even so Algy should have known better than to discuss his plans with two complete strangers. And now the thing was what to do.

Drummond had left the bar shortly after, and up till dinner time I had no chance of a private word with Longworth. I made him one or two covert signs when the sailor was not looking, but he missed them all. In fact he seemed to me to be wilfully dense. He must know that I was about somewhere, even if he didn't actually recognize me.

At dinner it was just the same. I came in to find him sitting at the long table between an elderly lady and a man who looked like a prosperous farmer. And not once did he even glance in my direction though I tried to catch his eye on several occasions.

The sailor had beckoned to me as I came in to sit at his table, but I had pretended not to see. I wanted peace and quiet to think out this new development. If Algy went to the Friar's Heel that night he was for it. That much was obvious. Unless, of course, Drummond proposed to be there, too, and bring the matter down to brute force. But even if he did, surely he must realize that it was very unlikely it would help us to find his wife's hiding place.

Or did Drummond intend to lie hidden in the hope of getting a clue, and to use Longworth as a decoy without whom the clue would not be given? That, of course, was possible. But what the damned fool seemed to fail utterly to realize even now was the folly of doing such a thing in his present disguise. Already the sailor suspected him: once let him be discovered at the Friar's Heel, even if his great strength did enable him to get away, suspicion would become certainty. Then they would either move Mrs Drummond, or finish her off right away, and we should be in a far worse position than we were now.

If only he would leave the thing to me. It seemed such an obvious solution to the whole matter. Instead of which, here they were blundering round, suspected by everybody and finding out nothing.

At length I finished my dinner, and went into the lounge. I had seen Longworth go out previously, but there was no sign of him as I sat down. And as I tried to drink some of the concoction that passes in the average English hotel for coffee, the sailor went by towards the door.

"Goodnight, mate," he called out.

"Where are you off to?" I asked carelessly.

"Going to see some friends out Netheravon way," he answered with a wink. "At least—a friend."

He went out under the pleasing delusion that he had deceived me, and I sat on. Where was Algy?

A quarter of an hour passed: a half, and at length I could stand it no longer. I would chance it and go to his room. I got up and strolled over casually to the office. There was the entry in the book right enough—A. Longworth, Room 15. I went upstairs; the room was facing me. And after a quick glance round to see that no one was about I opened the door and went in.

The room was empty, and I stood there wondering what to do next. It seemed obvious that he must have left the hotel, and if so he was probably on his way to Stonehenge by now. And the only thing to do as far as I could see was to follow him. After all, who knew what he might be up against, and even if Drummond was there a third person would do no harm.

I decided that I would walk. The night was fine though dark, and an hour, I calculated, would just about see me there. Then I would lie concealed unless my help was wanted, and find out what I could.

It was just about eleven when I reached the slight hill that passes the monument. I was walking on the grass beside the road to deaden the sound of my footsteps, and when I got level with the great stones I sat down for a while to reconnoitre. I could see them dimly outlined in the darkness some hundred yards away, and I craned my eyes to see if I could make out any sign of movement. There was nothing: all was silent and motionless, until after a while I began to imagine things.

I recalled that vigil of the other night by the stranded motorcar, and realized that unless I did something soon my nerves would begin to go. And one thing was obvious: if I did want to find out anything I would have to go nearer.

I put a leg through the wire fence, and even as I did so I heard a sound that froze me into immobility and brought me out in a cold sweat. It was a shrill scream of fear, and the voice was the voice of a man.

It came from the direction of Stonehenge, and I crouched there listening with every sense alert. The scream was not repeated, though it seemed to me that I heard a hoarse worrying noise for a time. Then utter silence.

Suddenly I became aware of something else. I was still standing half straddled over the fence, when I felt by the faintest movement of my legs that someone else was touching the wires. And not very far away either.

I peered into the darkness: was that the dark outline of a man—or was it only a little mound? It was moving, I could swear it was moving. But it was moving away from the road and towards Stonehenge.

Then came the next unexpected development. This time there was no mistake about it: someone was scrambling through the fence without taking any precautions whatever. The wires literally twanged, and once again I crouched down waiting. Well for me that I did so: well for me that I was not still in the place where I had sat down first.

For a moment later a man, bent almost double, came swiftly past right over the spot from which I had only just moved. The fence was between us but even so, he was so close that I could have touched him, and how he missed seeing me I do not know. But I saw him, and long after he had vanished into the darkness I sat there motionless, trying to puzzle out this new development. Even without the momentary glimpse I had got of his face, another sense would have proclaimed the truth. The man was a coal-black negro.

I looked round again: the mound was no longer there, and after a little hesitation I too started to crawl cautiously towards Stonehenge. Whether I liked it or not, the reason of that dreadful scream had got to be discovered.

Foot by foot I wormed my way forward, peering ahead at every step to try and see the other man who I knew must be somewhere in front of me. Suddenly from about twenty yards away came the faint glow of a screened electric torch. I stopped instantly: without realizing it I had almost reached one of the great stones. And for a space I stared at the terrible spectacle the light revealed.

Lying on his back, his legs sprawling drunkenly, was a man, and it only needed one glance to see that he was dead. There were ghastly marks round his throat, and his head lolled sideways. The poor brute had been throttled by a man of immense strength, and it looked to me as if his neck had been broken.

It was not Algy Longworth: the dead man was a complete stranger. But who was the man who held the torch? His face was in shadow: I could not see the outline of his body. Was it the sailor? Or was it the man with the damaged hand? I craned forward, and as I did so the torch was extinguished. I had a blurred impression of movement, and then silence. The man, whoever he was, had gone. I was alone with the dead body. And even as I realized it and began to wonder what I should do next, I heard the faint thrumming of a motor car from the road. Then came the slight squeak of a brake and the sound of a door being opened. I looked round. Whoever it was was running without lights.

Very cautiously I backed away from the murdered man. An unlighted car stopping where this one had seemed too suspicious for my liking. And having gone what I thought was a safe distance I lay down and waited: waited until the next thing happened, a thing which almost made me throw caution to the winds.

"To the right," came the voice of a man, speaking low. "You have your torch?" came the answer, and the man grunted assent.

And the second speaker was a woman. I could see them dimly outlined against the darkness not five yards away. But it wasn't that that filled me with a wild excitement: it was the smell of a scent like jasmine—and yet not quite jasmine. It was the woman herself—Irma—our arch-enemy. They moved away, and I wormed after them. "Here he is," said the man's voice. "I'll switch on the torch for a second."

Once more came the faint glow, and then a sharp exclamation from her. "This isn't one of them. I've never seen this man before in my life."

The torch was extinguished. "Darling—Are you sure?"

"Of course I'm sure," she said fiercely. "I know the whole brood by sight. That is no more Longworth than you are."

"Then what on earth was he doing here?" muttered the man.

"How should I know?" she answered. "That fool Pedro has killed the wrong man."

"Unless this man is a new member of their gang," said her companion.

She almost spat at him.

"I'm not concerned with new members. I want the old lot."

"My beloved," came his voice, vibrant with love and passion, "can't you chuck it? This is all such a ghastly risk. Drummond is dead already: you've got his wife. Isn't that enough?"

"It is not," she said coldly.

"Well, what are we going to do about this body?" he asked wearily.

"Every moment we're here increases our danger."

"Are those sheds over there empty?"

"But the risk, *cherie*. It is bound to be discovered."

"Not until we have finished," she said in a peculiar voice. "Send Pedro back from the car to carry it there."

They were moving away, back towards the road. And to my mind there returned those strange words of hers—"After, I will come to you." And her voice as she said the word "Finished," had been the same. What was in this strange woman's brain? What dark, hideous plan had she conceived? Because the conviction was growing on me that she was not only a woman obsessed with an idea—she was mad.

And who was this man, her companion, who evidently loved her? Where did he come in? Did he hope for reward after her plans were fulfilled—did he hope for her? What wouldn't I have given for the due to the events of the night. Who was the dead man? Who was the man who had first examined him and then disappeared into the darkness?

And then the noise of the car starting recalled me to the present. Pedro must be the black man I had seen dodging past me down the road, and I had no wish to meet Pedro whatever. Crouching low, I dodged away from the place where the body lay. I had seen enough. I would go back to the hotel and think things over tomorrow.

I reached the railings, and cautiously crawled through them. Then I started on my three-mile walk. From behind me came the harsh cry of a night bird, and once I paused and listened. It seemed to me that I heard a strange, worrying noise, followed by a sharp shout that was instantly suppressed. With an involuntary shudder I walked on till the dim outline of the giant stones were hidden by the hill. Nothing would have induced me to return to the place again. But I couldn't help wondering what further horror had happened there. Had the negro suddenly encountered the other wanderer by night? And who was it who had shouted?

One ray of light, and one ray only shone in the general fog. They had intended to kill Algy Longworth that night: they therefore intended to kill Darrell and Jerningham. The last lingering doubt that this woman intended to play the game had been dispelled. And it was therefore imperative that they should be warned. They must at all costs be kept away from the place. Once they were caught, the end would come at once: nothing could save Drummond's wife. This woman Irma would imagine that we were all accounted for, and no further reason would exist for delay. So Algy would have to be sent away as soon as possible, and told to stop away until at any rate I had discovered the headquarters of our enemy.

It ought not to be difficult, I reflected. Surely someone in the neighbourhood must have seen the negro. He would be a conspicuous figure in a locality like this. And once he was identified the house was identified. And once that was done, there was one thing on which I was absolutely determined. The police must be informed. If Drummond wouldn't do it, then I would. It was essential: the house must be completely surrounded by a cordon of men. The time for fooling with matters was past: things were altogether too serious. We were up against a mad woman and a man who was infatuated with her. And they would have to be put under restraint, or else exterminated.

Then another thought struck me. What if I informed the police at once or first thing next morning of what I had seen? Told them that in one of those old disused military sheds they would find the dead body of a man, and that the murderer was a negro. That would take them direct to the place and settle things. As a foreigner, I took it, he would have to be registered: his address would, therefore, be known. The only trouble was that my own doings might require a little explanation. Why was I masquerading about in a disguise? Why bad I entered my name in the hotel books as Seymour when it was really Dixon? Well—I should have to tell them everything, that was all, though I frankly did not relish the idea of trying to make a stolid local police officer believe me. The whole thing sounded too much like a nightmare induced by a surfeit of lobster.

I paused to light a cigarette, and as I did so I saw a red light on the road ahead of me. It was the tail-light of a car, and it was stationary. It seemed to be about a hundred yards away, and for a moment or two I stared at it thoughtfully. True, there was nothing inherently suspicious about a stationary motor car, but tonight I was in a mood to suspect anything.

I crept cautiously a little nearer. Something had evidently gone wrong, I could see the outline of the chauffeur as he peered into the bonnet. Another man was standing beside him holding an electric torch in his hands, and the chauffeur was tinkering with a spanner.

Suddenly the man holding the light turned it for a moment on to the chauffeur's face, and I stopped abruptly. For the chauffeur was the man who had sprung at me out of the ditch three nights before, and whose hands I could still feel on my throat. No doubt about it now: the car in front of me belonged to the enemy. And surely, unless it was a very amazing coincidence, it must be the same car that had stopped by Stonehenge earlier.

I crawled into the hedge and tried to decide on a line of action. There in front of me lay the means of running the gang to earth if only I could seize it. But how? Once the defect was put right the car would be off, and manifestly I couldn't follow it on foot. I cursed myself for not having come on a bicycle: then I might have had some chance. Now it was hopeless. And yet I knew that if I could but track that car to its destination our problem was solved.

I crept a little nearer, and suddenly an idea dawned on me. The luggage grid was down at the back. Suppose I managed to get on that! It would have to be done with the utmost care: the exact psychological moment would have to be seized. Just as he let in his gear would be the time. And if I was spotted, I would pretend that I was trying to jump a ride. Disguised as I was, the chauffeur would not recognize me: the woman, anyway, did not know me, and the only danger was the other man of whose identity I was still in ignorance. Still, it was worth the risk: the information, if I could get it, would be so invaluable.

The chauffeur was closing the bonnet. The man who had been holding the light opened the door and got in. The moment had come. Stooping low, I ran the few yards to the back of the car, just as I heard the noise of the self-starter. Then the engine was raced for a few seconds, and I gripped the grid with both hands, and swung myself on to it. We were off.

A wild feeling of triumph swept over me: so far, I had not been spotted. But it didn't last long, and if the road had not been good, it would have lasted an even shorter time. For sheer discomfort commend me to a ride on the luggage grid of a fast car. Several times I was nearly shot off as we went over bumps. In addition, the car was over lubricated, and emitted a dense cloud of blue smoke from just underneath me. But for all that, I felt it was worth it: I'd done the trick. I'd succeeded where, at any rate up to date, the others had failed. All that was necessary now was to hang on until we reached our destination, drop off as the car slowed down, and escape into the darkness. And in spite of my extreme agony, I almost laughed as I pictured Drummond's face the next morning when he heard the news.

I felt the brakes being applied and heaved a sigh of relief. And then the car swung right-handed, and turned through a gate. I could tell by the scrunch of gravel under the tyres that we were in a drive, and suddenly a light inside the car was switched on. That was a complication I had not thought of, for now the ground behind the car was illuminated through the back window. And if either of the occupants happened to look out they were bound to see me when I dropped off. I hesitated, squeezing myself as close as possible to the car. Should I chance it? And while I was trying to make up my mind, the car stopped at the front door.

Now I thought detection was certain, but still my luck held. The man and the woman passed into the house: the door closed behind them. And the next instant the car moved on. Once again did I get ready to jump off, when the noise of the gravel ceased and I realized we were in the garage. Moreover, it was a big garage, and the chauffeur had driven the car in as far as it would go so that I had at least ten yards to cover before reaching the door. I heard him get down and start fiddling with some tools on a bench. Should I make a dart for it now? Then the lights were switched off, and he yawned prodigiously. He had evidently finished for the night, and I only just had time to dodge to one side of the car as he came by on the other.

He heaved on the sliding doors, and they met with a clang. A key turned: his footsteps died away. And I couldn't help it—I laughed. The situation really had its humorous side. Without doubt I had successfully tracked the tiger to its lair—so successfully that I was inside while the tiger was out. And as my position came home to me I stopped laughing. The humour of the situation lay with the tiger.

I started to make a tour of inspection. The main doors were locked: there was nothing to be hoped for in that quarter. And a brief survey of the windows showed that none of them were made to open. Cautiously I felt my way along to the further end. A wooden bench littered with spanners and things filled three-quarters of it: in the other quarter, and my hopes rose as I saw it, was a second door. I tried the handle. It was locked. That finished it. I was caught like a rat in a trap. With the arrival of the chauffeur next morning I must be discovered. Nothing could prevent it.

What a drivelling idiot I had been! I had accomplished absolutely nothing. I didn't even know where I was, which would have been some recompense. Then, even if they kept me a prisoner, I might have found an opportunity of communicating with Drummond. As it was, all that I had succeeded in doing was to get locked up in a unknown place.

What about breaking one of the windows? It gave me a possibility of escape whereas if I waited there was none. But I soon realized the difficulty of the idea. The panes were small—far too small for me to squeeze through. It would mean smashing wood and everything, and there, not ten yards away, was the house. Still, it was a possibility. I was bound to be heard but in the general confusion I might escape. And even as I was turning the matter over in my mind I stiffened into sudden rigidity. A light was shining below the bottom of the second door, and I could hear footsteps approaching.

The key turned, and I dodged behind the car. A man came in, and I could hear him cursing under his breath. He had an electric torch in his hand, and he appeared to be searching for some tool on the bench. His back was towards me, and for a moment I had the wild idea of hurling myself on him and taking him unawares. I think if I had had any weapon in my hand I would have done so and chanced it.

He found what he wanted, and left the garage. My opportunity, if it ever really had been an opportunity, had gone. But had it? For he had left the door wide open.

Light streamed in, and I crept a little nearer. He was walking along a short passage, and a further door at the other end was open. It led into a room, and it was from the room that the light came. The passage was evidently to enable one to reach the garage from the house under cover, but it was not of such prosaic details that I was thinking. It was the brief glimpse I had obtained of the interior of the room that made me rub my eyes and wonder if I was dreaming.

The entire furniture appeared to consist of big stones. I had seen no chair, no table, only square and oblong stones. At least, I thought they were stones: they certainly looked like stones—stones about three or four feet long and a foot thick. And if they were stones, what in the name of fortune were they there for? Had I come to a private lunatic asylum? Was the whole place bughouse?

He had half closed the second door behind him so that I could no longer see anything from the garage. But I could still hear, and the noise was the noise a stonemason makes when chipping with a cold chisel.

I crept even nearer. Confound the risk, I thought; I was caught, anyway. And by this time my curiosity was so intense that it banished fear. At last I got near enough to see into the room, or, rather, into a part of it. And what I saw confirmed my opinion. They were bughouse: the whole darned lot of them.

The room was a big one, and the first impression that it gave was that it had been specially prepared for some mystical religious ceremony. The walls were completely concealed with black curtains, and a thick black carpet covered the floor. On this carpet, in the portion of the room that I could see, big greyish-white stones were lying about apparently haphazard. Some were on their sides: others stood endways. Some lay isolated: others were arranged as a child might arrange bricks. One particular group that I could see consisted of four stones on end and spaced at intervals of about a foot, with a fifth laid flat across their tops. In short, the whole effect was that of a stonemason's yard arranged by its owner when under the influence of alcohol.

Through the black curtains the lights stuck out—big, white, frosted lights that seemed to hang unsupported in the air. And after a while, as I looked at the one opposite me, it began to have the most extraordinary effect on my brain. First it would diminish in size, receding into the distance until it was only the size of a pin's head; then it would come rushing towards me, blazing bigger and bigger till it seemed to fill the whole room. I found myself swaying, and with a monstrous effort I looked away. Almost had I walked towards that light, self-hypnotized.

I forced myself to think of other things, and after a while the influence waned. What on earth was this extraordinary room? What was the man doing on the other side of the door? I could not see him, but steadily, monotonously, the chip, chip, chip went on. And then it suddenly stopped.

I glanced up only to shrink back against the wall of the passage. Where she had come from I did not know, but there, standing in the middle of the room, was the woman. It was the first time I had seen her without a hat, and for a while I could only gaze at her speechlessly.

She was dressed in some sort of loose white robe, and as she stood there outlined against the black background, a hand resting lightly on one of the big stones, she seemed like the priestess of some ancient cult. Her beauty was almost unearthly: her whole appearance utterly virginal. In her eyes there glowed a strange light—a light such as might have shone in the eyes of a martyr. And I felt that her soul was all the depth and height of space away.

It was incredible to think ill of such a woman—to believe her capable of evil. Almost did I believe that she was someone else—someone I had not seen before. To think that it was she who had planned the death trap at the Mere; to think it was her I had heard talking coarsely and brutally at Stonehenge not two hours ago seemed unbelievable. And then it came once more, that faint scent like jasmine—and yet not quite jasmine.

"Have you finished?"

She spoke quietly, and now her voice was a delight to hear. And then she stiffened and drew herself up. Into her face there came a look of disgusted contempt. But the poor fool kneeling at her feet, with his arms round her knees, was oblivious of it. He was stammering wild words of love, was the man who looked like Lakington; and so engrossed was I in the scene that the fact of my unknown man being the man who looked like Lakington seemed almost trivial. What did it matter who he was, poor devil: he was just an actor in the game that is age-old.

"When, my beloved, are you coming to me?"

Again and again he said it, his voice shaking, his hands trembling. And she just stood there, utterly aloof: to her he was non-existent. Her eyes were fixed in front of her, and once her lips moved as if she was speaking to someone no earthly vision could see. Even as I had seen her speak at the Mere. "Have you finished?"

With a sigh of utter weariness the man rose to his feet. "Yes," he said. "I have."

She smiled, and held out her hand. "Good. For now there must be no delay, my friend. Pedro's mistake has forced our hand. By the way, is he back?"

The man shrugged his shoulders. "I don't know. Probably by this time."

"Anyway, I have written a letter which must be delivered to one of the three tomorrow morning. We know that Longworth is here, so he will therefore be the one. Listen, I will read it to you:

"'My friends, the game has begun to pall. My revenge is sufficient. If you will follow the bearer of this you will come to your destination. And the widow shall be handed over to you. If you don't: if you are afraid to come, you will still be quite safe. No further steps will be taken against you. You will not be worth it. But Phyllis Drummond will die. So take your choice. Her life lies in your hands.

"'But let me repeat the warning given to your late lamented leader. My information is good, so no police. Otherwise Phyllis Drummond will die before you get here.'"

"But, *carissima*," cried the man, "will they come on that? It seems such an obvious trap."

"Quite clearly, Paul," she said, "you have much to learn concerning the mentality of Englishmen of their type. They will come, even if a cordon of machine-gunners stood in their way. And we shall be ready for them."

"And then? After it is over?" He stared at her hungrily as if trying to read her very soul.

"After it is over," she repeated coolly. "Why, then, my dear Paul, we shall see."

"But you promised," he muttered. "You promised by all you held sacred. Beloved"—his voice grew urgent and pleading—"for nearly a year I have worked unceasingly to give you your revenge. Worked without reward: at times without thanks. Only hope has kept me going, *carissima*—the hope that when all was over you would come to me. And now you say, 'We shall see.' Never have I kissed your lips during all these long months. Irma—say to me, promise me again—that I have not worked in vain."

"No, *mon ami*," she said. "You have not worked in vain."

With a cry of joy he snatched one of her hands and smothered it with kisses. And over his bent head I saw her face. She was shaking with hideous, silent laughter. I craned forward fascinated: that such a change could take place in any human being's expression seemed impossible. No longer a priestess of unearthly beauty, but evil incarnate that made one shudder to look at.

Suddenly the man straightened up, and instantly her face became a mask. Even did she go so far as to smile encouragingly at the poor fish.

"No, Paul," she repeated. "You have not worked in vain. Tomorrow night. . . ."

The sentence was never finished, too late I realized that in my absorption I had stepped into the light. For a moment or two she stared at me in silence. Then—"Who is that man?"

Like a flash her companion swung round. "Why," he said softly, "it's the bank clerk. Have you come to see my collection?" He was moving towards me as he spoke, and in his right hand there gleamed a wicked-looking automatic. "Come in, bank clerk," he said, still in the same deadly soft voice. "I am honoured indeed, even if the hour is a little unconventional."

Chapter 14

In Which I Meet Mrs Drummond

The situation was undeniably awkward. The fact that I had realized all along that detection was inevitable made it none the less unpleasant when it came. And I liked neither the look of the automatic nor that on the man's face. I stepped into the room.

"I fear it must seem a little strange," I began, making a valiant endeavour to keep my voice steady.

"It does," he agreed suavely. "May we be favoured with an explanation?"

I plunged desperately. "To tell you the truth," I said, "I lost my way. I went out for a long walk tonight, and after taking one or two turnings I realized I hadn't the faintest idea where I was. Passing along the road I saw this house, and I came up to see if someone could put me right. I couldn't get any answer, but I saw your garage door was open. So I went in, meaning to ask when the car returned. And I suppose I must have fallen asleep, for when I woke up the car was back and the door locked."

"I see," said the man. "It seems a pity that such a big discrepancy exists between the first few words of your explanation and the rest."

"I don't understand what you mean," I remarked, uncomfortably conscious that a pulse was hammering in my throat.

"You prefaced your interesting little story," he explained, "by the five words, 'To tell you the truth.' Why not do so?"

With a faint feeling of relief, I saw that the automatic was no longer in his hand. "I am not accustomed—" I began haughtily.

"Be silent," said the woman imperiously. "Do I understand you know this man, Paul?"

"I met him at Stonehenge yesterday afternoon, my dear," he remarked. "A bank clerk with lengthy holidays. South Africa last year, Australia next. I must apply for a position in that bank."

His eyes were boring into me, and I could have kicked myself with mortification. I, who had thought that my playing of the part had been perfect—that I alone was unsuspected. I tried another bluff.

"You are very clever, sir," I said coldly. "But not quite clever enough. My father keeps one of the few remaining private banks in which I am a clerk. But, as you will understand, not an ordinary clerk. And to broaden my mind he has allowed me to travel extensively."

"Most interesting," he answered. "And most considerate of your father. Anyway, that's better than the one before. You're improving."

"Stop all this nonsense," said the woman harshly. "Why wasn't I told about this man?"

"My dear," he said pleadingly, "what was the use?"

"On your own showing," she snapped, "you suspected him. Why wasn't I told?" Her voice was vibrating with anger. She swung round on me. "Who are you, you little rat?"

"My name is Seymour," I stammered.

Suddenly her mood changed, and she lit a cigarette.

"Put him in one of the seats," she ordered quietly.

"This way, Mr Seymour," said the man.

"And what if I refuse," I blustered.

For a moment he stared at me—thin lipped and motionless. "Just this," he said gently, "I will blow out your brains where you stand."

"A messy proceeding." I strove to speak jauntily. "But may I ask—"

He whipped out his revolver and covered me. "Move," he snarled. "And move damned quick. Come here."

He crossed to one of the stones. So did I. The more I saw of that man, the less I liked him.

I found that the stone at which he was pointing had been fashioned into a sort of rough seat. "Sit down, and put your arms where I tell you. There—and there."

I obeyed: there didn't seem anything else to do. And then there came a sudden click, and I felt two thin steel bars close over my wrists. I tugged and he laughed quietly. "I wouldn't waste your time," he remarked. "You're as much a part of the furniture now as the stone you are sitting on."

"Look here, sir," I said, "this is going beyond a joke. I admit that I had no right whatever to be in your garage, but that doesn't afford you any justification for treating me like this."

He took no notice. He was speaking in low tones to the woman. And suddenly she nodded and came towards me. For a time she stood in front of me staring into my eyes, and then she spoke. "Do you know Hugh Drummond?"

Now subconsciously, I suppose, I had been expecting that question, and on that one little effort of mine I do flatter myself.

"Hugh Drummond." I looked at her blankly. "I've never heard of the man in my life."

Still she stared at me, but my face gave nothing away. And at last she turned and spoke to the man.

"Well," I heard him say, "we might try."

She crossed to a door hidden in the curtains and disappeared, leaving me alone with the man.

"What has happened," he said suddenly, "to that egregious fraud who was pretending to collect butterflies?"

"I haven't any idea," I answered. "He left the hotel before dinner."

"Say nothing about him," he said curtly. "It will pay you not to."

"I wasn't proposing to," I remarked. "I fail to see the slightest reason for discussing a casual hotel acquaintance, or what bearing he has on my present position."

"If you hadn't been a damned fool you wouldn't be in your present position. Now the truth, my friend. Who are you, and how did you come here?"

"I have nothing to add to what I have already said," I answered.

He stared at me moodily, and I grew more and more puzzled. Try as I would I couldn't get a line on his mental attitude. If, as I now knew, he had spotted Toby Sinclair as a fraud, and me also, one would have expected him to show signs of gratification, even of triumph at having caught one of us so easily. Instead of which he seemed positively annoyed at my presence. True I had interrupted him in the middle of his love-making, but I felt that didn't account for it.

"You must be one of them," he said half to himself. "And that butterfly fool as well. Damn it! you swarm like rabbits."

I said nothing. Light was beginning to dawn on the situation. Our thin lipped friend wanted the lady, and wanted her quickly. But before he got her he had, in the vernacular, to do a job of work. And that job had consisted up till now of disposing of the six of us. He believed that three were accounted for: the others were to be settled in the near future. And now he was confronted as he thought with further additions to the party, and therefore further delay in obtaining his purpose.

"How the devil did you get here?" he repeated angrily.

"I have nothing to add to what I have already said," I repeated.

"Damn you," he snarled. "You'll smile the other side of your face before long. It may amuse you to know that you'll never leave this room alive."

"That," I remarked with a confidence I was very far from feeling, "remains to be seen."

He took out his cigarette case savagely and started pacing up and down. And I for the first time since I had come into the room began to examine it more thoroughly. And the more I examined it the more amazing did it become. The whole of it was in keeping with the part I had seen from the passage. Stones and yet more stones, placed apparently indiscriminately. And yet, were they? Was there not some definite design? And as I stared round trying to find the solution I noticed a thing which gave me a queer little thrill. There were other roughly shaped seats beside the one I was sitting in—five others, making six in all. And each one was fitted with the same steel bars that encircled my own wrists. Six chairs, and six of us. What fantastic scheme had been evolved in that woman's deranged brain? Time, I reflected grimly, and time alone would tell.

The sound of a door opening made me turn my head. Irma had returned. But now another woman was with her—a woman who was blindfolded. And with a sudden quickening of my pulse I realized that this must be Phyllis Drummond herself.

She had evidently been awakened from sleep. Her bare feet were thrust into slippers, and she had slipped a *peignoir* over her pyjamas. Her face under the handkerchief that covered her eyes was pale but absolutely determined. Guided by her captor's hand on her arm she walked firmly and without hesitation until she was halted in front of my chair.

"What new foolery is this?" she asked scornfully, and I metaphorically took off my hat to her. Captivity had not broken her spirit.

"No foolery at all, my dear, but a very pleasant surprise for you."

Mrs Drummond's hands clenched convulsively. "You don't mean that Hugh has found me?" A faint smile passed over Irma's face, the news of Drummond's supposed death had evidently been suppressed. "Not quite that," answered the other, "but one of his friends has."

"Then," said Mrs Drummond breathlessly, "he has succeeded. And so I am free to go. Who is it? Is it you, Peter?"

With a quick movement Irma whipped off the handkerchief and for a while Drummond's wife stared at me blankly. Then she turned wearily to her captor. "Why torment me?" she said. "What's the good? You know Hugh's friends. I've never seen this man before in my life."

And Irma who had been watching her intently relaxed and turned to the man. "That's genuine," she said briefly.

"Is this by any chance," I remarked ponderously, "a private lunatic asylum?"

"You may well ask, sir," said Mrs Drummond. "I don't know who you are, or how you came here, but there is at any rate one mad person present. And that is this woman."

Irma laughed, and lit a cigarette. "Dear little Phyllis," she murmured. "Always so direct and positive, aren't you? And now that you've been introduced to this room a little sooner than I had intended, tell me what you think of it?"

Mrs Drummond looked about her, a look of complete bewilderment spreading gradually over her face.

"What on earth does it all mean," she said at length. "What are all these stones for?"

"A model, my dear," answered the other gently, "that it has taken Paul much labour and trouble to construct. A model that is accurate in every detail."

"A model of what?"

"Of Stonehenge. One or two of the stones have been left out, but all the important ones are here. There for instance you see the Friar's Heel, and that one is the altar stone. You know the legend, of course. Some authorities do not believe in it, but it's a very pretty fairy story anyway. It runs that when the first rays of the rising sun on Midsummer Day shining over the Friar's Heel strike this third stone, the name of which I have not yet told you, the ceremony begins."

Her voice was soft and almost caressing, nevertheless my lips were dry. For I knew what the third stone was.

"It must have been an interesting ceremony, Phyllis. Can't you see those wild-eyed priests clad in fantastic garments? Can't you see that great rolling plain and the waiting multitude of savages—waiting in the hush that comes before the dawn for the first gleam of the sun above the horizon?"

I was staring at her fascinated: her eyes were glittering feverishly—her cigarette was forgotten.

"A minute more—and a sigh runs round the spectators. A few seconds, and the excitement grows. You can feel it—hear it like wind rustling in the trees.

"Inside the sacred circle stand the priests—some by the altar stone, some by this third stone here. All eyes are turned towards the east to greet the arrival of their god. This is the day on which he vouchsafes them his visible presence longest: this is the day on which it is meet and proper that he should be propitiated and thanked. An offering must be made: a sacrifice given.

"And on this third stone, waiting, too, for that first ray to strike her, lies the sacrifice. For those around her, for the hushed multitude outside, the moment that is just coming means life—the continuation of the benefits their god has bestowed on them since last Midsummer Day. For her it means—death: the stone on which she lies is the Slaughter Stone."

She fell silent, and I glanced at Mrs Drummond. She was staring at the speaker with a dawning horror in her eyes, and suddenly she bit the back other hand to keep back a cry. She knew—and I knew. But after a moment she pulled herself together with a great effort.

"Most interesting," she remarked steadily. "And did you have all these stones put up so that you could play charades on them?"

Slowly the madness faded from the other's face, and she flicked the ash from her cigarette on to the carpet. "That's it," she smiled. "A little game of let's-pretend. We shall be playing it tomorrow, my dear—or rather tonight. What part would you like to take?"

The silence grew unbearable, and yet once again did I take off my hat to that poor girl. She was powerless: she was trapped—but she was white clean through.

"I am not very good at acting," she said indifferently.

"Yours will be a passive—even if a very important role," returned the other. "No histrionic ability will be required."

"And may I ask," I remarked politely, "if I am to be privileged with a part. I must say I don't think much of the comfort of your stalls."

For the moment at any rate my role was clear: I must remain the outsider who had blundered into a madhouse. Slowly the woman turned and stared at me.

"I think you will look nice as a dead-head," she murmured.

"Am I to understand that the rest of the audience will have paid for their seats?"

"They will at any rate have worked hard," she returned. "But I can assure you there will be no jealousy on that account. The unexpected guest is always welcome."

"Charming," I said cheerfully. "At the same time, if it is all the same to you, I would rather like to know the hour the show starts so that until then I can enjoy my very short holiday in the manner I had intended to. Frankly this seat is giving me cramp."

I winked ostentatiously at Mrs Drummond: obviously this female must be humoured. But there was no response from her: somewhat naturally she accepted my role at its face value.

"This gentleman knows nothing about your wicked game," she burst out. "It's unfair, it's unjust to keep him here."

"To know nothing about the play is always an advantage," returned the other. "However, I grow weary. We will retire, my dear Phyllis—so that we shall both be fresh for the performance."

She led the way to the door, and I was left alone with the man.

"Look here, sir," I said angrily, "this has gone far enough. I admit that what I told you sounds a bit fishy: nevertheless it happens to be the truth. And I insist upon being allowed to go. Or if you wish to give me in charge then send for the police. But this is preposterous. You now know that I am not one of them, whoever 'they' may be."

"And you," he retorted calmly, "now know altogether too much. So for the purposes of this entertainment—positively for one night only—I fear you will have to be treated as if you were one of them."

He strolled through the door leading to the garage, and I heard the chink of metal against metal as he put the tools back on the bench. My last hope had gone, my last bluff had failed. When Mrs Drummond had failed to recognize me, and Irma herself had said "that's genuine," there had seemed for a while a possibility of escape. Now there was none. Now everything must depend on Drummond. He would follow the other three, of course, but without any idea of the strength he was walking into.

I counted them up in my mind. There was the man called Paul, the chauffeur, the man with the damaged hand; the sailor—and last but not least the negro. So many I knew of personally; how many more there were remained to be seen. And what chance had Drummond against a bunch like that? If only I could have got away I could have warned him. I began to tug desperately at the steel bars until a woman's laugh made me look up suddenly. Irma had returned.

"You can save yourself the trouble, bank clerk," she said mockingly, and at the sound other voice Paul returned.

"I suppose we had better gag him, my dear," he remarked, and she nodded carelessly.

"Yes," she said. "Gag him—and then go."

"This is an outrage," I spluttered, and the next instant he had deftly slipped a gag into my mouth, and then wrapped a handkerchief round me.

"If I hear a sound," he said quietly, "I shall come down and finish you off on the spot. *Carissima*, you must be tired." He crossed to the woman. "Won't you come to bed?"

"Go," she said curtly. "I shall come in a few minutes."

He went unwillingly, and for a while the woman stood motionless staring in front of her. The strange look had returned to her eyes:

she had forgotten my existence. Noiselessly she moved about on the thick black carpet, the incarnation of grace and beauty. First to one stone, and then to another she glided, as a hostess might move round her drawing-room, giving it the finishing touches before the arrival of her guests.

And then at last she paused before the altar stone. She knelt down and ran her fingers along underneath it searching for something. At length she found it and pulled it out. It was the photograph of a man.

Fascinated I watched her as she kissed it passionately: then she placed it on the altar in front of her, and bowed her head as if in prayer. I heard the murmur of her voice, but the actual words I could not distinguish. And after a while I began to feel drowsy. The gleaming white light opposite seemed to be growing bigger and bigger my head lolled back. And on the instant I was wide awake again.

Part of the roof was glassed in, like the roof of a racquet court, and some of the panes were open for ventilation. And staring through one of the openings was a man. His eyes were fixed on the kneeling woman: his face was inscrutable. Then he glanced at me, and for a brief second our eyes met. In am instant he had disappeared, and I was left trying to fit this new development into the jigsaw. For the man who had been staring through the skylight was the sailor.

Still her voice droned on musically, but I paid no attention. It confirmed, of course, my knowledge that the sailor was one of them, but why should he be on the roof? Spying, presumably: spying on the woman. And when he realized that I had seen him he had disappeared at once for fear I might say something.

"My lover! My god!"

Her words, clear at last, came through the silent room, and once again I looked at her. With her hands clasped together she was rocking to and fro on her knees in front of the photograph.

"Tonight, I come to you, my beloved."

And the lights shone on, gleaming like great stars against the black curtains. And the carpet seemed to glisten like some dark mountain pool deep hidden in the rocks. And the great white stones that rose from it took unto themselves life, and joined in a mighty chorus—"My beloved."

I closed my eyes: I was dreaming. It was some dreadful nightmare.

"My beloved, I come to you."

The sailor was shouting it: the man who had sprung at me out of the ditch was shouting it: Paul, his face a seething mass of black passion, was shouting it. I was shouting it, too—shouting it better than anyone—shouting it so well and so loudly that the woman herself, Irma, looked into my eyes and praised me. I could feel her fingers on my eyelids, from a great distance she nodded as if satisfied. Then came darkness. I slept.

It was daylight when I woke, cramped and stiff in every limb. There was a foul taste in my mouth, and I wondered if I had been drugged. I had noticed nothing peculiar on the handkerchief, but only on that supposition could I account for my condition. My head ached, my eyes felt bleary, and I'd have given most of my worldly possessions for a cup of tea.

By a stupendous feat of contortion I twisted my head so that I could see my wrist watch, only to find that the damned thing had stopped. Not, I reflected, that it mattered very much what the time was: an odd hour or two this way or that was of little account situated as I was. And after a while I began to curse myself bitterly for having been such an utter fool. If only I hadn't shown myself in the passage: if only. . . .

But what was the use? I hadn't slipped off the car: I had shown myself in the passage. And here I was caught without, as far as I could see, a chance of getting away. What made it more bitter still was the knowledge I possessed, the invaluable knowledge, if only I could have passed it on. Why, if Hugh Drummond only knew, he, with his marvellous shooting ability, could dominate the whole scene from the roof. But he didn't know, and all he would do would be to walk straight into the trap after the other three.

After a while my thoughts turned in another direction—even less pleasant than the first. What was in store for us? Was it all some grim, fantastic jest, or was it a revenge so terrible that the mere thought of it made me almost sick? Could it be conceivably possible that this foul woman intended to kill Mrs Drummond in front of us all? And afterwards deal with us?

It seemed inconceivable, and yet the trap at the Mere was just as dastardly. It was no good judging her by ordinary standards: therein lay the crux. She was mad, and to a mad woman everything is conceivable. Anyhow the present was bad enough without worrying over the future.

Faintly through the wall I heard the self-starter being used, and then the car leave the garage. That must be the note going to Darrell and Co. Would they walk into it blindly, or would they take some rudimentary precautions? Would they believe that this woman did really intend to set Mrs Drummond free if they came?

From every angle I turned the thing over in my mind only to arrive at the same brick wall each time. Whatever they did do or didn't do, I was out of the picture. I was powerless to help them in any way so there wasn't much use worrying.

"Have we slept well?" came a sardonic voice from the door.

Paul, with a sneering smile on his thin lips, was standing there looking at me. Then he came over and removed the handkerchief and the gag. For a time I could only move my jaws stiffly up and down, and make hoarse grunting noises—a thing which seemed to cause him unbounded amusement.

"Damn you," I croaked at last, "did you dope me last night?"

"A very efficacious and but little known narcotic, Mr Seymour," he remarked suavely, "was on the handkerchief I put round your mouth. Was your sleep dreamless and refreshing?"

"For God's sake," I muttered, "give me something to drink. My tongue feels like a fungoidal growth."

"A defect, I admit," he said, "in that particular drug. It leaves an unpleasant taste. And so I have much pleasure in telling you that it is on the matter of breakfast that I have come."

"Breakfast," I shuddered. "If I saw an egg I'd be sick."

There came a little click from behind my chair, and the steel bars slipped off my wrists.

"Stand up," he said. "At the moment the warning is unnecessary, I know. But bear in mind that freedom from your late position does not imply any further concession. So—no monkey tricks."

He was right: at the moment—and for a considerable number of moments—the warning was unnecessary. Both my arms had gone to sleep: and as soon as I got up I was attacked by the most agonizing cramp in my left leg. But at last I managed to regain some semblance of normality.

"Where's that drink?" I muttered.

"All in due course," he returned. "Owing to the fact that certain small preparations have to be made here for our little entertainment tonight we have to find other accommodation for you today. It would be a great pity if the element of surprise was lacking. And so you will come with me, Mr Seymour: and you will bear in mind that I have a revolver in my hand, Mr Seymour, and that my finger is on the trigger, Mr Seymour. And that should you give me the slightest trouble, you wretched interfering little busybody, that finger will connect with the trigger and the result will connect with you. So, hump yourself."

I could feel the muzzle of his gun in the small of my back as he pushed me towards the door. But I didn't care: anything was better than the atrocious discomfort of that stone seat. Moreover a drink appeared to be looming on the horizon.

The door led into the hall. No one was about, and still in the same positions we reached the foot of the stairs.

"Up," he said curtly.

At a turn in the staircase stood a grandfather clock, and I saw it was half past nine. So I reckoned I must have slept for five or six hours.

"Through that door," he ordered.

A man I had never seen before rose as we came in. But I didn't care about him: my eyes were riveted on a teapot.

"Charles will be your companion for today," he remarked. "And you had better look at Charles." I did: then I returned to the teapot. As an object to contemplate Charles did not appeal to me.

"Charles has orders," continued the other, "to deal faithfully with you in the event of the slightest trouble. That is so, isn't it, Charles?"

"I'll deal with 'im faithfully, guv'nor," he chuckled. "'E won't try nothing on twice, I gives yer my word. Why, I'd eat a little mess like that."

He emitted a whistling noise through a gap in his teeth.

"Paint the wall wiv 'is faice, I will," he continued morosely.

"A character is Charles," said Paul to me. "Equally handy with his fists or a knife. So be careful, Mr Seymour—very careful."

I gulped down my cup of tea and began to feel better. "I am sure I shall find him a most entertaining companion," I murmured. "Now don't let me detain you any more, little man. Run away and have your children's hour with the bricks downstairs. Or are you going to play puffers in the passage?"

And, astounding to relate, it got home. For a moment I thought he was going to hit me. His face was white with rage, his fists were clenched—evidently a gentleman without the saving grace of humour. But he controlled himself and went out slamming the door behind him, and I began to feel better still.

Anyway my limbs were free, and I'd had something to drink. Moreover there were cigarettes in my pocket. "Charles," I said, "will you smoke?"

Charles said—"Yus," and I began to take close stock of Charles. And one thing was quite obvious at first glance. He was perfectly capable of painting the wall with my face if it came to a trial of strength. So that if I was going to turn the change of quarters to my advantage it would have to be a question of brain and cunning and not force. And the first and most obvious method seemed bribery.

I led up to it tactfully, but diplomacy was wasted on Charles. At the mention of the word money his face became quite intelligent.

"'Ow much 'ave you?" he demanded.

"About thirty pounds," I answered. "It's yours here and now if you'll let me go, and then there's nothing to prevent you clearing out yourself."

"Let's see the colour of it," he said, and with a wild hope surging up in me I pulled out my pocket book. If I got away at once I'd be in time.

"There you are," I cried. "Twenty-eight pounds."

"Looks good to me," he remarked. "Though I ain't partial to fivers myself. Some suspicious blokes takes the numbers. You ain't suspicious are you, matey?"

He slipped the bundle into his pocket, and I stood up.

"Is it safe now," I said eagerly.

"Is wot safe now?"

"For me to go, damn it."

"Go where?"

"Out of the house, as you promised."

"Naughty, naughty," he said reproachfully. "Do you mean to say that that there money was hintended as a bribe?"

I stared at him speechlessly.

"And I thort as 'ow it was just a little return for the pleasure of be'olding my faice."

"You confounded scoundrel," I spluttered. "Give me back my notes."

Charles became convulsed with an internal upheaval that apparently indicated laughter.

"Yer know, matey," he said when he could at last speak, "I didn't know that they let things like you out of a 'ome."

Once more the convulsion seized him, and a dull overmastering rage began to rise within me. The limit of my endurance had been reached. I felt I didn't care what happened. Damn Drummond and all his works: damn the moment I'd ever let myself in for this fool show. Above all, damn this great hulking blackguard who had pinched my money, and now sat there nearly rolling off his chair with laughter.

And suddenly I saw red. I sprang at him and hit him with all my force in the face. Then while he was still too surprised to move I got in a real purler with the teapot over his right eye. And after that I frankly admit I don't remember much more. I recall that he did not remain too surprised to move for long. I recall seeing something that gleamed in his hand, and feeling a searing, burning pain in my forearm. I also recall that an object which felt like a steam hammer hit my jaw. Then—a blank.

Chapter 15

In Which Some of the Others Join Me

When I came to myself I was back in the room below, fastened to the same seat as before. The filthy taste was in my mouth again, so I guessed they had used the narcotic on me once more. But this time that wasn't my only trouble. My jaw felt as if it had been broken: and my arm, which some one had bound up roughly, ached intolerably.

For a while I sat there motionless. I was feeling dazed and drowsy. I'd almost come to the end of my tether. A sort of dull apathy had told of me. I felt I didn't care what happened as long as it happened quickly.

The room was absolutely silent, and after a time I forced my brain to work. I was alone: I was ungagged. Supposing I shouted for help. There was a bare chance that I might be heard by some stray passer-by. Anyway it was worth trying.

"Help!" I roared at the pitch of my lungs. "Help!"

I listened: still no sound. Very good: I'd try again. I opened my mouth: I shut it. Or perhaps it would be more correct to say it shut itself.

A huge black hand had suddenly materialized from nowhere—a hand with the fingers curved like a bird's talon. I stared at it fascinated, as it moved gently towards my throat. There was no hurry, but the utmost deliberation in the whole action. And this time I nearly screamed in sheer terror.

The fingers closed round my throat, and began playing with it. Still quite gently. No force was used; but every touch of those fingers gave its own message of warning.

As suddenly as it had appeared, it went, and I sat there sweating and silent. So I was not alone: somewhere behind me, out of sight, was that cursed nigger Pedro. The hand that had closed on my throat was the actual hand that had murdered that poor devil the night before. And as if he had read my thoughts there came from above my head a hideous throaty chuckle. Then silence once again.

Gradually I grew calmer, though the thought of that great black brute lurking behind me was horrible. If only I could see the devil it would be better. But he remained out of sight, and after a time I began to think he must have gone. Into the garage perhaps—the passage leading to it was behind me. Whether he had or whether he hadn't, however, I dismissed the idea of calling for help.

To distract my mind, I studied the room with closer attention. I could see more than half, and I wondered what the small preparations were that Paul had spoken of. As far as I could see nothing was changed: the same stones, the same carpet. And then it struck me that on one of the stone seats was what looked like a block of wood. It was about the size of a box of a hundred cigarettes, and a cord stuck out from one end on to the carpet.

I looked at the other seats. A similar block was on each one of them, and by pushing myself backwards in my own, I could feel the sharp edge against my spine.

By twisting my head I could just see the cord attached to it. It was a long one, and I followed it idly with my eyes across the carpet until it disappeared behind the next stone. Part of the preparations evidently, but with what purpose was beyond me. Just as everything else was beyond me. Time alone would show.

But that fact didn't stop one thinking. Round and round in my head ran the ceaseless question—what was going to happen that night? From every angle I studied it till my brain grew muzzy with the effort. What was going to be done to us? Did that woman really mean all she had implied, or had it been a jest made to frighten Mrs Drummond?

After a while I dozed off, only to wake up sweating from an appalling dream in which two of the great stones were being used to crush my head by the nigger. Looking back now I suppose I was a little light-headed, but at the time I wasn't conscious of it. I had lost a good deal of blood from the wound in my arm though I didn't know it then. And as the day wore on, and the room gradually grew darker and darker, I sank into a sort of stupor. Vaguely I heard odd sounds, the car in the garage, a man's voice in the hall, but they seemed to come from a long way off. And the only real things in my mental outlook were those cursed white stones.

They moved after a while, passing me in a ceaseless procession. They heaved and dipped and formed fours till I cursed them foolishly. And something else moved, too—a great black form that flitted between them peering and examining. Twice did I see it, and the second time I forced myself back to reality.

It was the negro, and he seemed intensely interested in everything—almost childishly so. He touched stone after stone with his fingers. Then he picked up one of the little blocks that I had noticed, and examined it closely, grunting under his breath.

Suddenly he straightened up and stood listening. Then with a quick movement he replaced the block, and vanished behind me just as the door into the hall opened and Paul came in. He crossed to my stone and stood looking down at me, while I feigned sleep. And after a time he too began to stroll round amongst the other stones.

He examined each of the blocks, and the cords that ran from them. And as I watched him out of the corner of my eye I noticed a thing I had missed before. On the altar stone was a little black box, and all the cords appeared to lead to it. He seemed particularly interested in that box, but in the bad light I couldn't see what he was doing. At length, however, he put it down, and lighting a cigarette once more came and stood in front of me. I looked up at him dully.

"You really are the most congenial ass I've ever met, Mr Seymour," he said pleasantly. "Did you honestly think Charles would let you go?"

"I've given up trying to think in this mad house," I retorted. "When is this ridiculous farce going to end?"

He made no reply for a while, but just stood staring at me thoughtfully. "I really am rather interested in you," he said at length. "It would be most devilish funny if you really have got nothing to do with them."

"I've already told you that I don't know what you are talking about," I cried. "You're making a fearful mistake. I don't know who you mean by them."

He began to chuckle. "'Pon my soul," he said, "I'm almost beginning to think that you don't. Which makes the jest excessively rich."

"A positive scream," I agreed sarcastically. "Would it be too much to hope that I might be permitted to share it?"

"I fear," he answered, "that you might not quite appreciate it."

He continued to chuckle immoderately.

"You will in time, I promise you," he went on. "And then you will see how terribly funny it all is. I must say," he continued seriously, almost more to himself than to me, "I did think yesterday that you and the butterfly gentleman were mixed up in it."

"I wish to Heaven," I said wearily, "that you would realize that I haven't the remotest idea what you're talking about. And I further wish you to be under no delusions as to what I'm going to do when I do manage to get out of this place."

He started laughing again. "What are you going to do?" he asked. "Don't, I beg of you, terrify me too much!"

I stuck to it good and hard. Useless it might be, but at any rate it was better than nothing. "I shall go straight to the police," I said, "and lodge a summons against you for assault and battery. And as for that cursed ruffian upstairs...."

"Poor Charles," he remarked. "You dotted him one with the teapot all right. Well, thank you for your kindly warning. You'll have some other privileged spectators coming to join you soon—three of them." He strolled to the door, and looked back as he reached it. "I can keep no secrets from you, bank clerk," he said. "You have an indefinable attraction for me. Do you see those little blocks in the seats?"

"Yes," I said.

"There is one in yours, just behind you."

"I've felt it already," I remarked.

"Well, be very careful how you feel it," he said gently. "Do nothing rough with it. Treat it as a mother treats a sickly child—gently and tenderly. Because it happens to be gun-cotton. Admittedly a safe explosive—but one never knows."

For a moment I was absolutely speechless.

"Gun-cotton," I stammered at length. "Good God! man—are you joking?"

"Far from it," he said. "But I can assure you that there's no chance of it going off—yet." He smiled genially. "The fact of the matter is, bank clerk, that you have butted your head into some rather dirty work. I don't mind admitting that there are moments when I think it is almost too dirty. But"—he shrugged his shoulders—"when the ladies get ideas in their charming heads, who are we to gainsay them?"

"If by the ladies you allude to that partially demented female who was talking such infernal rot last night," I said grimly, "I'll tell you one idea that she has got wedged in hers. She's got about as much use for you as a Cockney has for a haggis."

"I don't understand you," he said softly, but I noticed that, of a sudden, he was standing very still.

"Then I'll make myself clearer," I remarked. "You cut no ice with her, Paul: she loathes the sight of your face. I watched her last night when you were pulling out the knee clutching business, and her expression was that of one who contemplates a bad egg from close range."

"You are pleased to be insolent, Mr Seymour." He was still standing motionless by the door.

"I am pleased to be nothing, you flat-headed skate," I answered. It struck me that a little of Drummond's vocabulary might assist. "But if you imagine that after you've done whatever fool tricks you are going to do you're then going to land the beauteous lady you're making the deuce of an error. Nothing doing, Paul: you can take my word for it."

"But for the fact," he remarked after a time, "that the death you are going to die is such a particular choice one, I would strangle you here and now for those words."

"Doesn't alter the fact that she loathes the sight of your face, laddie," I mocked. "And I certainly don't blame her."

He sprang across the room towards me, and I don't think I have ever seen such a look of demoniacal rage on any man's face before. In fact, but for the interruption, I believe he would have carried out his threat. As it was he managed to control himself with a monstrous effort as the door opened and the woman herself came in.

"Quick, Paul," she cried. "They are coming—the three of them. Where's Pedro? Charles is here but we want the nigger. And gag that fool of a clerk."

He stuffed a gag into my mouth, and glared at me. "One sound, and I'll knife you," he muttered. "Pedro!" He looked over my shoulder. "Where is the damned fool?" he said irritably. "I've hardly seen him the whole day? Pedro!"

There was a guttural grunt, and then the huge nigger shambled past me. His head was down, and in the dim light he looked a terrifying sight.

"Get behind the curtains, Pedro. And don't kill. We want them alive in the chairs. Charles—get the other side of the door."

Sick with anxiety I waited. Could nothing be done to warn them? They were walking straight into the trap, and suddenly the full realization of our position seemed to strike me. All very well to gain a little cheap satisfaction by taunting the man over his love affair, but it didn't alter the fact that once these three men were caught the odds against us were well-nigh hopeless. Drummond couldn't fight half a dozen men, especially when two of them had the strength of the negro and the one called Charles.

The woman had left the room: the three men were hiding behind the curtains, so to all appearances except for myself it was empty. And then I heard Darrell's voice in the hall.

"So we meet again, *madame*," he said gravely. "As you probably know we have come without informing any one, trusting that you will keep your side of the bargain."

"Quite like old times seeing you," she answered. "And Mr Jerningham and Mr Longworth, too."

"Shall we cut the conversation, *madame?*" he remarked. "At your instigation three men—one of whom was Hugh himself—have been foully murdered. So you will pardon me if I say that the sooner you hand Mrs Drummond over to us the better I shall be pleased. In your letter you said that your revenge was sufficient. Let us then be done with it."

"We seem much milder than of yore," she mocked.

"You have Mrs Drummond in your power," he said simply. "We have no alternative. Well, *madame*, we are waiting."

"Yes, *mes amis*, you are right," she answered after a pause. "We will be done with it. You shall have Phyllis. And believe me I am almost sorry now that I ever started it. Moods change. A few weeks ago there was nothing I desired more than the deaths of all of you. Today I regret the Mere. Come this way."

"One moment, *madame*. Does she know that her husband is dead?"

"No—she does not. Mr Darrell, it is easy to say, I know, but I wish he were not."

"A pity you didn't think of that a little earlier, *madame*," he said grimly. "Where are we to go? Why cannot Mrs Drummond be handed over to us in this hall?"

"You will soon see why," she answered, appearing in the door. "Besides I particularly want to show you all this room."

I gave an agonized guttural choke but it was no good. As she had doubtless anticipated they paused inside the door, completely taken off their guard by the strangeness of their surroundings.

"What on earth," began Jerningham, and even as he spoke the three hidden men sprang on them.

In a few seconds it was all over. Paul had a revolver in Jerningham's neck. Charles gave the same attention to Darrell. And poor little Algy Longworth was the negro's share. He was merely picked up like a kicking baby and deposited in a seat. Then the steel bars were turned and he sat there glowering.

"You damned dirty nigger," he shouted angrily.

"Silence, you little rat," said Irma. "Get the other two fixed. Shoot, Paul, if they give any trouble."

But the muzzle of a revolver in the nape of a man's neck is a good preventer of trouble, and soon the four of us were sitting there like trussed birds.

"So it was a trick, was it?" said Darrell quietly.

The woman began to shake with laughter.

"You fools," she cried, "you brainless fools. Did you really imagine that I was going to hand Phyllis over to you and let you walk out of the house. You must be mad."

She turned on Charles and the nigger.

"Go! Get out! But be around in case I want you. Paul—you can ungag the bank clerk."

Her glance roved from one to the other of us.

"Four," she said musingly. "And there should have been six. You see, Darrell, that there are six seats prepared for your reception."

Her eyes were beginning to glitter feverishly, and as she stood in the centre of the room her body swayed gracefully from side to side as if she was dancing. To me it was not unexpected, but the other three were staring at her in amazement. As yet they had not seen one of her outbursts.

"Still we must make do with four, I suppose," she went on. "Unless, Paul, we sent out for two more. No—better not. Let us keep our final meeting as intimate as possible. And we already have one stranger."

"Where is Phyllis Drummond?" said Jerningham.

She turned and looked at him dreamily.

"Phyllis is waiting." she answered. "For days she has been waiting for you to come, and now very soon she will join you."

"And what then," snapped Darrell.

"Why then, *mon ami*, you shall all go on a journey together. A long journey. Ah! if only Hugh was here: if only my circle was complete. Then indeed the reunion would be a wonderful one."

And now the crazy glitter in her eyes grew more pronounced till I marvelled that the man called Paul could ever have hoped for any return for his love. The woman was frankly crazy, and stealing a glance at him I saw that he was staring at her with a dawning horror in his face.

"*Carissima*," he muttered. "I beseech of you, do not excite yourself."

"But as it is we shall have to make do with four." Her voice had risen. "Four instead of six. And the principal guest not here. Why—the whole lot of you could go if only Drummond was here. But I did my best, Carl—I did my best."

She had turned to the altar stone, and was speaking to it.

"I did my best, beloved—I did my best. And his end was not unworthy. Gassed—and drowned like a rat in a trap."

She threw herself across the stone, her arms outstretched, and for a space there was silence in the darkening room. Then abruptly she rose and swept to the door.

"At nine o'clock, Paul, we will begin."

"Look here," I said when she had gone, "Paul—or whatever your name is—what is the good of going on with this?"

He stared at me dully.

"The woman is clean plumb crazy. She is as mad as a hatter. So what are you going to get out of it? You can't marry a mad woman: you can't even make love to her."

He muttered something unintelligible under his breath.

"For God's sake, man," I went on urgently, "pull yourself together. Set us free, and let us go."

"She'll be all right—after," he said at length. "Quite all right—after." He turned towards the door, and in desperation I played my last card.

"You poor ass," I cried, "there isn't going to be an after for her. When she has finished us, she's going to commit suicide. And whatever you choose to do with a lunatic, you're stung good and strong with a corpse."

It was no good. He opened the door and went out. In fact I doubt if he even heard what I said, and with a feeling of sick despair I looked at the others.

"So they haven't spotted you, Dixon," said Darrell in a low voice.

"Not yet," I answered. "I don't think it ever dawned on them that I was one of the three they think were drowned at the Mere. But, for a while they suspected me of being another member of the bunch—a new one. Then Mrs Drummond rode them off."

"You've seen her?" said Jerningham eagerly.

"Last night," I said. "She was brought down here blindfolded and suddenly confronted with me. And there was no mistake about her failure to identify me being genuine. Not that it matters much," I went on gloomily. "We're hopelessly for it unless Drummond can do something. Why in Heaven's name did you fellows walk into it so easily?"

"Because he told us to," answered Darrell calmly.

"Told you to," I echoed in amazement.

"A short note," he said. "Just—Follow the messenger—all three of you. Be surprised at nothing. And tell Dixon that he must not reveal my identity until he hears the Anthem whistled once."

"He knows I'm here?" I cried. "But I don't understand."

"Frankly—no more do I," said Algy. "What's this damned stone quarry?"

"It's a model," I said, "of Stonehenge. Look here, you fellows, I'll tell you all I know. I can pretend that we are strangers if anyone comes in. But there is no reason why we shouldn't talk in view of the position we are in—its most damnably serious."

"Fire ahead," said Jerningham quietly.

I told them everything; what I knew, and what I only suspected. I told them of the dead man at Stonehenge, and the scene of the night before. And they listened with consternation growing on their faces.

"It was our last hope," I said, "trying to make that man realize she was mad. But he's wild about her—absolutely wild."

"You really think she's going to commit suicide," said Darrell doubtfully.

"I do," I answered. "Though the point is of academic interest only as far as we are concerned. She is going to do all of us in first."

"Man—but it's a fearful risk." said Jerningham.

"Don't you see," I cried, "that she doesn't care a damn about the risk. What does the risk matter to her if she's going to join Carl, as she thinks, after? And that poor fish, Paul, is so infatuated with her that he is prepared to run any risk to get her."

We argued it from every angle whilst the room grew darker and darker. To them the only thing that mattered was that Drummond had told them to come: that Drummond had something up his sleeve. But try as I would, I couldn't share their optimism. What could he do alone—or at best with Toby Sinclair to help him? The odds were altogether too heavy. Had we all been free it would have been different. Then we could have put up a good show. As it was the thing seemed hopeless to me. And yet he had deliberately told these three to walk into the trap. It was incomprehensible.

It appeared that they had not seen him, but had only received the note. And the previous night Algy Longworth had also got a note which explained his movements to me. It had contained instructions to the effect that he was to announce publicly his intention of going to Stonehenge after dinner, that as he valued his life he was not to go but was to take a walk in the opposite direction.

"If I had gone," he said, "I suppose I should have shared the fate of the poor devil you saw dead. I wonder who he was."

"Ask me another," I remarked. "He was a complete stranger to me. But he was undoubtedly murdered by that foul brute of a nigger."

Conversation became desultory. All our nerves were getting frayed. The light had almost gone; we were just vague shapes to one another as we sat there fastened to those fantastic stones, waiting for nine o'clock.

"I can't believe it," burst out Jerningham once. "Damn it—it's like a nightmare."

No one answered; only the throaty chuckle that I had heard before came from somewhere behind me. "It's the nigger," grunted Darrell. "Get out, you filthy brute."

He chuckled again, and then like some monstrous misshapen animal he began to shamble round the room. I could just see him in the darkness peering first at one thing and then at another. He went to the two unoccupied seats and began fiddling with the mechanism that moved the two curved steel bars. He worked it several times, chuckling to himself like a child, and suddenly came Jerningham's voice strained and tense.

"Come and do that to my chair, nigger. I'll give you some cigarettes and money if you do."

But the black man took no notice. He had transferred his attentions now to the black box that lay upon the altar stone. That occupied him for a long while, and all the time the throaty chuckling continued. Every now and then came the chink of tin on stone: then, as silently as he had come, he vanished again.

It was the suspense of waiting that was so appalling, and I began to long for nine o'clock. A mood of dull resignation had come over me. I felt I simply didn't care. Anything—so long as they got on with it. And as if in answer to my thoughts the door leading into the hall slowly opened, and a clock outside began to chime.

"Nine," muttered somebody.

The final act was about to begin.

Chapter 16
In Which We Have a Rehearsal

I think my main feeling was one of intense curiosity. There was no light in the hall, but a faint lessening of the general darkness marked the door. For a time nothing happened, then something white appeared in the opening, and the room was flooded with light.

The woman Irma was standing there clad in the same white garment she had worn the preceding night. Behind her hovered Paul—his face more saturnine than ever, but it was on her that all our attention was concentrated. In her hands she held some largish object which was covered with a silken cloth, and after a while she advanced to the altar stone and placed it there reverently. Then she removed the wrap, and I saw that it was a full size plaster cast of a man's head.

"Dashed if it isn't our late lamented Carl," muttered Darrell.

The woman took no notice, she was staring intently at the cast. Once or twice her lips moved, but I heard no words, and for a time her hands were clasped in front of her as if in prayer. Then quite suddenly she turned her back on the altar and began to speak, whilst we watched her fascinated.

"A few months ago," she said, "I stood beside the wreckage of Wilmot's giant airship, and over the charred body of my man I swore an oath. That oath will be finally fulfilled tonight."

Her voice was quiet and conversational.

"But for an accident last night—a mistake on the part of one of my servants—I should not have sent you three the note I did. But Pedro, whom you have doubtless seen, killed a man at Stonehenge, and that necessitated a hastening in my plans. Why did you not go to Stonehenge, Longworth?"

"Got hiccoughs after dinner, darling," said Algy cheerfully. "Tell me, my poppet, is that a new line in nightdresses?"

And just as Paul became livid with rage when I had jeered at him that morning, so now did the woman turn white to the lips with passion.

"You dog," she screamed. "How dare you? Strike him, Paul—strike him across the face."

Then she controlled herself.

"Stay," she said in a calmer voice. "He is not worth it. I will continue—for there is much to say. But for that accident, I might—in fact I think I would—have given you one further clue. And yet I do not know: the game in very truth had begun to pall since Drummond died. You were only the puppies that followed your master. He was the one I wanted—not you. However, it was not to be, and because the finish comes tonight I thought that Phyllis should have you with her as she cannot have her husband. As yet she does not know that you are here: she does not even know her husband is dead. That she shall learn later—just before the end."

She paused, and I saw that Darrell was moistening his lips with his tongue, and that Jerningham's face was white. There was something far more terrifying in this calm matter of fact voice than if she had ranted and raved.

"This fourth man," she continued, "this bank clerk presented a conundrum. Believe me, sir," she turned to me, "I have no enmity against you. It is a sheer misfortune that you should be here, but since you are, you've got to stay."

"Please don't apologize," I said sarcastically. "Your treatment of your guest has left nothing to be desired."

But she seemed to have forgotten my existence: her real audience consisted of the other three.

"The Friar's Heel," she remarked. "You solved that quicker than I thought you would. And here you are. This gentleman has doubtless already told you that these stones form a model of Stonehenge. And you wonder why I should have taken so much trouble. I will tell you.

"Revenge is sweet, but to taste of its joys to the utmost, to extract from it the last drop of satisfaction, it must be as carefully planned as any other entertainment. That is why I regret so bitterly that it was Drummond himself who died at the Mere. I like to think of him struggling in that room—struggling to breathe—and knowing all the time that it was I who had done it. But I would far sooner have had him here; because he has escaped the supreme thing I planned for him."

With one hand outstretched she stood facing the other three.

"He killed my man. You know it. You cannot deny it."

"If by that you mean he killed Carl Peterson, I do not deny it," said Darrell calmly. "And no man ever deserved death more richly."

"Deserved death!" Her voice rose. "Who are you, you dogs, to pronounce judgment on such a man?" With an effort she controlled herself. "However, we will not bandy words. He killed my man—even as I shall shortly kill his woman."

She fell silent for a while staring at the plaster cast, and I saw Darrell's anxious eyes roving round the room. They met mine for a moment, and he shrugged his shoulders helplessly. It was out now: there was no bluff about it. Death was in sight, and the manner of it seemed of but little account. Death—unless. . . .

Feverishly I stared around. Death, unless Drummond intervened. I looked up at the roof, remembering the sailor of the night before. But this time it was empty. And all the time the man called Paul stood watching the woman with sombre eyes.

"It has not been very easy, Darrell." She was speaking again. "My servants have blundered. Mistakes have been made. But from the moment she fell into my hands the final issue has never been in doubt. I might have had to forego this. I might even have had to forego getting the lot of you. But her life has been forfeit since that moment. I have played with her at times, letting her think that she would be free if you found her, and she, stupid little fool, has believed me. Free!" She laughed. "There have been times when only the greatest restraint has prevented me killing her with my own hands. And now I am glad, for I would like you to see her die."

"*Carissima*," said the man called Paul, "is it wise to delay? All has gone so well up to now, and I fear something may happen."

"What can happen," she said calmly, "who can interrupt us? The time has passed when there was danger of surprise. Your police, Darrell, are stickers. And although I did not think you would enlist their aid, there was the little matter of the blood in the ditch. I felicitated dear Phyllis on that. Paul tells me that she practically killed him with one blow of that heavy spanner—naughty girl."

"For God's sake get on with it, woman," said Jerningham harshly.

"The essence of satisfactory revenge, my friend," she remarked, "is not to hurry. The night is yet young."

I closed my eyes. The powerful gleaming lights against the black made me drowsy. It was a dream all this—it must be. In a few moments I should awake, and see my own familiar room.

"What think you of the setting of my revenge?" From a great distance her voice came to me, and I forced myself back to reality again.

"Stonehenge—in miniature. Theatrical—perhaps. But the story fascinates me. And because in this year of grace the real place cannot be used it was necessary to make a model." With brooding eyes she stared in front of her. "We will rehearse it once, Paul. I am in the mood. Turn out the lights."

"*Carissima*," he protested, "is it wise?"

"Turn out the lights," she said curtly, and with a muttered oath he obeyed.

"I am in a strange mood tonight," Her voice—low and throbbing—came to us out of the darkness. "It is true that I have rehearsed it before, that I know exactly every effect. But I would postpone it awhile. Besides it may be that you, who will watch the real performance, can suggest something at the rehearsal. Think well, you watchers: use your imagination, for only thus will you appreciate my plan.

"Night. Darkness such as this. Around us on the grass a multitude who wait."

I sat up stiffly: was it imagination or had something passed close to my chair?

"They wait in silence, whispering perhaps amongst themselves of what is about to happen. They have seen it before—many times, but the mystery of what they are about to see and the wonder of it never palls.

"Darkness—and then in the east the faint light that comes before the dawn. Look!"

It was clever—damnably clever. How the lights had been arranged to give the effect I cannot say, but at the end of the room behind the Friar's Heel there came a faint luminosity. It was more a general lessening of the darkness than anything else, and one could just see the outlines of the stones against it.

"A murmur like a wave beating on the shore—then silence once again. A gentle breeze, faint scented with the smell of country kisses their faces, and is gone, whilst all the time the dawn comes nearer: the tense expectancy increases."

I couldn't help it. I was fascinated in spite of myself. My reason told me that all these elaborate preparations were nothing more nor less than the preliminaries to cold-blooded murder. And yet, theatrical though they might be, and were, they were also artistically impressive. I remember that I found myself thinking what a marvellous stage effect it would be.

Gradually the light behind the Friar's Heel increased, and then the woman began to sing. Her voice was small but true, and she sang in a tongue I did not know. It was a wild barbaric thing that sounded like one of those bizarre Magyar folk songs. And the effect was incredible. I found myself sweating with sheer excitement, all danger forgotten; and the others said after they had felt the same. The light grew brighter: her song wilder and more triumphant. And then suddenly she ceased.

"It comes," she cried. "The god comes. And as the first rays fall on the slaughter stone, and the woman who lies there, the sacrifice is made."

Out of the lessening darkness came a rim of golden light. It appeared behind the Friar's Heel, and gradually grew larger and larger, even as the sun appears above the horizon, a yellow ball of electric light being raised slowly on a winding gear. So said reason. But imagination saw the scene of countless centuries ago.

"The shadows shorten," she whispered. "Soon they will reach the slaughter stone and pass it by. This time there is no victim—but next. . . . My God! What's that?"

Her voice rose to a sudden shrill cry, and for a while we all stared stupidly. For now the slaughter stone was bathed in light, and on its smooth surface was a gruesome object. One end was red with dried up blood, and the other had a nail.

The man called Paul moved slowly towards it.

"It's a man's finger," he muttered, and his voice was shaking.

"A man's finger," repeated the woman. "But how did it get there? How did it get there?" she screamed. "How did it get there, you fool?"

And Paul could give no answer.

"A man's finger," she said once more, and glancing at her I saw that every drop of blood had drained from her face. "Where is Grant?"

"Grant," said Paul stupidly. "Why do you want Grant?"

"Drummond shot his finger off," she answered. "In the room below the Mere. Get him. Get him, you wretched fool, at once."

"But will you be all right," he began, and again from behind me came a throaty chuckle. "Great Scott! the butterfly man."

I turned round. Sure enough there was Toby Sinclair, powerless in the hands of the negro. The mystery of the finger was explained.

"Damn you!" he cried, "this is an outrage."

"Put him in a seat, Pedro," said the woman, and Toby was forced into the chair next to mine.

"If it isn't Mr Seymour," he fumed angrily. "Are these people mad? Is this place a lunatic asylum?"

He subsided into angry mutterings, and I said nothing. For now I was too excited to speak. It was evident that the game was beginning in grim earnest.

"Get Grant," said the woman, and Paul left the room.

She stood motionless leaning against the altar stone whilst that damnable nigger shambled round the room and then disappeared again. Toby Sinclair still continued to curse audibly, and the other three stared in front of them with eyes bright with anticipation. What was going to happen next? Once Sinclair stole a glance at me and winked, and I must confess that wink heartened me considerably. Because even now I saw very little light in the darkness.

The door opened, and Paul came in followed by the man with the damaged hand.

"Grant," said the woman quietly, "is that your finger?"

He gave a violent start: then he picked it up with a trembling hand. "It is," he muttered foolishly. "At least, I—I think it is. It must be."

"Do you recognize any of these men?" she went on.

"I recognize those three," he stammered, and Darrell nodded pleasantly.

"A little morning exercise by the waters of the Mere," he remarked.

"And what of the others?" she said.

He looked at Toby and me, and shook his head.

"I've seen them," he said. "At Amesbury. And I thought"—he looked sideways at Paul—"I thought. The boss," he went on sullenly, "said that I was to say nothing about them."

For a moment she stared at Paul with a look of such concentrated cold fury that I almost felt sorry for the man. After all, swine though he was, he did love her, and had only embarked on this affair for her sake. But what she was going to say to him we shall never know, for at that moment there came a diversion.

The man with the damaged hand had suddenly come very close to me and was peering into my face. Then with a quick movement he seized my moustache and tore it off.

"God in Heavens!" he muttered, "it's one of them. One of the three that were drowned."

A dead silence settled on the room, which was at last broken by Toby. "What about *Opsiphanes syme*?" he burbled genially.

Another dead silence, broken this time by the woman. "So Drummond is not dead," she said softly. "How very interesting."

"I seem to recall," drawled Jerningham pleasantly, "in those dear days of long ago, that our lamented friend whose repulsive visage adorns the altar had frequent necessity to remark the same thing."

And then Paul spoke with sudden fear in his voice. "It's a trap. An obvious trap. He's probably got the police with him."

"There wasn't a soul outside when I came in," said Grant. "There hasn't been a thing past the gate since eight o'clock."

"Go out," said the woman, "and mount guard again. Paul—fetch Phyllis."

For a moment or two he seemed on the point of arguing with her: then he thought better of it and both of them left the room.

"So you are Sinclair," she said, coming over to Toby.

"Quite right, sweet girl of mine," he answered. "And how have we been keeping since our last merry meeting?"

"All of you except Drummond." She was talking half to herself. "Helpless: at my mercy."

A triumphant smile was on her lips, and as it seemed to me with justice. It exactly expressed the situation, and now that the momentary excitement of the finger episode had worn off I began to feel gloomier than ever. It was all very well for the others to be flippant, but unless they were completely blind to obvious realities it could only be due to bravado. We were absolutely in this woman's power, there was no other way of looking at it. That their mood might be due to a blind unquestioning faith in Drummond's ability was also possible, but unless he came with four or five exceptionally powerful men to help him, this was going to be a case of the pitcher going to the well once too often. For what none of them seemed to realize was the fact that this woman was careless of her own life. There lay the incredible danger. Discovery meant nothing to her provided her revenge had come first.

I came out of my reverie to find Darrell's eyes fixed on me. "Learnt that tune yet, Dixon?" he said.

Toby Sinclair was humming the Froth Blower's Anthem, and I nodded. I was free now to give Drummond away, but what earthly good it was going to be heaven alone knew.

"A new recruit, dear Irma," went on Darrell. "You will be pleased to know that it was he who solved most of your clues."

She turned her strange brooding eyes on me. "How did you get out of the Mere," she asked curiously.

"A little substitution," I remarked. "The gentleman you left below arrived too soon, and then I sat on the water handle by mistake."

"I am glad," she said. "The audience will now be complete."

"Think so," said Jerningham mockingly. "One seat, and a rather important one, still remains to be occupied."

"It is possible that it may remain unoccupied," she said enigmatically. "Good evening, Phyllis. Your husband's friends have all arrived, as you see."

Mrs Drummond stared round with a wan little smile. "Hullo! chaps," she said. "Where's Hugh?"

"The Lord knows, Phyllis," answered Darrell. "We don't."

"He will come," said Mrs Drummond calmly. "Don't worry."

"You think so," answered Irma. "Good. And anyway why should you worry. Whether he comes, or whether he doesn't, the result as far as you are concerned will be the same. In fact I am not sure that my revenge would not be all the sweeter if he didn't come—until too late." Once more she was leaning against the altar stone, with one hand resting on the bust of Carl Peterson. "Imagine his feelings for the rest of his life if he arrived to find you all dead, knowing that at last he had failed you."

"May I remind you once again of the number of times we have heard remarks of a similar nature from your late lamented—er—husband—" said Jerningham with a yawn.

"And may I remind you," she answered, "of my original little verse to Drummond concerning the Female of the Species. I shall wait a little, and then we will proceed. Should he come in the interval I shall be delighted for him to participate in our little ceremony. Should he fail to appear he will not. He will merely find the results. And should he be so injudicious as not to come alone he will encounter two locked doors, doors which will take even him some time to knock down. He will hear you screaming for help inside here—and then—"

Her voice rose: her breast heaved: she was tasting of her triumph in advance.

"Bonzo's meat cubes are highly recommended for preserving a placid disposition," said Algy brightly. "You'll split a stay lace, my angel woman, unless you're careful."

"Why do we delay, dear one?" said Paul anxiously. "Let us be done with it now, and leave him to find what he will find."

But she shook her head. "No: we will give him half an hour. And if he is not here by then. . . ."

I thought furiously: every moment gained might be an advantage. "How is he to know anything about it," I said. "If he is where I last saw him, he is in Amesbury. And it will take more than half an hour get a messenger to him and for him to reach here."

She looked at me thoughtfully. "Is he also disguised like you and Sinclair?"

"He is," I said shortly. "He has a large black beard. . . ."

"You fool," howled Sinclair. "You damned treacherous fool. My God! We're done."

I stared at him stupidly, and a sudden deadly sick feeling came over me. "But," I stammered, "I thought. . . ."

I looked across helplessly at Darrell. What had I said? Surely the message was clear, to say who he was after I heard the anthem once.

"I could kill you where you sit, you cur," went on Sinclair idly, "if only I had my hands free."

"You seem to have said the wrong thing, Mr Dixon," said Irma pleasantly. "So dear Hugh is disguised in a large black beard, is he? I don't think I should like Hugh in a black beard. Well, well! I wonder what little amusement he has in store for us. We will certainly wait, Paul, until he arrives. I couldn't bear to miss him in a black beard."

"He had a scheme," said Sinclair furiously to the other three. "An absolute winner. But everything depended on his disguise. You fool, Dixon: you fool."

"Shut up, Toby," said Mrs Drummond peremptorily. "I'm sure Mr Dixon didn't mean to do any harm, and anyway—" she turned to me—"thank you a hundred times for all you've been through on my behalf."

I looked at her gratefully, though I was too much upset to speak. I simply couldn't understand the thing. Evidently Drummond had altered his plans since he'd sent the message through Darrell. But if so—and he didn't want me to comply with his first instructions—why hadn't he sent countermanding orders through Sinclair? And after a while I began to feel angry: the man was a damned fool. From beginning to end he had bungled every single thing. It was I who had borne the burden and heat of the whole show. And what possible hope had he got of deceiving anybody with that absurd false beard?

"And have you any idea if our friend is coming soon?" pursued Irma sweetly. "Or shall we send a note to Amesbury, addressed to Mr Blackbeard?"

"You needn't worry," said Sinclair sullenly. "He's coming all right."

He glowered vindictively at me, and I glowered back at him. I was absolutely fed up—so fed up that I almost forgot what was in store for us. Of all the bungling, incompetent set of fools that I had ever known this much vaunted gang won in a canter. And their so-called leader was the worst of the lot.

My mind went back to Bill Tracey's remarks about him and the extraordinary things he had done. I'd tell Bill the truth when I next saw him. I'd put him wise. And then my stomach gave a sick heave: I should never see Bill again. The sweat poured down me. My anger had gone—reality had returned. In a short while this astounding farce would be over, and I should be dead.

The room swam before me. I could only see the faces of the others through a mist. Dead! We should all be dead. By a monstrous effort I bit back a wild desire to shout and rave. That would be the unforgivable sin in front of this crowd. They might lack brains, but they didn't lack courage. I pulled myself together and stared at them. Boredom was the only emotion they displayed—boredom and contempt. This foul woman could kill them all right: she could never make them whimper. "I'm damned sorry," I said suddenly. "But for God's sake don't think it was treachery."

For a moment no one spoke. Then—"Sorry I said that," said Toby gruffly. "Withdraw it and all that sort of rot."

Silence fell again: the only movement was Paul's restless fidgeting. The woman still leaned gracefully against the altar stone. Mrs Drummond sat motionless, staring at the door.

"He will probably be coming soon, Paul," said Irma suddenly. "And it would be better not to give him any warning. Gag them."

"What about the girl?" he said.

"Gag her as well, and put her in the vacant chair for a time."

"Don't touch me you foul swine," said Mrs Drummond coldly. "I will go there."

"And then when dear Hugh comes," said Irma, "he shall take your place, Phyllis. Whilst you will be placed elsewhere."

She clenched her hands, and for a moment the feverish glitter returned to her eyes. Then she grew calm again.

"Now turn out all the lights except the one at the end."

And so for perhaps ten minutes we sat there waiting. Once I heard Pedro's throaty chuckle that seemed to come from the passage leading to the garage: and once I thought I heard the sound of a car on the road outside. Otherwise the silence was absolute.

Through the open skylight I could see the stars, and I began wondering what had become of the sailor. Somewhere about the house I supposed: one of the infamous gang. And then I started to wonder how Drummond would come.

Should I suddenly see his bearded face peering through at us—covering the woman with a revolver? But the stars still shone undimmed by any shadow, and after a while my brain refused to act. My arm was throbbing abominably. My thoughts began to wander.

I was back in my club, and the woman Irma was the Wine Steward. It was absurd that I couldn't get a drink before eleven o'clock in the morning in my own club. A fatuous wartime regulation that should be repealed. I'd write to my MP about it. Everybody ought to write to their MP about it. Here was that doddering ass old Axminster coming in. Thought he owned the place because he was a peer. . . . What was he saying? I listened—and suddenly my thoughts ceased to wander.

It wasn't Axminster: it was the man with the damaged hand. "A big bloke with a black beard is dodging through the bushes towards the house," he said. "What are we to do?"

The woman stretched out her arms ecstatically. "Let him come," she cried triumphantly. "Pedro." Came another throaty chuckle from behind me. "Come into the room after him, Pedro. Don't let him see you. Then I leave him to you. But don't kill him."

CHAPTER 17

In Which the Curtain Rings Down

As long as I live I shall never forget the tension of the next few minutes. The light was so dim that the faces of the others were only blurs. Paul had joined the woman, and they were standing side by side against the altar stone. The door in the hall was ajar, and the hall itself was in darkness so that it was impossible to see anything distinctly.

"He had a scheme: an absolute winner."

Sinclair's words came back to me, and I wondered what it was. Had I really done the whole lot of us in by my indiscretion? But at last the period of waiting was over. Drummond's voice could be heard in the hall.

"Very little light in this house."

The woman by the altar stiffened. "His voice," she said exultingly. "Drummond at last."

And then, or was it my imagination, there seemed to come a funny sort of hissing noise from the hall. Had the negro got him already? But no, he was speaking again. "I am a police inspector, and I wish to see the lady of the house on a very important matter."

In the dim light I could just see Darrell's expression of blank amazement, and I sympathized with him. Was this the brilliant scheme? If so, was a more utterly fatuous one ever thought of. Why, his voice gave him away.

"A very serious matter. I may say that I have two plain clothes men outside. What is that door at the end there? Don't attempt to detain me. Oh! I see—you're leading the way, are you."

The door opened, and there stood Drummond. I could just see his black beard, but it wasn't at him that I looked for long. He took a couple of steps into the room, and like a shadow the negro slipped in—dodging behind the curtain. I heard hoarse gurgling noises coming from the others as they strove to warn him, but Paul had done his work too well.

With a swift movement he stepped back and shut the door, so that Pedro was not more than a yard from him.

"Good evening. Inspector. Your voice is very familiar."

"A little ruse, my poppet," said Drummond pleasantly, "for getting into the august presence. May I say that I have a revolver in my hand, in case you can't see it in this light? And will you and your gentleman friend put your hands up. I've dealt with one of your myrmidons outside in the hall, and my temper is a bit ragged."

With a faint smile the woman raised her hands, and Paul followed suit.

"How are you, *mon ami*," she said. "We only required you to complete the family circle. In fact I was desolated when I thought you'd succumbed at the Mere."

I worked madly at the handkerchief with my jaws. Why didn't he come further into the room? At any second the negro might spring on him.

"And what is this ridiculous entertainment?" he asked.

"Specially staged for you, Hugh," she answered.

"I'm sorry you've wasted your time," he said shortly. "A truce to this fooling. I've had enough of it. You and the swine with you are for it now."

"Are we?" she mocked.

"Yes—you are. Come here, you swab. I don't know your name, and I don't want to, but hump yourself."

"And if I refuse," said Paul easily.

"I'll plug you where you stand," answered Drummond. "I don't know how my wife and friends are secured, but set them free. And no monkey tricks."

And then, with a superhuman effort, I got the handkerchief half off my mouth.

"Look out behind," I croaked, and even as I spoke the gleaming white teeth of the negro showed over his shoulder. That was all I could see at that distance, but I could hear.

There came a startled grunt from Drummond, that foul throaty chuckle from the black man, and the fight commenced. And what a fight it was in the semi-darkness. I forgot our own peril, forgot what depended on the issue in the thrill of the issue itself. Dimly I could see them swaying to and fro, each man putting forward every atom of strength he possessed, whilst Irma swayed backwards and forwards in her excitement, and the man Paul went towards the struggling pair in case he was wanted.

"Leave them, Paul," she cried tensely. "Let Drummond have his last fight."

And then Darrell got his gag free. "Go it, Hugh; go it, old man," he shouted.

I heard someone croaking hoarse sounds of encouragement and suddenly realized it was myself. And then gradually the sounds ceased, and my mouth got strangely dry. For Drummond was losing.

From a great distance I heard Darrell muttering "My God!" over and over again to himself, and from somewhere else came pitiful little muffled cries as Mrs Drummond realized the ghastly truth. Her husband was losing.

It was impossible to see the details, but of the main broad fact there was no doubt. At long last, Drummond had met his match. The nigger's chuckles were ceaseless and triumphant, though Drummond fought mute. But slowly and inexorably he was being worn down. And then step by step the black man forced him towards the chair where his wife was sitting.

"Take Phyllis out, Paul," cried Irma suddenly. "Take her out."

Foot by foot, faster and faster the pair swayed towards the empty seat. Drummond was weakening obviously, and suddenly with a groan he gave in and crumpled. And then in a couple of seconds it was over. He was flung into the chair, and with a click the steel bars closed over his wrists. He was a prisoner, the family circle was complete.

With a heart broken little cry his wife, who had torn off her gag, flung her arms around him and kissed him.

"Darling boy," she cried in an agony. Then abruptly she straightened up and stood facing her enemy. And if her voice when she spoke was not quite steady, who could be surprised?

"You foul devil," she said. "Get it over quickly."

And Pedro's evil chuckle was the only answer. I glanced at Irma, and for the time she was beyond speech. Never have I seen such utter and complete triumph expressed on any human being's face. She was in an ecstasy. Standing in front of the bust of Peterson, she was crooning to it in a sort of frenzy. The madness was on her again.

"My love, my King: he has been beaten. Do you realize it, my adored one? Drummond has been beaten. You are here, my Carl: your spirit is here. Do you see him—the man who killed you—powerless in my hands?"

Gradually she grew calmer, and at length Paul spoke.

"There is no reason for more delay now, *Carissima*," he said urgently. "Let us finish."

She stared at him broodingly. "Finish—yes. All will be finished soon, Paul. But for a few minutes I will enjoy my triumph. Then we will stage our play."

She looked at each of us in turn—a look of mingled triumph and contempt. "Ungag them, Paul, and Pedro—you attend to the white woman should she give trouble."

She waited till Paul had obeyed her, gloating over us, and the full realization of our position came sweeping over me. Great though the odds against him had been, some vestige of hope had remained while Drummond was still free. Now our last chance had gone: we were finished—outwitted by this woman. And though nothing could have been more utterly futile and fatuous than Drummond's behaviour, I felt terribly sorry for him.

Still breathing heavily after his fight, he sat there with his chin sunk on his chest looking the picture of despondency. And I realized what he must be going through. Beaten, and knowing that the result of that beating meant death to us all and to his wife. And yet—angry irritation surged up in me again—how on earth could he have expected anything else? If ever a man had asked for trouble he had. Now he'd got it, and so had we.

All the fight seemed to have gone out of him: he was broken. And when I looked at the others they seemed broken too—stunned with the incredible thing that had happened. That Drummond, the invincible, should have met his match at last—should be sitting there as a helpless prisoner—had shattered them. It was as if the Bank of England had suddenly become insolvent. And it was like Peter Darrell to try and comfort him.

"Cheer up, old son," he said lightly. "If that nigger hadn't caught you unawares from behind, you'd have done him." And Drummond's only reply was a groan of despair, whilst his wife stroked his hair with her hand, and Pedro, like a great black shadow, hovered behind her.

"Possibly," answered Irma. "That 'if' should be a great comfort to you all during the next half hour."

"All is ready," said Paul. "Let us start."

"Yes, we will start. But, as this is our last meeting, are there any little points you would like cleared up or explained? You, my dear Drummond, seem strangely silent. It's not surprising, I admit; complete defeat is always unpleasant. But, honestly, I can't congratulate you on your handling of the show. You haven't been very clever, have you?

In fact, you've been thoroughly disappointing. I had hoped at any rate, for some semblance of the old form, certainly at the end, but instead of that you have given no sport at all. And now—it is over."

She fell silent, that strange brooding look on her face, until at length Paul went up to her. "For Heaven's sake, *Carissima*," he said urgently, "do not let us delay any longer. I tell you I fear a trap."

"Why do you fear a trap?" she demanded.

"They have come into our power too easily," he said doggedly. "They have walked in with their eyes open, it seems to me."

"All that matters is that they have walked in," she answered. "And now, whatever happens, they will never walk out again. Do you hear that, Drummond, I said—whatever happens."

He made no answer until the negro, with a snarl of rage, thrust his evil face close to him.

"I hear," he said sullenly.

"It matters not," she cried triumphantly, "if a cordon of police surround the house; it matters not if they batter at the doors—they will be too late. Too late!" She breathed the words deliriously; the madness was coming on her again.

"But," stammered Paul, "how shall we get away?"

She waved him from her imperiously. "Be silent; you bore me," Once more she turned to the plaster cast. "Do you realize, my Carl, what has happened? They are all here—all of them. Drummond and his wife are here; the others are here waiting to expiate their crime. Their lives for yours, my King; I have arranged that. Is it your will that I delay no longer?" She stared at the bust as if seeking an answer, and somebody—I think it was Algy—gave a short, high-pitched laugh. Nerves were beginning to crack; only Mrs Drummond still stood cool and disdainful, stroking her husband's hair.

Suddenly the wild futility of the whole thing came home to me, so that I writhed and tugged and cursed. Seven of us were going to be killed at the whim of a mad woman! Murdered in cold blood! God! it was impossible—inconceivable. . . . Why didn't somebody do something? What fools they were—what utter fools!

I raved at them incoherently, and told them what I thought of their brains, their mentality, and the complete absence of justification for their existence at all.

"I told you she meant to kill us," I shouted, "and you five damned idiots come walking into the most obvious trap that has ever been laid."

"Shut that man's mouth," said Irma quietly, and for the second time Pedro's huge black hand crept round my throat, squeezing, throttling, so that, half choked, I fell silent. After all, what was the use? Mad she might be and undoubtedly was, but as she had said to Drummond, we were finished, whatever happened. And it was more dignified to face it in silence.

"We will begin," she said suddenly. "Paul, get Phyllis."

With a little cry, Mrs Drummond flung her arms round her husband's neck. "Goodbye, my darling," she cried, kissing him again and again. But he was beyond speech, and at length the negro seized her and dragged her away.

"Let me go, you foul brute," she said furiously, and Paul, who was standing by the stone of sacrifice, beckoned to her to come. Proudly, without faltering, she walked towards him.

"Lie down," he said curtly.

"Get it accurate, Paul," cried Irma anxiously. "Be certain that it is accurate."

"I will be certain," he answered.

And then for the first time I realized that there were ropes made fast to rings in the stone. She was going to be lashed down. She didn't struggle even when Pedro, chuckling in his excitement, helped to make her fast. And on her face was an expression of such unutterable contempt that it seemed to infuriate the other woman. "You may sneer, my dear Phyllis," she stormed. "But look above you, you little fool; look above you."

With one accord we all looked up, and at the same moment a small light was turned on in the ceiling. And when he had seen what it illuminated Ted Jerningham began to shout and bellow like a madman. "Stop it, you devil," he roared. "Let one of us go there instead other. My God! Hugh. Do you see?"

But Drummond was still silent, and after a while Jerningham relapsed into silence too. And as for me, I was conscious only of a deadly feeling of nausea. Hanging from a rafter was a huge, pointed knife. It was of an uncommon Oriental design, and it looked the most deadly weapon.

"Yes, Hugh—do you see?" cried Irma mockingly. "Do you see what it is that hangs directly above your wife's heart? It has been tested, not once, but many times, and when I release the spring it will fall, Hugh. And it will fall straight." And still Drummond sat silent and cowed. "But I shall not release it yet: that I promise you. There is a little ceremony to be gone through before our finale. The rest of them have seen it, Drummond, but to you as my principal guest it will come as a surprise. And after it is over, and the knife that you see up there is buried in Phyllis's heart, your turn will come."

She was rocking to and fro in her mad excitement.

"Paul has arranged it," she cried exultingly. "Clever Paul. Behind each one of you is enough explosive to shatter you to pieces. But Paul has so arranged it that even as Phyllis waits and waits for death to come—so will you all wait. You will see it creeping closer and closer, and be powerless to do anything to save yourselves. I shall light the fuse, and you will see the flame burning slowly towards this little box. And when it reaches that box—suddenly, with the speed of light, the flame will dart to the gun-cotton behind your backs. For the fuse that connects the gun-cotton to the box is of a different brand to the one I shall light. Paul knows all these things: Paul is clever."

And now the madness was on her in earnest. She walked to and fro in front of the altar stone, her arms outstretched, worshipping the plaster cast of Peterson. "Is my revenge worthy, my King?" she cried again and again. "Does it meet with your approval? First she shall be killed before their eyes, and then they will wait for their own death. They will see it coming closer every second, until, at last. . . ."

"Great Heavens! man," shouted Darrell to Paul, "you can't let her go on. The woman is mad."

But he took no notice. His eyes were fixed on the woman who had now become silent. She seemed to be listening to a voice we could not hear, and something told me that we were very near the end. "Put out the lights, Paul," she said gravely.

I took one last look round the room; at Mrs Drummond, lying bound, with the black man gloating over her; at Irma, standing triumphant by the altar stone; and finally at Drummond. Even now I could hardly believe that it was the finish, and that he had nothing up his sleeve. But there he still sat with his head sunk on his breast, the personification of desolate defeat. And then the lights went out.

Once again we were plunged in darkness that could be felt, but this time it was not a rehearsal. In a few minutes that knife would fall from the ceiling, and the poor girl would be dead. And we should see it actually happen. The sweat poured off me in streams as the full horror of it came home. I scarcely thought of what was going to be the fate of the rest of us afterwards. To be lying there bound, knowing that at any moment the knife might fall, was enough to send her crazy. More merciful if it did.

"A model of Stonehenge, Drummond. You have realized that?"

At last he seemed to have recovered the use of his tongue. "Yes, I have realized that." His voice was perfectly steady, and I wondered if even now he realized what was coming.

"And the stone on which Phyllis lies is the stone of sacrifice. Do you think she is a worthy offering?"

"Do you really mean to do this monstrous thing, Irma Peterson?" he asked.

"Should I have gone to all this trouble," she mocked, "if I didn't?"

"And yet, when on one occasion you asked me, I spared Carl's life. Do you remember?"

"Only to kill him later," she cried fiercely. "Go on, Drummond: beg for her life. I'd like to hear you whining."

"You won't do that," he answered. "If I ask you to spare her it is for a different reason altogether. It is to show that you have left in you some shred of humanity."

"As far as you are concerned I have none," she said. "As I say, should I have done all this for nothing? Listen, Drummond.

"It was in Egypt, as I told you in my first letter, that the idea came to me. By the irony of fate, it was suggested to me by a man who knows you well, Drummond. You and dear Phyllis had been staying at the same house with him, and he was so interested to find out that I also knew you. He told me about this splendid game of hidden treasure, and it appeared that you had won. I asked him the rules, and he said they were exceedingly simple. Everything depended on having good clues. I trust that mine have been up to standard."

She paused, and no one spoke.

"From the game, as you played it then, to the game as you have played it now, was but a short step. Preparation was necessary, it is true; but the main idea was the same. I would give you a hidden-treasure hunt, where the prize was not a box of cigarettes, but something a little more valuable. And I would leave you to think"—her voice rose suddenly—"you poor fool, that if you succeeded you would get the prize."

She laughed, and it had an ugly sound.

"However, of that later. Having made my preparations, the next thing was to obtain the prize. That proved easier than I expected. Twice, but for one of those little accidents which no one could foresee, Phyllis would have got into a special taxi in London—a taxi prepared by me. But I could afford to wait. For weeks you were watched, Drummond—and then you went to Pangbourne where you began to realize that I was after you. And then came the opportunity. A hastily scrawled note in your handwriting—Paul is an adept at that, and I had several specimens of your writing—and the thing was done.

"'Bring the Bentley at once to Tidmarsh, old girl. A most amazing thing has happened.—H.' Do you remember the note, Phyllis? I don't blame you for falling into the trap: it said neither too much nor too little, that note. And so I got the prize at a trifling cost. It was naughty of you to hit him so hard, my dear, as I've told you before. Paul said it was a positively wicked blow."

Once again that mocking laugh rang through the room, but I hardly heard it. With every sense alert, I was listening to another sound—the sound of heavy breathing near me. Something was happening close by—but what? Then came a groan, and silence. "What was that? Who groaned?" Her words came sharp and insistent.

"Who, indeed?" answered Drummond's voice. "Why don't you continue, Irma Peterson? We are waiting for the theatrical display."

"Pedro! Pedro! Is Drummond still in his chair?" Came that same throaty chuckle, followed by Drummond's voice again: "Take your hands off me, you foul swab."

"It is well," she said, and there was relief in her voice. "I should not like a mistake to occur now. And, with you, Drummond—one never knows."

"True," said he, "one never knows. Even now, Irma—there is time for you to change your mind. I warn you that it will be better for you if you do."

"Thank you a thousand times," she sneered. "Instead, however, of following your advice, we will begin. The sacrifice is ready; we have delayed enough." Once more I became conscious of movement near me, and my pulses began to tingle. "Just for the fraction of a second, Drummond, will you again see Phyllis alive: then the knife will fall."

The faint light was beginning behind the Friar's Heel, in a couple of minutes it would be all over. Unless.... unless.... My heart was pounding; my tongue was dry. Was it the end, or were strange things taking place?

"The dawn," she cried. "You see the dawn, Drummond. Soon the sun will rise, the rays will creep nearer and nearer to Phyllis. And then.... See.... the rim is already there. It is coming, Drummond, coming. Have you any last message, you poor damned fool, for her? If so speak now for my hand is on the lever of the knife."

"Just one," said Drummond lightly, and to my amazement his voice did not come from the chair in which he was imprisoned. "Every beard is not false, but every nigger smells. That beard ain't false, dearie, and dis nigger don't smell. So I'm thinking there's something wrong somewhere."

There was a moment's dead silence, then she gave a little choking gasp. Came a streak of light as the knife shot down, a crash, and on the stone of sacrifice lay the bust of Carl Peterson, shattered in a hundred pieces. For a while I couldn't grasp it. I stared stupidly at the woman who was cowering back against the altar stone; at the crumpled figure of Paul lying on the ground close by me. And then I looked at the nigger, and he was grinning broadly.

"So it ain't poor dear Drummond in dat chair," he chuckled. "That is my very good friend John Perkins, and when you thought John was talking, it was really dis nigger what spoke, so you see you weren't quite as clever as you thought, my poppet."

Suddenly she began to scream hysterically, and Drummond raced round the chairs setting us free.

"Guard Phyllis," he shouted, as the door opened and Charles followed by the chauffeur came rushing in. It lasted about five seconds— the scrap—but that five seconds was enough. For when it was over and we looked round for Irma she had gone. Whether there was some secret door which we didn't discover, or whether she fled through the passage into the garage we shall never know. But from that day to this there has been no trace seen of her. And I don't even know the ultimate fate of the various men of the house party. Having caught the lot, including Charles, we put them in our chairs. And then Drummond lit the fuse and we left them bellowing for mercy.

"Let 'em sweat for ten minutes," he remarked. "I've disconnected at the junction box, but they don't know that I have. Now then, boys, once again—and all together—Froth Blowers for ever."

We stood in the road and we yelled at the tops of our voices. And it was only when we'd finished that I suddenly remembered the sailor.

"That's all right, old boy," laughed Drummond. "Been retrieving any more bad plums out of waste paper baskets lately?"

And so the game ended, and I know that that night I was too tired even to think about the strangeness of it, much less ask. It wasn't till lunch next day that Drummond cleared up the loose ends. I can see him now, lolling at the end of the table with a lazy grin on his face, and a tankard of beer beside him.

"You'll probably curse my neck off, chaps," he said, "for keeping you in the dark, but honestly, it seemed the only way. It was touch and go, mark you—especially for Phyllis, and that was where the difficulty came in!"

"For the Lord's sake start at the beginning," said Darrell.

"In the first place, I wasn't too sure that they really did think we'd been killed at the Mere. And so it became absolutely vital that I should not be caught. But how to arrange it, and at the same time lull her suspicions, and make her think she'd got me, was the problem. Obviously by providing myself with a double, which is where dear old John came in. He acts for the movies, and he'd grown that awful fungus for a part he has to play shortly. When it is removed, however, he really does look rather like me; moreover he's the same build. So off we set—me as a sailor, him as me—without the smell of an idea as to what we were going to slosh into down here.

"Then came an amazing piece of luck. We motored down—John and I—and we passed the house of last night. There was of course nothing suspicious about it—nothing to mark it as the spot we wanted. Except one thing, and therein lay the luck. As we went past the drive another car coming towards us slowed up, evidently with the intention of turning in. And sitting beside the driver in the front seat was the gent called Paul. That settled it."

"Why?" I asked.

"You couldn't be expected to know," he answered, "but I should have thought old Toby's grey matter would have heaved to it, especially as he spotted the astounding likeness to the late lamented Lakington. Don't you remember the message Phyllis scrawled with her finger, in the blood at the back of her seat? *LIKE LAK*. It couldn't mean anything else, unless it was the most astounding coincidence. So we were a bit on the way, but not far. We'd found a house connected with them, but whether Phyllis was inside or not I hadn't an idea. However, being a bit of an adept at exploring houses at night, I intended to do so until you two bung-faced swabs went and made fools of yourselves at Stonehenge that afternoon."

"Never," he grinned cheerfully, "in the course of a long and earnest career have I heard two people give themselves away so utterly and so often as Toby and Dixon did that afternoon. It was staggering, it was monumental. And the man they deliberately selected to be the recipient of their maidenly confidence was Paul himself. Beer—more beer—much more beer."

"Damn it, Hugh," cried Sinclair.

"My dear lad," Drummond silenced him with a wave of his hand, "you were the finest example of congenital idiocy it has ever been my misfortune to witness. The stones of Stonehenge are little pebbles compared to the bricks you dropped, but I forgive you. I even forgive jolly old Dixon's scavenging propensities in waste paper baskets. Such is my nature—beautiful, earnest and pure. But you assuredly caused me a lot of trouble: I had to change my plans completely.

"Paul obviously suspected you. No man out of a lunatic asylum could possibly avoid doing so. And as I had no possible means of knowing that all he wanted to do was to get on with the job, I had to assume that he would pass on his suspicions to Irma, and proceed to rope the pair of you in. Time had become an urgent factor. So I wired Algy, and when he arrived, I told him by letter what to do. He was to announce loudly that he proposed to go to the Friar's Heel by night, but as he valued his life, he wasn't to do anything of the sort."

He leaned back in his chair, and looked at me with twinkling eyes. "You may be a damned idiot, Joe," he said, "but I looks towards you and I raise my glass. Had it remotely dawned on me that you were going there yourself, I'd have given you the same warning. But it didn't."

"You knew I was there?" I stammered.

"Laddie," he remarked, "hast ever listened to a vast herd of elephants crashing their way through primeval forest? Hast ever heard the scaly rhinoceros and young gambolling playfully on a shingly shore whilst they assuage their thirst? Thus and more so, was your progress that night. Like a tank with open exhaust you came into action. Like a battalion of panting men you lay about, in the most obvious places you could find, and breathed hard. You were, and I say it advisedly, the most conspicuous object in the whole of Wiltshire."

He frowned suddenly.

"You know what we found there, the others don't. Some poor devil who looked like a clerk—stone dead. What he was doing there we shall never know, but it was perfectly obvious that he had been mistaken for Algy. The nigger had blundered, and it was a blunder which might prove awkward. You heard them talking, Joe—Paul and Irma: but it didn't require that confirmation to see how the land lay. All along I had realized that Phyllis and I were the principal quarry. If she got you so much the better, but we came first. And what I was so terribly frightened of, as soon as I saw that body, was that Irma would get nervous, and believing I was already dead, would go back, finish off Phyllis straight away, and then clear out. I still had no definite scheme; I didn't even have a definite scheme after I'd functioned with the nigger. In fact I didn't really intend to fight him at all.

"I suppose he must have smelt me or something, at any rate he came for me. And by the Lord Harry, it was touch and go. However"—he shrugged his shoulders—"I pasted him good and hearty in the mazzard, and that was that. In fact he is in an awkward predicament that nigger. I dragged him into one of those disused sheds, and handcuffed him to a steel girder. Then I put his victim beside him. And he will find explanations a little difficult.

"The trouble was that all this had delayed me. I hadn't got a car, only a bicycle—and that house had to be explored at once. My hat! laddie," he said to me, "I didn't expect to find you as part of the furniture. How on earth did you get there?"

"On the luggage grid of their car," I said.

"The devil you did," he grinned. "The devil you did! Joe—you are a worthy recruit, though when I saw you through the skylight I consigned you to the deepest pit of hell. But, thank Heavens! you didn't give away the fact that you'd seen me."

"I thought you were one of them," I said.

"I know you did, old boy," he laughed, "What we'd have done without your thoughts during this show I don't know. They have all been so inconceivably wide of the mark that they've been invaluable."

"Don't pay any attention to him, Mr Dixon," said his wife.

"My darling," he protested, "I mean it. Joe has been invaluable. The air of complete certainty with which he proclaimed the exact opposite to the truth has saved the situation. I've been able to bank on it. And once I realized what that foul female intended to do I wanted every bit of assistance I could get.

"The first alternative was to try and get you out of the house single-handed, but I dismissed that as impossible. I didn't know your room, the house was stiff with men, and—most important of all—that woman would have shot on sight.

"The second alternative was to get all the bunch into the house without arousing her suspicions. And when I heard her reading the letter she was sending Algy I realized we were getting on. John and Toby could be brought in at a suitable time, and there only remained the problem of what I was going to do. I confess I didn't think of it. John suggested the nigger. It was a risk, but it proved easier than I thought."

"Damn it, Hugh," cried Darrell, "why didn't you say who you were in the afternoon? You were alone with us, and if you'd set us free then we could have tackled the whole bunch."

"Because, Peter," said Drummond gravely, "it would have taken us some minutes to tackle them. It would have taken Irma half a second to kill Phyllis."

"At any rate," said Jerningham, "you might have let us know. Jove! old boy, I never want to go through twenty minutes like that again."

"I know, chaps—and I'm sorry. I'd have spared you that if I'd thought it safe. But then you would all of you have been acting, and I wanted the real thing. I knew that Dixon thought John was me, and would tell you so, too. And I wanted you all to carry on as if you thought so. The rest you know. It was easy for me to talk every time instead of John, with the room in semi-darkness as it was. And I think you'll admit we staged a damned good fight."

"When did you spot it, Phyllis?" said Darrell.

"When I kissed John," she laughed.

"And very nice too," grinned that worthy. "Unrehearsed effects are always best."

Drummond rose and stretched himself.

"All over, chaps, all over. Back to the dreary round. Algernon," he hailed a passing waiter, "bring, my stout-hearted fellow, eight of those pale pink concoctions that the sweet thing in the bar fondly imagines are Martinis. I would fain propose a toast. But first—a small formality. Mr Joseph Dixon will place his hand in his pocket and extract there from coins to the value of five shillings. I will then present him here and now with the insignia of the Ancient Order, feeling that he has well merited that high honour. Our anthem he knows; he has already sung it twice in his cracked falsetto. The privileges attendant to our Order you will find enumerated in this small book, Mr Dixon, and they should be studied in the solitude of your chamber when alone with your thoughts. Especially our great insurance treble which guards your dog from rabies, your cook from babies, and yourself from scabies. Great words, my masters, great words, I perceive that Algernon, panting and exhausted after his ten-yard walk, is with us again, carrying the raspberry juice with all his well-known flair. Lady and Gentlemen—to our new Froth Blower. And may I inquire which of you bat-faced sons of Belial has pinched the five bob?"

Temple Tower

Chapter 1

In Which the "Maid of Orleans" Leaves for Boulogne

The *Maid of Orleans* drew slowly away from the side. Leaning over the rail was the usual row of cross-Channel passengers calling out final goodbyes to their friends on the quay. An odd Customs man or two drifted back to their respective offices: the R.A.C. representative raised protesting hands to High Heaven because one of his charges had departed without his *triptyque*. In fact, the usual scene on the departure of the Boulogne boat, and mentioned only because you must start a story somewhere, and Folkestone harbour is as good a locality as any.

Standing side by side on the quay were two men, who had been waving their hands in that shamefaced manner which immediately descends on the male sex when it indulges in that fatuous pursuit. The targets of their innocent pastime were two women, whose handkerchiefs had fluttered in response from the upper deck. And since these two charming ladies do not come into the matter again it might be as well to dispose of them forthwith. They were, in short, the wives of the two men, departing on their lawful occasions to Le Touquet, there to play a little golf and lose some money in the casino. Which is really all that needs to be said about them, except possibly their last remark chanted in unison as the ship began to move:

"Now mind you're both good while we're away."

"Of course," answered the two men, also in unison.

And here and now let us be quite clear about this matter. Before ordering a dinner the average man consults the menu. If his mouth is set for underdone beef with horseradish sauce it is as gall and wormwood to him to be given mutton and red-currant jelly. Similarly, before reading a book the average reader likes to have a pointer as to what it is about. Does it concern the Sheik of fiction carrying off a beautiful white woman on his thoroughbred Arab; or does it concern the Sheik of reality riding a donkey and picking fleas out of his *burnous*? Does it concern a Bolshevist plot to blow up the policeman on point duty at Dover Street; or does it concern the meditations of an evangelical Bishop on the revised Prayer-Book? And honesty compels me to state that it concerns none of these things, which is just as well for all concerned.

But it occurred to me that the parting admonition of those two charming ladies might possibly be construed to mean that they feared their husbands would not be good during their absence. Far from it: such a thought never even entered their heads. It was just a confirmatory statement of a fact as certain as the presence of Nelson in Trafalgar Square.

"Dear lambs," they remarked to one another as the boat cleared the harbour, "it will do them good to have a few days' golf all by themselves."

However, I still haven't given this pointer. And with it the last hopes of those who insist on a love story will be dashed to the ground. They must have received a pretty severe jolt when this matter of husband and wife was alluded to, though a few of the more optimistic ones may have had visions of a divorce looming somewhere, or even a bit of slap and tickle. Sorry: nothing doing. So if this is the mutton of my restaurant analogy you know what to do. But don't forget this book weighs as much as *Pansy, or the Girl who Lost All for Love*, and will do just as much damage to the aspidistra if you hit it.

Another thing, too, which it does not concern is golf. On that fact, I must admit with shame and sorrow that these two miserable men had deceived their trusting wives. The larger and more nefarious of the two had actually addressed his partner in crime at breakfast that morning on the subjects of handicaps and niblicks and things, and what they were going to do during their few days at Rye. His eye had not twitched: his hand when he helped himself to marmalade had been steady. And yet he lied—the dirty dog—he lied.

And his companion in vice knew he had lied, though, to his everlasting shame, he said no word. Both of these scoundrels allowed their wives to leave them for a perilous sea voyage with a falsehood ringing in their ears. Which shows you the type of men you're dealing with. However—that's that: I'll get on with it. Still not given the pointer? Oh! read the darned book and find out for yourself.

I will take the larger one first. His height was a shade over six feet in his socks: his breadth and depth were in proportion. Which, in boxing parlance, entitles him to be placed among the big men. And big he was in every sense of the word. His face was nothing to write home about, and even his wife admitted that she only used it to amuse the baby. Anyway, looks don't matter in a man. What does matter is his condition, and, reverting once more to boxing parlance, this man looked what he was—trained to the last ounce.

It has always been a bit of a marvel to me how Hugh Drummond kept as fit as he did, in view of his incredible capacity for lowering ale. Nevertheless, the bald fact remains that in the matter of fitness he had all of us beat to a frazzle. I particularly wish to emphasise that fact, because I believe that this is the first occasion that one of his really intimate friends has written about him. Take, for instance, the extraordinary adventure with that crazy woman, Irma, on Salisbury Plain. Joe Dixon wrote that, and Joe, good fellow though he is, hardly knew Hugh at all. But fourteen years have gone by since I first met him, in the front line near Arras, and in fourteen years one gets to know a man. From which it will be inferred that I was the other of the two nefarious scoundrels who had stood waving to their trusting wives from the quay.

Now, as will perhaps be remembered by those who have followed some of our adventures in the past, we got mixed up with a bunch of criminals shortly after the war. Their leader was a man named Carl Peterson, who was killed by Drummond in Wilmot's giant airship just before it crashed in flames. And that led up to the amazing happenings on Salisbury Plain that I have already alluded to, when Peterson's mistress kidnapped Drummond's wife and nearly got the lot of us. But she escaped, and the first thought that had sprung to my mind on getting Hugh's letter was that she had reappeared again. Up till now I had had no chance of speaking to him privately, but as the boat disappeared round the end of the jetty, I turned to him eagerly:

"What's the game, Hugh? Is it Irma on the scene again?"

He held up a protesting hand.

"My dear Peter," he remarked, "have you noticed that the sun is in the position technically known as over the yardarm?"

"And as the Governor of North Carolina said to his pal, let's get to it," I answered. "What about the Pavilion Hotel?"

"It is a wonderful thing being married, Peter," he said thoughtfully as we strolled along the platform.

"Marvellous," I agreed, and glanced at him sideways: there was a certain note in his voice that confirmed my suspicions.

"And," he continued, "it is good for all of us to sacrifice something in Lent."

"It is June," I answered, "but the principle holds good."

"Peter," he said, as we fell into two easy chairs in the lounge, "your brain has probably jumped to the fact that it was not entirely due to a desire to beat your head off on Rye golf links that I engineered this little affair at Le Touquet. Waiter—two large tankards of ale."

"Some such idea had dawned on me," I agreed. "It seemed so remarkably sudden."

"My dear old lad," he said with a grin, "you can't imagine the diplomacy I had to use. I first of all suggested that we all four should go to Le Touquet—a proposal which was jumped at by my devoted spouse. I then wrote you that masterpiece of duplicity."

"Masterpiece it may have been," I laughed, "but it gave me brain fever trying to think of an excuse that would hold water."

"What did you cough up finally?" he asked.

"I wrote to my lawyer," I said, "and told him to write to me and say he'd got some urgent business on my dear old grandmother's will. Sounded a bit thin to me, I confess, but, by the mercy of Allah, it went down. And Molly was deuced keen to go."

"So, bless her, was Phyllis," answered Hugh. "Thin or not, Peter, it worked. For a few days we are going to be bachelors. And much may happen in a few days."

"As you say," I agreed, "much may happen in a few days. At the same time, you haven't answered my first question. Is it Irma?"

"It is not, bless her. Maybe another time, for I should hate to lose her. But this time it's something quite, quite new."

He drained his tankard and pressed the bell.

"We will have the other half section, while I put you wise. Mark you, Peter, it may be the most hopeless mare's nest, and if it is we can always play golf. But somehow or other I don't think it is. In fact, in my own mind, I'm quite certain it isn't. You don't know this part of the world at all, do you?"

"Not a bit," I said.

"Well, the first thing to do is to give you a rough idea of the lie of the land. Once we leave Hythe we come to a large stretch of absolutely flat country which is known as Romney Marsh. The word *marsh* is a misnomer, as the soil itself is quite hard and gives very good grazing. There are a few small villages dotted about, and an odd farmhouse or two, but the prevailing note is solitude. Motor charabancs cross it daily from Hastings and Folkestone, and the roads are good but a bit narrow. But it is a solitary sort of place for all that; you feel that anything might happen on it.

"A few centuries ago it was covered by the sea, which came right up to the foothills, so that all of Romney Marsh is reclaimed land. And from those hills you get the most marvellous view away towards Dungeness and Lydd—if you like that type of view, that's to say. Open, free, with the tang of the sea in the wind. I love it; which was one of the deciding factors that led me to take our present house. It has a clear sweep for miles right out to sea, and I've installed a powerful telescope on the terrace—a telescope, Peter, which has been and is going to be of assistance. However, to return to our muttons. As I've told you, the Marsh itself is sparsely populated. The only considerable towns are Rye and Winchelsea—which can hardly be said to be on Romney Marsh at all. Rye is set on a sort of conical hill, and must in the olden days have been almost completely surrounded by water. But except for them, and Lydd, where the artillery range is, and New Romney, there's not much in the house line, and those that are there belong principally to small farmers.

"About a week ago—to be exact, the day before I wrote to you—I was undressing to go to bed. It was fairly early—not more than eleven or a quarter past—and after I had got into pyjamas I sat by the open window having a final cigarette. My dressing-room faces over the Marsh, and I could see the lights of a passing steamer going West. Suddenly, from the very middle of the Marsh itself, there came a red flash lasting about a second; then a pause, and a moment afterwards it was blue. They were repeated half a dozen times—red, blue, red, blue— then they ceased altogether.

"For a while I sat there staring out, wondering what on earth they could mean. By putting a couple of matches on my dressing-table I got the rough alignment so that I could get the direction in the morning—but I was sorely tempted to go out and investigate then and there. However, I decided not to; Phyllis was in bed, and I was undressed. And if the truth be told, Peter, even at that early hour the possibility of a little fun had struck me, and I didn't want to run the risk of cramping our style. So I didn't mention anything about it to the dear soul. That it was a signal of some sort seemed fairly obvious, but for what and to whom? The first thought that flitted across my mind was that smugglers were at work. For if rumour speaks the truth there is the devil of a lot of smuggling going on since these new silk duties were put on. There are stories told of fast motor-boats, and mysterious motor-cars that go careering about in the middle of the night. However, when I began to think things over a bit, I dismissed the smuggling theory. To put it mildly, it seemed unlikely that men engaged in such an extremely secret and risky business would take the trouble to advertise themselves by flashing red and blue lights all over the place. Besides, one would have expected the signal—if such it was—to be given towards the sea, and this was given towards the land. So I washed out smugglers. The next solution that presented itself was that it wasn't a genuine signal at all, but the work of some boy with a developed film sense. A joke inspired by 'Dandy Dick—the Cowboy's Terror,' or something of that sort. And leaving it at that, I fell asleep.

"The next morning I was up early. A mist was lying over the Marsh which lifted after a while, and I took a squint over my two matches. They, of course, gave me the right direction, but not elevation. That I had to guess. As I've told you, there are very few houses about, and there was only one through which the line of my matches passed. Moreover, as far as I could judge, though things look very different by day to what they do at night, that house gave me approximately the right elevation. So I went downstairs and focussed my telescope on it.

"It was, as I expected, an ordinary farmhouse. There seemed to be a couple of outhouses and four or five biggish trees. Moreover, the whole property stood isolated by itself, like a little island rising out of a lake. As far as I could judge, it stood about a quarter of a mile from the main road between Rye and New Romney, and was connected to it by a rough track. I could see no sign of life, until the front door opened and a woman with a pail in her hand came out and went into one of the outhouses. In every respect a peaceful country scene.

"However, I waylaid the postman that morning and got some more information from him. It appeared that the place was known as Spragge's Farm. It belonged to a man of that name, and had belonged to his father and grandfather before him. The present man lived there with his wife, and, I gathered, was not a popular individual. He was surly and morose, and had the reputation of being a miser. Apparently he was quite well off, but he refused to keep a servant, making his wife do all the menial work. He had a ferocious temper, and on two or three occasions had been run in before the local Bench for actual physical violence to one of his farm hands, the result being that now he could get no one to work for him. Following up my second theory I asked if he had any children, and was told that he hadn't. But, I gathered, he occasionally took in a lodger who wanted quiet and rest. I further gathered that the usual duration of the said lodger's stay was not extensive, as he got neither rest nor quiet for his money.

I asked if he had one now, but that the postman couldn't tell me. He hadn't heard of one, but then, Spragge's Farm wasn't on his beat. So having found out mighty little, I thanked him and he went off. And then, after he'd gone a few yards he turned round and came back. It appeared that he had suddenly remembered that the cards which Spragge had put in one or two of the shops in Rye, advertising that he took in boarders, had been removed recently, the assumption being that possibly he had given up that side line. And that comprised all the information I got.

"Off and on through the morning I had a look at the place, but nothing of the slightest interest did I see. Once a man came out who I assumed was Spragge himself, and I saw the woman two or three times, but except for that there was no sign of life about the farm. And after a while I began to wonder if the whole thing wasn't capable of some perfectly ordinary explanation; or possibly that the farm itself was not the origin of the lights.

"And then, Peter, there occurred the thing which caused my letter to you and the departure of our women-kind today."

Hugh lit a cigarette, and I followed suit. Up to date it struck me that the doings had been hardly such as to awake feverish excitement in the breasts of the troops, but I knew my man. Domesticity might have dulled him a little, but he could still spot the genuine article like a terrier spots a rat.

"We will now leave the Marsh," he continued, "and come to the higher ground where my house is. I've got no one near me—my next neighbour being about half a mile away. He, too, commands a view right out to sea, but there all similarity ends between us, I trust. His name is Granger, and he's a gentleman I've got remarkably little use for. In appearance, he is small and measly looking: you see smaller editions in a bit of ripe Stilton. As far as I know he lives alone, save for two servants—one a great bullock of a man who looks like a prize-fighter, the other an elderly female who cooks. I got those details from my own staff, because I've never been inside his house myself. In fact, the only time I've met the blighter is occasionally out walking, when he is invariably accompanied by this professional pug. And it was on one such occasion that he stopped and spoke to me.

"'Captain Drummond, I believe,' he said.

"I admitted the soft impeachment, and wondered what was coming.

"'You and your wife must forgive my not calling on you,' he went on jerkily. 'I am a recluse, Captain Drummond, and my health is not of the best.'

"He rambled on, and when he'd finished I assured him that it did not matter in the least, and that we quite understood. I didn't add that the only thing we wouldn't forgive him for was if he did call, and we parted, leaving me with two very distinct impressions.

"The first was that, in spite of his name, the man was not pure English. There was a distinct trace of an accent in his voice, though I couldn't decide what. The second was that he was afraid of something. The whole time he was talking to me his eyes had been darting this way and that, as if he was perpetually on the lookout for some unexpected danger. Of course, it might have been only a mannerism, but that was the impression he gave me, and subsequent gossip confirmed my idea. The man was frightened, though whether of a specific individual or of people at large I didn't know.

"It appeared he had taken the house very soon after the war, and had immediately proceeded to fortify the place like a prison. There was already a high wall all round the house, and his first act was to have the top of it covered with a double row of long crossed steel spikes. His next performance was to have the existing open gates for the drive replaced by two heavy wooden ones whose tops were also covered with the same contraption of spikes. These were kept permanently locked, and the only way of getting in was through a small wicket let into one of them. But this was also kept locked, and before it could be opened a tremendous ceremony had to be gone through. My informant on all this once again was the postman. When the time came for the various errand boys to bring the provisions for the day, the prize-fighter took up his position by the wicket gate. When the bell rang he opened it and took the meat, or whatever it was, from the boy. Then everything was shut up again as before. The same with the postman, too. On the rare occasions when Mr. Granger got a letter he handed it to the bodyguard through the gate; he was never allowed to go up to the front door.

"But that wasn't all; I've only mentioned the outer line of defences up to date. The inner was just as thorough. Every window in the house was protected on the outside by iron bars, exactly like a prison cell. Even the attics had them; not only the ground floor rooms. That work was done by a local man, so the countryside got full information—but a London firm was employed for other things, of which only vague rumours got round. Burglar alarms of the most modern type were installed, and trip wires in the grounds which rang gongs, and the Lord knows what else.

"However, there is no good elaborating the details. I've told you enough already to show you that my neighbour not only resented intrusion, but was determined to stop it. Naturally, in a country place like this the inhabitants buzzed like a hive of bees with curiosity, though when I took my place three years after, the excitement had died down. They had become used to him, and the generally accepted theory was that he was an eccentric who lived in terror of burglars. Colour was added to that idea by the doctor who, on one occasion, was called in to see him. It appeared that everything short of blindfolding the medico was done to prevent him seeing anything. He was rushed from the wicket gate to the front door, through the hall and up to the bedroom. And when he got there the prize-fighter remained in the room. Mark you, Peter, the doctor man told me this himself.

"He waited for the servant to go, and when he showed every intention of staying, he stuck in his toes. He told Granger, who was in bed, that he was not in the habit of having a third person in the room when he was examining a patient unless that person was a qualified nurse. Granger answered very querulously that the man was his confidential valet and that he wished him to stay. The doctor replied to the effect that he didn't care a damn what he was, but that if he didn't clear out of the room Mr. Granger would have to obtain another doctor. Well, the long and the short of it was, that, after a while, and very reluctantly, the servant left the room, and the doctor got on with his job. As he said to me, he didn't really mind in the slightest if the man remained or if he didn't, but he was determined to see what would happen if he insisted.

"After he had made his examination, and prescribed something or other, he glanced round the room.

"'Lovely things you've got here, Mr. Granger,' he remarked casually.

"The invalid struck a little bell beside the bed, and the servant entered so quickly that he must have been just outside the door.

"'Show the doctor out,' said the sick man irritably. 'And I'll let you know, Doctor Sinclair, if I want you again.'

"Now the doctor, though one of the best, has the devil of a temper. And he let drive at that.

"'Your case is not one that I care to continue treating,' he said coldly. 'It is not your bodily health that requires attention, but your manners. My fee is half a guinea.'

"For a moment or two, so he told me, he thought the prize-fighter was going to strike him, but Granger pulled himself together.

"'Forgive me, doctor,' he said. 'I'm not feeling my best today. Yes, there are some lovely things in this room, and, in fact, all over the house. That is why I have taken these somewhat elaborate precautions against unauthorised people gaining an entrance. A burglar's paradise, my dear sir; a burglar's paradise. I trust you will forgive my momentary irritability, and continue as my medical attendant.'

"By that time Sinclair's anger had evaporated, and he said no more. And when he did go back next day the valet made no attempt to remain in the room. Even the precautions of the first day were relaxed a little, and he didn't have the impression that he was being marched along under an armed guard. But no time was wasted lingering about the house, and no further mention was made of what was in it.

"This yarn of the doctor's, as I say, was taken by most people to confirm the theory that Granger was frightened of burglars. And one has certainly heard of cases where miserly eccentrics have lived for years surrounded by their treasures, and protected by every sort of mechanical device. But though I said nothing about it at the time the solution didn't quite satisfy me. Even the most suspicious recluse would hardly suspect a respectable medical man of any desire to steal the spoons. So, why these elaborate precautions on the occasion of his visit? Was it eccentricity on Granger's part which was almost akin to insanity: the result of a fear so great that he suspected any and everyone without exception? Or was it something deeper than that; and if so, what?

"Well, I set to work to puzzle it out. The first idea that occurred to me was that he was afraid for his life. That, again, was open to the same objection. You don't expect a doctor to pinch your spoons, but even less do you anticipate that he will murder you. So I dismissed that theory, and tried another. Was there something to conceal in the house which he didn't wish the doctor to see? Remember, the doctor is the only human being, as far as I know, who has ever been in the house from the outside world. I worked along that line for a bit, saying nothing to anybody, and the more I thought of it the more did I become convinced that I was on the right track. Of course, it was possible that he was afraid that the doctor might spot some of the inner secrets of his defences, but again the same darned old objection. If he did he was hardly likely to run round revealing his discovery to bands of burglars. So what was the mystery? If I was right, what was hidden inside? Was it a human being? Possibly, but the idea presented difficulties. Remember, Granger has been there for six years, and, in spite of all his safeguards, it would have been difficult to keep a fourth person in the house for all that time without someone spotting it. And if it wasn't a human being it must be some object. But surely it would have been perfectly simple to hide it away so that the doctor couldn't see it during his quick walk through the house.

"So there I was up against a blank wall once more. And after a while I gave up worrying over the blamed thing; it wasn't worth it. Perhaps someday the mystery, if any, would come out, and in the meantime I, outwardly, at any rate, subscribed to the theory that Mr. Granger was an eccentric old man who did not want to be disturbed, and had taken damned good care that he shouldn't be. Sorry for all this hot air, Peter, but I had to make it clear to you. We will now get on a bit quicker. The morning after I had seen the lights on the Marsh I went out for a stroll to the village. And that meant I had to go past Granger's house. Now don't forget that all my cogitations on his *ménage* had taken place months ago: I had long given up worrying my head about it. So that what happened cannot be fancy or imagination due to my suspicions. About a quarter of a mile before I got to his gates who should I see coming along the road but the man himself and his tame bruiser. Now on the rare occasions when I had met him we had always stopped and had a few words—generally platitudes about the weather. And as usual I halted as I came abreast of him and passed the time of day. He was a bit more affable than usual for some reason: in fact, he even managed to crack a smile over something that I said. And then, for some unknown reason, I mentioned the lights I'd seen on the Marsh. It was just a sudden impulse said without thought.

"Good Lord! Peter, I thought the man had gone mad. He stared at me with dilated eyes, and his lower jaw was shaking like a man with ague. And the pug wasn't much better.

"'Red and blue lights,' he stammered foolishly. 'Red and blue lights.'

"He was croaking in his agitation, and clutching the valet's arm with two trembling hands.

"'Where did you see them, Captain Drummond—these lights?'

"But by that time I'd taken a pull at myself: evidently there was a mystery in the offing, and I wasn't going to be too specific.

"'Somewhere on Romney Marsh,' I said vaguely. 'Why? What's all the excitement about?'

"Red and blue,' he almost screamed to the valet. '*Santa Maria!* Gaspard—it is he.'

"'Shut up,' growled the pug, though his own forehead was wet with sweat.

"But the other was beyond hope: he was in a state of gibbering terror.

"'Back to the house,' he kept on muttering. 'Hurry—for the love of the Virgin.'

"And away the pair of them went down the road with Granger clawing at the valet, and the valet glancing this way and that over his shoulder, as if he expected someone to materialise out of the hedge. For a while I stood staring after them foolishly: the whole thing was so totally unexpected. Then I followed them at a discreet distance, feeling a strong desire to laugh. They looked so damned ridiculous. Granger, as I think I've mentioned, is a little man, and to see him hopping along beside that vast bullock of a valet who every now and then broke into a shambling run had its humorous aspect. They reached their front gate, and while the pug was fumbling with his key to open the wicket Granger kept dancing about in his agitation. Then they disappeared, and I heard an iron bar clang home. The fortress had been reached in safety."

Hugh paused and looked at me with a grin.

"Getting a bit nearer the meat juice, ain't we, Peter? Why should the fact that a red and blue light had been flashed on Romney Marsh inspire terror in the breasts of our Mr. Granger and his pugilistic companion? And no mild form of terror either. For if I'm a judge that man was sick with fear for his life."

"It would seem," I murmured mildly, "that the problem is one which can hardly be solved on paper. And since our wives are at Le Touquet, it might help to pass the agonising time till they rejoin us, if we—"

"Good lad," he laughed. "I knew you would."

"But, look here, Hugh," I said, "has nothing more happened? Have you seen the lights again?"

"Only once—three nights ago."

"And you haven't been down to this place—Spragge's Farm?"

He shook his head.

"I thought I'd wait for you, Peter. It seemed a crime to keep a thing like this to oneself."

"Just one small point, old man," I put in. "What about the police? If your surmise is right: if this man Granger is in fear of his life why hasn't he told the police about it? Or has he? Because if so—"

"He hasn't, Peter," he interrupted. "That I know. The local inspector is a great pal of mine. And since that very objection occurred to me, I made a point of meeting him. I brought the conversation round to

Granger—never a difficult thing to do. And I'm convinced that if he had asked for police protection I should have heard of it. Therefore he hasn't. Why not? Because, laddie, he dare not. That's my answer to it. It's what I have thought all along. There is something that man has got to conceal, and he dare not run the risk of bringing the police in."

"It sounds feasible," I agreed. "Anyway what's the next move?"

"A couple of short ones. Then lunch. And after that we'll lay out a plan of campaign."

He led the way and I followed: thus it had always been in the past.

CHAPTER 2

In Which We Meet Two New Allies

I don't pretend for a moment, of course, that there was the slightest excuse to be offered for us. Manifestly the matter was no business of ours. If Mr. Granger chose to barricade his house with iron spikes it was his affair, and no one else's. Still I regret to say that there are people in this world who are as irresistibly drawn to a thick-ear atmosphere as a cat is to a saucer of milk. And Hugh Drummond was one of them, having been born that way.

In that way he differed from me: I only acquired the liking by force of his example. And I am bound to admit that had I been the one to see a red and blue light flashing on Romney Marsh, and realised that such a harmless, even peculiar phenomenon produced terror in the breast of my next-door neighbour, I should not have proceeded farther with the matter.

Wherefore the difference of our mental attitudes during lunch is easily understandable. Mine was principally concerned with our official position in the matter: his was entirely occupied with whether the thing was likely to produce some sport.

"My dear Peter," he said, as the waiter brought the coffee, "we haven't got any official position in the matter. So that's that, and there's no use worrying about it. But it is manifestly the duty of every law-abiding citizen to investigate such a strange pastime as flashing coloured lights on the Marsh. Maybe it is some new method of catching moths: maybe not. Anyway we're darned well going to see."

"And the first move?" I asked.

"Is to call at Spragge's Farm," he answered.

"We are not to know that his notice about rooms to let has been withdrawn. We will therefore, on the way back, present ourselves at the door, and you will ask if he can put you up. Say that you're suffering from nervous breakdown due to backing three winners in succession, and demand to see what accommodation he has to offer. Then say you'll let him know. We'll both keep our eyes skinned and perhaps we'll see something."

"Right ho!" I said resignedly. "As long as I'm not expected to stop at the bally place, I'll put up the palaver."

We paid the bill, and left the dining-room. Hugh's car was outside the hotel, a Bentley Sports model: and ten minutes later we had dropped down the hill to Sandgate and were running along by the sea towards Hythe.

"From now on, Peter," he said, "until we get actually to Rye itself the ground is dead flat. When we get out a bit further you'll see the range of hills away to the right where my house stands."

It was a hot, lazy afternoon, and the heat haze shimmered over the country which stretched dry and parched on each side of the road. Even the usual breeze which one gets in the locality had died away, and the few cattle we saw were standing listlessly in what shade they could find. The disused red water cistern on Littlestone golf links dropped away behind us, and the Martello Towers ceased as we turned away from the sea after New Romney.

"Dungeness away there to the left," said Hugh briefly. "And Lydd. Now we're on the Marsh proper."

The road was good but narrow, with a deep ditch on each side, and he pointed out the spot to me where a motor charabanc had skidded and overturned one night, pinning the occupants underneath it till they were drowned in six inches of water.

"These grass sides to the road get slippery at times," he explained. "And then you want to watch it."

At length he stopped the car and lit a cigarette.

"Now, Peter," he said, "we approach our destination. That place there in front of us is Rye. Cast your eyes two fingers right and you will see on the hill an imposing red brick edifice. That is the house of Drummond. Straight in front of us you will see a smallish house in a clump of trees: that is Spragge's Farm. One finger to the right of my house, also on the hill, you perceive another house. That is our friend Granger's prison. Now you get the geography of the part that concerns us. And the great point, as you will notice, is that if, as I am tolerably certain, those lights were a warning of some sort, Spragge's Farm is as good a place as any on the Marsh for Granger to see them from."

"Correct," I agreed. "Now what am I really to say to Spragge?"

"Any darned thing you like," he laughed as we started once more. "It's only a preliminary reconnaissance, and we can't expect much luck."

It was fortunate we didn't, because we had none at all. The farm stood about a quarter of a mile from the road, and a rough drive—little more than a stony lane—led up to it. A gate barred the entrance, and leaning over it was a morose looking individual smoking a pipe. He stared at us with scarcely veiled hostility as we pulled up, and made no effort to move.

"This is Spragge's Farm, isn't it?" said Hugh politely.

"It is," grunted the man without removing his pipe from his mouth.

"Do you know if Mr. Spragge is anywhere about?"

"I'm Mr. Spragge. What might you be wanting?"

Hugh's fingers began to drum on the steering wheel, and it wasn't difficult to tell exactly what he was wanting. But to clip a man over the jaw is not conducive to further conversation, and his voice remained studiously mild.

"I was told, Mr. Spragge," he said quietly "that you had a room to let at your farm. My friend here is anxious for a place where he can finish—er—a book undisturbed. If your room is free he would like to see it."

The man removed his pipe, only apparently to enable him to spit with greater ease. Then he stared insolently from one to the other of us.

"You were told wrong," he grunted. "I've no room to let, and if I had I choose who I put up."

"Your choice must be fairly limited I should imagine," remarked Hugh, "if this is a fair sample of your manners. Nice chatty little fellow, aren't you, Mr. Spragge?"

The man straightened himself up, and the veins on his forehead began to stand out like whipcord.

"Look here, you damned dude," he said thickly, "you get out of this before I lose my temper. I speaks how I like, and to whom I like. But unless you're out of this pretty quick, I'll pull you out of your car and little pansy-face beside you as well."

Hugh laughed pleasantly.

"And why should I get out of this, Mr. Spragge? This road is as much mine as yours, and you've no idea what a pretty picture you make leaning against that gate. True, your face leaves much to be desired, and your clothes are deplorable, but the general picture—the *tout ensemble*—of the Englishman guarding his home is quite wonderful. Don't you agree, Peter?"

I glanced at him out of the corner of my eye, and saw the old well-remembered look on his face. He was deliberately goading the man on, though for what purpose I couldn't quite make out. This man Spragge was a powerful looking brute, and I failed to see any object in starting a rough house. And that was exactly what seemed imminent. With a flood of blasphemy the farmer flung open the gate, and slouched over to the car; and as he came Hugh opened the door and stepped into the road.

"You" snarled Spragge. "I've warned you once: now you can have it."

I almost laughed: how many men had said words to that effect in days gone by? And with the same result. Spragge shot out a fist like a leg of mutton, which encountered air, and the next instant he was lying flat on his back in the middle of the road, completely knocked out.

"Quick, Peter," said Hugh urgently. "Sling the blighter into the back of the car, and we'll take him to the farm. Heaven forbid, old man," he chuckled as the Bentley spun up the track, "that we should be so grossly inhuman as to leave this poor injured fellow lying in the road. His wife's tender care is essential, and—keep your eyes skinned. We might spot something."

We pulled up at the door, and almost immediately a woman appeared. She was a worthy helpmeet to Mr. Spragge: in fact I have seldom seen a more forbidding looking pair. Tall and gaunt, with a thin saturnine face and bony hands, she looked an even more unpleasant customer than her husband. He was a powerful, foul tempered brute: she looked the personification of evil.

"What has happened?" she asked harshly.

"Mrs. Spragge, I assume?" remarked Hugh politely. "I regret to state that your husband's jaw has encountered a hard substance, which has temporarily rendered him unconscious. So, my friend and I, at great personal inconvenience, have brought him to the dear old homestead. Shall we bring him in?"

Spragge was already beginning to stir uneasily, so there was no time to be lost if we were to get inside the house.

"I don't understand," she said angrily. "What has happened to the fool?"

"Far be it from me, madam," murmured Hugh, "to cavil at the excellent description of your spouse. But he will doubtless tell you all about it when he is his own bright self again."

We had slung him out of the car and laid him on the grass, and as Hugh spoke I suddenly became aware of a noise that rose and fell regularly. It came from the inside of the house, and at that moment, Hugh evidently heard it too. He grinned faintly, and looked at the woman.

"How nice it is to have a little peaceful nap in the afternoon," he murmured. "But you should never take in a lodger that snores, Mrs. Spragge."

"Get out of this," came a thick voice from behind us. Spragge, who had come to, had raised himself on his elbow, and was glaring vindictively.

"Splendid," cried Hugh. "Our own bright boy again. A little *arnica* applied by mother, and the face will be as good as new. But tell me, who is the human fog-horn within?"

"Look here, mister," cried the woman shrilly, "you be off. This farm ain't no business of yours, and I'll thank you to get into your car and clear out."

"The ingratitude of woman," said Hugh resignedly. "After all I've done for poor Mr. Spragge too. Well, Peter, never shall it be said that we stayed where we weren't wanted. We'll go. But do tell little Ferdinand when he wakes that he ought not to sleep on his back."

He swung the car round, and as we went down the drive I glanced back. The man had scrambled to his feet, and was standing by his wife. And the two of them stood there motionless watching us, until we turned out of the drive into the main road.

"Not much out of that, Peter, I'm afraid," said Hugh. "All that we have established is that the Spragges are a very unsavoury pair, and that they have a man who snores staying in the house. But whether the man who snores is the red and blue light merchant, or whether it is any of them, Heaven alone knows. And as far as I can see there is only one way to find out."

"Which is?" I asked.

"To go there by night," he answered.

"That's when the activity is likely to occur. And I've somehow or other got a hunch that our musical sleeper is going to turn out to be very much in the picture. Let's go back to the house now, so that you can dump your kit: then we'll have dinner at the Dolphin in Rye, and do a bit of night work after. Jove! Peter, I'm beginning to feel quite young again."

"You'll be younger before you've finished," I said resignedly. "They tell me a few months in prison is a wonderful rejuvenator."

But he only grinned; in an affair of this sort he was beyond hope.

"Prison be blowed, old boy. We may be a pair of thugs, but we are young men from the Christian Association compared to this comic bunch. Besides, we can always retire from the contest if we want to."

At that it was my turn to grin: a lion can retire from its kill if it wants to. At any rate time would show: up to date beyond putting Mr. Spragge to sleep we were blameless.

The Bentley swung to the left as we came to Rye, and we took the circular road around the hill on which the town is built.

"Up that cobbled road to the right, Peter," said Hugh when we had gone halfway round, "is the Dolphin Inn. A famed resort for smugglers in the old days, and an extraordinarily good pub now. On your left is the road to Hastings, but we go straight on up to the higher ground."

We crossed the railway line, and another three miles brought us to Hugh's house, where I dropped my baggage. As he said, the view over the Marsh was wonderful: it lay spread out in front of us like an aeroplane photograph.

"If you look through the telescope," he remarked, "you'll see it is focussed on Spragge's Farm."

I adjusted the eyepiece and found that I could make out every detail of the house. Almost could I see the handle on the front door so powerful was the instrument. But though I kept my eye glued to it for fully five minutes I saw no sign of life. The place was deserted: presumably Mr. Spragge was dealing with the *arnica*, and the mysterious sleeper still snored.

"When you're ready, Peter," he said, after, he had had a look himself, "we might stroll along past friend Granger's place. I'd like you to cast an eye on his preparations."

I was ready, and so we once more took the road. A short ten minutes' walk brought us to our destination, and assuredly Hugh had not exaggerated when he called it a prison. The wall was about ten feet high, and constituted a fairly formidable obstacle in itself. But what made it practically impassable was the arrangement of steel spikes on the top. They faced in all directions: and each one was about two feet long. There was no gap anywhere: they continued over the massive wooden gates that formed the entrance. And by standing away from the wall I could see the top story of the house inside: every window was guarded with iron bars as Hugh had said.

"The gentleman certainly seems to resent intrusion," I remarked, and even as I spoke a small two-seater went past us and stopped outside the gates. A young man was driving it, and by his side was an extremely pretty girl. For a time they sat in the car looking somewhat dubiously at the prospect confronting them: then they both turned round and looked at us. And after a moment or two the man got out and came over to us. He was a cheerful looking youngster with a snub nose and freckles, and when he spoke he had a perfectly charming smile.

"Excuse me," he said, "but is either of you Mr. Granger?"

"Not guilty," remarked Hugh. "The gentleman you're after is inside the fortifications."

"I say," he went on a bit awkwardly, "you'll understand I don't want to be rude, or any tripe of that sort, but what kind of a bird is he?"

"Why do you ask?" said Hugh.

"Well—er—the lady with me has taken on a secretarial job with Mr. Granger. And dash it all, this bally place looks like an inebriates' home."

"It's not that as far as I know," said Hugh. "But frankly I shouldn't call it the sort of household that I'd like a girl I knew to go to."

"You hear that, Pat," he sung out. "This gentleman thinks the show is a dud."

The girl got out of the car and came and joined us. Though usually of an unobservant nature, I noticed that there was a ring on her engagement finger, and with the acumen of Sherlock Holmes I arrived at what turned out to be the correct solution.

"Can't help that, Freckles," she said calmly. "Dud or no dud, I've had fifty of the best out of the old bean and that's that."

"You could send the money back," he said doubtfully.

"Easily, little bright-eyes," she laughed, "if I had it to send. Unfortunately all that remains is twelve shillings and fourpence halfpenny."

"That's a bit of a snag," he admitted. "But look here, Pat, I don't like the smell of this place at all."

"Nor do I," she agreed frankly. "But what can I do?"

"Can you tell me anything about this gentleman, sir?"

He turned again to Hugh with a worried look on his face.

"Practically nothing, I'm afraid," said Hugh. "He came here some years ago, and had all these affairs erected round the house. He calls nowhere and sees no one, and the only other occupants of the house are a man and his wife."

"There is a woman there then. That's good."

The youngster looked vaguely relieved.

"But may I ask exactly how you came to hear of this job?" said Hugh to the girl.

"Quite easily," she smiled. "I had my name down at a bureau in London for secretarial work. Ten days ago I went in to find if anything was doing, and the woman who runs it offered me this. It might have been anybody else, only I happened to be the first. And the terms were so very good that I jumped at it. Five pounds a week, and fifty on account."

"Ten days ago," said Hugh thoughtfully, glancing at me, and it was clear what he was thinking. If this girl had only heard of it then the offer must have been made before the appearance of the lights on the Marsh.

"Have you any idea what your work is to be?" went on Hugh.

"Not the slightest," she answered. "Presumably an ordinary secretarial job."

Once again Hugh glanced at me: then he lit a cigarette.

"Well, as I told this gentleman," he remarked, "it's not the sort of house I'd choose for a rest cure. But I may be wrong: I've never been inside myself. Only there is one thing you ought to know."

And then very briefly he told her about the mysterious signals from Spragge's Farm. She listened in silence, but the result was a foregone conclusion. Her mind was made up, though Freckles did his best to dissuade her.

"Can't you possibly chuck it, Pat?" he said earnestly.

"How can I, you mutt?" laughed the girl. "I tell you I've spent the fifty quid."

"And I'm overdrawn," he muttered. "Hell!"

"Look here," began Hugh and I simultaneously.

The girl gave us both a delicious smile.

"Sweet of you both," she said. "I know just what you were going to say. But I couldn't dream of it. After all this old bird can't eat me. I shall be all right, Tom: don't you worry."

"But I *do* worry," answered the youth. "So would anybody who saw what sort of a house it was."

"Go and press the bell, my pet," she said firmly. "It's little Patricia for the shore. Go on, you ass: we can't stand here in the road all day."

He went over reluctantly and did as he was told, and suddenly Hugh spoke.

"Look here, Miss?"

"Verney," said the girl.

"Mine is Drummond: and this is Peter Darrell. What I was going to say was this. My house is the next one to this—about half a mile away towards Rye. Now everything may be quite O.K., but in case— only in case, mind you— it isn't, it will help you to know that we're near at hand. So one or other of us will make a point of being here between two and three each day. Of course it's quite on the cards that you'll be able to take a walk: in fact, if I were you I'd insist on it. Then if anything crops up you can come and tell us. But if by any chance he keeps you inside or makes you stop in the garden, and you want to get at us, just write a note, put it in an envelope with half a brick inside and bung it over the wall. You can spot the place—close by the gate, and we'll be here to get it."

"Thanks most awfully," said the girl gratefully, "though I'm quite certain it won't be necessary. Oh! my goodness, what an awful looking man!"

The peephole in the gate had opened suddenly, and staring through it was the man who I placed at once as the pugilistic servant. He was certainly not a prepossessing sight as his narrow eyes took us in in turn, and the girl's exclamation was very natural. Suspicion was in every line of his face, and it was not until he saw Hugh that his expression cleared.

"This lady," said Hugh, "has come to do secretarial work for Mr. Granger. Presumably you are expecting her."

The man made no reply, but stared up and down the road. Then at last we heard an iron bar clang and the gate opened just sufficiently to let him through.

"Come quickly," he said in a harsh voice. "Mr. Granger expects you, but we had forgotten your coming."

"My trunk is in the car," said the girl. "Get it, please. Don't touch the typewriter: I will carry that myself."

"Pat: I don't like it." Freckles made one final, despairing attempt. "Can't you possibly get out of it?"

"I can't say that I like it very much myself, Tom," she said quietly, "but I'm going through with it for all that."

The man, with the trunk on his shoulder, stood in the open gateway beckoning to her urgently.

"So long, old son," she said with a smile. And then turning to Hugh she held out her hand. "Between two and three: I'll remember."

She took her machine out of the car, and the iron bar clanged to inside.

"Damn it," began Freckles, "she oughtn't to have gone. She—"

He paused suddenly, and at the same time I felt the flesh at the back of my scalp begin to tingle. For from inside the wall there came the deep-noted baying of a hound. It rose and fell, in a snarling roar of incredible ferocity: then as suddenly as it had begun it ceased, and only the faint noise of rattling bars could be heard.

I looked at the boy: he was as white as a sheet. And the next moment he had sprung forward and was pounding with his fists on the gate.

"Pat," he shouted, "Pat. Are you all right?"

Came her answer, faint and a little tremulous.

"It's all right, Tom. It's locked up."

For a while we stood there looking at one another, whilst the colour slowly came back to his cheeks.

"By Jove! that gave me a shock," he said at length. "I ought never to have let her take this filthy job," he added savagely.

On Hugh Drummond's face there appeared his habitual cheery smile.

"My dear fellow," he cried, "from the little I know of the adorable sex, the question, as they say in Parliament, did not arise. Miss Verney had determined to take the job, and that was that. Don't you worry: we'll look after her."

"I suppose you're right," said Freckles gloomily. "Anyway, I'm going to put up at the pub here till I'm certain she's all right."

For a moment Hugh hesitated, and I could see he was summing the boy up.

"Look here," he said after a while, "don't bother about a pub. Come and put up with me."

"Do you really mean it?" He stared at Hugh doubtfully. "I mean—dash it—you hardly know me. You don't even know my name."

"I'll trust you not to steal the spoons," laughed Hugh. "But it would be an advantage to know your name."

"Scott," said Freckles. "Tom Scott. And it's really most awfully good of you. I'd love to stay with you if you don't mind."

"Shouldn't have asked you if I did," said Hugh. "Let's get into that bus of yours and push back to the house."

"It may take a bit of time to start her," said the proud owner. "I picked her up cheap."

At the end of five minutes his prophecy had proved correct. Acting under instructions, I had pulled out a wire and received a severe electric shock: Hugh had stamped on a button, causing a loud explosion and a discharge of grey smoke through the radiator. But finally she commenced to fire on at least two of the four cylinders and we started, the driver's face wreathed in a complacent smile.

"The steering is a bit dicky," he explained as we missed a milestone by an inch. "Wants knowing. Nearly took a tramcar coming over Vauxhall Bridge this morning."

"Do you mean to say," gasped Hugh, who was precariously clutching at the sides of the dickey, "that you drove this abom—this affair out of London?"

"Rather," said Freckles. "Why not?"

"To the left here," muttered Hugh feebly. "And for God's sake don't kill the cat. She has maternal duties to perform at the moment."

A frightful crash occurred in the bowels of the machine, and we came to a halt.

"When the brakes don't act, I put her into reverse," explained Freckles, and Hugh nodded weakly.

"I no longer have any fears for Miss Verney," he remarked. "Her perils at present are as nothing to driving out of London in this machine. However, young fellow, we'll have it pushed round to the garage and then we must have a little talk. Because there are one or two things you've got to get into your head."

He led the way into the house, and we followed him.

"I'll show you your room afterwards," he said to Scott. "But after that motor drive I want a nerve tonic. Help yourselves, you fellows: it's all on the sideboard."

We took our drinks outside and sat down.

"Now I suppose I'm right," began Hugh, "in assuming that you are responsible for the ring on Miss Verney's finger?"

"That's so," said Freckles with a grin. "We fixed it a month ago, but since neither of us has a bean the outlook is a bit grim."

"You've got plenty of time before you," laughed Hugh. "However, just at the moment we'll leave your matrimonial prospects. You heard what I said to your fiancée about those lights on the Marsh, didn't you?"

"Rather," cried the boy. "What's the game do you think?"

"That," said Hugh, "is exactly what Darrell and I had decided to find out. We still propose to find out, but now you and Miss Verney have come into the picture."

"I wish to heaven she hadn't," said Scott gloomily.

"If she hadn't you wouldn't have either," remarked Hugh. "And we shouldn't be sitting here drinking a whisky and soda and having this talk. But she did and there's no more to be said about it. Now let me say at once that I do not believe she is in any danger, so you can set your mind at rest over that. But I do believe that she's in a house where some pretty funny doings are going to happen in the near future. It's obvious that her boss is terrified to death of something, though what that something is we know no more than you. But we propose to have a dip at finding out tonight."

"How?" cried Scott eagerly.

"I don't know whether you heard me mention Spragge's Farm. If you look through that telescope you'll find that it is focussed on it. And that is the house from which the lights have come. It therefore looks as if there was a connection between it and Mr. Granger's terror, which has only arisen since the signal was given. This afternoon Peter and I, by a little subterfuge, got as far as the front door, but we couldn't get any farther. However, it was enough to prove that there is someone else in the house beside Spragge and his wife, because we heard the blighter snoring. Tonight we propose to investigate again, and you can come too if you like."

"If I like," cried Freckles joyfully. "Lead me to it."

"But on one condition," said Hugh quietly. "There seems to me to be every prospect of a bit of fun, and fun is too hard to come by to run any risk of having it spoiled. If you come in with us, Scott, you have got to do as you are told. No fancy tricks of your own or anything of that sort—do you get me?"

"Absolutely," answered the other. "I'll do just what you say."

"Good," said Hugh. "Now come here, and let me feel your muscle. Not too bad. Got it cranking that infernal contrivance of yours, I suppose. Anyway, don't forget the golden rule—if you've got to hit, hit first."

"I say you really are a priceless pair," said Freckles ecstatically.

"We may get a bit of sport," said Hugh casually, and then his eyes narrowed suddenly. "Isn't that a car, at the turn-off to Spragge's Farm?"

He went to the telescope and focussed it.

"A big yellow one, Peter," he said. "There's a woman in the driver's seat with a man beside her. And leaning over the gate talking to them is our Mr. Spragge himself unless I'm much mistaken. Now I wonder if they've got anything to do with it. Hullo! They are turning round, and going back towards Rye. Going like hell into the bargain. Come on, let's hit the Bentley. We might spot something."

"A Bentley," sighed Freckles. "Indeed and in truth the Lord is good. And incidentally, Drummond, if it's any good to you at any time, I'm used to driving the breed."

"Good," said Hugh. "It may come in handy."

We fell into the car, and he let her out. He drove, as he did everything else, magnificently, and in four minutes we struck the top of the hill leading down to Rye. Now as I say, Hugh had trodden on the juice, and yet, roaring up the hill towards us was a big yellow car driven by a woman with a man sitting beside her. And another in the back seat. I had a fleeting glimpse of a beautiful, rather scornful face bending over the wheel, and a man with a small pointed beard sitting beside her: then they had flashed past.

"See which way they go, Peter," sang out Hugh, braking hard.

"They've turned off towards your house," I said.

"And towards Granger's," he answered, swinging into the entrance of a house to turn. "By George! They must have travelled."

"An Isotto straight twelve," remarked Freckles casually. "But you've got the legs of them in this. Oh! If Mother only knew what her baby boy was doing instead of sitting in Prodom and Peanut's office, the old girl would pass right out."

"You are a reprehensible young devil," chuckled Hugh as we started up the hill again. "But the girl at the wheel, Peter, was undoubtedly a pippin of the first order."

And as from a great distance I heard the voices of two adorable ladies in the Hermitage at Le Touquet wondering how the dear lambs were enjoying their golf.

We swung past the entrance to Hugh's house, and then he slackened speed a little.

"No good looking as if we were racing them," he said. "And if they've got anything to do with it By Jove! Peter, they have."

The yellow car had stopped at the entrance to Granger's house. The occupants were still sitting in it, and were apparently studying the place. But as we passed they all three stared at us.

"Don't look round," said Hugh quietly. "Though I'm afraid we've committed a tactical bloomer. Do you think they spotted us as the car they met on the hill?"

"The chauffeur bloke at the back did," said Freckles.

"Damn!" said Hugh. "However it is done now. We'll go back to Rye by another route. Now I wonder where that bunch come into the picture. In fact, I wonder the hell of a lot of things."

Chapter 3

In Which We Come to Spragge's Farm By Night

The Dolphin Inn at Rye is almost too well known to need description. It stands halfway up a steep cobbled hill in the centre of the town, and to its hospitable doors come all sorts and conditions of men. Tourists, artists, golfers—all may be found there—discussing everything from the history of the Cinque Ports to the Putt that Failed on the Last Green. Of old, when the sea lapped round the foothills of Rye, and in later years too, it was a well-known haunt of smugglers, as Hugh had said. Many a cask of old brandy, many a roll of silk had come in through the front door, which the most drastic search by preventive men had failed to reveal. There were stories told of secret passages, and sliding panels by means of which the Excise men were outwitted; but in the present year of grace the only sliding panel in evidence is the one through which the barman hands out the necessary.

It was half-past six when we entered the lounge hall, having left the car at the bottom of the hill. Two old ladies were sitting in one corner immersed in guide books, whilst another was occupied by an elderly clergyman. There was plenty of room for us, but Hugh went straight through to a small room which led off the main hall.

"The only untouched part of the hotel," he remarked. "This room is as it was when the place was built."

Nearly the whole of one end of it was occupied by a huge fireplace, in which as the guide book put it, *"it was the custom on special occasions to roast an ox whole."* The special occasions presumably were when a particularly good haul of contraband had successfully eluded the coastguard men. On each side of the fireplace the wall consisted of a sort of scroll-work, long since blackened by the smoke. The shelves were filled with pewter—some valuable, but for the most part modern stuff. And perhaps the most interesting thing in the room was an old map worked in embroidery, showing the country in 1723. Even as late as that the sea was very nearly up to the outskirts of Rye, and almost the whole of Romney Marsh was covered with water.

"Looks a bit different, doesn't it?" said Hugh, studying it idly. "Where we dotted old man Spragge one this afternoon was a bally lake. There's where his farm is, Scott," he went on. "And that is our destination tonight. By Jove!" he added with sudden interest, "That must be Granger's house. I'd no idea it was so old. A convent: that accounts for the wall round it."

"Naughty girls—the nuns," said Freckles. "Do you know the story. . . .?"

But we never heard this bright particular gem, because at that moment two men came in, one of whom hailed Hugh with a shout of joy. He wore a Guards tie, and his face seemed vaguely familiar to me.

"You old blighter," he cried. "Fancy meeting you here."

"Hullo! John James," said Hugh. "How's yourself? You know Darrell, don't you?"

"I met you once in the pavilion at Lord's," cried the newcomer, and then I placed him. He was whisky or beer or something, and rolled in money. Sir John Jameson, Bart., was his name, and he had recently come into the title. Moreover he had a big place somewhere in Kent.

"This is Scott," went on Hugh. "Sir John Jameson."

"This undoubtedly calls for a drop of the old and bold," said John James. "By the way, this is Piggy Heythrop, who suffers from the delusion that he can beat me at golf. Waiter—five martinis. Well, old lad—what are you doing down here?"

"I've rented a house for the summer called Bay Trees. Principally because there isn't one."

"The devil you have," cried the other. "Why, man, that house used to belong to my governor. And the one next door as well. Look here, Hugh, we've got back to Laidley Towers: you and your lady wife must come over and stop."

"Hold hard a moment, John," said Hugh. "You say the next-door house used to belong to you. Which one do you mean?"

"Temple Tower. Used to be a convent. The old man sold 'em both about twenty years ago. Personally I was rather sorry about Temple Tower. It's got a very interesting history. I wonder who has it now."

"A very eccentric individual," said Hugh. "By name of Granger. He's barricaded the place like a prison: put two-foot spikes round the top of the wall, and bars on every window. He's got a menagerie in the garden, and any caller is examined through a hole in the gate before he is let in. It would take a cross between a monkey and a mongoose all its time to get in, let alone a human being."

John James stared at him thoughtfully.

"What an extraordinary bloke," he remarked. "Doesn't sound as if he was all there. Still I bet I'd penetrate the fastness: once, that is, I'd negotiated the wall."

"What do you mean? "said Hugh sitting up with a jerk,

"I told you the place had belonged to us," said the other. "Well—it used to be a convent."

"I know that," said Hugh. "Just seen it marked on the map."

"And the nuns, bless 'em, though forbidden to receive male visitors through the front door got away with the goods through the back. There's an underground passage leading from an old crypt in the garden which runs into one of the cellars."

"Are you certain?" cried Hugh.

"Of course I am, old boy. Mr. Monk, having said his little piece in the crypt, toddled along the passage to pay his respects to the lady of his choice in the house. Why, we've got an old plan of it hanging up in the hall at Laidley Towers."

"Have you ever been along this passage, John?" demanded Hugh.

"Can't say I have," admitted the other. "As a matter of fact, it's not quite as plain sailing as it sounds. You see. . . ."

"How much did you beat him by?" said Hugh suddenly, "We must have a game one day, John."

"What's that?" stammered the bewildered baronet. "I—er. . . ."

"How are the links playing, John? Must be a bit dry, I suppose."

And it was then I became aware that someone else had entered the room. It was the bearded man who had been sitting by the girl in the car. Hugh went on calmly talking golf: John James, though still looking slightly dazed, followed his lead, until Heythrop, happening to look at his watch, gave a startled exclamation.

"Good Lord! John—it's nearly half-past seven."

"The devil it is," cried the other. "We must go, Hugh. Got the most ghastly collection of county bores dining. Look here—I'll come over and see you tomorrow sometime."

"Splendid," said Hugh. "We might have a four ball."

He followed them into the hall, and under cover of some desultory conversation with young Scott I took stock of the bearded gentleman. He was a good-looking man of his type, but the type was not one that appealed to me. His features were aquiline: his mouth full and red under the carefully trimmed beard. His clothes were perfect—rather too perfect, and though they carried the unmistakable stamp of an English tailor, in some strange way they served to accentuate the fact that the man who wore them was not an Englishman. His hands were beautifully kept: his pearl tie-pin was a little too ostentatious. In fact, the man was overdressed: he didn't fit into the picture. He gave the impression of the exquisite hero in musical comedy.

He looked up suddenly, and found my eyes were fixed on him.

"A very interesting part of your country," he said suavely.

"Most," I answered shortly, feeling a little annoyed at having been discovered staring at him.

"And this inn certainly belies the terrible reputation enjoyed by your country hotels abroad," he went on politely.

"A reputation which I fear is thoroughly deserved," I answered as affably as I could. After all, there was no good showing my feelings, though I found myself disliking his voice even more than his appearance. It was oily and sleek—if a voice can be sleek: and underlying it was another quality which for the moment I could not spot. Then I got it—it was cruelty: I could imagine the man opening his flat gold cigarette case, and extracting one with the utmost deliberation, just in order to keep his victim on the rack a little longer so that he might gloat over him.

We talked on casually, and all the time I was wondering what nationality he was. Italian possibly, though his English was faultless. The girl, in the two quick glimpses I had had of her might well have been Italian. And what was their relationship to one another? I knew that he was studying me also, though our conversation was confined to banalities: studying young Scott too with his heavy lidded eyes.

"Golf," he was saying, "is a game which I unfortunately have never had the opportunity to master."

"Master!" broke in Freckles with a laugh. "You're in the same boat as a good many other people."

"So I believe," he said politely. "And yet it seems to the outsider that it should not be hard to hit a stationary ball with some degree of precision. Dear me—what's that?"

From outside had come a sudden crash, followed by a loud "Damnation," in Hugh's voice. I rose at once, followed by Scott, and went into the hall. Standing outside the door was Hugh staring upwards; at his feet, smashed to pieces on the cobble, was a heavy chimney-pot.

"Confound it," he exploded when he saw me, "this cursed thing only missed me by about a foot."

Attracted by the noise the boots had appeared, and two or three of the guests were staring out of the window.

"Very sorry, sir, I'm sure," said Boots scratching his head. "Such a thing ain't never happened before, not to my knowledge."

"And if it happens again somebody is going to get a thick ear," said Hugh grimly. He was still staring upwards and his mouth was set in a hard line. Then with a little shrug of his shoulders he entered the hotel.

"I must apologise for my language," he said with a smile to the clergyman.

"My dear sir," said the cleric benignly, "a mild expletive is surely permissible under the circumstances. Why, if that heavy thing had hit you on the head it might have stunned you."

Hugh gave a short laugh.

"As you say, it might have stunned me," he agreed. "But it didn't. I am going to wash, Peter, and then we might have some dinner."

We followed him to the lavatory, and he carefully closed the door.

"Ever heard of a chimney-pot falling on a dead calm day?" he said quietly.

"What do you mean?" said Freckles looking startled.

"I strolled down to the bottom of the hill to see John off," went on Hugh. "And also to put him wise to one or two things. Then I came back, and was standing outside the door lighting a cigarette. A sitting target, though I must say it never dawned on me that anything of that sort was likely to happen. But luckily the blighter missed."

"You think someone pushed the thing over deliberately?" cried Freckles.

"I don't think: I know. I saw his shadow move."

"Then why not go and have a look-see," said the boy.

"Because the shadow will have moved a considerable distance by now," answered Hugh dryly. "In other words we'd find nothing, and merely make ourselves look fools. But don't be under any delusions, you fellows: that was a deliberate attempt by someone to lay me out."

"It can't have been the bearded gentleman," I said. "He's been talking to us ever since you left."

"I don't know who it was," said Hugh drying his hands, "But if he, or they, are prepared to go to the length of attempted murder it proves one thing at any rate. We're up against a pretty tough lot. It's all right, young fellow," he went on as Scott's face fell. "This bunch is outside the garden wall: your girl is inside."

But to me privately as we went out, leaving Freckles to the basin, he was not so optimistic.

"We were fools, Peter," he said. "We ought never to have allowed that girl to go inside that house. I'm not frightened of anything happening to her now: what I am afraid of is what is going to take place if this lot, whoever they are, do get inside."

"You think that's the game?" I asked.

"Granger is the game," he said. "And if the mountain won't go to Mohammed, Mohammed must go to the mountain. Granger has gone to ground in his house, and nothing short of an earthquake is going to get him out. Therefore to get him, they've got to get into the house. *Voila tout.*"

"We might send her a letter telling her to leave," I suggested.

He shrugged his shoulders.

"From what I saw of the girl," he laughed, "I think she'd tell us to go to blazes."

Young Scott joined us and we went in to dinner. And though Hugh deliberately kept the conversation on outside topics, I couldn't keep my mind off the problem that confronted us. The whole thing seemed so utterly disconnected: that was the trouble. What link bound the bearded man and his companions with the snorer at Spragge's Farm? What was the signification of the red and blue lights? Above all, if Hugh was right, and he was not a man who made mistakes on matters of that sort, who was it who had deliberately tried to lay him out with the chimneypot? And why?

The bearded man was eliminated, which left of those we knew the girl and the chauffeur. But even granted it was one of them the second question remained unanswered. Why? Even if we had aroused their suspicions by going back on our tracks in the car, their return for it seemed a little drastic.

Another alternative came into my mind: supposing it wasn't them at all? Supposing we had struck some completely new factor in the situation? Again came the same unanswerable question. Why? What had we done—or rather what had Hugh done—to give any possible reason for trying to kill him? The only person who could legitimately feel that way was Spragge, and it seemed well nigh incredible that that worthy should have secreted himself on the roof on the bare chance of laying him out.

From Spragge my thoughts turned to the snorer. He was a possibility. True he hadn't seen us as far as we knew, but Hugh was an easy man to describe. Supposing Spragge had told him what had happened in the afternoon: supposing the man was a criminal and thought detectives were after him, and had determined to try to get rid of them? . . . And then I gave it up: it was obvious that that solution wouldn't hold water. Genuine detectives don't go about the country in racing

Bentleys slogging people over the jaw. And further he had no possible means of knowing that we were going to be at the Dolphin.

We were halfway through dinner when the bearded man and the girl entered. She swept past us as if the whole of Rye belonged to her, but her companion paused by our table and nodded to me.

"I must congratulate you, sir," he said turning to Hugh, "on your narrow escape. I was talking to your friends at the time, and the crash was terrific."

"Thank you very much," said Hugh gravely. "It's the worst of these old houses: anything might happen."

"Precisely: anything might happen," agreed the other, and with a bow he passed on to his table.

"Unless I am much mistaken," said Hugh thoughtfully, "the time is coming in the very near future when that gentleman's face will disappear through the back of his skull. He is the type of mess I like not: moreover he is undoubtedly one of the players. So here's to hoping."

We finished our dinner in silence, and it was not until the coffee came that any further allusion was made to the subject. Hugh, I could tell, was trying to puzzle things out in his own mind as I had done, and Freckles—the confounded young scoundrel—couldn't keep his eyes off the girl.

"What's the plan of campaign, Hugh, for tonight?" I asked, after the waiter had left us.

"I've been thinking over it, Peter," he answered, "and I've come to the conclusion that the safest way of tackling it if we want to find out anything, will be to approach the house from the other side—that is from the sea. I figure it out this way. We are obviously under suspicion: it is known that we are taking an interest in Spragge's Farm, in that swab over there all covered with hair, in Granger's house—in fact, in the whole outfit. If, as is more than likely, we are all three seen leaving Rye in the Bentley and taking the road towards Spragge's Farm, the betting is a fiver to a dried pea that we shall be followed. We'll have to leave the car in the road, and that gives us away completely. So my suggestion is this. There is a road—it's pretty bad, but it will serve—that runs past the golf links and goes down to the sea. True we still have to leave Rye in the direction of the farm, but as long as they don't find the car in the road it doesn't matter. In fact it's rather to the good; it may help to put 'em off the scent if they think we've gone on towards Folkestone. So we'll leave the car on the sea road, which incidentally peters out into nothing, strike inland on foot, and approach Spragge's Farm from the rear. And after that, it's on the lap of the gods. Ever done any night work, young Scott?"

"What sort of night work?" demanded Freckles.

"Moving about country at night, of course."

"Can't say I have," admitted the youngster.

"Well, keep close to me, and do exactly as you are told," said Hugh. "And pay attention to where you put your clumsy great feet. We'll want silence, and don't forget it."

"Do you think there is a chance of a scrap?" he asked eagerly.

"I haven't the faintest idea," said Hugh. "But I want to avoid one if possible. We want to find out all we can, and not be discovered doing so."

"What time do you suggest starting?" I asked him.

"Let's see," he calculated. "It will be a good hour's walk—perhaps more. Allowing for the car journey—say an hour and a half. So if we leave here as soon as we've finished dinner, we ought to strike the farm about eleven thirty."

He finished his coffee and got up. And for the first time to my knowledge the girl showed herself aware of our existence. Her glance rested on Hugh—coolly and thoughtfully: then I was honoured and after that young Scott. Then she returned to her dinner as if we had been summed up and dismissed, for all the world like a man turning down three horses that had been brought out for his inspection. I said as much to Hugh as we left the coffee-room, and he smiled slightly.

"Bless her heart," he laughed. "I wonder if it was she who tried to anoint my head with the chimneypot. Incidentally, I wonder what their names are. Presumably they are staying here since she has changed for dinner."

We opened the hotel register, and looked at the last three entries.

Paul Vandali.

Madame Vandali.

Jean Picot.

"H'm," grunted Hugh. "If the names are genuine, they mark the chauffeur down as French, and the other two as Southerners of sorts. Possibly Italian. However, we shall doubtless find out in time. Now you fellows, smoke if you want to, because once we start walking it will be a case of no lights."

We strolled down the hill, and I noticed that Hugh was glancing from side to side. But the road seemed deserted, and we got into the car without having seen a soul.

"One hour at this time of night ought to be enough to make Folkestone," he said as we got in.

"Did you see him, Peter?" he asked me as we drove off.

"Not a sign," I said surprised. "Where was he?"

"In the shadow of that big warehouse place. Mr. Jean Picot for a tozzy. I couldn't make out his face, but there was someone there crouching against the wall."

"Then let's hope you put him off," I remarked.

The night was a perfect one for our purpose. Already dark, it would be darker still, as the moon was not due to rise till three o'clock. A faint breeze was blowing, and in the distance the light of a signal gleamed like a great red star. For the first half mile the road ran dead straight: then came a T bend. To the left lay the road to Folkestone and to the proper entrance to Spragge's Farm: to the right lay our route to the sea. And so it was with some surprise, after what he had said at dinner, that I found Hugh swing left-handed when we got there.

"There are no flies on those birds," he said briefly. "And on these marshes you can see the headlights of a car for miles."

He drove on for perhaps another mile until he came to a small track leading off the road. Then he switched off the headlights, and turned the car.

"I'm taking no chances, Peter," he said as we drove slowly back with only the small side lamps alight. "We're up against brains this trip."

We got back to the bend without having met anyone, and took our proper road. He was still driving without headlights and so our progress was slow. Gradually the road got worse and worse, until the murmur of the sea on the shore to our right told us we had struck the coast. To our left lay the sand dunes, and Hugh continually peered in that direction as if looking for some landmark .

"There's a path somewhere about here which leads a little way into the dunes," he explained. "It will give us a bit of cover for the bus. Here it is."

We swung along it, and after going about twenty yards he pulled up. The car was almost hidden from the road: certainly at night no one passing along would be likely to spot it. And there we left it, and struck inland on foot, Hugh leading. At first the going was bad: the low sandhills so beloved of golfers exercise no attraction for the mere pedestrian. But after a while it got better, and the loose-shifting soil gave place to firm reclaimed ground.

We walked in silence; only the harsh cry of a stray night bird broke the stillness of the night. In the distance the lights of Rye glittered from the hill: in front of us darkness save for an occasional gleam from some cottage.

Suddenly Hugh paused, and we came up with him. He was standing on the edge of a dyke—one of the many which intersect the Marsh in all directions. But for some reason or other this one seemed to interest him.

"I've never seen one so broad," he explained. "This is more like a miniature canal. However, it seems to be leading in the right direction. We may as well follow it up."

We walked on once more, sticking to the bank, until once again he paused, this time with a low whistle of surprise. A boat was in the water completely covered with a tarpaulin, and even in the darkness it was easy to see that it was no ordinary row-boat. He scrambled down, and lifted up the covering: then he came up and joined us again.

"A motor-boat and a powerful one," he said thoughtfully. "Now I wonder if that is also part of the jigsaw. Or is it just a perfectly harmless machine belonging to some perfectly harmless individual?"

"Useful for smuggling," I suggested.

"Quite," he answered. "Or as a line of escape. Do you notice, Peter, that the dyke narrows and becomes congested with weeds from here inland? Whereas the other way presumably it is clear right down to the sea. However, there is no good wasting time. We'll just make a mental note of the fact that it is here."

We pushed on again still keeping to the edge of the dyke. And now there were more signs of life. We saw sheep in a field to our left, and also a few cows.

"This is probably Spragge's ground," said Hugh. "We must begin to go warily. Hullo! Is that our friends, I wonder?"

In front of us about a mile away we could see the headlights of a car. It was moving fast in the Folkestone direction, and for a while we stopped and looked at it. At one moment it seemed to be coming straight towards us: then as the road jinked we saw only the reflection of the lights travelling sideways across our front. And so we stood until the glare had almost faded away to our right: almost but not quite. For Hugh had been correct in his tactics: it was our friends as he had predicted. The reflection became stationary in the sky: shifted as the car turned, and then became again the headlights returning on the same road. And to me there seemed something strangely ominous in that powerful silent light searching the country for us, with people who we even now knew would stick at nothing, in the car behind it. Was the girl driving again, with Paul Vandali sitting beside her; or were other unknown people on the trail too?

"Let's hope that has put 'em off the scent anyway," said Hugh as the light disappeared in the direction of Rye. "It's lucky we took the sea road."

Once more we struck out along the bank of the dyke. We walked in single file with Hugh leading and young Scott in the centre. Sheep were becoming more plentiful now, and suddenly Hugh came to an abrupt halt.

"There's the house," he said in a low voice as we joined him. "Straight in front of us."

It lay there black and silent. No chink of light came from any window: no sound broke the stillness save the faint creaking of the branches of a tree. A little to one side lay the outhouse we had noticed that afternoon and suddenly Hugh clutched my arm.

"There's a light filtering through a crack in the wall, Peter. In the outhouse. Don't you see it? And, by Jove!" his grip tightened, "we're not the only prowlers abroad tonight. Somebody passed across the light just then."

We stood there motionless, scarcely breathing, staring into the darkness. I could see the light distinctly now, shining probably through the hinge of the door. But no further shadow blotted it out: the other nocturnal wanderer, whoever he was, was lying up in the darkness now like us.

"It is the possibility of a dog that I'm afraid of," whispered Hugh. "It might have been one of the household who is walking about."

Cautiously, a step at a time, we crept nearer. And after a while I became conscious of a curious noise. It would last for perhaps ten seconds: then cease abruptly. And after a pause it would be repeated. Hugh heard it too: I could just see the outline of his face beside me peering ahead trying to locate it.

For the third time it came: but on this occasion an unmistakable sound of splintering occurred in the middle, and one part of the problem was solved. Someone was sawing wood, and I almost laughed. If after all our elaborate precautions we were to find old man Spragge cutting up tomorrow's firewood the jest would be rather rich.

As we drew nearer it was obvious that the sound came from the outhouse: saw, pause, saw, pause. And whoever it was who was producing it he certainly wasn't working overtime. The pauses grew longer, the noise shorter, and when at length we reached the wall of the building the sawing seemed to have ceased altogether. From inside came the occasional sound of a person moving about, and once some tool fell with a metallic clang on the floor.

We were some two yards from the chink of light, and I could see that Hugh was looking keenly all round us. It was obvious what was worrying him, and I, too, searched the darkness intently. If we had seen the other watcher in the light from the door, he, in his turn, would be able to see us if we peered through. And that was the last thing we wanted. If he was a member of the household he would give the alarm: if he was one of the opposing side we should have given ourselves away completely. And so for five minutes we stared into the night, but without success. No trace could we see of him: he seemed to have vanished completely.

At last came Hugh's whisper in my ear—"We'll chance it, crouch low," and inch by inch he edged his way to the door. I followed close behind him on my hands and knees, with the youngster just on my heels. I could hear his excited breathing, and truth to tell I was getting well worked up myself. Were we going to see anything inside, or would it turn out to be a false alarm?

Very gradually Hugh straightened himself up until he could see through the crack. For a moment or two he stared and I saw a look of amazement appear on his face. Then he went on and I took his place.

The scene was an astounding one. The illumination came from half a dozen candles which stood on a rough carpenter's bench. A saw and some tools were scattered about, but it was the worker himself who fascinated me. He was sitting on an overturned box, and in the course of my life I have never seen a more bestial face. He was clean shaven save for a short moustache. His mouth was a little open as he worked, and the light shone on a row of yellow teeth, from which two were missing. His nose was flattened, and a great red scar ran down one cheek from the temple almost to the chin. His eyebrows were bushy, and once when he happened to glance up I saw his eyes glaring with a kind of animal ferocity. He paused in his work, too, at that moment and shook both his fists in the air as at some imaginary enemy. And his expression was that of a homicidal maniac.

Never, in fact, unless I had seen it, would I have believed that any living thing, who bore the outward semblance of a man, could have presented such an utterly devilish appearance. He fascinated me, so that I stared and stared until Hugh nudged me in the ribs. And then only did I force myself to look away from him at the work he was doing.

At first I couldn't make it out. He had beside him two or three slats of wood each about a foot long, two inches broad and an inch thick. There was an augur hole at each end of the slats, and through these holes he was passing two ropes. And then it suddenly dawned on me:

the man was making a rope ladder. I looked on the floor at his feet, and saw the ends of the top ropes were attached to a canvas sack about the size and shape of a bolster. And at last I got it, but not before Hugh had pulled me forcibly away, and performed the same office on young Freckles, who had nearly given the whole show away by an audible gasp when he had looked in.

"Damn it," muttered Hugh irritably, "you blokes might have been getting your money's worth at a peep-show in a circus."

We were sitting on the ground some sixty yards away from the house, under cover of a hedge.

"I saw all there was to see in two seconds," he went on. "And for the love of Pete don't forget we're not the only people here tonight."

"What was that horror doing?" said Scott. "I've never seen such an awful looking specimen in my life."

For a moment or two Hugh hesitated.

"Well, young fellow," he said at length, "I fear that his present mission in life is fairly obvious. When you see a man making a rope ladder it is safe to assume he wants to climb something. And when you further see a big canvas sack at one end of the rope ladder, it is not difficult to spot what it is he wants to climb. That sack will just lie nicely between the spikes on Granger's wall, and will anchor the top of the ladder into the bargain. And when he gets to the top he can sit on the sack, throw the ladder down the inside of the wall, and there you are."

"You mean to say," stammered Freckles, "that that beast, that damned murderous swine, is going to get into Temple Tower? With Pat there? Not on your life, Drummond. If you won't go for him now, by God, I will!"

He had scrambled to his feet, and I could hear his quick agitated breathing.

"Sit down and shut up," said Hugh curtly. "I am not going for him now, and he'd eat you with one hand. Sit down, youngster," he went on kindly. "I guess it is a bit of a shock to you, but we've got to do a bit of thinking. No good has ever come yet of barging in like a bull in a china shop, and whatever may be that beauty's intentions in the future, he's perfectly safe where he is at present."

Chapter 4

In Which the Necessity for Sparking Plugs is Proved

And so for the next quarter of an hour we sat there discussing the thing in whispers. The feeling of incongruity, almost of the ridiculous, in three grown men prowling about Romney Marsh at night, which I at any rate had experienced, even if only slightly, had disappeared: we were face to face with reality, and pretty grim reality at that.

That this horrible, bestial individual was preparing to get into Temple Tower was obvious. And that his reason for doing so was not to pay a polite call was equally obvious. That it had been Granger who was in his mind when he had paused in his task and shaken his great fists in the air I was sure. But beyond that there was still much that was obscure. We had learned something of vital importance it was true, but the one ray of light we possessed only seemed to make the surrounding darkness more impenetrable.

Was this brute sitting in the outhouse the man we had heard snoring? Was he the man who had flashed the red and blue warning to the house on the hill? Whose was that other shadowy form that we had seen cross the light through the door? And most curious of all, what was the connection if any between this animal man and the Vandalis? Were they working in conjunction, or was the maker of rope ladders playing a lone hand?

That his object was to get at Granger was, as I have said, clear. And as Hugh said, if Granger knew that this specimen was after him his precautions were comprehensible. But was it only his life they were after, or was there something concealed in Temple Tower that they wanted as well?

"I give it up," said Hugh at length. "We don't know enough yet to say. But our evening has not been wasted: we've got another player taped all right. And as I don't think we can do more, I suggest home and hitting the hay. The only thing I wish is that we could spot that other bloke, but it is hopeless on a night like this."

But we were destined to have one more glimpse of him. Even as we rose the door of the barn opened, and the ladder maker stood there framed in the light. We had only seen him sitting before; standing up he seemed more horrible than ever. He was a short man, but his arms were abnormally long, and he looked for all the world like a huge misshapen ape. Then he turned back, blew out the lights, and as he did so we crept nearer the house. It was just possible we might learn something, and the night was yet young.

He opened the door and went in, and shortly afterwards a light shone through the curtains of one of the rooms facing the road. As luck would have it the window was open, and as we crept along the side of the house we heard voices.

"It is cursed foolishness, I tell you," came in Spragge's snarling voice. "You've done it twice now, and it is bound to attract attention."

"I agree with Spragge." It was Mrs. Spragge speaking. "Those two men this afternoon—what were they doing except trying to find things out?"

And then I, at any rate, got the shock of my life. For the voice that answered them was soft and musical. It was as if one had suddenly discovered some priceless gem of beauty in a filthy pigsty. At first, in fact, I could hardly believe that it was the bestial monstrosity speaking.

"*Mes amis*," he said gently, "it is for the last time. My ladder is nearly finished; soon, very soon the moment will come. It matters not to me what these two Englishmen suspect: maybe it is just idle curiosity on their part. It is no offence against your laws to flash a red light and then a blue across the Marsh. There is nothing here which all the world may not see. But those lights—they are seen by him. And he knows what they mean. And his soul is sick with terror because he knows that death is near. Moreover he knows"—and now the voice grew, if anything, more gentle and sweet—"that that death will not be quick. Not for him the swift bullet that shatters the brain. But a death of lingering agony—a death which makes him welcome death as a lover welcomes his mistress. My arms will be about him, and when I have torn him limb from limb my hands will squeeze the last fleeting breath from his body. Ah! Yes—he knows. Once more shall he see the lights, to remind him that I am still here. And then we will go to bed."

"You talk too much," grumbled Spragge. "And don't you forget, Mister, what you promised us after it was all over."

"I shall not forget," said the other contemptuously. "Now turn out the light."

Came a sudden darkness, and we crouched there enthralled. Had it been said blusteringly, had the voice been what one would have expected from such a being, half the effect would have been lost. But those soft melodious, gentle words carried with them an icy thrill, impossible to set down on paper. And whatever might have been Granger's crime in the past, I felt sorry for him if this man ever got hold of him.

Suddenly there came a sharp hissing noise, and a bright red light shone out. And then things happened quickly. I had a brief glimpse of a man silhouetted in the light not twenty yards away: of the beast-faced ladder maker staring out above our heads, and then the light went out. He too had seen the man, and with a grunting cry he hurled himself through the open window and crashed past us so close that we could almost have touched him. For a while we heard him blundering round in the darkness, searching for the other watcher. The instant he had jumped past us Hugh, fearing that Spragge might join in the search, had risen and led the way round the house in the direction away from the front door. Which was just what did happen, and for some ten minutes, hidden behind a small tool shed we listened to the two men as they searched. But it was useless—the mysterious unknown had disappeared completely—and at length they gave it up and returned to the house.

"Couldn't find an elephant on a night like this, let alone a man," came Spragge's growling voice. "It's your damned fault anyway, playing with those fool lights."

"My friend," said the other, "the man was there anyway. The light merely discovered him."

"Probably that swine who was here this afternoon," said Spragge, and then their voices died away as they got round the corner of the house.

The front door shut with a bang, and still we stayed on. Was anything further going to occur? Would the ladder maker still insist on flashing his signal across the Marsh, or would he follow Spragge's advice and give it up? Apparently it was to be the latter, for shortly after a light appeared in one of the upper windows. Then that, too, went out, and the house was in darkness. The charming trio had retired for the night.

"Come on," said Hugh. "I think we've seen all we are likely to tonight."

We skirted along by the footpath until we reached the dyke, and though it seemed to me that the need for precaution had gone, I noticed that Hugh still moved with the utmost caution. And it wasn't until we had put a good half mile between us and the farm that he relaxed his vigilance.

"There is an air of efficiency about this bunch," he remarked, "that behoves us to be careful. Spragge and his spouse are negligible: even the handsome bloke making ladders seems to have his intentions cut and dried. But it is the others."

"Do you think there were more than one there tonight?" I said.

"Ask me another," he answered. "There may have been half a dozen for all I know. On the other hand, the man who showed up in the light, and the man who crossed the outhouse door may be one and the same person. But one thing is cleared up anyway: he and that horrible brute are not working in collusion."

"It is possible," said Freckles, "that he is a detective who is after the other swine."

"As you say, young fellow, it is possible," agreed Hugh. "The trouble is that there are the hell of a lot of things that seem to me to be possible. But one thing is quite definitely certain. We've got to get that girl of yours out of Temple Tower in the near future. She's not in any danger tonight—so there is no need to worry at the moment. But in view of the prospective caller, I think she will have to have a telegram recalling her to London."

"I've never thought of such a specimen," said Freckles. "He made one positively sick to look at."

"You noticed his slight accent, Peter," said Hugh. "And the way he started, *Mes amis*. The whole darned bunch are foreigners."

"What I principally noticed was his voice," I said. "A voice like that from such a man is the most astounding thing I've ever known."

We walked on briskly. Now that the thing was over for the night the thought of bed was becoming increasingly attractive, especially as our long spell without movement at the farm had made us all a bit chilly. The motor-boat loomed up as a welcome halfway landmark, and shortly after we left the dyke and struck off right-handed.

"Sometime," said Hugh, "when we've got a spare moment, we might follow that dyke down to the sea. Though it seems pretty obvious that it must be clear. Also we might make a few discreet inquiries concerning the boat itself."

At last the car hove in sight, and with a sigh of relief young Freckles fell into the back seat.

"Thank the Lord no one has pinched that," he remarked sleepily. "Every garment I possess is full of sand, and—Good Lord! Won't she start?"

Most emphatically she wouldn't start: moreover the engine, when Hugh pressed the self-starter, was making the most peculiar noise.

"What the devil has happened.?" he said grimly. "Has she been tampered with?"

He got down and opened the bonnet: then he gave a low whistle. He had flashed an electric torch on to the engine, and by its light, propped up inside, I saw a piece of paper.

"This is no business of yours, Captain Drummond," he read out slowly. "There are quite enough people engaged in it already without you butting in. This is only a small warning and punishment for what you have done up to date: next time, if you should be so ill-advised as to let there be a next time, you will be hurt."

"Is that so?" said Hugh softly, and then he began to laugh. "Stung, you fellows, stung good and proper. We're either here for the night or we've got to walk."

"What's happened?" demanded Freckles.

"Our friendly correspondent, my lad," said Hugh, "in addition to embarking on a literary career has amused himself by removing all the sparking plugs. And cars have grave difficulty in running without sparking plugs."

"Haven't you got any spare ones?" I asked.

"One—possibly two. But not six. Damn it—I'm not a walking garage."

"Where is the nearest garage?" cried Freckles.

"Rye," said Hugh laconically. "And even if we got there the chances of waking them up are remote."

We looked at one another blankly—the significance of this new development was overshadowed for the moment by the physical annoyance of the thing. We were all tired, and here we were, four or five miles from anywhere, planted with an immovable motor-car.

"Well, there's only one thing to be done," said Hugh at length. "One of us must go to Rye and throw bricks at the first garage until someone does appear on the scene. Let's toss: odd man out goes,"

"It would be me," said Freckles resignedly, as we looked at the coins, "Well, chaps, when my bloodless body is found dead in a ditch, tell Mother that it wasn't the effect of alcohol."

We watched him go off down the road, and Hugh grinned.

"A good youngster," he said. "Very good,"

And then he grew thoughtful again, studying the paper he held in his hand. The words were printed in block capitals, so there was no handwriting clue to be obtained. The message was in pencil, evidently done on the spot, as the paper had been roughly torn out of a notebook.

"Can you remember, Peter," he said at length, "whether we mentioned the fact that we were coming to Spragge's Farm tonight when we were in the Dolphin? I know we talked about it at dinner, and at my house, but on neither of those two occasions could we have been overheard."

I cast my mind back.

"I think we did," I answered. "I think it was mentioned when we were in that small room looking at that old map. But there were only the three of us there at the time."

We might have been overheard from the hall," he remarked.

"As far as I remember only the parson and those two elderly women were in the hall. Anyway what is the great idea?"

"Nothing much," he admitted. "But what I was wondering was whether it was a pure fluke that this car was found here by whoever wrote that message? Or did the other side know we were coming?"

I saw his point, but I could no more supply the answer than he could. As far as we knew we had not been overheard, but only as far as we knew.

"It's becoming increasingly obvious," he went on, "that a considerable number of people are involved in this. That man we saw silhouetted in the light was neither Vandali nor the chauffeur. Of that fact I'm perfectly certain. He was too tall for the first, and too slight for the second. Further, I don't think that it can have been he who wrote this note, unless by some extraordinary chance he was actually lying up in these sandhills when we arrived. Even then it takes time to remove six sparking plugs, and write a note. Yet he was at Spragge's Farm before us."

"Incidentally, how did he know your name?" I said.

"That's easy," he remarked. "It's written on a plate on the instrument board, even if he didn't know it before. But if my suspicions are right he did know it before, just as he knew our plans before. The key to this mystery, Peter, or at any rate one of them, lies in the Dolphin Inn. The little episode of the chimney-pot is all part and parcel of it."

"But look here," I objected, "if that's the case: if they knew we were coming here why did that car go along the other road? Of course, it's possible that it wasn't their car at all, but some other people who had taken the wrong road."

"And another thing is possible too," he said quietly. "That it was their car, and when they drew blank on the main road they knew we must have come along this one."

"But that disposes of your own theory that they knew our plans," I cried.

"Does it?" he said. "I don't agree. They knew part of our plan, but not all of it. They knew we were coming to Spragge's Farm, but they did not know we were coming by the sea route."

"I don't see," I began densely.

"Lord! Man, it's plain," he cried. "If, that is to say, my supposition is correct, and the finding of the car was not a fluke. Where did we discuss approaching the Farm from the sea? In the dining-room, where we know we were not overheard. Where did we discuss the main idea of going to the Farm? In the little room."

"Where," I interrupted, "we know with even greater certainty that we were not overheard. Confound it all, old boy, we three were alone in the room. The only people within range were the padre and those two old trouts knitting. You surely don't suspect one of them?"

"Every man who wears a dog collar isn't of necessity a parson," he said obstinately.

"Well, anyway," I remarked, "it can't have been the cleric who bunged the chimney at your head, because he was in the hall the whole time."

"Perhaps you're right, Peter," he said, but it was quite obvious he didn't think so. However, he said no more, and after a while, I began to doze in the sand . I calculated that it would be daylight before Freckles could possibly be back, and sleep seemed better than an insoluble argument. In fact, the only thing that mattered as far as I was concerned was that, fluke or no fluke, the darned blighter had successfully kept me out of my bed.

It was the sun's rays shining direct on my face that woke me. Hugh was still sitting beside me, and as I stirred he looked round.

"I hope to heaven nothing has happened to that youngster," he said in a worried voice.

I was wide awake in an instant: that possibility hadn't dawned on me up till then.

"I ought to have gone myself," he went on. "He's but a baby. I'll never forgive myself if he's come to grief."

He rose and stared down the road, and I joined him. Visibility was poor, as the ground mist had not yet lifted, and after a while he began to fidget uneasily.

"I've got a good mind to go and look for him," he said. "It's three hours now since he started."

"But surely," I said, "they wouldn't be such fools as to lay him out. They don't want to attract attention to themselves."

"I don't think they are going to kill him and leave him in a ditch," he grunted. "But we're up against an absolutely unscrupulous bunch, Peter. And whoever removed our plugs must have known one of us would go for more. What easier than to lie up—then dot that boy one as he passed? Just to make him talk when he came to. He's loyal all right—but don't forget his girl is there. And that would tend to spoil his nerve."

"Look here, Hugh," I said seriously, "we'll have to hand this thing over to the police. All joking apart, it's got a bit beyond our form. As you say yourself, that girl is inside Granger's house."

"I suppose you're right, Peter," he said regretfully. "But it does seem cruel hard, doesn't it? The point about the whole thing though, is this. What are we going to say to the blighters? After all, as far as I can see, the only actual offence that has been committed as yet, is the removal of our plugs. And we don't know who did it. Making a rope ladder is a perfectly legitimate occupation: flashing red and blue lights is not a criminal offence. The person to go to the police, if anyone, is Granger himself. And he won't. It's not all as easy as it looks, you know."

I was silent: what he said was undoubtedly true. Even if we showed them the note written by the unknown, our case was decidedly thin. More than likely they would regard it as a stupid practical joke, and in addition to that, view us with considerable suspicion for our share in the night's activities. At the same time one could not get away from the feeling of responsibility with regard to the girl, and I could see that Hugh was not too happy in his mind about it either.

"It is this way as I see it, Peter," he went on after a while. "And honestly it is not because I want to keep this bit of fun and laughter to ourselves that I say it. If we tell the police what little we know about this show up to date our connection with it automatically stops. We pass out of the picture. Now the police are trammelled by all sorts of rules and regulations: in other words they are not free agents. They have to obtain warrants and things of that kind before they can move a step. Would it not therefore be better to keep matters in our own hands at any rate until we know a bit more? Then if we think it necessary, or if there seems to be the slightest danger threatening that girl we'll tell them all we know."

"You darned old hypocrite," I laughed. "Have it your own way."

And once again we fell silent, staring down the road. The mist was lifting gradually, though it was still impossible to see any distance.

Out to sea was a tramp homeward bound, and the occasional wail of a siren showed that the fog was not confined to the land.

And suddenly Hugh heaved a sigh of relief; a figure trudging wearily along had come in sight. It was Freckles with the parcel of plugs clutched in his hand.

"Hell take it," he said as he came up. "I've had the most frightful time. An old woman in a nightcap bunged a bucket of water over me in one garage: thought I was tight or mad. No one could understand why I wanted six of the damned things. I've walked about eighteen miles."

"Did you see anyone on the way, young fellow?" asked Hugh.

"Not a soul," grunted Freckles. "Except a tramp asleep in a ditch. Lucky devil—I very nearly joined him."

He got into the car, and lay back wearily.

"Home, John, home. I'm just about done in."

"Right ho! My son," said Hugh. "You shall be between the sheets very soon now."

He tightened up the last plug, and closed the bonnet.

"Hop in, Peter," he cried. "Taking everything into consideration I'd sooner get past the coastguard station before they are all awake. What the dickens is that?"

We had gone over a bump in the road, and an extraordinary metallic clang had come from behind the car. He got out, and I followed him. And when we got to the back of the car, for a moment or two neither of us spoke. There are times when the power of speech fails one.

Hanging on to the luggage grid, attached by a short piece of string, were our six original sparking plugs. And in the middle of them was another small note.

"Your plugs, I believe," read Hugh, and just then Freckles' face appeared over the hood.

"What did you say?" he spluttered.

"Keep calm," said Hugh weakly. "Remember your aged mother."

"You mean to tell me," remarked Freckles, in a choking voice, "that those plugs were there all the time?" He swallowed once or twice, and over the next minute I will draw a decent veil. Even Hugh listened in admiration to the flood of rhetoric that poured forth, and he is no mean artist in that line himself.

"Laddie," he said gravely, when Freckles paused for breath, "I had no idea that such language was known to anyone under forty."

"I would put him," said Freckles broodingly, as the car drew up at the house, "on a hard concrete surface. And then I would cover him all over with sparking plugs. And then having pegged him down I would take a roller of medium weight, and passage it backwards and forwards over his vile body, pausing occasionally to jump on his stomach with hobnailed boots. Yea—thus and more would I do to that offspring of Beelzebub. And if any sparking plugs were over I would ram them down his mouth with a sledgehammer."

"Run away to bed," laughed Hugh and Freckles departed muttering horribly. And not until his door had closed did Hugh grow serious again. He wanted less sleep than any man I've ever known, and my immediate need of it had been met by the two hours I had had in the sand dunes. And now as we stood by the dining-room window staring over the Marsh I could see his brain was busy once more.

"What was the idea, Peter, of that little jest?" he said at length. He was holding the note in his hand as he spoke. "Was it in reality what he says here—a small warning and punishment?"

"Why should you think otherwise?" I asked.

"This morning," he said, in an unusually quiet and serious tone of voice for him, "I had a very queer sensation. I got it first of all when you were asleep. I suddenly became convinced that there was someone else there. I saw no one: I heard no sound. Nevertheless the feeling was strong on me that we were not alone: that somebody else was watching us. In those sand dunes, of course, you could hide a battalion of infantry. Footmarks disappear as soon as they are made. It was hopeless to try and explore, but for all that I believe there was someone there."

"And if there was," I said, "what do you deduce from it?"

"That the object of the plug episode was a little deeper than appears on the surface: that there was more in it than to make us temporarily annoyed and inconvenienced. Mark you—I don't know. It is all surmise on my part, and surmise moreover based on what may be a false start. There may have been no one there at all. But if there was then I think that the main object of the thing was to enable the watcher to take stock of us considerably more closely than any of the opposing side have been able to up to date."

"Assuming for the moment that you are right," I said, "have you any theory as to who the watcher was?"

He shook his head.

"None at all. I've got no theories on the thing at all. But one thing I do know, though you will probably call me every kind of an ass for saying so. I feel it instinctively. There is someone in this show who is infinitely more dangerous than that specimen making the rope ladder, or than the Vandalis. I sense his influence behind them. Whether he is the leader or not, or whether he is quite separate I can't tell you—but he's there. Further, I believe that it was he who first of all tried to out me with the chimney-pot, and having failed there decided on other measures and lay up this morning to study us."

"The man we saw at Spragge's Farm," I suggested.

"Possibly: possibly not. Time will show. But the solution lies at present in the Dolphin, and when you turn in I'm going to see what there is to be seen there. Probably nothing, but there's no harm in having a try."

"I'll come with you," I said, but he refused to allow me to.

"I can do without sleep," he remarked, "and you can't. Go and turn in, old boy, and I'll have a bit of shut-eye this afternoon."

I went up to my room and slowly undressed. In front of me lay the Marsh, bathed in the early morning sunshine. The mist had quite gone: only a haze over the sea still remained. For a while I stood by the open window staring at Spragge's Farm, but there was no sign of life. Then with a feeling that the whole thing was an unreal dream I got into bed. And the next thing I knew was the sound of Hugh's voice.

"Wake up, Peter. It is half-past twelve. Time for a spot of lunch."

"Did you find out anything?" I said as I scrambled out of bed.

"Not very much," he answered. "I went over the list of visitors, but got no farther. There is, however, one thing I noticed that gives one to think a little. The Vandalis' room is Number 18. Now Number 18 is on the first floor. It stands at the corner of the passage, and is directly above the little room leading off the hall. Do you see the significance?"

"Not at the moment," I said. "We weren't talking loud enough to be overheard through the ceiling. Besides Vandali was in the room."

"But the lady was not," he retorted. "Think again, Peter. Number 18 undoubtedly possesses a fireplace, though I haven't been into it to see. The flue of that fireplace must lead into the main one which communicates with the huge chimney in the room below—a chimney which would act as a glorified megaphone. It is a point anyway to bear in mind."

He left me to finish dressing, and ponder over this fresh development. It undoubtedly was a point to bear in mind; and if he was correct it accounted for a great deal. More than likely words spoken in the little room below, even in a low tone, would be heard perfectly distinctly by anyone listening-in just above the chimney.

"John is coming to lunch," he said as I joined him below. "Moreover, he is bringing the plan of Temple Tower. And that is another point, Peter, which is going to have a bearing on the situation. The possession of that plan is a very big asset in our favour. For without it, as far as I can see, no one is going to get inside the house. Our friend of the Marshes may get inside the grounds, but there he will stick."

He swung round as a car pulled up at the door.

"Here he is. Morning, John. Got the necessary?"

"I have not," said the other coming into the hall. "Look here, Hugh, you didn't play a damn fool practical joke on me last night, did you?"

"Not that I'm aware of," he answered. "Why?"

"You remember that plan I was telling you about—the one of Temple Tower?"

"I do," said Hugh, sitting up suddenly. "You were going to bring it over this morning."

"I know I was. And I haven't, for a very good reason. Someone broke into Laidley Towers last night, and stole it."

CHAPTER 5

In Which We Come to the Wood at Temple Tower

For a while we stared at him in silence, and at that moment Freckles came down and joined us.

"You're certain, John," said Hugh at length, "that it isn't hidden away in a drawer somewhere?"

"Of course I'm certain, old man," answered the other. "The darned thing was framed, and it used to hang in a corner of the hall. When I went to get it this morning it wasn't there. I sent for the butler, and he swore on his Bible oath that it was there yesterday. Besides, there is more to it than that. It appeared that when we were at dinner last night, a man called to see me. One of the footmen answered the door, and told him that I had a party. The man looked all right apparently, and when he said that he would wait and that I was not to be disturbed on any account, the footman showed him into a room off the hall. Then the darned fool forgot all about him for some time. As soon as he remembered he went back to the room, and found that the bird had gone. He made a hurried survey, and when, as far as he could see, nothing was missing, he decided that his best policy was to say nothing about it. Of course when I found out what had happened, I gave him hell. He was very contrite about it: assured me again and again that the man had looked like a gentleman: that he had driven up in a car and all that. But when it came to describing him to me it was hopeless. He gave a description that would fit a hundred people. And all he could really say was that he would know him again if he saw him."

"It just bears out what we were saying, Peter," said Hugh thoughtfully. "Where were we discussing the plan? Why, in the little room again. And we were overheard there. It stands to reason. An old plan of Temple Tower is of no earthly value to anybody, unless they are connected with this business. A pony to a tanner it is the woman. By the way, John, I suppose it wasn't our bearded friend who visited you?"

"Not unless he'd shaved off his beard. Even my mutton-headed poop would have noticed that amount of face fungus. But there is one rather important point, which I forgot to tell you yesterday. The plan was framed, and on the back of it is some writing. And that writing gives the clue to the secret entrance. The plan, of course, shows where it is approximately, but without the writing at the back you can't get in."

"And you haven't any idea what is written there?" I asked.

"Not the remotest. Dash it, old boy! I was only about eleven years old at the time."

"As you say, John, that is very important," said Hugh. "Because what it boils down to as far as I can see is that unless the bloke that pinched it takes it out of the frame it is useless to him."

"That's about the long and the short of it," agreed the other

"Gosh! You fellows," cried Hugh, "I'd give something to see a little daylight in this. Anyway, let's go and gnaw a bone."

And all through lunch we argued it backwards and forwards. Was it the man we had seen at Spragge's Farm who had stolen the plan, or was it, perhaps, Jean Picot the chauffeur?

"That's a point, John," said Hugh. "Go and ring up your place and find out if the footman can say what sort of a car it was the man came in. See if he remembers the colour: that might help."

But again we drew blank. The car had not been left at the front door, and the man had no idea on the subject.

"The more I see of it, Scott," said Hugh as we finished lunch, "the more do I think that the first real daylight we shall get is from Miss Verney. I want you and Peter to be there from two to three this afternoon, in case she gets a note over the wall. I'm going to turn in for a couple of hours, and then this evening our work really begins."

"The Marsh again?" asked Freckles.

"No, young fellow—Temple Tower," said Hugh gravely. "If anybody gets inside that wall we're going to follow."

And so two o'clock found Freckles and me ensconced in the little wood which lay opposite the front gate. Hugh had turned in: John James had returned to Laidley Towers with the definite intention of getting some kit and then coming back to the house. As he pointed out, it was his plan, and if there was any fun and laughter going begging, he was going to have a dip at it.

Not unnaturally, the boy was a bit on edge, and I certainly didn't blame him. All that we could see of the house was the tower: the rest of it was hidden by the wall. And in the hot, drowsy afternoon the whole place looked more like a prison than ever. Even to me it was so gloomy as to be depressing, and I hadn't got my fiancée inside.

We hardly talked at all, and when we did for some reason or other, we found ourselves whispering. Save for the drone of countless insects, the silence was absolute: even the birds seemed stricken dumb. Once a farm wagon creaked slowly by, the driver half asleep: but except for that the road was deserted. And after a while Freckles began to doze.

I suppose I must have followed his example, because I distinctly remember that I had a brief vivid dream of the beast-faced man at Spragge's Farm. And then, quite suddenly, I was wide awake. Something had moved not far away, and the sound had roused me. I sat up and glanced at my watch: it was a quarter to three. I looked at Freckles: he was sleeping peacefully. Then I stared round me: what was the noise I had heard?

The undergrowth was dense: I could see nothing. But that noise which had sounded like the cracking of a twig must have been caused by something. Or somebody. And then—I cannot explain it—I began to be aware of a peculiar sensation, a sensation I had never experienced before. Someone was watching me; I knew it.

Once again I stared all round me; once again I saw nothing save the brambles and trees. But the feeling grew on me, till it amounted to a certainty. I was being watched. Back to my mind came Hugh's words of that morning: he, too, had felt the same sensation in the sand dunes. And after a while I could stand it no longer: I got up. Still no sound: still no sign, but the feeling remained. The silent watcher was still there. I took a few steps forward, and there came the sudden crack of another twig. And now I knew I was right: we were not alone in the wood.

Absurd I know, and I am almost ashamed to admit it, but for some reason or other the most unreasoning panic began to get hold of me. And only by taking a firm pull at myself did I remain where I was. In the middle of a summer's afternoon, for a grown man to be frightened in an English wood was utterly ridiculous, and yet the plain fact remained that I was. The noise had seemed to come from the direction in which I was facing, and acting on a sudden impulse I plunged into the undergrowth. There was nothing—nothing at all. A bird startled by the noise flew away chattering angrily, but of anyone human there was no sign. I took a few more steps, peering in every direction, with the same result. And then, suddenly, I heard Freckles calling me, and his voice was urgent.

"Darrell! Darrell! Where are you?"

"Here I am," I answered. "What's the matter?"

I found him sitting up, rubbing his eyes with the back of his hand.

"I must have been dreaming," he said slowly. "And yet I could have sworn I was awake."

"What did you think you saw?" I asked.

"It is a most extraordinary thing," he said, "but I thought I saw a black figure through those bushes over there. It was all black, standing between those two trees. Just at first I thought it was you, until it moved: then I saw it wasn't. And then it suddenly vanished."

"Let's go and have a look," I said: and together we walked over to the two trees. But there was no one there, and though we stood listening intently we heard no further sound. The wood had relapsed into its drowsy silence once more.

"A trick of the light most probably," he said. "Some shadow or other."

"Shadows don't come and go," I answered. "As a matter of fact for the last five minutes I've had the impression that we were being watched."

"But, damn it," he cried, "if there really was someone there, what was he doing in that extraordinary rig. He was absolutely black, and a most peculiar shape."

"What do you mean by a peculiar shape?" I said.

"I'm blowed if I know what I do mean," he answered, scratching his head. "But he didn't look normal."

"When you say black," I persisted, "do you mean he was a nigger?"

"No; he didn't seem to have a face at all. He was just a black outline." He gave an irritable laugh. "Confound it, Darrell, I'm not tight. And I know I was awake. What the deuce is in this wood?"

"It's a bit too big a proposition to explore at the moment," I said. "I think we'd better return to our observation post; we don't want to miss the letter if it comes."

We went back to our original position and lay down again. And for the next ten minutes while we waited I have no hesitation in admitting that I frequently found myself looking over my shoulder into the shadows behind us. What was this mysterious being that I had heard, and Freckles had seen?

After a while I glanced at my watch: it was ten minutes past three. And I was on the point of suggesting that we should give it up, when something skimmed over the wall and fell in the road, not two yards from where we were lying. It was the letter, and it had hardly reached the ground before Freckles had it in his pocket.

"Pat," he called out in a low voice. "Pat."

"Hullo!" I just heard her answer from the other side.

"Are you all right, darling?"

"Yes, quite. Look here, Tom...."

But whatever she was going to say we missed, because at that moment Freckles glanced up the road. He let out an urgent "Shut up," and bolted back under cover beside me.

"The Vandalis," he muttered, and even as he spoke I heard the roar of their car in the distance. It drew up almost in front of us, but fortunately in such a position that we could see the gate. The woman was driving, and we wormed our way a little further forward in order to see better. The whole thing was evidently cut and dried beforehand, and a direct frontal assault was the plan. Vandali got out of the car, looking even more overdressed than he had in the Dolphin, walked over to the bell and rang it. Then he lit a cigarette, and coming back to the car, stood leaning against it and talking to the girl. Once I thought he must have seen us, because he stared perfectly straight at me, and seemed to pause for an instant in his conversation. But he gave no further sign, and a few moments later, the hole in the gate was opened and Gaspard looked out.

Vandali turned round, and for a while he and the girl stared at him in silence. Then Vandali spoke.

"Is Mr. Granger at home?"

"That's as may be," retorted the other. "Who are you, and what do you want?"

"My name doesn't matter. But I wish to see your master."

"Well, he don't wish to see you, nor anyone else."

He made as if to shut the hole in the gate, but Vandali stepped forward.

"Wait a minute, my friend," he said. "You know who is down there on the Marsh, don't you?"

"I don't know what you are talking about," said Gaspard hoarsely.

"Don't lie: it is foolish," said Vandali. "You know that you are found at last—or rather your master is. And you know what that means."

Gaspard moistened his dry lips with his tongue.

"Tell me who you are," he repeated.

"As I said before," answered Vandali, "it doesn't matter who I am. But go and tell your master that someone who knows everything is outside and wishes to speak to him. And tell him further that he need have no fear."

For a while the man hesitated: then he slammed and bolted the panel of the opening and we heard his steps departing up the drive.

"I wonder," said Vandali thoughtfully to the girl, "if it will work the trick. We hit the mark all right over Marillard. Still it is only guesswork."

"Guesswork that is a certainty," she answered impatiently. "My dear Paul, look at the house, look at the precautions he has taken against anyone getting in. Of course it is the man."

"I suppose you are right," he agreed. "Anyway, we can but try the bluff?"

He lit a cigarette, and stood leaning against the car.

"And if the bluff doesn't succeed?" she remarked, "what then?"

"I see nothing for it," he said, "but the police."

The panel suddenly opened again, and he swung round. And framed for a moment in the hole in the gate was an unpleasant shifty-eyed face. The owner himself, I decided, and evidently Vandali had come to the same conclusion.

"Mr. Granger, I believe," he said quietly.

But if he expected any further conversation he was doomed to disappointment, A querulous voice said: "I don't know you: go away," and then the panel slammed to again.

"Wait a moment," called out Vandali. "I know you don't know me, but I know you."

"Go away," shrieked the voice from the other side of the wall.

"Listen to me, you fool," snarled Vandali, losing his temper, "or it will be the worse for you. Unless you consent to see me, and discuss things, I will put the police on to you."

A peal of cackling laughter was the only reply, and I saw the girl put her hand on Vandali's arm and whisper something.

"Look here, Mr. Granger," he said more calmly, "we'll give you a day to think it over in. Tomorrow at about this time we will return. And then I advise you, for your own sake, to see me."

But there was no reply, and after a time, with a shrug of his shoulders, Vandali got back into the car. And the girl was just leaning forward to press the starter, when a noise like a young explosion occurred at my elbow. As I pointed out to Freckles afterwards, he might have controlled himself for another half second, but he merely retorted that half a second can be longer than an eternity if a fly goes up your nose. Anyway, the bald fact remains that the uproar of Freckles' sneeze literally shook the countryside. And the girl drew back from the self-starter, and then they both stared straight at us.

"Botanising?" said Vandali quietly.

"No. Only studying the habits of the lesser *carnivora*," burbled Freckles. "I say, laddie, he didn't seem to like your face, did he?"

Vandali got out of the car, and slowly crossed the road.

"Spying, I see," he remarked curtly.

Freckles grinned amiably and sat up.

"Blessed if it isn't my old friend from the Dolphin," he said. "And what are we doing in the fragrant countryside this afternoon?"

"May I ask what *you* are doing lying concealed here?" said Vandali angrily.

"*Tush! Tush!*" said Freckles, "and likewise *pish, pish!* I must buy you a little brochure on manners for men with beards. Can you advance any reason why I and my dear old friend Abraham de Vere Potbelly should not lie in the verdant hay, studying the beauties of nature?"

"Look here, my young friend," said Vandali quietly, "I would strongly advise you not to play the fool with me."

"God forbid, my dear old lad of the village," cried Freckles earnestly, "that I should ever play anything with you. I should hate to. I don't think you'd make at all a suitable companion for me. In fact I know my aged mother would object most strongly. 'Percy,' she would say, 'have nothing to do with that rude man. Give him the raspberry at once.'"

The veins were beginning to stand out on Vandali's forehead, but he managed to control himself, and turned to me.

"Since this boy seems partially insane," he said, "might I ask you to be good enough to tell me what the great idea is?"

"What the devil has it got to do with you?" I said curtly. "As far as I know we have as much right to lie in this wood, as you have to drive your car along the road."

"I see," he answered slowly. "Well, I hope you have profited by your eavesdropping."

"Immensely, thanks," said Freckles. "And now don't let us keep you any more. I would fain resume my studies of nature."

"Come along, Paul," cried the girl imperiously. "You are only wasting time."

"Madame," said Freckles tragically, "you wound me to the very core. Surely, surely, to engage in playful badinage with one of my engaging countenance cannot be regarded as wasting time. But I do wish you'd get him to cut the grouse moor on his face. That's given him the once-once," he continued with a grin as the car drove off. "But there is no doubt, laddie, that the girl is a decided pippin."

"I wish you could have controlled your nose," I said irritably. "Damn it! People in Rye must have heard you."

"It was a bit of a break," he admitted. "Still I do not see that it has done much harm. We've had a pleasant little chat, and I suggest that we now ooze back to the house, and read Pat's letter."

There certainly seemed to be no object in staying where we were, and I was on the point of agreeing, when suddenly the panel in the gate was cautiously opened, and Granger again looked out. We were standing in the middle of the road, so it was useless to try and conceal ourselves. He stared at us with utmost hostility, but Freckles, completely unperturbed, seized the opportunity.

"Good-afternoon," he cried cheerily. "Do you mind telling Miss Verney that I am here. Scott is my name."

"Are you friends of Captain Drummond?" answered Granger, with a look of relief replacing the anger.

And then there occurred the most extraordinary thing. Granger's expression changed suddenly. And it changed so suddenly that we could do nothing but stare at him blankly. His jaw dropped, and a look of terror appeared on his face, such as I have never seen before or since. For perhaps a second he stood there: then the panel clanged to.

"What the devil is the matter with the man?" stammered Freckles.

"It was not us," I muttered. "He wasn't looking at us."

We swung round quickly, and peered into the wood, the same thought in both our minds. And this time I, too, saw it—a great black shape that seemed to flit between the trees until it vanished. For a moment or two we stood there undecided, then we pulled ourselves together and gave chase. But it was hopeless. Once I thought I saw it in the distance between two trees, but when we got there, there was nothing. And after a while we gave it up and returned to the road mopping our foreheads.

"So it wasn't my imagination after all," said Freckles. "What is it, Darrell?"

"Ask me another," I answered. "But whatever it is it put the fear of God into our friend Granger. I've never seen a man look more terrified in my life.".

"I wonder if it is that swine from Spragge's Farm masquerading about in disguise," he said as we strolled back to the house. "What defeats me is that it seemed such a rum shape." He stopped, struck with a sudden thought. "I suppose it is human, isn't it?"

"Good Lord, man!" I cried irritably, "There are enough complications in this affair already without introducing a bally ghost. Besides, ghosts do not step on twigs and break them."

"That is so," he admitted. "But it really was the most extraordinary object. It didn't seem to have a face."

We walked on in silence until we reached the house. Up to date every single hour seemed to have produced a new development, and I fully expected to find that something more had happened in our absence. But in that I proved to be wrong. Hugh was taking his ease in a long chair on the veranda, and assured us that nothing had disturbed his siesta. He hoped that we were not as hot as we looked, whereat we cursed him for a lousy knave, and demanded beer in tankards. But all his air of laziness vanished when we began to tell him what had happened.

"You are absolutely certain about this peculiar thing you saw in the woods?" he said. "But, of course, you must be. You couldn't both have imagined it. Very strange: very strange indeed."

He lit a cigarette thoughtfully.

"I wouldn't be surprised if you are not right, Scott," he went on, "and it is not our friend from Spragge's Farm."

"Whose name would seem, from what Vandali said, to be Marillard," I put in. "But my impression of the thing we saw in the wood was that it was considerably taller."

"Anyway," said Hugh, "whether it is him or not, we've arrived at two definite conclusions. Granger is frightened of it, and he is not frightened of the Vandalis. Therefore it would seem that it and Vandalis are working separately. Am I right or wrong?"

"Don't ask me," grunted Freckles. "The whole thing at the present moment is completely above my form. But there is one point that sticks out a bit, and that is the fact that the Vandalis know about Marillard, and that Granger is frightened of him. So that if the 'it' is Marillard, even though they may be working separately, the Vandalis are using him as a weapon for their own ends."

"Life is certainly a trifle complicated," murmured Hugh. "However, let us hear what your perfectly good girl has to say on the matter."

"Great Scott! She has written a three volume novel," said Freckles as he opened the letter. "Er—and the first paragraph, chaps, does not seem to bear directly on the subject."

"You surprise me," said Hugh gravely. "The first paragraph may therefore be omitted."

"It certainly will be," laughed the other. "Here is where she really gets going."

He settled himself comfortably in his chair.

"This is the most amazing household," he began. "I'll start at the beginning and try not leave out anything. The first excitement occurred the instant the gate was shut—and you heard it. The dog, I mean, if such an animal can be called a dog. It is the size of a calf, and I suppose it saw a stranger. Instantly it hurled itself against the bars of its cage, roaring—there is no other word for it—with rage. Its eyes were red, its great fangs were showing, and the front of the cage shook so much that I feared it might give way.

"'What an awful brute,' I said to the man who had opened the gate. His name is Gaspard, and he and the dog are a pretty pair.

"'You're right,' he said. 'And he runs loose at night. Don't forget that.'

"He flung open the front door, and then I really thought for a moment or two I had come to a madhouse. A nasty-looking little man, who subsequently turned out to be my employer, was coming downstairs as I stepped into the hall. The instant he saw me he started shouting, 'Who's that woman? Who's that woman?' at the top of his voice. I stood there wondering whether to laugh or be angry, while the servant man said something to him which seemed to reassure him. At any rate, he came shambling forward, and muttered some sort of an apology.

"'You must excuse me, my dear young lady,' he said, 'but I am a great recluse. My nerves are not all they might be.'

"'So I see,' I answered. 'I presume you are expecting me.'

"'Of course, of course,' he muttered. 'Just for the moment I had forgotten you were coming—that is all. Let me see—you come from Miss Mudge's bureau, don't you? Now you would like to see your room, I'm sure. Gaspard—tell your wife to show this young lady to her room. And then later we will go into your duties. Tell me, as you came in, did you see anyone outside in the road?'

"'I came with my fiancé,' I said. 'And there were two gentlemen who told us which the house was.'

"I could hardly get the sentence out before he was shouting for Gaspard.

"'Did you see the men?' he stuttered. 'The two men outside?'

"'Only Drummond and a friend of his,' said Gaspard.

"'Who was the friend?' he cried.

"'If you want to know,' I said coldly, 'his name was Darrell.'

"He stared at me suspiciously, and I suppose he noticed I was looking a bit surprised. Anyway, he made an attempt to pull himself together.

"'I don't encourage strangers. Miss....'

"I told him my name.

"'Ah! Yes, of course. I remember now. No, Miss Verney, I don't encourage strangers. As I told you, I am a recluse, and I keep myself to myself.'

"I forbore to make the obvious retort that no one was likely to object, and he went rambling on, evidently trying to put me at my ease. And then at last the woman arrived, and I escaped upstairs.

"'Mr. Granger seems in a very nervous condition,' I said to her.

"She was a furtive-eyed creature and very uncommunicative.

"'So would you be if you never stirred outside the house,' she muttered morosely. 'Here's your room.'

"She flung open a door, and walked in in front of me. And then Gaspard brought in my box, and the pair of them went out and left me alone. The room was quite comfortable, though the furniture was very plain. And like every other room in the house, there were steel bars over the window.

"I got unpacked, and shortly afterwards the woman brought me some tea.

"'When you've finished, ring the bell and I'll take you to Granger,' she said.

"I noticed the omission of the *mister*, but said nothing. As a matter of fact, it only confirmed what I'd thought ever since I got into the house, that they were all of much the same class. However, I finished my tea and went off to interview the gentleman. His room is at the top of the house, and is, if possible, more heavily barricaded than the rest. The door is about three inches thick, and you can hardly see out of the window for bars. He was sitting at his desk when I came in, and I took a pew opposite, from which I could study him more fully than I'd been able to up to date. He is the most terrible little man, Tom: perfectly frightful. He is like some kind of insect with a rash on it, and but for the fifty quid I think I should have left then and there.

"However, he started explaining what he wanted me to do. And after a time I had to stop him: he was so incoherent and rambling that I could not make head or tail of what he was saying. In addition to which he kept popping up to have a look out of the window, until I could have shied the inkpot at his head.

"'You must forgive me, Miss Verney,' he said several times, 'but I have had a great shock just lately.'

"I said nothing, of course, but presumably he was alluding to the signals Captain Drummond was talking about. And quite obviously the man is in a pitiful condition of nerves. However, to get back to the point. After he had hummed and hawed for some time, and told me that he would want me to write letters and that sort of thing for him, he suddenly asked me if I knew anything about jewellery and precious stones. I said I knew very little.

"'I have one or two beautiful bits of stuff,' he rambled on. 'I have been an ardent collector for years.'

"Which, of course, was very nice, but what it had to do with my duties as his secretary was a little obscure. So I brought him back to the point.

"'I should like to know, Mr. Granger,' I said, 'what will be the arrangement over going out. There seemed to be a great deal of difficulty over getting in: I hope it won't apply to getting out.'

"'That we will arrange,' he cried. 'Just at present it would be better, I think, for you to take your walk in the grounds. There are reasons, important reasons. But one thing, as you value your life, you must not forget—do not go out after dusk.'

"'You mean the dog?' I said.

"'Yes—and other things, too. Soon I hope the danger will be over, but for the next few days do not forget my warning.'

"And then I could not help it: I just had to ask him:

"'Why have you got your house barricaded like a prison?' I said.

"'I have an enemy,' he answered; 'an unscrupulous enemy. He believes I did him a wrong—years ago. As if one could do such as he a wrong. But I'll beat him, I'll beat him.'

"He was literally jibbering in his excitement, and for some time I thought he was going to have a fit. Then the upheaval passed.

"'A vile criminal, Miss Verney: a man debased beyond words.'

"Bearing in mind the speaker, I thought that a bit rich.

"'Do not be alarmed,' he continued, 'if you hear things at night, out in the grounds. You will be quite safe. Well, well, we will finish our talk tomorrow. A letter or two, and your outings. We must discuss them: we must certainly discuss them.'

"And with that I left him. Honestly I do not think the man is quite all there, and as for his remarks about the criminal outside, the man is as crooked as a corkscrew himself. However, it is past eleven now, and I am going to bed. My dinner was sent up to my room, and I have not seen Mr. Granger again. But an hour ago I heard the most frightful quarrel going on between him and Gaspard, and it sounded to me as if Gaspard was drunk. Anyway, I have locked my door, though, to give the devil his due, neither of them has given me any trouble at all. Good-night: I'll finish this effusion tomorrow, though whether I will ever get it to you or not remains to be seen."

CHAPTER 6

In Which We Come to Temple Tower

"By Gosh! The old thing has spread herself," said Freckles. "There is a further vast instalment."

"Get on with it," cried Hugh. "It strikes me Miss Verney has her head screwed on in exactly the right way."

"She is not too dusty," conceded her fiancé graciously. "Now this whack of stuff is headed Mid-day."

"Had a perfectly good night," she begins, "though I woke up once with that beastly dog baying at something outside. However, I soon fell asleep again, and did not wake till after eight. All of which matters not: I'll get on with it. I received his majesty's command to wait on him at ten o'clock. Now you know my watch has never been quite itself again since it fell in the river at Henley, and sure enough it had apparently gained about twenty minutes this morning. The result was that little Patricia, with pencil and paper complete, fresh and radiant in the morning sunshine, popped into the sacred room at twenty to ten instead of ten. Not, you would have thought, a very frightful crime, but you should have seen the result. His lordship was kneeling by the side of the fireplace, holding something in his hand. As soon as he heard the door open he thrust whatever it was back into a recess, which he closed. Then he scrambled to his feet in a fury.

"'I said ten,' he stormed.

"'I thought it was ten,' I remarked amiably. 'My watch must have gained.'

"Then I sat down with paper and pencil, and waited for him to start. After a bit he calmed down and took a seat at his desk.

"'You must make allowances for me, Miss Verney,' he mumbled. 'My health is not very good.'

"'That's all right,' I said. 'It was my fault for coming too soon.'

"And once more I waited for him to begin. At last he got under way, and dictated three short letters—all of them business, and all of them trivial to a degree. Then he stopped.

"'Is that all?' I said.

"'All for this morning,' he answered. 'As a matter of fact, Miss Verney, my correspondence is very small. Being the recluse I am, I know but few people.'

"'If this is a fair sample of a day's job,' I remarked, 'I shall certainly not be overworked. I will go and type these now, and bring them to you to sign.'

"I got up and went to the door and just as I was opening it I heard him muttering in his beard again: there are times when he talks exactly like a man with his mouth full of fish-bones. So I waited for him to get it off his chest, and if you can explain it I shall be glad, for I certainly can't.

"He first of all started on the question of outings. He mumbled and he grunted, and repeated his warning of last night about the immediate future. Then without a word of warning he suddenly asked me if I'd like to go to London. I stared at him blankly and asked him if he meant alone, or was he going, or what.

"'Alone,' he said. 'All alone in a nice first-class carriage.'

"Honestly, Tom, I don't think the man is all there. I half expected him to go on and say something about the pretty puff-puff. However I waited, and let him get on with it in his own way.

"'You see, Miss Verney,' he said for the twenty-fourth time, 'I am a recluse. I dislike intensely going outside my own grounds. And one of the things that I shall wish you to do for me will be to make frequent trips to London on very confidential business.'

"'That seems quite clear,' I said. 'But what sort of business? Because I have got no knowledge of anything except typing and shorthand.'

"'You won't require any knowledge,' he assured me. 'All that I want is a nice-looking young lady whom I can trust implicitly.'

"And suddenly I remembered a thing which Miss Mudge had said when she told me of my being engaged. At the time I didn't think about it, but now it came back. One absolute proviso was that I must look a lady.

"'You see, Miss Verney,' he went on, 'my one hobby all through my life has been acquiring beautiful things. And recently a relative of mine has died, and left me a wonderful collection of old jewellery. Now this big place, as you will understand, costs a lot of money to keep up, and

I fear that, much as I regret it, I shall have to sell some of my things. And that is where I want you to help me.'

"'You mean,' I said, 'that you want me to take them up to London and sell them for you?'

"'That's it,' he cried. 'That is just what I want.'

But why not send for a good man from Christies,' I said, 'or a first-class jeweller to come here? I should probably be badly swindled.'

"He shook his head cunningly.

"'No, you won't,' he said. 'Not if you do it the way I say. You see,' he went on confidentially, 'it is like this. If I send for a first-class jeweller to come to me here, and he sees all my collection or even half of it, it stands to reason that he won't give me as good a price as if I sold each article separately. At the same time I obviously cannot ask a man to make fifty different journeys down here and show him the things one at a time. So I want you to make the fifty different journeys up to London. There are scores of first-class jewellers either there or in the big towns like Birmingham and Manchester, and if you go to a different one each time you will get the maximum price for each article. Look, for instance, at that.'

"He produced from his desk a small box, and opened it. Inside was the most lovely pearl and diamond pendant I have ever seen. The setting was old-fashioned, but even I could realise how valuable it was.

"'Now,' he went on, 'if you took that to a good man, and told him it had been left you by your mother or a relative, I am sure he would give you a thousand pounds for it.'

"'I should think it more than likely,' I said. 'But why bring in the bit about it having been left me? Why not simply say that I want to sell it?'

"'He might want to know how you got it.' he explained. 'And the one important thing. Miss Verney, is that the news should not be passed round among them that a big collection is being disposed of piecemeal. Once that is known, down will go the prices.'

"I suppose he is right, though I don't know much about these things.

"'I had intended,' he went on, 'when I first engaged you for you to start on that side of your duties at once. But now certain things have occurred which render it necessary for you to postpone it a little. So that for a few days, my dear young lady—just for a few days—your duties will not be very onerous.'

"With that I left him, and went and typed the letters. What is the meaning of it, Tom? One thing is perfectly clear: it is not for any secretarial work that I have been engaged. The main part of my job is obviously to sell his stuff for him. But it all seems so peculiar.

Incidentally when I took him back the letters to sign, he was down again on his knees by the fireplace, and he had completely forgotten all about them. Moreover he was furious at my walking in, though I had knocked twice.

"Lunch time—so I will stop. What do you think? It all seems very funny to me."

"And to me," said Hugh thoughtfully, as Freckles folded up the letter. "But not inexplicable, once one thing is granted."

"And that is?" I asked.

"That the stuff to be disposed of is stolen," he answered. "If this collection he talks of was honestly come by, the simplest method by far of disposing of it would be to do what Miss Verney suggests, and have a really good man down from London. Obviously he dare not. So he has hit on this distinctly clever method. If Miss Verney walked into a shop with an ornament such as she mentions, it would arouse no suspicions. It is just the sort of thing she might have been left by a relative. And a good man would give her a fair price for it. If Granger walked into a shop with it they would probably ring up Scotland Yard after one look at his face. And if he took it to an ordinary fence he would get a third of its value."

He rose and began to stroll up and down.

"We are on the line," he said: "I am sure of it, though we are the deuce of a long way from spotting the whole thing. Our friend at Temple Tower is obviously in possession of a big lump of stolen property which he intends to sell. For that purpose he engages a lady secretary, who without suspicion can get a good price for it. Then suddenly along comes the bird at Spragge's Farm who puts the fear of God into Granger. He is probably a man whom Granger double-crossed, and who is entitled to his share of the swag. So that necessitates Miss Verney's activities being postponed until he is disposed of one way or the other. Does that sound feasible?"

And the more I thought of it the more it did, though, as Hugh said, there were still a lot of unaccountable things. Where, for instance, did the Vandalis come in? Were they also entitled to a share in the stolen property? And, if so, why had Granger not recognised them? And then last, but certainly not least, whose was that mysterious black figure that had flitted silently through the wood, and which inspired Granger with such ghastly terror? Was it the man from Spragge's Farm, or was it yet a further complication? A sudden exclamation from Hugh interrupted my thoughts. He was standing with his eye glued to the telescope, and the instrument was focussed on Spragge's Farm.

"Activity," he remarked, "on one of the fronts. There is a car standing outside the farm—a thing that looks like a tradesman's van. They are all three of them there, the two men and the woman, and they are putting something into it. By Jove!" he went on excitedly after a moment, "I believe it is. It is just about the shape. They are putting the rope ladder on board, you fellows. Now the woman has gone into the house, and one of the men has clambered into the back of the car. They're off."

And now it was easy to see the car coming along the track away from Rye, and after a while we lost sight of it.

"I wonder what that signifies," said Freckles.

"It signifies that the ladder is finished," said Hugh gravely. "And it also signifies, if I mistake not, that the game is shortly going to begin in earnest. That car can get to Temple Tower from the opposite direction. Come on: we've got to take the road once more."

"But he surely won't try and climb the wall by daylight?" I cried.

"No: but it is more than possible that he is going to hide the ladder nearer the scene of action by daylight," said Hugh. "And if he hides it anywhere he is going to hide it in that wood. There is no particular hurry because it is going to take that car at least half an hour to get there going by that route. But I think we'll just stroll along and see what happens."

And so once again did we find ourselves lying up in our hiding-place opposite the gate of Temple Tower, only this time Hugh was with us. Moreover I noticed that he, every now and then, threw a glance over his shoulder into the gloom of the wood behind, as if he expected to see that mysterious black figure. But on this occasion there was no sign of it: the wood was silent and deserted. And after a time I even began to wonder if the whole thing had not been a trick of the light, and whether we hadn't imagined it all.

Ten minutes passed, quarter of an hour, and then we heard the sound of a car in the distance. Very cautiously we peered out, and Hugh gave a little grunt of satisfaction.

"It is the one I saw," he muttered, and we waited breathlessly to see what would happen. Forty yards away from us it pulled up, and Spragge, who was driving, said something to the passenger hidden behind. And the next moment the ladder maker emerged.

I don't know about the others, but to me he seemed even more repulsive in the daylight than he had the night before. He peered up and down the road; then, seeing there was no one in sight, he hauled his ladder out of the body of the car. The rope part was wrapped round the central bolster, and its general appearance was that of a gigantic sausage. Then, putting it under his arm, he dived into the undergrowth.

We could hear him crashing about, and then, after a short silence, he emerged, and again went to the back of the car. This time he pulled out a wooden pole about the length of a hay-rake. At one end he had constructed a sort of cradle, and its object was evidently to enable him to hoist the ladder into position on the wall. He went into the wood once more: then, reappearing a second time, he vanished into the back of the car, which drove rapidly past us towards Rye. His preparations were finished: he was ready for the night's work.

We waited till the car had disappeared, and then stepped out on to the road.

"There would be no harm," remarked Hugh, "in investigating our friend's handiwork. And there is one rather useful point. If he makes as much noise moving about at night as he did then, he won't be hard to follow."

We found the ladder and the wooden cradle without difficulty. They had been roughly pushed under some blackberry-bushes, with but little attempt at concealment. Relying on the fact that there was no one about, all he had done was to put them sufficiently far from the road to escape the eye of a stray passer-by.

"A sailor, I should think," remarked Hugh thoughtfully, as he examined the ladder. "That canvas and tarred twine seem to smack of the sea."

"Do we leave them there?" asked Freckles.

"We do, my lad," laughed Hugh. "Because unless I am very much mistaken tonight's entertainment is going to help us considerably to elucidate things. It is all right, young fellow," he went on reassuringly. "Miss Verney is not going to come to any harm—that I promise you. Let's stroll back and see if John has returned to the fold."

And even as he spoke he swung round with that characteristic movement I knew so well. He was peering into the undergrowth with every muscle braced, and every nerve alert. But nothing moved: the silence was still absolute. And after a while he relaxed and stepped out of the wood into the road.

"What did you see?" said Freckles eagerly.

"Nothing," he answered curtly. "I thought I did for a moment, but it was my imagination. Come on: let's get back."

He said no more until we were in the house, and then he waited till Freckles had left us alone.

"Peter," he said gravely, "the plot thickens."

"You did see something in the wood, then?" I remarked.

"I saw your mysterious black friend," he answered quietly. "He is very good at concealing himself, but I happen to know a trick or two concerning that game myself. He was about twenty yards away from us."

"But then why didn't we go for him?" I cried bewildered.

"There is one little point that I have learned in the course of my life, Peter," he answered, "that rather influenced the situation. A man without a gun is at a considerable disadvantage when opposed to a man with one. We were in the former category: he was in the latter. Had we moved, we were for it: he'd got us covered."

"But do you really think he would have dared to have shot the three of us close to a main road?" I objected.

"I don't suppose he wished to for a moment," he agreed. "At the same time, had we gone for him then and there he might have been forced to. And I wasn't for taking the chance. Peter," he went on in a lower voice, "there is a damned sight more in this affair than is at present sticking out on the surface. We are up against something pretty big, and we have got to move warily. But there is one thing I can promise the gentleman in the wood: two people can play at his game. My hand may have lost its cunning to a certain extent, but I think I can still guarantee to stalk the stalker. And next time he will not be the only one with a gun . Don't say anything to the youngster."

I did not, though I couldn't prevent myself from thinking over this new development. That Hugh was perhaps mistaken never entered my head: he simply was one of those men who did not make mistakes on matters of that sort. He had the eyesight of a lynx, and if he had seen an automatic, then there was an automatic. And as he said, it put matters on a different footing. If the owner of the gun was prepared, if forced to it, to kill three men close to a main road, the affair was bigger than we had at first thought. But who was he: what was he: where did he come in? Was he acting in collusion with the ladder maker Marillard? Or was he another quite separate cog in the machine? One thing was certain, whatever he might be: he was a very dangerous addition to the other side. And a further thing, too, was certain. The possibility that it might be Marillard himself who was masquerading in some disguise was disposed of: that at any rate we now knew.

John James had appeared on the scene in time for dinner, eager to hear if any further doings had taken place. And having been posted up to date there was nothing further to do but to wait for darkness before once again treading the familiar road to Temple Tower. Hugh was unusually silent as we sat outside finishing our brandy, and I guessed that he was trying to piece together the jigsaw in his mind. And it came as a feeling of relief when, at a quarter to ten, he got up and said it was time to start.

"Come into my study for a moment, Peter," he said to me. "Look here, old boy," he remarked when he had shut the door, "here is one for you. I daren't trust either of the other two with a gun, but you are used to them."

I slipped a vicious-looking little Colt into my pocket, and I could see the outline of another in his.

"Needless to say, don't use it unless it is absolutely essential," he warned, "But also, needless to say, don't forget that our friend of the wood carries one himself."

We rejoined the others, and Hugh looked at them critically. Freckles was obviously on edge with excitement, and Hugh smote him on the back.

"Easy does it, young fellow," he laughed. "And don't forget—not an unnecessary word, not an unnecessary sound. And if I tell you to do something, jump to it. Now we'll go in two pairs. I'll go first with Scott, and we will go beyond the spot where we know the ladder is hidden. Peter, you follow with John, and go to ground where we were this afternoon. Give us two or three minutes' start."

It was practically dark when we reached our hiding-place. We had passed no one on the road, nor had we seen any sign of the other two who were some three or four hundred yards ahead of us.

"How long are we likely to have to stop here?" whispered John James to me.

"Ask me another," I answered. "Presumably until our friend from Spragge's Farm considers it safe to start work."

Half an hour passed, an hour, and then quite suddenly from inside the grounds there came the most terrible sound. It rose and fell in a deep throated snarling roar, savage beyond description. For perhaps a quarter of a minute it continued: then it ceased as abruptly as it had commenced.

"Good God! what was that?" muttered John James in a shaking voice.

"The Pekinese," I answered, none too steadily myself. "I've heard the brute once before."

And at that moment I heard Hugh's voice, low and urgent.

"Peter, where are you?" He loomed out of the darkness. "We have been stung," he said. "The ladder has gone. We have been sitting here all this time like damned fools, and the enemy is inside."

We scrambled to our feet, as Scott joined him.

"When I heard that hound," he went on, "I began to wonder. So I had a look. It is not there. Our friend is inside the wall. Moreover," he continued grimly, "the dog seems to be aware of the fact."

"What do we do now?" I asked.

"Go round the wall," he answered, "keeping your eyes skinned for the ladder. We ought just to be able to see that bolster thing against the sky. If we can't we are done, because the ladder itself will be inside. I'll lead: Peter, you bring up the rear."

We started off in single file, keeping to the road. As Hugh had said, it was possible to see the top of the wall outlined against the sky, and there had been no sign of the canvas sack when we reached the corner. There we struck away from the road at right angles, still following the wall. And as luck would have it we had come the right way. Not fifty yards from where we had turned we saw it on top of the wall.

"Now," said Hugh, "which of you two is the lightest? Scott, I should think. Up you go, young fellow, on my shoulders: get astride that bolster and pass the ladder over to this side."

It proved easier than one would have thought, and ten seconds later Freckles was sitting astride the wall and Hugh was climbing up the ladder. Then he threw it over to the other side and disappeared down it, leaving Freckles to pass it back for us. John James went next and I followed, and three minutes from the time we had found it we were all inside.

There was plenty of cover to conceal our movements as we crept cautiously forward. The whole place was unkempt and badly looked after. Thick undergrowth grew between the trees, and there was no semblance of even the crudest track or footpath. At last we came to an opening. Ahead of us, some fifty yards away, lay the house, and a light was burning in one of the ground-floor windows. Then suddenly another light went on, this time on the second floor, and outlined against it was the figure of a girl. She was peering out, and Freckles gave a quick exclamation.

"Shut up," growled Hugh. "Not a sound."

It was Miss Verney, and after a time she put out the light again. Once more the house was in darkness save for the ground-floor room.

"I want to see into that room," whispered Hugh. "Skirt round to the left, keeping under cover."

We followed him, dodging from tree to tree, until he halted before another open space. In front of us was what looked like an old ruined wall, as far as one could see in the darkness. It was broken down and crumbling, and in some places was on a level with the ground.

"The old chapel," he muttered, and John James grunted assent.

And we were just on the point of going on when there came the sound of voices from the house. It was too far off to hear what was said, but they were loud and angry. Both were men's, and it was obvious that a quarrel was going on. And then, just for an instant, I saw the two of them silhouetted against the light, and recognised Granger and the servant Gaspard. Granger was shaking his fists in the air, and Gaspard was standing sullenly with his hands in his pockets. Then they disappeared, and the light went out.

"Damn," muttered Hugh. "However, let's go on and have a look at the chapel. Careful where you put your feet: it is going to be awkward if someone sprains his ankle."

We crept on till we came to the crumbling stonework. It was grass-grown and afforded treacherous walking, rendered all the harder by the darkness. Twice did I dislodge a stone with my foot, and I was just beginning to wonder what good Hugh hoped to do when I heard him give a gasp of surprise. I peered ahead: he was bending over something on the ground.

"Peter," he muttered, "look at this."

This was the dog—stone dead. It was an enormous brute, and its body was arched, and its great fangs gleamed white in a last death snarl. And in the air there hung the smell of burnt almonds.

"Prussic acid," he said. "I wondered what had silenced it so suddenly."

And then he straightened up, and his hand went to his revolver pocket.

"The dog is dead," he muttered grimly, "but the man who did it—isn't. Keep your eyes skinned."

Instinctively, we closed up; there was something terrifying about that gloomy, silent house and the rank undergrowth, even without the additional knowledge that we were not the only watchers. The whole place smelt of decay, and I was on the point of suggesting to Hugh that we should go, when there came from the house the sound of bolts being drawn. Someone was coming out.

The door opened, and in the dim light from the hall we saw for a moment the outlines of Granger and the servant. Then it clanged to again, and we heard the bolt shoot home.

"Nero; where are you, you brute?"

Gaspard's voice came through the darkness: evidently he had been shut out of the house to find out what had happened to the dog. He went plunging into the undergrowth, calling and whistling, whilst we still stood there undecided what to do.

"Nero. Nero."

His voice was coming closer, and Hugh signed to us to move back under cover. And then quite suddenly there came a shrill scream of terror, followed by a horrible choking noise. The calls for Nero ceased abruptly: and after a moment or two the choking noise ceased too. The same thought was in all our minds: what was happening in the darkness close by? What had caused that sudden scream of mortal fear?

Like a shadow Hugh glided away in the direction of the sound, and we followed. Every now and then he paused and peered ahead, but in the gloom of the undergrowth it was impossible to see anything. And it so happened that it was my lot to make the discovery. I was the last of the four, and quite by chance I was staring at a bush to my left. And it seemed to me that something moved.

I went nearer, and only by the greatest self-control did I check a cry myself. A great black object was lying on the ground, and as I approached it suddenly rose. It seemed to unwrap itself, and I felt instinctively that it was staring at me. Then, with a sort of snarling hiss, it vanished, and I saw what it had left behind.

"Hugh," I said shakily, and in a second he was with me.

"Good God!" he muttered, and pulled out a tiny electric torch. Gaspard was lying there, his face red and swollen, and a glance showed that he was dead. He had been throttled: the marks on his throat were plain to see.

"It was the black figure," I said. "It was lying on top of him, and when it heard me, it got up and vanished."

"It strikes me we are dealing with a homicidal maniac," he remarked, and his voice was hard. "And with that brand one shoots on sight. Let's see if we can't get a sight. Back to the ladder, and move."

He led the way, and we followed as quickly as we could. But to keep up with Hugh in the dark was an impossibility, and he was soon far ahead of us. At last the wall loomed up in front, and it was as we reached it that the sharp crack of a revolver brought us all up standing. It came from the direction of the road, and a sick feeling of fear got hold of me. Which of them had fired?

"Hugh," I called out, regardless of who might hear. "Where are you?"

"All right, Peter," came his welcome voice, and to my amazement I realised that he was the same side as we were.

"That shot!" I said. "Who fired it?"

"I can't see through a brick wall," he answered, "so I don't know. But with luck we may find out soon. He was over the wall when I got here, and the ladder is the other side. Up you go, Scott, and pass it back."

Once again we repeated the performance of crossing, but this time Hugh was off like a flash the instant he reached the ground. And it was just as we were wondering whether to follow him or not that the final shock of the evening occurred. A voice with a slight American twang came out of the darkness from close by.

"May I ask what you guys think you are doing?" it said. "Or would it be indiscreet?"

"Who are you?" I cried. "And where are you?"

"Who I am doesn't matter at the moment," went on the voice. "Nor where I am. But I have a gun in my hand, which I shall have no hesitation in using, if necessary."

"A game at which two can play."

Hugh's voice, doubly welcome this time, showed that he had returned.

"By the sound you are both new ones to me," said the unknown quietly. "I am thinking we'd better have a little light on the scene, or else someone will be making a bloomer."

"Then I will supply it," snapped Hugh.

He switched on his torch, and focussed it on the stranger. He was standing about five yards away, a thin, hatchet-faced man of about fifty. In his hand was a revolver, but it was banging loosely by his side, and he made no move to raise it. For a while he stood there in silence: then he smiled faintly and spoke.

"I trust the inspection is satisfactory," he remarked. "But in case you want anything more, do you recognise that?"

He opened his coat, displaying the badge of the New York police.

"I do," said Hugh. "Was it you who fired that shot?"

"It was not," answered the other. "And if you will deflect your torch a little lower you will see why, though you will have to come nearer."

He was still holding his coat open, and as we got close to him we could see a bullet hole clean through it on a level with his waist.

"Touch and go, gentlemen," he remarked. "And now, if you have satisfied yourselves that I am not the villain of the piece, I would strongly suggest that you put out that torch. There are people abroad tonight who are attracted to torches, and next time it may not be my coat."

For a moment or two Hugh hesitated, then he switched off the light.

"May I ask what your name is?" he said.

"Certainly, though I fear it will not convey much to you. My name is Matthews—Victor Matthews. Am I right in supposing that you are the gentlemen who were wandering around Spragge's Farm last night?"

"You can suppose any damned thing you please," snapped Hugh. "What I want to know, Mr. Matthews, is what you are doing prowling about here?" The other laughed.

"I have always heard," he said, "that offence is the best defence. But really, sir, don't you think your remark is a bit cool? You may remember the badge I showed you, which, at any rate, gives me an official standing. But as far as you gentlemen are concerned, I fail to see that you have any—certainly none that permits you to break into the private grounds of a house in the dead of night. However, you need not fear: I shall say nothing about it. In fact, I am profoundly relieved to see you. I have played a lone hand long enough. And if you are prepared to assist me, no one will be more pleased than myself. Did you find anything of interest inside there tonight?"

"We found," said Hugh quietly, "a dead dog and a dead man."

"Dead man!" cried the other sharply. "Who—*le Rossignol*?"

"The how much?" cried Hugh: prizes for French have hitherto eluded him.

"The Nightingale," said Matthews. "The man you saw at Spragge's Farm, making that ladder."

"No: it wasn't him," said Hugh. "It was Gaspard, Granger's servant. And he had been killed by a mysterious being in black."

"Throttled, of course," said the other.

"How do you know that?" asked Hugh suspiciously.

"Because," said Matthews, "the mysterious being in black, as you call him, who very nearly finished me off, is known, amongst other things, as the Silent Strangler. So he has killed the servant, has he?"

"We came on him in the act," said Hugh.

"Then that accounts for his rapid retreat," remarked Matthews thoughtfully. "Well, gentlemen, do we work together, or do we not? I can only assume that you have come into this show out of idle curiosity, or for sport. Am I right?"

And now it was Hugh's turn to laugh.

"I have heard worse guesses," he said. "What do you think, Peter?"

"I certainly think that if Mr. Matthews can explain some of these mysterious happenings we should join forces," I said.

"I can explain almost everything," he answered quietly. "But I do not think this is either the time or the place. So let us put things in order here, and go. It will be dawn soon."

"But look here, chaps," objected Freckles, "what about the bloke from Spragge's Farm—the Sparrow or whatever he is called? He must still be lying about all over the place."

It was perfectly true: in the general excitement the ladder maker had been forgotten.

"You saw no signs of him inside?" asked Matthews.

"Not a trace," said Hugh. "And even if we didn't see him, I should have expected to hear him. He is not a silent mover. Incidentally, I wonder if he came at all tonight."

"He must have, to put the ladder there," said John.

"Not of necessity," answered Hugh. "Don't forget that this man in black saw him hide it and knew where it was."

"How do you know that?" cried Matthews.

"Because we encountered the gentleman in the wood this afternoon. Only, as he was armed and we weren't, we left him alone."

Matthews whistled softly.

"You can thank your stars that you did," he remarked. "Or we should not be having this conversation now. Anyway, gentlemen, I look at it this way: If *le Rossignol* is inside there, let him remain: he will do no harm. He will kill Granger if he gets a chance, but, believe me, that doesn't matter. And if he is outside, again, let him remain there."

"That is all jolly fine and large," cried Freckles, "but a great friend of mine—a lady—is inside there, too."

"What's that?" said Matthews. "A lady? How is that?"

"My fiancée is doing secretarial work for Granger," explained Freckles.

And once again Matthews whistled softly.

"Splendid," was his somewhat unexpected remark. "Perfectly splendid."

"I am damned if I see anything splendid about it," grunted Freckles.

"But I venture to think that you will," answered the other. And then his tone changed. "Gentlemen," he said briskly, "we cannot stand here all night. You, of course, must do exactly as you like. But may I ask what you were proposing to do if you had not run into me?"

And for a while no one answered. It was a bit of a poser: what was there to be done?

"As I thought," continued Matthews, "you don't know. And I don't blame you. To be quite frank, gentlemen, you have put yourselves in a position that is a little difficult to explain. If you go to the police you have to admit that you have broken the law yourselves, and you have to tell them a story which will take a bit of swallowing. I know it is true: you know it is true, but—well, I won't labour the point. I think you would find the atmosphere a little incredulous, to put it mildly. So I have a definite proposition to make to you. Do nothing at all until you have heard my story. As I told you, I can explain everything—or almost everything. Then you must do as you see fit—go to the police or not, as you like. In return, you shall tell me all you know, and between us, gentlemen"—his voice rose in his excitement—"we will beat the most dangerous criminal that lives in the world today."

"Yes, but what about my fiancée?" cried Freckles.

"I give you my solemn word that she is in no danger," said Matthews quietly. "But if you are under any apprehensions, get her out of the house tomorrow. Anyway, you can't now. And, as I said before, I think you will understand, when you have heard my story, why I was pleased when I heard that one of our side was in the house. Well, gentlemen, what do you say?"

And at last Hugh spoke.

"Agreed," he said laconically. "You had better come to my shanty."

"Good!" cried Matthews. "Then the first thing to do is to remove that ladder and hide it in a different place. And after that we will go to your house, and I will tell you a story which, though long, I think you will find not uninteresting."

Chapter 7

In Which Victor Matthews Begins His Story

"For the purposes of this argument, Mr. Matthews," remarked Hugh, "you had better assume that we know nothing."

We had all returned to his house, and having hunted round for bacon and eggs, had first of all had some breakfast. The ladder had been carefully hidden in the undergrowth, and we had seen no further trace of the man in black. And now, seated on the terrace, with the mist stretching like a white sea below us, we waited eagerly for him to begin.

"All right," he answered, "I will assume that you know nothing. And, as a matter of fact, gentlemen, I am very certain that you do know nothing of what I am going to tell you. Because I am going back to the year of grace 1881. It was in that year that the inhabitants of Bordeaux had an unsuspected honour accorded them—so unsuspected, in fact, that most of them are still probably unaware of it. Under the very shadow of the Cathedral of St. Andre a male child was born into the world. The question of nomenclature was a little difficult, since the mother had no idea who was the proud father, but she compromised by calling the child Jean and giving it her own surname of Marillard.

"From the very first, I should imagine, the child was a most unprepossessing specimen. It was abnormally ugly, and that fact, coupled with the sneers of its companions over the question of its birth, combined to make its life intolerable. Anyway, it never had a fair chance, and as a result, the boy's character grew from bad to worse. He was an incipient criminal from the start, and his surroundings nurtured the growth, until, at the age of sixteen, he was nothing more nor less than a savage young animal. And if yon chose to turn up the archives of the Bordeaux police you would there find records of positively murderous assaults perpetrated by this youth, in many cases on men years older than himself. He was possessed of incredible strength, and at times he was perfectly uncontrollable. He also possessed another strange characteristic—a very soft and melodious voice."

The speaker smiled slightly and waved his hand in the direction of Spragge's Farm.

"Thus the propitious beginning of Jean Marillard, now, as you will see, in his forty-seventh year. However, to return to his earlier days. He was eighteen years old, as far as I remember, when he decided that he had had enough of Bordeaux and drifted to Paris, where he naturally became associated with the lowest type of Apache. And you must remember, gentlemen, that in those days the Apaches were Apaches—not harmless citizens earning an honest penny by dressing themselves up for the part for the benefit of credulous tourists, as is the case today. Like to like: it was but in the nature of things that young Marillard should consort with the most vicious of the whole tribe. And it was then that he received his nick-name of 'the Nightingale.'

"For the next year or so his history is unimportant. He remained submerged in the underworld of Paris, a skulker in dark corners. And then, with the invention of motor-cars, came the great opportunity. The thing has been done, of course, *ad nauseam* since, but the first motor bandit gang was the one of which the Nightingale was a prominent member. It is all a question of proportion, and just as in these days a racing car, with its eighty miles an hour, has the advantage over other users of the road, so, then, did some ancient Peugeot capable of only twenty.

"And now I must leave him for a moment and introduce you to some other characters in the story. Only two are of any importance, and one of those two...."

He paused, and a strange, almost dreamy, look came into his eyes.

"One of those two is the most powerful and dangerous man in the world today. I will take the other first. His origin is completely obscure. Half an Englishman, half Heaven knows what, he was in his way as dangerous a man as the Nightingale. But it was a very different way. The Nightingale, to do him credit, feared no man. He fought in the open—fought like a beast perhaps—but face to face. Also he was loyal to his pals, which was just what the other was not. A slimy, mean, creeping little beast, who conformed to no standard at all save what suited himself best. They called him *le Crapeau*, which I always thought was an insult to such an intelligent beast as the toad. And unless I am very much mistaken—in fact, I know I am not mistaken—the Toad is your next-door neighbour, who now passes under the name of Granger. When I say 'passes under,' for all I know Granger may really be his name."

"Do you mean to say," shouted Freckles, "that that is the man who Pat—who Miss Verney is working for?"

"Don't alarm yourself, Mr. Scott," said Matthews quietly. "You already have my word for it that your fiancée is perfectly safe. Moreover, I think it is more than likely that you will finally come to the conclusion that the luckiest thing she ever did in her life was to go there."

"What on earth do you mean?" said Freckles, staring at him blankly.

"May I finish my story, and I think you will see what I mean?" said Matthews. "Where was I? Ah! Yes—the Toad. There were three other members of the gang, who do not concern us at all now, since they are all dead. For the sake of clearness, however, I will give you their nicknames. One—a great hulking brute of a man—was called the Butcher. He was a slaughterer pure and simple: a man with no brain, but of great strength. The second was a deadly shot with a revolver, who was known—why I can't tell you—as the Snipe. And the last member calls for no particular description. He had no nickname, and was called Robert.

"Now, I do not propose to weary you with a full account of their activities. Many of them were quite insignificant: many were even stupid. Remember that motor-cars were a new toy then for everyone, and our friends were no exception to the rule. They behaved, in short, on frequent occasions like children who are showing off, and they were treated accordingly by the authorities. Until the day came. . . ."

Once again he paused, that same dreamy look in his eyes.

"Gentlemen," he went on quietly, "you may think that what I am about to tell you is an exaggeration: that I have a bee in my bonnet on this particular subject. You may think that such a being as a master criminal is merely part of the stock in trade of the sensational novelist—a fiction of the films. You are wrong. It was in 1898 that a strange sinister influence began to make itself felt throughout the underworld at Paris, and not only through the underworld, but through that section of society that reacts instantly to it—the police. At first the influence was vague—more a suggestion than a definite force. Incredible rumours flew round, and no one knew what to believe. The police, as a body, scoffed openly at the whole thing: so did some of the Apaches. For gradually these rumours crystallised into one central idea: that a power had arisen which was definitely controlling the criminal activities of Paris, and controlling them for its own ends.

"What the power consisted of no one knew: who wielded it, no one knew. But after a year had passed the scoffing ceased: the thing was a proven fact. An intelligence was at work more powerful than the police, more cunning than the Apaches.

"How came the proof, you ask? I will tell you. Not by any single dramatic stroke, but by a series of incidents, which, though small in themselves, when taken cumulatively, afforded irrefutable evidence. Men who had received orders from an unknown source, and had disregarded them, were found dead: and no one knew the hand that had struck them down. The police, too, did not escape: *gendarmes* who had interfered with the unknown's plan were killed. Some were shot: a few were knifed, but his favourite method was to strangle his victims. In fact, a reign of terror started, the more terrifying because of the air of mystery that surrounded it. Men spoke together in bated whispers, glancing fearfully over their shoulders, for no one knew who was a spy or who was not . The King of the Underworld had arrived."

Victor Matthews paused to light a cigarette, whilst we waited eagerly for him to continue. Amazing though the story was, it was his quiet way of telling it that made it so impressive.

"It was in 1900," he continued, "that a further development took place. He was cunning, this man—and clever. He knew to a nicety the French nationality: his psychology was perfect. Up to date, he had maintained his air of mystery: from now on he would give them something concrete to catch hold of. And so it was that there gradually came into circulation a series of exquisitely drawn little pictures. A man would find one in his pocket when he came to undress, with no idea as to how it had come there. And with each of them would be some definite order, written in block capitals. And if those orders were disobeyed, the recipient would later be found dead, with the same device pinned to his coat. Here is one that I kept for many years."

He pulled out his pocket-book, and even as he had it in his hands, his eyes dilated and he sat motionless, staring at a tree just behind my seat.

"My God!" he muttered. "Look at that."

"What the devil," began Hugh, and then he came over to where I was sitting. And in silence we all stared at a small piece of paper which we had failed to notice in our absorption up till then. It was about two inches square, and was fastened to the tree by a drawing-pin. And in the centre of it, drawn in ink, was a perfect representation of a hunchback.

"Is that the device you mean?" said Hugh quietly.

For answer Matthews unfastened his pocketbook, and from it he took the exact replica of the paper pinned to the tree, save that it was yellow with age. But the drawing was the same—a hunchback.

"I took this one," he said gravely, "from the body of a man who was found strangled one morning behind a lot of crates in the Gare de Lyons. He had in his pocket a third-class ticket for Marseilles, but he had not caught his train."

For a while we were all silent, each busy with our own thoughts. This sudden verification of Matthews' story, coming, as it were, out of the blue into a sunny English garden, seemed well-nigh uncanny. Almost mechanically Hugh went to the telescope and stared through it. And after a while he swung round and faced us.

"How the devil did that get there?" he said.

Matthews gave a short laugh.

"Your activities are evidently known. Captain Drummond, and are not approved of. *Le Bossu Masque* must have put it there himself."

"*Masque?*" I cried, and Matthews nodded.

"Yes: I was coming to that, when this somewhat dramatic interruption occurred."

"Damn the fellow," spluttered Hugh. "Having the gall to come into my garden and stick his cursed bits of paper all over the view. If I catch the blighter I'll turn his hump into a goitre in his neck. However, Mr. Matthews, please pardon the natural annoyance of a respectable English householder. Let's hear some more."

"Well, as I was saying," continued the other, "it was in 1900 that that design began to become familiar with the population of Paris. That it was a further development of the same man, we knew; his methods remained exactly similar to those he employed when he was unknown. Only now he began to grow more daring. Up till then, his orders had always been transmitted in writing: now he commenced to issue them verbally. And this, of course, was seized on as a golden opportunity by the police. In every community there are men who can be bought, and the underworld of Paris is certainly no exception to the rule. And so as soon as this new development became known plans were very carefully laid to catch him. With great secrecy, and through the most trustworthy channels possible, it was communicated to certain likely quarters that in the event of anyone receiving a message from *le Bossu*, with instructions to meet him personally, the police were to be at once communicated with. And a very big reward was promised if the information led to his capture.

"Sure enough, one day we got a ring on the telephone. And a guarded voice informed us that *le Bossu* had summoned the speaker—a particularly unpleasant form of brute known as the Rat—to go to a small hotel not far from the Gare de l'Est at ten that night. The police surrounded the place: every entrance to the hotel was picketed when the Rat arrived. He was presumably to receive more detailed instructions in the hall as to which room he was to go to, and we gave him orders to communicate the number to the man at the door. It had been decided to allow him a little time with *le Bossu* so that we could find out what scheme that gentleman had in view, and it was ten minutes after the Rat had disappeared upstairs that we rushed the room.

"Now, gentlemen, I was in the passage outside the room from the time the Rat went in. And I will swear that no one came out. Yet, when we went in, he was lying stone dead in the middle of the carpet, with a knife driven up to the hilt in his back."

"Good Lord!" said Freckles, a cigarette he had forgotten to light between his lips. "But how did the fellow get away?"

Matthews shrugged his shoulders.

"The window was open, and so that was where he escaped, presumably. But that was only one case out of a dozen."

"Hold hard a minute," said Hugh. "Had no one in the hotel seen the man who took the room?"

"The room had been booked by telephone," said Matthews. "And the hotel, though small, is a busy one. Numbers of men had been in there that evening, and it was quite impossible to say which of them it was."

"But a hunchback is a pretty conspicuous figure," I objected.

"Ah! But was he a hunchback? True, he had adopted this device, but that was no proof that he was one himself. Or possibly the hump was detachable—a specially assumed disguise."

"Yes—that's true," agreed Hugh.

"You may take it from me, gentlemen," went on Matthews, "that we took every possible, and impossible, theory into account. But the plain, bald fact remained that under the very noses of the police the Rat had been murdered, and the murderer had vanished into thin air. However, I must get on: that is all ancient history and is nothing whatever to do with our little affair today, save that it gives you a good idea of the type of man we are dealing with."

"Awfully jolly," murmured Freckles. "He sounds an absolute topper."

"I'm coming now to the part that really concerns us," continued Matthews. "And to make it clear to you, I will take it as it actually happened, not as we found it out at the trial of the Nightingale. He was our informant when, unfortunately, it was too late. As you will understand, after the episode of the Rat, and several others of a similar type, it had become impossible to carry on with the method we had originally hoped so much from. No one dared run the risk, though we doubled and trebled the money offered. But certain facts leaked out from the men who had seen him, and two of these were early established. First—he had a hump, though, as I said before, whether it was genuine or not we didn't know. Second—he was always masked. There was not a soul in the whole underworld of Paris who could claim to have seen his face.

"It was in September, 1902, that the Nightingale received a message which caused him to turn pale with fear—a summons from *le Bossu Masque*. The Nightingale and his gang had, as I have already told you, been playing about with their motor-car, and enjoying themselves in their own mild way. If the truth be known, I think they were rather frightened of the machine: certain it is, they had no notion of its possibilities as an instrument of crime. And to them, pottering along with their little footpad tricks, came this sudden summons. The car, driven by the Nightingale alone, was to be taken to the small town of Magny, halfway between Paris and Rouen, and there further instructions would be given him."

Matthews smiled slightly.

"I can imagine the feelings of *le Rossignol*," he went on, "as he drove out through the Porte Maillot on that fine September morning. The ever-present fear of the driver of those days that the car would break down was for once forgotten: he probably prayed devoutly that it would. But his prayer was unanswered, and at eleven o'clock he drew up outside the Hotel du Grand-Cerf, in Magny, and proceeded to fortify himself with some alcohol.

"Lunch time came, and with it a wild hope that there was some mistake, and that he was to be allowed to continue his normal life undisturbed by *le Bossu Masque*. Vain thought: the summons came as he finished his meal. A letter was handed to him by the *garçon*, which he opened with trembling hands. It ran as follows:

"'At eight tonight you will take the road to Gisors on foot. Four kilometres out of the town, on the left of the road, is a small copse. In the centre of the copse is a wood-cutter's shed. Go there.'

"He told us at the trial, that three times that afternoon did he get as far as the local *gendarmerie*, only on each occasion to have his courage fail him at the last moment. Poor devil! One can hardly blame him. No one knew better than he what had been the penalty for treachery in Paris. And if it occurred in Paris with the whole force of police available, what chance had a couple of stout local *gendarmes* at night in the middle of a wood? And so eight o'clock found him taking the road for Gisors. He trudged along whistling, probably to try and keep his spirits up, until at length the copse on the left of the road loomed up out of the darkness. Like all town-dwellers the country at night was full of nameless terrors for him, even on normal occasions. The sudden scream of a night-bird could make him sweat with fear far more easily than any report of a revolver. So it isn't difficult to imagine his feelings on this far from normal occasion, when he struck into the trees and began to search for the wood-cutter's shed.

"At last he found it. It was in pitch darkness, and when he tried the door it was locked. (Interrupting myself for a moment, I think at the trial, when all this came out, that our friend made as good a story as he could out of it, to try and enlist sympathy. But even granted that, I'll bet he had a pretty grim half-hour.) After a while he sat down, and took out a packet of Caporals. A cigarette, he reflected, might help to quieten his nerves. And even as he felt in his pocket for a match a hand came out of the darkness and took the cigarette out of his mouth.

"Frozen with horror he sat there, leaning against the wall of the shed. Speech he could understand: the roar of Paris he was at home in, but that silent action in the middle of a deserted wood, where he had believe himself to be alone, literally petrified him with terror. His tongue was cleaving to his dry mouth: he couldn't even scream. Somewhere close to him was that most dreaded being in Paris—the masked hunchback.

"The sweat ran in streams from his forehead: his teeth chattered. If only this other one would speak: if only something would happen to break this ghastly silence! But there was nothing—nothing save the faint creaking of the trees in the night breeze. At last he forced himself to look round: there, standing just behind him, was the figure of a man. He could make out no details: only the outline could be seen against the blackness of the wood. And after a while he scrambled to his feet.

"'I have come,' he said in a shaking voice.

"'Why do you suppose, *Rossignol*, that I chose a spot like this for our rendezvous?'

"According to Marillard at his trial the voice of *le Bossu* was the most terrible thing he had ever heard. It was never raised, and his own description of it was that it sounded like drops of iced water boring into his brain.

"'That we should be secret, *M'sieur*,' he stammered.

"'And that is why you propose to light a cigarette in the middle of a dark wood,' went on the voice. 'That you were a fool I have long known: I perceive that you are an even more incredible imbecile than I suspected.'

"'Pardon, *M'sieur*,' muttered *le Rossignol*. 'I am not used to the country: I did not think.'

"'Precisely: you did not think. In future, you will think. Now pay very close attention. Tonight you will sleep at the Hotel du Grand-Cerf. Tomorrow you will return to Paris. The day after you and the Snipe will take the car and go to Chateaudun. You know the road?'

"'No, *M'sieur*. But I will find out.'

"'Yes: you will find out. You leave Paris through the Porte d'Orleans. The distance is one hundred and twenty-five kilometres. Arrived there you will put up at the Hotel de la Place, and see that your car is refilled with petrol and oil. Place also in your car two bottles of wine and food sufficient for two of you for a day. The rest of your gang will go there by train. They will put up at the Hotel St. Louis. Repeat what I have said.'

"In a trembling voice *le Rossignol* repeated his instructions.

"'Good. You will then await further instructions. And be careful, *Rossignol*, to put a guard on your tongue. Too much wine may be dangerous. If you serve me well, it will be to your advantage. If you fail—you will not do so twice. It is my pleasure to employ your car for other purposes than frightening old women in the street.'

"'*Oui, M'sieur*. I will not fail. The Porte d'Orleans, you said?'

"But there was no answer: *le Rossignol* was alone. As he had come so did *le Bossu Masque* go—in utter silence. And an hour later a badly shaken Apache entered the Hotel du Grand-Cerf and called for wine. Whatever the future might hold, this nerve-wracking first fence was safely over. That eerie wood was a thing of the past: in the inn was warmth and comfort and, most important of all, light.

"Now there were many people who, when they heard the story I have just told you at the trial, laughed it to scorn. Why, they demanded, these elaborate and theatrical details? Why this meeting in a deserted wood at what must have been great inconvenience to *le Bossu* himself, if all that transpired could as easily have been done in Paris itself? But they didn't see what I and one or two others saw. They didn't understand that *le Bossu* was a master of criminal psychology. He realised the immensely more powerful effect that he would produce on the mentality of a man like Marillard, if he met him as he had done, rather than in Paris, which was *le Rossignol*'s own atmosphere. It was the terror of the unknown that he was exploiting—the most potent terror of all, especially to a man of low mental calibre. He was proposing to use this gang for his own ends, and none knew better than he that fear was the safest way of keeping their mouths shut. However, that is all in parenthesis. Subsequent events prove only too clearly that I and the others who thought as I did were right. So we will pass on to the day but one after, which found *Rossignol* and the Snipe installed in the Hotel de la Place at Chateadun, while the Toad and the other two were in the Hotel St. Louis. The car had been filled up with petrol and oil: all instructions had been carried out, and there was nothing to do but to wait.

And now we come to one of the most amazing crimes that has ever been perpetrated in France: the crime, moreover, that is the direct cause of this present state of affairs here. Strange, you will think, that such a long time has elapsed, but the reason for that you will understand when I have finished. Many of the actual details of the crime, I can, of course, only fill in by guess-work: for many we have to take Marillard's unsupported word, on an occasion, too, when admittedly he was trying to make out the best case he could for himself. Still, the story hangs together, and I can vouch for its main essentials.

"About three miles out from Chateaudun, on the road to Vendome, there stands the Chateau du Lac Noir. It is a magnificent old building standing in enormous grounds. It dates, I think, from the thirteenth century, and until quite recent years was the property of the Due de St. Euogat. However, he had found keeping up the place beyond his means, and he had sold it about ten years previously to a Russian—Prince Boris Marcovitch. He was a man of fabulous wealth, whose only hobby in life was collecting. He didn't confine himself to one particular line: anything that attracted his attention and that he liked, he bought. But if there was one thing that he did have a predilection for, it was precious stones—particularly emeralds. I have talked to men who had seen his collection, and they have, one and all, assured me that it was unique in the world.

"He was a man of peculiar tastes—this Russian Prince. He rarely, if ever, left the *chateau* grounds, and when he wanted company he imported it wholesale from Paris. It didn't seem to matter very much to him whether he knew the people or whether he didn't. He would write to a cousin of his who lived in the capital, requesting him to bring down a party. Perhaps a dozen girls and some men would arrive, and then for twenty-four hours there would take place what can only be described as an orgy. Drink flowed like water, and the only person on whom it had no effect was the Prince himself.

"I remember a man who had attended one of them describing the end of the performance to me.

"'I was pretty well tight myself,' he said, 'but not as bad as the rest. The whole lot of them, men and women alike, were sprawling round the table dead drunk. In the earlier part of the debauch the Prince had been the leader of the revels: now he sat at the end of the table twirling a wine-glass between his fingers and with a look of ineffable contempt on his face. His thoughts were so obvious that he might have spoken them aloud.'

""'You boors: you loutish swine—why in heaven's name did I ever have anything to do with you?'"

"So my informant told me, and I had confirmation from other sources. He seemed to be a man who from time to time had to break out, and then was sickened by the reaction when he had done so. But his disgust would only last a couple of months at the most. Then another of the same sort of parties would be given, to be attended with the same result.

"It is perhaps unnecessary to say that, whatever was the effect on the host, his guests thoroughly enjoyed the entertainment—particularly the ladies of the party. The Prince would think nothing of giving each girl a present worth a hundred pounds when they left, and since most of them came from the ranks of the Casino de Paris or the Folies Bergeres, you can imagine their feelings on the matter. And so when it was noised abroad in the theatrical set in Paris that a supreme debauch of all was planned, the Prince's cousin became amazingly popular. It was to be a fancy-dress affair, and everyone was to come as an Apache. It got round of course to Police Headquarters, but it was none of our business what the Prince chose to do in his *chateau*. Our only concern was the prevention of crime, and it was on that account that a week before this historic party I found myself getting out of the train at Chateaudun. You will understand that I was unofficially attached, and Grodin, my immediate superior, thought that I could give the Prince a friendly warning better than one of the regular men.

"He saw me at once when I arrived, and as I looked at that refined aristocrat I marvelled that he could ever give way to these appalling excesses.

"'*Monsieur le Prince*,' I said, when he had glanced at my card, 'I wish to assure you that my visit is entirely unofficial. But we understand that you are giving a party here shortly, and that your guests are coming as Apaches.'

"'Correct, Mr. Matthews,' he remarked. 'Is there any objection?'

"'None, sir,' I said. 'But in view of your magnificent collection we wondered at headquarters if you would like any police protection for the night in question?'

"He drew himself up and stared at me coldly.

"'May I ask why I should require protection against my own guests?'

"'You will pardon me, sir,' I said doggedly, 'but I intend no reflection on those of your guests whom you know personally. It is, however, a well-known fact that many of the people who accept your hospitality are quite unknown to you.'

"'Proceed, sir,' he said quietly.

"'And such an opportunity as this is the very one to attract the attention of *le Bossu Masque*.'

"He began to laugh silently: then he rose and pressed a bell.

"'Come with me, Mr. Matthews.' He gave an order in Russian to a servant who entered. 'I have heard rumours of this mysterious *Bossu Masque*, and I can assure you that nothing would please me more than if he should honour my party with his presence.'

"He was leading the way into the garden as he spoke.

"'He might succeed in giving me what I find so difficult to experience today—a genuine thrill. On the other hand—he might not. In my spare time, Mr. Matthews, I have sought to improve a natural aptitude in the use of firearms, and you shall judge for yourself whether my efforts have proved successful.'

"He had halted by a small garden table on which a waiting servant had already placed a case containing two revolvers. Once again he gave an order in Russian, and the man took up a position twenty yards away, holding my visiting-card in his outstretched hand. There came a crack, and the visiting-card was no more. Then the man threw an apple in the air. The Prince shot twice. He got the apple with the first, and the largest bit of it with the second."

"Good shooting," said Hugh. "I used to be able to do that myself, but I have my doubts if I could do it now. Sorry to interrupt. Go on, Mr. Matthews."

"As you say. Captain Drummond—good shooting, marvellous shooting. He laid down his revolver, and turned to me with a smile.

"'That, sir,' he said, 'is why I say that on the other hand—he might not. For I should have not the smallest hesitation in killing him on the spot.'

"I bowed: there seemed nothing more to say.

"'I understand perfectly,' he continued, 'the object of your visit. And I am greatly obliged to your headquarters for their courtesy. But I can assure you that I am quite capable of dealing with any uninvited guest myself; and, as for the others, I have implicit confidence in my cousin.'

"So I returned to the station and to Paris. I reported the result of my visit to Grodin, who shrugged his shoulders.

"'Well, anyway, he can't blame us if anything does happen,' he remarked, and at that we left it. We had done all we could: we had warned him. And, as Grodin pointed out, *le Bossu Masque*, up to date, had confined his activities to Paris and its suburbs."

Victor Matthews paused and lit a cigarette.

"Eight days later," he said quietly, "we received a frenzied call on the telephone from the Chateaudun police. In the early hours of the morning Prince Boris Marcovitch, while at supper with his friends, had been shot dead through the heart, by *le Bossu Masque*, and practically the whole collection had been stolen."

"Good Lord!" cried Hugh, "this beats the band. Take a breather, my dear fellow, and have a drink."

CHAPTER 8

In Which Victor Matthews Ends His Story

"I was afraid you might find the story a little long," said Matthews, as the butler brought out the tray.

"Long be blowed," cried Hugh. "It is the most extraordinary yarn I ever listened to. Sounds like a book."

"Truth is stranger, Captain Drummond. The old tag. I think that beer looks very promising."

He took the glass, and raised his hand in a toast.

"I'm just trying to think," he went on after a while, "of the best way of telling you the remainder. I think perhaps I shall make it most interesting if I first of all give you the story as it was told us on our arrival at the Chateau du Lac Noir by the guests who had been detained there by the local police pending our coming.

"There were fourteen of them in all—eight women, and six men. And their condition, as you can imagine, was pretty bad. In addition to this appalling affair, which in itself was sufficient to upset anyone, the whole lot of them had been extremely drunk the night before. And they looked like it.

"However, by dint of questioning and piecing together their various stories, we managed to arrive at a fairly accurate account of what had happened. They had arrived by the train which reached Chateaudun at four o'clock the previous day. As usual they had been met at the station by the Prince's private carriages, and taken straight to the *chateau*, where the Prince received them. Champagne and caviar had at once been served, which sent them all upstairs to change for dinner in an expansive mood.

"Dinner itself started at eight-thirty and was preceded by more rounds of a special aperitif known only to the Prince, so that even at the beginning of the meal several of them were talking out of their turn. And by eleven o'clock most of them were riotously tight. Two girls from the Folies Bergeres were dancing on the table: in fact, an extra special debauch was in full swing. The hours went on: more drink arrived, and yet more drink, until many of the guests were frankly and unashamedly asleep. Only the Prince remained his normal self, though he was drinking level with them all.

"Now it was his custom to hold these carousals in the huge old banqueting-hall. It was a lofty room with a broad staircase at one end leading up to the musicians' gallery. They had long since faded away, completely worn out, and in the general din probably no one even noticed that they had ceased playing. And so you can visualise the scene. The candles guttering on the table around which sprawled the drunken guests; and sitting at one end, with a look of scornful weariness already beginning to show on his face, their host. The staircase was behind his left shoulder, the top half of it in semi-darkness, as were the portraits of the Prince's ancestors which stared down on the revellers from the walls.

"Suddenly one of the men who was singing some maudlin song broke off abruptly and leaned forward rubbing his eyes. What on earth was that strange object on the staircase? Was it really there—or was the great black shadow his imagination? Then it moved and he lurched to his feet. Grim reality struggled through the fumes of alcohol, and he hiccoughed out a warning.

"The others looked up: a woman screamed. And cold as ice the Prince turned round to find himself facing a masked hunchback. There was a moment of dead silence—then he rose to his feet. And even as he did so a solitary shot rang out from the stairs, and the Prince pitched forward on his face—stone dead.

"The guests, sobered by this utterly unexpected tragedy, huddled together like sheep. *'Le Bossu Masque'* passed from lip to lip in fearful whispers. And still this monstrous figure stood there motionless, his revolver still in his hand. Suddenly the door from the servants' quarters opened and five men came in. Save for the fact that they were masked they might have been five of the guests, because they too were dressed as Apaches. Two of them advanced to the terrified guests, and each of them carried a revolver. No word was spoken; evidently the whole thing had been planned beforehand. While the two of them guarded the guests, and the sinister masked hunchback stood in silence on the stairs the other three systematically looted the place. They smashed in cabinets and wrenched open drawers, while the man whose collection they were taking lay dead by his own table.

"It lasted nearly an hour so we are told. The stuff was carried out through the front door, the looters returning each time for more. And then at length they finished, and the three men who had been removing the stuff disappeared. There was the sound, and of this they were one and all quite positive, of a motor-car driving away—then silence. Slowly the two men who had been covering them the whole time backed to the door and disappeared also. And with that pandemonium broke loose.

"As mysteriously as he had come *le Bossu Masque* had vanished. The thing was over and finished; only broken cabinets and a dead man, who stared at the ceiling, remained to prove that it was ghastly reality and not a drunken dream. Completely sobered by now the men of the party dashed round the house, only to find that every servant had been bound and gagged. So they did the only thing there was to be done and sent for the local police.

"Well, that was the situation that confronted us on our arrival. Two things were established at once. *Le Bossu Masque* had added yet another murder to the long list already to his credit; and the fact that a motor-car had been used, and that there were five Apaches in the raid, made it practically certain that the gang involved was *le Rossignol*'s. So the first thing obviously to do was to try and lay that gang by the heels, which should have proved an easy matter. They have their invariable haunts to which they always return sooner or later, and we anticipated no difficulty whatever in catching them. But two days went past; three; a week; and still there was no sign of them. And it became increasingly obvious to me that the reason was simply and solely that they were acting under orders from *le Bossu Masque* himself: it was his brain we were contending against—not theirs.

"Then came a new development. In a wood not far from Chartres a shepherd found a deserted motor-car. It had been forced in through some undergrowth, and was completely hidden from the road. Indeed, but for the fact that he thought he had seen a snake, and had gone into the bushes after it, the car might have remained there for months without being discovered. Of the gang, however, there was still no trace, nor of the loot they had taken—loot which, on the Prince's cousin's valuation, was worth, at a conservative estimate, half a million pounds.

"And then at last came the final development of all. The telephone bell rang in our office, and a voice came over the wire. It was disguised, but not quite sufficiently. Before he had said a sentence I knew it was the Toad speaking, though I didn't let on that I knew. And his information was to the effect that *le Rossignol*'s gang were lying up in a wood halfway between Mamers and Alençon. He was speaking from a public telephone call office so it was hopeless to try and track him through that. But I passed on the word that the Toad was back in Paris, and sat down to think it out.

"If you look at the map you will see that the wood mentioned by the Toad is some sixty miles west of Chateaudun, while the wood where the car was found is about twenty miles due north. That seemed peculiar in the first place. In the second, what had caused the Toad to split? That it was quite in keeping with his nature I knew, but the Toad never did anything without a reason. And what was the reason in this case? Why had he turned traitor? Was he doing it on his own account, or was he doing it under orders from *le Bossu Masqué*? Had that gentleman decided that now the cat had pulled the chestnut out of the fire for him, its services could very well be dispensed with?

"However, the first thing to be done was to verify the Toad's information. The wood he mentioned was surrounded by a cordon of armed police, who gradually closed in on the centre. And what he had told us proved correct. The gang was there; at least, three of them were. Who fired the first shot I don't know, but men's fingers are quick on the trigger in cases like that. Sufficient to say that two of the police were killed, and two were wounded, before the three bandits fell riddled with bullets. Finding themselves cornered, half starving, dirty, and unkempt, the Snipe, the Butcher, and the man called Robert fought like rats in a trap and died. But of the Nightingale there was no trace. Nor, again, was there any sign of the stolen property, though we searched the wood with a fine-tooth comb. And so there we were up against a brick wall once again. It was true that three of the gang were dead, but they were the three least important ones. *Le Bossu Masqué* had completely vanished: so had both the Nightingale and the Toad. Had they split up the loot between them, or what had they done with it? Were they hanging together or had they fallen out? Those were the questions we constantly asked one another, and as constantly failed to answer.

"And then, one day about a fortnight after the fight in the wood, we caught the Nightingale. With his voice and terrible appearance he was altogether too conspicuous a character to escape notice. And the police found him hiding in a back slum in Rouen, and promptly despatched him to us in Paris, where he first of all told us that part of his story that I have already told you.

"If you remember, we left him and his gang at Chateaudun

putting up in the two hotels of the town, and having arrived there on the day of the Prince's party. They were completely in the dark as to what their further orders were to be: all they had to do was to sit and wait. Their instructions came to them at eight o'clock that night, and were simple in the extreme. They were to wait until eleven, and were then to proceed by car to the Chateau du Lac Noir. The motor was to be left in the shadow of some trees a hundred metres from the front door, and they were to remain hidden in the trees, also, until they saw a light flash twice from the bedroom window over the front door. They were then to proceed to the back door, where they would again receive instructions.

"They waited until, at two-thirty, they saw the light. When they got to the back door they found it open, and confronting them in the darkness of the passage the dim black figure of the *Bossu Masque*, who ordered them to pick up some coils of rope and follow him.

"They obeyed: as *le Rossignol* said—'*Messieurs*, we dared not do otherwise. We were more frightened of *le Bossu Masque* than of all the fiends in hell.'

"Suddenly he flung open the door into a lighted room, and there confronting them they saw the four men-servants, who, following the example of those upstairs, were a bit fuddled themselves. Incidentally, of course, we knew all this part of the story already. But confirmation is always valuable, and we thought it a good thing to let him tell the yarn in his own way. They trussed the servants up, and then they received their final instructions. When they heard a shot they were to go straight into the banqueting-hall: the Snipe and he were to cover the guests, the other three were to loot the place. And he told us then exactly the same story as we had already heard from the guests.

"So far, so good—but what we wanted to know was still to come.

"'Be very careful now, *Rossignol*,' said Grodin sternly. 'You have spoken the truth up to date: see that you continue doing so.'

"'By the Holy Virgin, *M'sieur*,' he exclaimed passionately, 'no word but the truth shall pass my lips. And if it does then may I be stricken dead, and have to forego my revenge on that festering sore *le Crapeau*.'

"Grodin glanced at me—that was a bit of news. But he merely told *le Rossignol* curtly to continue.

"It appeared, then, that the Snipe, the Butcher, and Robert were to find their way by cross-country trains to Mamers, from which place they were to go to a wood between there and Alençon.

"'And of those three, *Messieurs*, I can tell you no more. I saw in the paper that they were dead. How, if I may ask, did you find them?'

"'The Toad gave them away,' I said quietly, and for a moment we thought he was going to have an apoplectic fit. The veins stood out on his forehead, and a flood of the most filthy blasphemy poured out of his lips. We let him finish: as far as his feelings about the Toad were concerned, we had a certain sympathy with him.

"At last he pulled himself together and continued. His orders and the Toad's were to take the car, with the loot inside it, on the road towards Chartres. After they had gone twenty kilometres, they would find a track leading off to the right. They would know it, because there were three tall trees at the junction. They were to proceed along this track for two kilometres, where they would find a disused quarry. In the quarry was a shed, and in that shed they were to put the car. Under no circumstances were they to move out of the quarry, or light a fire, or attract attention to themselves in any way. But if, by any chance, they were discovered by some wandering pedestrian, the pedestrian was to wander no more. And they would receive further instructions in due course.

"Now I may say at once that we subsequently verified this statement. We found the track, and the quarry, and the actual wheel marks of the car in the shed.

"Well, it appeared that they sat there the whole of the next day. They had the bread and cheese and wine which *le Bossu Masque* had ordered them to put in the car, so they were not hungry. And, incidentally, it struck me, even at the time, what astounding attention to detail that little fact showed. For if there is one thing that will overcome fear it is hunger, and but for having given them food one or other of them would most certainly have gone to the nearest village to get it.

"I will now try and continue in the Nightingale's own words.

"'It was about six o'clock, *M'sieurs*, that it happened. The sun was just setting, so I know the time. I had risen and was standing in the door of the shed, wondering what we should next be told to do. Suddenly I received the most terrible blow in the back of the neck, and I knew no more.'

"We looked at his neck, and there was an ugly looking scar about two inches long. In fact, anyone except an abnormality like the Nightingale would never have known any more.

"'When I recovered consciousness,' he went on, 'it was dark. At first I didn't know where I was, everything was a blank. And then, little by little, memory came back to me. The quarry—the affair at the *chateau*—the car. Mon Dieu! *M'sieurs*—sick and faint, I raised myself on my elbow. The car had gone: so had *le Crapeau*. I was alone in the shed. How long I had lain there I knew not: some hours, because the sky was studded with stars. And then there came a voice out of the darkness, and I nearly fainted with horror.

"'"*Rossignol*," it said, "where is the car?"

"'I was not alone: *le Bossu Masque* was there too.

"'"*M'sieur*," I cried, "I do not know. That accursed traitor *le Crapeau* struck me from behind with what must have been a spanner. See—I am wet with blood.'"

"'And, in truth, I was, gentlemen—soaked with it—my coat, my shirt, everything.'

"'"Accursed fool," went on the voice, and I could dimly see *le Bossu*' s outline in the gloom. "Blundering idiot. Do I plan with my great brain this wonderful coup in order that you should allow yourself to be sandbagged like an English tourist? And by *le Crapeau* of all people."

"'"*M'sieur*," I pleaded, "I did not suspect him. I was standing in the door wondering what our next instructions would be when he crept on me from behind."

"'"Be silent, worm," he said. "It is well for you, *Rossignol*, that your shirt is soaked with blood. Were it otherwise I might be tempted to think that this was a put-up job between you."

"'"By the blood of the Virgin, *M'sieur*," I cried, "I swear to you"

"'"Be silent," he snarled. "I said it was well for you that he hit so hard. It proves to me that you are only a fool and not a traitor. Were you the second, *Rossignol*, I would strangle you here and now with my own hands. As it is, your punishment is sufficient."

"'"But, *M'sieur*," I cried, "what am I to do?"

"'There was no answer, *le Bossu Masque* had gone. I was alone now, in very truth—miles from anywhere.'

"So did the Nightingale ramble on. We let him talk, but there was obviously nothing more that he could tell us. He was very incoherent as to dates and times, and I think he undoubtedly remained in that shed in a semi-delirious state for three or four days. How he finally arrived at Rouen we never found out: he hardly seemed to know himself. Anyway, the point was not important.

"He was brought up on a charge of robbery with violence, and sentenced to twenty-one years' imprisonment in Devil's Island. And with that we can leave him for the present. And with that also my story of the quarter of a century ago is practically finished. *Le Rossignol*, with a characteristic outburst of frenzied invective against the Toad, disappeared from the dock into twenty-one years of hell.

"And now, gentlemen, we pass out of the region of certain fact into the region of guesswork. To take the Toad first. I do not think there can be any doubt as to what he did. Overcome by the thought of so much loot, he determined to try and get it all for himself. He laid out the Nightingale, and went off in the car. What happened then we can only surmise. Perhaps he found that he couldn't manage the car: perhaps he lost his nerve. But somewhere in that area of country he hid the stolen stuff. Probably he put in his pocket sufficient jewellery to keep him in comfort for many a long day. But the bulk of the stuff he must have hidden, intending to go back for it when the hue and cry was over. Then he ran the car into a wood, hid it as well as he could, and disappeared. And it is a fact that he did disappear. Years passed by: the war came, but never a trace of the Toad did we see. He vanished from the underworld of Paris as completely as a stone vanishes in the sea. Many people thought he was dead, though, personally, I never agreed with them. But at last the whole thing was forgotten: even the search for the treasure was abandoned. That had really been hopeless from the first, unless we could lay our hands on the Toad and make him lead us to it.

"As to what happened to *le Bossu Masque* we are equally in doubt. Many people believed that he had caught the Toad, and had murdered him for his treachery, first compelling him to reveal the hiding-place of the loot. There was a great deal to be said for the theory, though, somehow, I never believed it myself. No body was ever found anywhere which could possibly have been the Toad's. And I felt tolerably certain that a big man like *le Bossu* would never have taken the trouble to follow an object of that sort out of the country merely to kill him. It was the loot he was after—not the Toad. We still felt his activities in Paris, though, as years went by, they seemed to grow less and less. And there are strange stories told of incredible deeds of heroism performed in the war by a masked hunchback, who appeared suddenly in different parts of the line. Fiction, of course, but *le poilu* likes his little bit of mystery—just as your Tommy does.

"And so we come to the present moment, and this strange reunion of the principals in that drama of nearly thirty years ago. As a matter of fact, you will see that it is not quite so strange as it would appear at first sight, but a perfectly logical affair.

"It starts with the release of the Nightingale from Devil's Island five years ago. I was then working with the police in New York, but not because I had to. I happen to be of independent means, and I work for the love of the thing, not for the salary. And the case of all others that intrigued me most during my whole career was the one I have just told you. It was unsolved: I felt I had been beaten.

"Now I have a fairly good knowledge of the criminal nature. And quite by chance I happened to learn that an uncle of *le Rossignol*'s had died leaving his money to his nephew. So I gambled on the result that twenty-one years in Devil's Island would produce on a man like the Nightingale, believing, as he did, that he was there principally because of the Toad's treachery. I chucked up my job, and got on the heels of the Nightingale.

"Well, my guess proved right. He was now, for a man in his position, comparatively affluent, which enabled him to be free from the necessity of working. And, as I thought would prove the case, he was obsessed with one idea, to the exclusion of everything else. And that idea was revenge on the Toad. If *le Crapeau* was still alive he was going to find him.

"Gentlemen, these past few years may seem to you to have been dull: to me they have been fascinating. Backwards and forwards, searching and ferreting, the Nightingale has chased his man. Old companions of twenty years previously have been interrogated: clues have been followed up, only to be discarded. And all the time, unknown to him, I have been sitting on his heels, patiently waiting. I knew that no one was better qualified to find the Toad than he was. He had access to information that I could never have got: in addition it was the sole driving force of his life.

"It is true, I admit, that at one period, when for months he seemed completely defeated, I very nearly gave it up. And then, quite suddenly out of the blue, there came the message that gave me the greatest thrill of my life. It was proof of what I had always thought in days gone by. Just an envelope handed to me by a *gamin* as I sat outside a cafe in Paris.

"'Keep out of this.' That was all that was written on the paper: that—and the drawing I hadn't seen for so many years. So *le Bossu Masque* was not dead: *le Bossu Masque* was on the trail, too. He also was following the Nightingale: he also was working on the same lines as myself. A strange situation as you will agree: I and that greatest of criminals both using the same dog to hunt our man, and the dog quite unconscious of the fact that he was being so used. It added zest to it, I can assure you. It meant sleeping with one eye permanently open: it meant that the whole time it was necessary to look in every direction, not only at the Nightingale. Several times I sensed his presence near me: how, I can't tell you. And remember the terrible handicap that I was working under. *He knew me, but I didn't know him.*

"However, that is neither here nor there. Just as the obsession of *le Rossignol*'s life was to lay hands on the Toad, so the obsession of mine became the desire to catch *le Bossu Masque*. It had turned into a duel between him and me. And that duel is now approaching its end."

For a moment or two Victor Matthews fell silent, his eyes fixed on the little drawing still pinned to the tree above my head. And we, enthralled though we were, let him take his own time.

"The rest," he continued after a while, "is fairly soon told. Little by little, from a clue here and a clue there, it became increasingly certain that the Toad had left France. But where had he gone, and had he taken the loot with him? And then came a sudden and astounding stroke of luck. The Nightingale, in the course of his search, had reached Boulogne, and one evening he was sitting in a small wine-shop on the Quai Gambetta. At the next table to him was a French *ouvrier*, and I venture to think that not even the *Bossu Masque* himself would have recognised me in that excellent workman. The cafe was fairly empty, and I was on the point of going when two French fishermen came in. They were both a little tight, and their conversation was clearly audible. But what principally attracted my attention was the fact that they obviously were full of money.

"At first I listened idly, and then a stray sentence struck my ear.

"'*Le moulin a Bonneval.*'

"The mill at Bonneval, and Bonneval was the name of a village between Chateaudun and Chartres. Moreover, it was the nearest village to the quarry where the motor-car had been hidden during the day. Isn't it an astounding fact how sometimes, after months and years of fruitless labour, a stray remark casually overheard may provide a clue? As it stood, of course, there was nothing in it—but the coincidence attracted my attention. It was well it did so: amazing though it seems that a chance remark was destined to end our search.

"I stole a glance at the Nightingale: he, too, had caught the phrase, and was listening intently. And after a while, as the full significance of their conversation sank into his mind, he began to quiver like a terrier when it sees a rat. Sometimes the men lowered their voices, but for the most part what they said was clearly audible. And one fact was soon established definitely. These two sailors owned the ketch *Rose Marie*, and they had recently smuggled over a cargo consisting of three large wooden cases, which had been landed on Romney Marsh somewhere between Rye and Dungeness. Further, that these cases had something to do with the mill at Bonneval.

"I give you my word that by this time I was almost as excited as the Nightingale himself. I remembered that there was an old disused mill, standing a little back from the road, about a kilometre north of Bonneval.

"Was it possible that that was the hiding-place which we had searched for in vain? And if so, who was the recipient of the cases on Romney Marsh?

"Then another thought struck me: was *le Bossu Masque* present? I glanced round the room: there were only some fisher-folk and a pale youth who looked as if he served in some shop. Honestly I could not think he was there, and yet—"

He waved his hand at the tree behind me.

"However," he continued, "it may be that he wasn't. The Nightingale is an easy man to track, and that may easily account for it. To return to that evening. The two sailors didn't say much more, but what they had said was quite enough to send the Nightingale flying over to England. He has one gift which you probably noticed the night before last—he speaks English fluently. And that was a considerable help to him. It was impossible for him to tell, of course, if the cases had been landed on Romney Marsh because the Toad was near at hand, or simply because it is an admirably situated locality for smuggling."

"Hold hard a moment," said Hugh. "How long ago did you overhear this conversation in the wine shop?"

"About six weeks," answered Matthews. "Rather more. Well, I can't tell you when the Nightingale first discovered that the man he wanted was your next-door neighbour. He's no fool, and presumably his suspicions at once fell on a house fortified like Temple Tower. So did mine. But the Toad is a secretive gentleman, and suspicion is not proof. Personally, I have not seen the man who now calls himself Granger, though I've lain up for hours waiting for him. I assume that the Nightingale has; at any rate, he has satisfied himself somehow that Granger is the Toad. And so his quest is ended: he has found his enemy. Theatrical as all those people are, he has flashed his warning across the Marsh—red and blue lights, the colours of the gang. For years that man—ever since *le Rossignol* was liberated from Devil's Island—has lived in fear of being found. And now he has been."

Young Freckles took a deep breath.

"I say, chaps," he remarked, "we are having a jolly party, aren't we? And how do the Beaver and the girl come in?"

"I was just coming to them," said Matthews. "Paul Vandali is one of those men, well-known to the police to be criminals, who have yet succeeded in steering clear of trouble. The only commandment they keep is the eleventh—thou shalt not be found out. The lady has not, I think, ever been united to Vandali in the holy bonds of matrimony, but she has been his inseparable companion for three years."

"I suppose he is not the *Bossu Masque?*" I asked.

Matthews shook his head.

"Quite impossible," he said. "He is not old enough. Vandali is a man of only about thirty five. So that rules him out. Oh, no! He comes in in a very different way. I have mentioned, if you remember, the Prince's cousin, who chose his parties for him. Now that cousin is also the Prince's heir, and he is alive today in Paris. He inherited all the Prince's money, and so is an extremely wealthy man. After the affair at the Chateau du Lac Noir, he offered an enormous reward for the recovery of the stolen property—no less than fifty thousand pounds. Naturally he, years ago, gave up all hope of getting it back, though the reward still stood. And then Vandali and the lady appeared on the scene. You have seen them, and you will realise that they are people who are quite at home in the highest society. At any rate, they met Count Vladimar—that is the cousin—at supper one night not very long ago. And the conversation came round to the affair at the Chateau du Lac Noir. My informant was the waiter—who was not a waiter. To be more explicit, the Paris police were after Vandali over a little matter at Nice. They had no proof, but they were trying to trap him in an unguarded moment. And the waiter was really a detective.

"Well, he got nothing from the meal which helped him over the Nice business, but what he did get was that Vladimar most categorically stated that the reward of fifty thousand pounds still held good. He said it with a laugh, almost as if he implied that it might just as well be a million for the good it would do. But the detective caught a very significant glance that passed between the two. And here they are.

"How they spotted this place I can't tell you. It may be that they, too, through friends in the underworld, have kept themselves posted in the Nightingale's movements, realising, as I did, that in him lay their best chance of being led to the treasure. At any rate, they are here."

Matthews paused and lit a cigarette.

"Well, gentlemen, so much for the past, and the original causes that have led up to the situation as it stands today. Of my doings since I have been here there is little to say. I have told you that the main obsession of my life is to lay hands on the man who nearly murdered me tonight. And I have been lying up in a small place in Rye, watching and waiting for what I knew must happen, sooner or later—his arrival. I have kept my eye on *le Rossignol:* you saw me the other night when I very foolishly got caught in the light. But until tonight I did not know *le Bossu* was here. I don't know quite what took me up there—restlessness, perhaps, or something deeper. It sounds strange, I know," his voice grew almost solemn, "but I veritably believe, though I have never seen him until tonight, that there is some channel of communication between him and me which cannot be explained by any natural means. Gentlemen, I have felt him near me in Paris: I know it. And tonight an overmastering impulse took me to Temple Tower, You know with what result. Suddenly I saw him—looming out of the darkness—right on top of me. And although I had half expected it, the shock at the moment was almost paralysing. I even forgot to draw my gun till it was too late: he had gone."

He paused, and a dreamy look came into his eyes.

"But he is here, and I am here, and this time it is the end, one way or the other."

For a moment or two no one spoke: there was something almost awe-inspiring in the quiet finality of his words. Just as at Spragge's Farm, the soft melodious voice of *le Rossignol* had seemed to ring Granger's death knell, so, now, did this second deadly hatred promise a fight to the finish.

"Enough, gentlemen," he went on in his normal voice. "No good has ever come of dreaming. Will you now return the compliment, and tell me what has happened to you? Then we will draw up a plan of campaign and decide what to do."

We told him everything: about the chimneypot episode, the sparking plugs, the stolen map, and Miss Verney's letter. And when we had finished, he smoked a complete cigarette before he spoke.

"Captain Drummond," he said quietly, "I congratulate you. I think your deductions are absolutely correct. Whether he meant to kill you with the chimney-pot, or only put you out of the way temporarily, is immaterial—but that was his first idea. And I think your appearance on the scene has changed all his plans. He has only just arrived, of that I am sure. He came expecting to find *le Rossignol* and me: instead, he finds all of you, to say nothing of the Vandalis."

He rose and began pacing up and down, his face working eagerly as he emphasised each point.

"What is the result? Merely that time becomes all important. He hears of the map belonging to Sir John: he steals it. Not knowing of the verse behind, he thinks that he has solved the method of getting in to Temple Tower. And he was looking for the entrance tonight when the dog found him. Probably alarmed by the din the animal made, he hid for a while nearby, and it was then that Gaspard stumbled on him, only to be strangled. Who knows why he did that? It is possible he did not know you were in the grounds, and thought he might gain access to the house by pretending to be Gaspard: it is possible he had no alternative. But of one thing, gentlemen, I am very sure: time is now even more all important to *le Bossu* than it was a few hours ago.

"In view of the fact that he did not gain access to the house, the killing of Gaspard was an error—a bad error. But it is done and cannot be undone. And of another thing I am very sure, too." His voice grew grave, and he stared over the Marsh thoughtfully. "If you heard the Vandalis' programme, Mr. Darrell, so did he. And I do not think it would find favour in his eyes—far from it. I hold no brief for either of them, but—"

He said no more, but the little shrug of his shoulders filled in the silence more ominously than any spoken word.

"Had he got into the house tonight, the Vandalis would not have mattered. But he didn't, and now they do. However, they can look after themselves: the point we have to decide is what we are going to do. Shall we call in the police, or shall we not? There are, it seems to me, two main objections. The first is this: What are we going to tell them? Nothing that we can do can bring the man Gaspard back to life, and if we tell them anything, we must tell them all. And frankly, gentlemen, though you are, of course, the best judges of that, I think an account of your recent doings, told in cold blood at a police station, might prove a little awkward."

"I know the Inspector pretty well," said Hugh, "but perhaps you are right."

"The other objection," went on Matthews, "is this. And to me it is a far bigger one. If we tell the police, and they take the matter up, we drop out, or at any rate you do. And"—he thumped his fist into his open palm—"for the local police to try and tackle *le Bossu* is about equivalent to asking a board school child to explain Einstein's Theory. They are naturally trammelled by the law, and *le Bossu* would laugh at them. No, gentlemen, the only way of catching him, if you are prepared to do it, is for us to join forces and act outside the law on our own. Keep the police out of it, and we will catch him. Let them in, and our hands are tied."

"My dear fellow," said Hugh with a grin, "no one loathes the idea of letting the police in more than I do. But do not forget there is a lady involved."

"I don't," remarked Matthews gravely, and turned to young Freckles. "I quite appreciate your position, Mr. Scott. But I am going to say something which I hope you will not consider impertinent. There is a reward of fifty thousand pounds at stake. Wait, please"—he held up his hand, as Freckles started to speak—"and then bite me afterwards. Captain Drummond, if I may say so, hardly seems to be a gentleman in need of money. I am in this show for one reason only—to get to grips with *le Bossu*. If between us we find that property, we get fifty thousand pounds. And do not be under any delusion. Count Vladimar can pay that sum without feeling it. Which brings me to my point. Your fiancée can be of invaluable assistance to us in finding it, and as a natural result would be entitled to the whole reward. Please understand me, Mr. Scott," he continued with a smile, which robbed his words of any offence. "But young ladies do not as a general rule take on jobs of that sort if their future husbands are wealthy."

"My dear old lad," laughed Freckles, "we haven't got a blinking bean between us, if that is what you mean."

Then here is an unprecedented opportunity of getting fifty thousand of the best," said Matthews.

"Be a bit more explicit," said Hugh after a pause.

"*Le Bossu* will return to Temple Tower," said Matthews quietly. "You disturbed him last night, but there is no power in Heaven or Hell that will deter that man from doing what he has come here to do. He may or may not kill *le Crapeau*, according to the mood he is in: but he has come to get the stuff stolen twenty-five years ago—the stuff which, as Captain Drummond says, Miss Verney has been engaged to sell. Well, gentlemen, my suggestion is this. Let us lie up and wait for him. In the past we have always laboured under the disadvantage of not knowing where he would turn up: this time that disadvantage is gone. We know exactly, and all we have to do is to wait for him. And this time," he added softly, "we are going to catch him. What do you say?"

Hugh glanced round at all of us.

"It seems to me," he said, "that Scott must decide."

"Well, old birds," answered Freckles, "it seems to me that if five of us can't tackle this bloke, the addition of a couple of policemen isn't going to help much. I'm all for Mr. Matthews' suggestion."

"Good," cried Hugh. "Then that's that. What do you want, Denny?"

The butler had come out of the house in an obvious state of suppressed excitement.

"Have you heard sir, what they've found in the wood opposite Temple Tower?"

"No," said Hugh quietly. "What?"

"A dead man, sir. Hidden in the bushes. A terrible looking thing he was, so the postman told me—more like a great monkey than a man. They say that he has been stopping at Spragge's Farm."

For a moment or two there was silence: then Victor Matthews spoke.

"How was he killed?" he asked.

And I think we all knew the answer before it came.

"Murdered, sir, so I hear. From the marks round his neck they say he was strangled."

CHAPTER 9

In Which I Meet "Le Bossu Masqué"

So *le Rossignol* had been there after all. His dead body must have been quite close to us during the hour we had lain up waiting, before we found that the ladder had gone. And horrible and repulsive though he had been, I could not help feeling a twinge of pity for the poor brute. I could imagine him there in the darkness of the wood searching for the rope ladder he had made so laboriously, and then suddenly feeling the grip of the silent strangler on his throat. Perhaps that same choking cry that Gaspard had given—and then silence.

"Your friend," said Hugh grimly, when the butler had gone, "is evidently no believer in half measures."

Matthews was silent: this new development seemed to have nonplussed him. He paced up and down with quick, nervous steps, and a look of frowning concentration on his face,

"This alters things, gentlemen," he said at length. "Now the police must come into the affair."

"True," remarked Hugh. "At the same time, I don't see why we should run round telling them what we know. In fact, it makes it even more difficult to do so, because we lay ourselves open to grave blame for not having informed them about what we knew of the Nightingale's intentions."

"That is so," said Matthews thoughtfully. "And as a matter of fact, it is even worse for me. Strictly speaking, if only as a matter of courtesy, I should have informed them of my presence here, and what I was doing. Instead of that, I am passing as an ordinary tourist. You are right. Captain Drummond. We must still say nothing about it. And there, going along the road, if I'm not mistaken, is the local inspector."

Hugh started to his feet.

"I'll get him in," he exclaimed, going towards the gate.

"Please don't mention who I am," called Matthews after him, and Hugh nodded in answer.

"Hullo! Inspector," he hailed, "what's this I hear about someone being murdered?"

"Quite right, sir," said the other gravely, halting by the gate. "Just come from there myself."

"Come in and have a spot of ale," said Hugh, "and tell us all about it. I think you know Sir John, don't you? And these are three other friends of mine."

"A bad business, gentlemen," said the Inspector, putting down his glass. "Very bad. And as far as I can see at present, there is no trace of a clue

"What happened?" asked Hugh. "I've heard vaguely from my butler, who had heard vaguely from the postman."

"It was Joe Mellor that found him, sir—him that keeps the dairy farm along the road there. Found him quite by accident, he did: or rather, not him, but his dog. He was walking past Temple Tower, and his dog was in the wood opposite. Suddenly it began to bark and make a rare blather, and Joe went in to see what was happening. He found the dog standing by some bushes, and, when he looked closer, he saw a man's leg sticking out. The rest of the body was carefully covered, and Joe tells me that he'd never have seen it but for the dog. He gives a pull on the leg and hauls out the body. Well, gentlemen, in the course of my life I've run across some pretty queer customers, but I give you my word that the dead man is the queerest. He don't look like a man at all: he looks like a great ape. A terrible face he's got, and not improved by the manner of his death. He was strangled, and the face is all red and puffy."

"You've got no clue at all?" asked Hugh. "No idea who the man is?"

"None at present, sir," answered the Inspector. "But I shall soon. Bill Matcham, who works down on the Marsh, happened to be passing, and the instant he saw him he recognised him as a man who had been lodging at Spragge's place. Maybe you know the farm, sir?"

"Vaguely," said Hugh casually. "Somewhere down there, isn't it?"

He waved a comprehensive hand at the Marsh.

"That's right, sir. And Spragge himself is a queer customer. Well, I don't mind if I do, sir." He took the refilled glass from Hugh. "Hot work this morning."

"By the way," said Matthews speaking for the first time, "for how long had this man been dead?"

"The doctor said somewhere about twelve hours, sir," answered the Inspector.

"So it happened last night," cried Hugh, in affected surprise.

"That's right, sir; last night sometime round about ten o'clock this man was strangled and his body hidden in the wood by Temple Tower."

"You've got something in your mind, Inspector," said Hugh quietly.

"Well, sir, we're all of us entitled to our thoughts, and maybe I have mine. Ever see anything of Mr. Granger, sir?"

Hugh smiled slightly.

"So that's how it is, is it? I can't say I do, Inspector. I've met him out walking once or twice, that's all."

"A queer gentleman, sir: very queer. Who ever heard before of a man coming to live in a place like this and fortifying his house with all them steel spikes and things, to say nothing of the bars all over the windows?"

The worthy officer put down his glass and wiped his lips with the back of his hand.

"Well, gentlemen, I must be going. This affair is going to keep me busy."

"But surely you don't suspect that Mr. Granger had anything to do with it?" said Hugh.

"I don't suspect no one, sir," answered the other. "All I say is that Mr. Granger is a queer customer, and this is a queer affair."

"A most sapient conclusion," remarked Matthews with a faint smile as the gate shut behind the Inspector. "One wonders what the worthy man would think if he knew that a precisely similar corpse lay inside the fortifications."

"One also wonders," said Hugh quietly, "what steps our Mr. Granger is going to take over that similar corpse."

But any surmises on that point proved unnecessary, for at that moment who should appear at the gate but Miss Verney. Even at that distance one could see that she was in a state of great agitation, and she had left Temple Tower in such a hurry that she had come without a hat. And as she stood there for a moment the Inspector returned and joined her. Then they both came towards us.

"She's found Gaspard's body," said Matthews with quiet conviction. "Be very careful what all of you say."

And he proved to be right. It appeared that, going out after breakfast, the first thing that had struck her was that the dog's kennel was empty. And then, in the distance, she had seen the brute lying asleep as she thought. For a time she had watched it, ready to dart back to the house if it moved. But after a while it had struck her that from its attitude it couldn't be asleep: one hind leg was sticking straight up in the air, and she had approached it cautiously to find that it was dead.

"I was so amazed," she went on, "that for a moment or two I just stood there staring at it. There was no sign of blood, or of any wound, and so I guessed it must have been poisoned. But who by? I had heard it baying furiously in the middle of the night, and then it suddenly stopped and there wasn't another sound. Still trying to puzzle it out, I walked on into the undergrowth. And there I found"—she grew a little white at the recollection, and her voice trembled—"the body of the servant Gaspard. He looked too awful, with his face all red and terrible. And I simply lost my head and flew to the gate and came here."

"An extraordinarily wise proceeding, Miss Verney," said Hugh quietly.

"May I ask who this young lady is?" said the Inspector.

"Miss Verney was engaged to do secretarial work for Mr. Granger," answered Freckles. "And her engagement is now terminated," he concluded firmly.

"This is most extraordinary," said the Inspector, scratching his head with a pencil. "I must go back there at once. One inside and—"

"Quite so. Inspector," interrupted Hugh with a warning sign. "But Miss Verney is a bit tired at the moment. I'll stroll with you to the gate. Come along, Peter, There is no good upsetting her any more," he went on as we got out of earshot, "by telling her about the other."

"What do you make of it, sir.?" said the Inspector as we came to the road.

"Well, from what Miss Verney said," remarked Hugh, "it would appear as if the servant Gaspard had also been strangled. And if that is so, the strong presumption is that the same man did both murders, and poisoned the dog."

The Inspector nodded portentously, and then lowered his voice impressively.

"What did I tell you, sir; what did I tell you? Mr. Granger is a queer customer."

"Queer customer he may be," answered Hugh. "But one thing is as certain as that gate in front of us. He had nothing to do with the two murders. With his physique, he could no more have strangled Gaspard than he could have strangled me."

"I don't say he did it, sir," said the other, "but you mark my words, he could tell a lot about it if he chose to."

"I wouldn't be surprised if you're not right," said Hugh gravely. "Drop in on your way back and let us know if you find out anything."

For a while we stood leaning over the gate, watching his retreating back.

"What do you make of it, Peter?" said Hugh suddenly.

"It is one of the most extraordinary affairs I've ever heard of," I answered. "Even with Matthews' explanation it's amazing enough: without it, as the Inspector is, no wonder he is scratching his head. It's a mighty lucky thing that *le Bossu* missed him."

"Mighty lucky," he agreed, lighting a cigarette. "He strikes me as being an extraordinarily sound sort of bloke. Extraordinarily sound," he repeated, as we started to walk back to the house. "In fact, I was proposing to ask him to come and stay here."

"Not at all a bad idea," I agreed. "Then we're all on the spot together."

We found him alone with John, the other two having disappeared somewhere, and Hugh at once proposed it.

"That's very good of you. Captain Drummond," he said. "But, frankly speaking, I don't think there will be much staying."

"What do you mean?" said Hugh, looking puzzled.

"Simply that matters have come to a head," he answered. "I am as certain as I can be of anything that *le Bossu* never intended to be in Rye today. He murdered *le Rossignol*, and then got into the grounds by the ladder, believing that, once he was inside. Sir John's plan would enable him to find the secret entrance. It didn't. Then the dog came for him and disturbed the household. Then Gaspard came, and he murdered him, once again believing that he would be able to get into the house—this time by the front door. And what defeated him was your sudden appearance. I know I've said much the same before, but when one is dealing with a man of his calibre there's no harm in being clear in one's head. He didn't mind in the slightest if these two murders were discovered after he had settled things with the Toad: but now the discovery has been made before the settlement. And that is why I say matters have come to a head and there won't be much staying before the end comes. We are going to find things moving at breakneck speed, and the only comfort is that even *le Bossu* can't do anything by day. But I think you can dismiss the idea of sleep at night for the next day or two."

"That's not likely to worry us," said Hugh. "And I quite see your point. Still, the offer holds if you care to make this house your headquarters."

"Thank you again," answered Matthews. "I won't bother to move my kit here, but if I may drop in when I want to I shall greatly appreciate it. And if I may stay now for a little lunch I should be most grateful."

"Of course, my dear fellow," cried Hugh,

And in view of our rather erratic timetable and hours at the moment, I'm rather in favour of a bit of food at once. It's twelve o'clock."

He shouted for Denny, who, accustomed as he was to Hugh's vagaries, betrayed no astonishment. And then, whilst we waited, we went on discussing from every angle what was likely to be the next move. With his previous knowledge of *le Bossu*, it was only natural that Victor Matthews should take the lead, but even he confessed himself beaten. How was the silent strangler to rectify his mistake?

"*Le Bossu* knows," he said, "as every other criminal knows, that the English police, once they get their teeth into a thing, never let it go. They may chew slowly, but they chew surely. And he must know that the discovery of these two murders is going to make the police swarm round Temple Tower, which is the last place he wants them at. So what is he going to do? Because he'll do something: of that you can rest assured."

And it is safe to say that not one of us there, in our wildest dreams, would have guessed what *le Bossu* did do that very afternoon—so staggering was it in its simplicity, so incredible in its ferocity. But of that in its proper place.

Lunch was over, and the first problem to be settled was what the girl was to do. She, on hearing the whole story, was as keen as mustard on helping, but Freckles—in fact, all of us—were absolutely opposed to her returning to Temple Tower. She already knew, at any rate, one of the secret hiding-places of the stolen jewels, and though she offered to go back, we vetoed it unanimously. And, finally, it was decided that she should stop at Hugh's house for the present at any rate, with Freckles as her guard, an arrangement which seemed to satisfy everybody concerned. John had decided to motor back to Laidley Towers, returning again in the evening, and as soon as he heard that, Victor Matthews asked for a lift to Rye. He was of the opinion that developments might take place there in connection with the two murders, and he had decided, if necessary, to tell the police something, if not all, of what he had told us that morning. Later, John might pick him up on his way back.

"What are you going to do, Hugh?" I said.

"I dunno, old lad," he answered. "Don't you worry about me."

And sure enough he disappeared soon after lunch and I was left to my own resources.

At first I tried to sleep, but I soon gave up the attempt. Sleep simply would not come, and after a while I decided to go for a walk. I gathered from Denny that there was a short cut over the fields which led to Rye, and with the idea of possibly getting a lift back in John's car I struck out along it. There was always a chance, I thought, of finding out something, and if not, Rye was a town well worth exploring.

It was a drowsily warm afternoon, and I walked slowly, my thoughts full of Matthews' astounding story. It seemed well-nigh unbelievable that this amazing crime of a generation ago should have its denouement in such a peaceful English setting. Who was he—this sinister being—who had baffled the whole French police force? Had we seen him in the Dolphin the night before? Was he the clergyman, as Hugh had half suggested?

Futile surmises: if Matthews didn't know, it was hardly likely that I should. But the problem haunted me: I couldn't get it out of my thoughts. And suddenly I arrived at a decision. I would stroll round Rye, and then go to the Dolphin for tea. With luck I might find the little room empty, in which case I would investigate the fireplace, and see if there was anything in Hugh's theory. It could do no harm, and it gave me an object for the afternoon. Possibly even, I might solve the problem of the identity of *le Bossu* himself.

A neighbouring clock struck three, and shortly after I reached the outskirts of the town. I strolled aimlessly round, looking into old curiosity shops for about half an hour: then, striking up the hill, I made for the Dolphin. Once I thought I saw Victor Matthews in the distance, but I wasn't sure, and I wondered how his line of inquiries was progressing.

The hall was deserted when I entered: so, fortunately, was the little room. And I made a dive at once for the fireplace. It was, as I have already said, an enormous affair, in which it was easy to stand with one's head and shoulders up the flue. I peered upwards, but could see nothing. Evidently there was a jink in the chimney which stopped the light. At any rate there was only blackness to be seen.

"Do you require tea, sir?"

I emerged hurriedly, to find a waiter staring at me.

"Please," I said, feeling remarkably foolish. "A wonderful fireplace, this."

"Yes, sir. It is very famous."

He stalked from the room, leaving me with the uncomfortable feeling that he regarded me with grave suspicion. Admittedly the beauties of the fireplace were best seen from the outside: at the same time I failed to see any reason why I shouldn't stand inside it if I wished to. However, having satisfied himself on his return that the fireplace was still there, he thawed somewhat under the influence of a substantial tip.

"Hotel pretty full?" I said casually.

"Yes, sir. They comes and goes," he answered. "Weekends we're always full up, but we've got some rooms now if you want one."

His interest waned when he found I didn't, and after a while he drifted away to some new arrivals in the hall. They were obviously American tourists motoring through, and therefore could be given a clean bill of health as far as I was concerned. Presumably, also, the waiter might be excluded, though his case was not quite so certain. I had already made up my mind that the most unlikely person would prove to be the man we wanted, and that even women must not be ruled out. After all, men had masqueraded in female clothes before now.

Other people came drifting in, and I eyed them all like a lynx. And then, after a while, the absurdity of the proceeding struck me: how could I possibly know? It was more than likely that *le Bossu* had already left the hotel, even assuming he had ever been there.

Suddenly my interest revived: Vandali and the girl had come into the hall. For a moment or two they seemed undecided as to where they would sit: then they turned and came into the little room. The girl swept past me as if unconscious of my existence, but Vandali gave me a curt bow.

"Been doing any more botanising?" he said sarcastically.

"Been getting the Yuletide welcome at Temple Tower again?" I returned.

He paused and stared at me, and I thought for a moment that he was going to have an actual discussion. Then apparently he thought better of it and he passed on and joined the girl. I picked up a paper and pretended to read. It was a day old but I wanted a screen from behind which I could study them. They had begun to talk in low tones, and it was impossible to hear more than an odd word or two. But it seemed to me that he was urging some line of action on her, and that she was opposed to it. What it was I had no idea, but once I distinctly heard him mention the word "police." I strained my ears, but they were sitting too far away. Only it became increasingly obvious that there was a fundamental difference of opinion between them over something, and that neither could apparently convert the other.

I laid down the paper and lit a cigarette. There did not seem to be much object in waiting any longer. I could not move closer to them without making things obvious, and they were evidently not going to raise their voices. And I was on the point of getting up when some dirt fell down the chimney at the end of the room and lay in a little heap on the whitened hearthstone. A very ordinary phenomenon, and yet—was it? I felt my pulse begin to go a little quicker. Had that dirt fallen naturally, or had it been disturbed by something? Was the hidden listener even now at his post! And yet how could he be unless he was in the room?

The other two had noticed nothing. For about five minutes they continued their conversation: then, shrugging his shoulders irritably, the man got up and left the room, whilst the girl picked up an illustrated weekly. In a fever of impatience I waited for her to go too: I wanted to have another look up the chimney. But apparently she had no intention of following her companion's example, and after a time she took out her cigarette-case.

I watched her out of the corner of my eye, as she began to hunt in her bag for a match. And it suddenly struck me that the opportunity was too good to miss.

"Allow me," I said, rising and striking one for her.

She thanked me, and a little to my surprise she laid down her paper as if quite ready to talk.

"A ghastly affair," I said, "these two murders."

"Two!" she cried, staring at me blankly. "Two!"

"Yes," I said. "One outside, and one inside the grounds of Temple Tower."

And now it was obvious that not only was the information a surprise to her, but it was a very agitating surprise.

"I heard of one," she said, "the one outside. But, tell me, who was murdered inside?"

"Mr. Granger's servant—a man called Gaspard. It appears that both men were strangled."

"But this is amazing," she cried. "You're sure it wasn't Mr. Granger who was killed?"

"Perfectly sure," I said. "The police are investigating both crimes now."

A look of relief appeared on her face, though her bewilderment was still obvious, and I tried to read the situation by the light of my inside knowledge of the Vandalis' plans. The reason for the relief was clear: it would have complicated things for them considerably if Granger had been dead.

"It is incredible," she said once again. "Who on earth killed the man outside?"

"The same person presumably who killed the one inside," I answered, but her remark, phrased as it was, threw a sudden ray of light on what she was thinking and the reason for her surprise at my news.

Evidently she must have assumed that *le Rossignol* had been murdered by Gaspard. And the information that Gaspard himself was dead completely nonplussed her. So much was apparent: what was not clear was whether or not she knew of *le Bossu*. Her expression at the moment seemed to be that of a person who had heard an inexplicable piece of news: but surely if she knew of *le Bossu* the matter ceased to be inexplicable at once. And as we continued to discuss the thing, I began more and more to feel sure that she did not know of the silent strangler. Which only tended to make it more baffling.

If Hugh's surmise was right: if our plans had been overheard by someone listening in the chimney, and if, further, the Vandalis' room was the one overhead, something must be wrong somewhere. He had put his theory forward when the idea was that the person who had heard our plans was the very woman I was talking to. Of course, it might well be that there was no one there at the moment, and that the dirt had fallen accidentally. And even as I thought so, some more fell down the chimney and lay in a little heap on the whitened hearthstone.

"I beg your pardon," I said, suddenly conscious that she had asked a question and was expecting an answer. "I didn't quite catch your remark."

"I asked if you knew anything about this man Granger?" she said.

"I fear I am only a stranger here," I answered lightly. "He seems a man of curious disposition."

"Is it worth while," she said coldly, "lying in quite such a stupid fashion? A man does not go and conceal himself beside the road on a hot summer's day for fun."

"Is it worth while," I answered equally coldly, "calling a man a liar until you are quite certain of your facts? The reason for my concealment, as you call it, was simple. Mr. Granger has recently engaged a secretary. She happens to be the fiancée of the youngster who was with me. And in view of the type of house it had been arranged that she should throw a letter over the wall telling him if she was all right. Hence our presence there."

She stared at me suspiciously, but with the serene confidence of having told the truth—or very nearly—I returned the look blandly.

"You mean to say that that is all you were there for?" she cried.

"What else is there to be there for?" I countered.

"A man doesn't fortify himself like that unless he is afraid of something," she said.

"Some such idea had occurred to me," I agreed.

For a while she smoked in silence: then she seemed to come to a sudden decision.

"What do you think he is afraid of?" she demanded.

"Presumably the entrance of callers," I remarked.

"Shall we cease to beat about the bush. *Monsieur?*" she said quietly. "For I really cannot believe that your ignorance is quite so profound as you make out."

"If it enabled me to talk a little longer with you, *Madame*," I replied, "I would wish it were even more profound."

She waved aside the clumsy compliment with a frown.

"You know who the man is who was found murdered in the wood." The remark was a statement, not a question.

"Let us suppose for the moment that I do. What then?"

"Why, then you must know everything," she cried irritably. "Why not come out into the open. *Monsieur?* There is plenty for all of us. And now that he is dead there is no hurry. We can take our time."

At last her meaning was clear, and with it the absolute certainty that she was ignorant of the existence of *le Bossu*. She believed that, with the murder of *le Rossignol*, the only people left to share the reward for the stolen property were themselves and us. But one thing it seemed to me she had overlooked even from her own point of view.

"*Madame*," I remarked, "we agreed, I think, that the object of the fortification was to keep out callers, and it would not appear to have been successful. Someone must have been inside the grounds last night."

"Precisely," she said, staring me straight in the face. "And that someone must have been a very powerful man. Almost as powerful as your friend who was in here a night or two ago."

For a moment I did not take her meaning. Then it suddenly dawned on me, and I burst out laughing.

"My dear lady," I cried, "you surely are not accusing us of having pulled off a double murder, are you? That is a bit too rich altogether."

She rose without answering, and with a feeling of relief I realised she was going. There was nothing more to be gained by prolonging the conversation, and I wanted to have another look up the chimney. It was certainly not my intention to enlighten her over *le Bossu*, and if she chose to pretend to me that she thought we had murdered Gaspard and *le Rossignol*, she was quite at liberty to do so.

I watched her step out into the hall, and stand there for a moment or two as if undecided where to go: then she turned and ascended the stairs. And I, after a swift look round to make sure I was unobserved, made a dart for the chimney. And this time it was not all darkness: Hugh was right.

About six feet above my head was a square opening through which a faint light was filtering. And even as I stared at it something moved behind it, and I saw a pair of savage eyes staring down into mine. Then they were gone, and I stepped out into the room again.

My pulse was beating a shade faster than usual, but my brain was perfectly cool. What was the next move? That those eyes had belonged to le *Bossu Masque* himself I felt sure, but what was going to happen now? According to Hugh, the Vandalis' room was above us, and *Madame* Vandali had just gone upstairs. So that she would be bound to find him, and what then? Because, from my reading of the case, she didn't know of his existence.

I waited—but there was no sound. Then I took another look up the chimney, but this time all was darkness. And after a while another thought struck me. If, as I believed, the Vandalis did not know about him, would he have dared to go into their room?

I went quickly out into the hall and looked upstairs. True enough. Number 18 was over the little room where we had been talking, and so far Hugh was right. But he had not seen the position of the opening in the chimney, and I had. And I saw at once that that opening could not have been made from Number 18, but must have come from the room next it. Number 19 was *le Bossu*'s room—not 18. The door was shut, and for a moment I had an insane impulse to stroll casually up the stairs, open the door, and walk in. I could pretend I had come into the wrong room by mistake, and he could not do me any harm in the Dolphin.

However, I decided against it, and walked over to the Visitors' Book. There was the entry right enough: "H. Thomas, London. No. 19."

"I see you have a Mr. Thomas staying here," I said to the girl. "I wonder if that is the Harold Thomas I used to play golf with? Is he a big man with a slight stoop?"

"He is a biggish man, but I don't think he stoops," she answered.

"Fair moustache?" I asked,

"I think he is clean shaven," she replied. "I really couldn't say for sure. But I expect he will be back for dinner."

"He is not in the hotel, then?" I said quietly.

"No. I haven't seen him all day."

She turned to a new arrival, and I went back into the annexe. What was to be done now? That the man who called himself Thomas was in the hotel I knew. But it was manifestly impossible for me to tell the girl how I knew it. If a man lays claim to having seen eyes peering at him out of chimneys, his audience is more than likely to make rude insinuations concerning alcohol. And yet it was utterly imperative that, somehow or other, I should see inside Number 19. How to do it: that was the problem.

I wandered restlessly back into the hall: what about sitting down in a spot which commanded a view of the room? And to my amazement I found, on looking up, that the door was open. Mechanically I ordered a whisky and soda: how did that fact affect things? Did it mean that the owner of Number 19 had gone out in reality, or what?

I finished my drink, and as I laid down the glass I came to a decision. I would go up and walk straight into the room. If there was any unpleasantness I could pretend that I thought it was my mythical Harold Thomas and apologise for my intrusion. But I should have seen the man we wanted: and that, so it seemed to me, was worth a big risk.

There was no one about, and so, putting a bold face on it, I walked straight up the stairs. Then for a moment I admit I hesitated: visions of being arrested as an hotel thief floated before me. But I banished them, and with a preliminary knock on the door, I went into Number 19.

There was no one in it, and I glanced quickly round. A weather-beaten suitcase stood in one corner: on the bed lay a pair of pyjamas. A man's toilet accessories—hair brushes, shaving gear, and the like—adorned the dressing-table. In fact, it was without exception the least suspicious looking room I have even been in. And then I suddenly became aware of a most peculiar noise. It came from the next room, and it sounded as if someone was drumming with his feet on the partition wall. It came fitfully, and then, after a while, it died away altogether, save for an occasional bump.

With its cessation I pulled myself together: there was no good my remaining there now that I had found the room empty. The bluff about Mr. Harold Thomas was all very well, but not having found him at home there was no excuse for my remaining in his room. I must go down and resume my watch in the hall.

And even as I came to that conclusion I happened to look in the glass in front of me. I could see over my shoulder the room behind me. The door was slowly shutting. With a great effort I forced myself to look round. Evidently Mr. Thomas had returned.

But it wasn't Mr. Thomas. Standing almost on top of me was a masked figure, that in the fading light seemed of monstrous size. In a flash I took in the hump on his back, realised it was *le Bossu Masque* himself, and then his hands shot out and he got my throat. I struggled wildly, and I am not generally considered a weakling. But in that man's hands I might have been a child. The silent strangler had got me.

Soon there came a roaring in my ears, and still the grip held. I was losing consciousness: he was throttling me. And the last thing I remember before everything went black was the look of fierce triumph in his eyes.

CHAPTER 10

In Which "Le Bossu" Retrieves His Error

When I came to myself, for a moment or two I could recall nothing. Then in a wave it all came back to me. Once again I saw that terrible figure crouching over me, and felt those vicelike hands on my throat.

Feeling a little dazed and sick, I scrambled to my feet. Of my assailant, there was no sign: the room was empty. And then another thing struck me: the kit that had been lying about was no longer there. Everything had gone, including the suitcase.

For a while I sat on the bed trying to pull myself together. My neck was most infernally sore: undoubtedly *le Bossu* well deserved his second nickname of the Strangler. Because it was useless to blind myself to the fact that had he wished to kill me he could easily have done so. Luckily he had not so wished, and I was still alive, but it was not due to any prowess on my part. He had decided to make me unconscious whilst he packed his things and left the hotel, and had calmly proceeded to do so.

I glanced at my watch: it was seven o'clock. I had been unconscious for roughly an hour. And it was as I replaced it in my pocket that my eye was caught by a big piece of folded paper lying half under the bed. I picked it up mechanically, and opened it out. And then, for a time, I stood gazing at it, literally unable to believe my eyes. It was the actual plan of Temple Tower which had been stolen from Laidley Towers the preceding night. I turned it over: on the back were written some lines in pencil.

I crossed to the window to examine it better: then, on second thoughts, I crammed it in my pocket. There would be plenty of time to study it later: the immediate necessity was to get out of the room. I calculated that he must have dropped it inadvertently when packing, and once he discovered his loss he would almost certainly return for it. And

I had no wish whatever to encounter the gentleman by myself again. True, I could accuse him of half murdering me, but who was there to prove it? A stiff neck gives no outward and visible sign of its existence; it would only be my word against his. Whereas it would be obvious to all concerned that I was in a room where I had no right to be.

I opened the door cautiously and peered out. And with a sigh of relief I saw that no one was about. Even if I was seen leaving the room I should render myself liable to suspicion, but luck was with me. And ten seconds later I was in the hall again, with the precious plan in my pocket. There was no hurry now: I could afford to take my time. And the best thing to do, it struck me, was to inquire into Mr. Thomas' movements. So I walked over to the office.

"By the way," I said to the girl, "has Mr. Thomas returned yet?"

She looked at me in some surprise.

"Mr. Thomas paid his bill and left half an hour ago," she said. "He didn't say anything about coming back."

"I must have misunderstood his plans," I remarked. "Did he say if he was returning to London?"

"He didn't say anything," said the girl. "But he can't get back to London tonight from here. The last train has gone."

I thanked her and let the subject drop. There was nothing more to be got out of her, and it seemed to me that she was already looking at me a little curiously. What had happened was clear. After laying me out he had calmly packed his kit and walked out of the hotel. And we were none of us any nearer knowing what he looked like than we were before. That was the sickening part of it. But I'd got the plan, and that was worth half a dozen stiff necks. I sat down in a secluded spot and ordered the largest whisky and the smallest soda that the hotel could produce. Then I pulled the precious piece of parchment out of my pocket and proceeded to examine it.

The plan itself was dated MLXXXII, which I calculated as 1532. And though my history was extremely rusty, I worked that date out as being in the reign of Henry the Eighth. It showed the original house of Temple Tower, though, of course, not under that name, and the guarding wall. It also showed another building situated about a hundred yards from the house, which I assumed must have been the now non-existent chapel. Connecting the two buildings from outside wall to outside wall, there ran the secret passage clearly marked on the plan. So that, at first sight, it appeared that once one was inside the grounds, with a tape measure, the entrance to the passage would be easy to locate.

"Good Lord! Darrell, where did you get that?"

I glanced up quickly, to find John James regarding me in amazement.

"Hullo!" I said. "Here's your bally old plan."

"So I see," he cried. "I didn't think it was a copy of the *Pink 'Un*. But how did you get it?"

"Sit down," I remarked, "and order the necessary. I could do with another. And I will tell you the doings."

"What's stung your face, laddie?" he said. "It looks kind of fixed in position."

"It is," I answered. "And it's all part of the doings."

He sat down, and I told him briefly what had happened.

"Well, I'm damned," he muttered, when I'd finished. "He's a cool customer. However, let's get back to the old plan. Turn it over, and we'll see what is on the other side."

The writing was crabbed and old-fashioned, and being in pencil, the words were none too easy to decipher. But at last we managed to make them out.

When tower and eastern turret come in line, a tree is found.
Thirty long paces north, and in the ground
The answer lies. But should you hear the sound
Of turning wheels—beware.

"Seems helpful," he murmured. "The only drawback is that we've got to get inside the grounds to make use of it. Moreover, we've got to get in by day."

For a moment or two I did not get his meaning.

"At night we probably shouldn't be able to see the bally turret," he explained.

"But look here," I said, "this bit of doggerel is only a repetition of the information in the plan. There's the passage clearly marked."

He shook his head.

"That's where you're wrong," he answered positively. "The plan only shows the spot where the passage passed underneath the old outside wall. The actual entrance was somewhere inside the chapel, just as the entrance the other end is somewhere inside Temple Tower."

"Then it seems to me," I remarked, "that I've got a stiff neck for nothing. For I'm darned if I can see how we're going to get into the place by day."

"It's just possible that the girl might be able to help us there," he said thoughtfully. "Scott's girl, I mean. She'll have to go back for her kit, and then she ought to have no difficulty in spotting the tree and marking it for us somehow. Anyway," he continued after a pause, "what do we do now, sergeant-major? There doesn't seem much good our sitting on here."

"Let's give it a little longer," I said. "I feel there is a bare possibility of our friend returning to find this. And it would be a pity to miss the blighter."

"Right ho!" he agreed. "As long as you like as far as I'm concerned. But my own opinion is that he's not going to come back for that. Why should he? He's read the verse at the back, and it's not difficult to remember. So that the plan is of no more use to him now, any more than it is to us."

"Perhaps you're right," I said. "Let's give it ten minutes or so, and then we'll push back for dinner."

I replaced the plan in my pocket, and lit a cigarette, whilst he got up.

"I'll wander down to the station," he said, "and get an evening paper. Then, if you're ready, we'll toddle when I get back."

He strolled out, leaving me to finish my drink. The lounge was empty, and the soft evening light slanting through the old-fashioned windows gave it a particularly peaceful aspect. Then four men, two of whom I recognised as golfers of Walker Cup repute, came in talking shop. And I wondered idly what they would think if I butted into their conversation.

"Excuse me," I might say, "interrupting your dissertation on putting, but have you seen a masked hunchback lying about anywhere? Because I've just been very nearly strangled by one."

I began to chuckle inwardly as I imagined their expressions. And yet it was true, damn it, it was true. It wasn't a dream, and it wasn't an attack of *delirium tremens*. Then the clergyman came in, with the two elderly ladies in tow, and one of the golfers, who had abandoned his hobby for the latest from the Stock Exchange, lowered his voice discreetly.

I lit another cigarette and wondered if by any chance *le Bossu* would return. Probably John James was right, and he wouldn't. And even if he did, unless he actually walked into Number 19, how should I know him? I glanced upstairs once again, and as I did so I suddenly remembered that strange drumming noise that I had heard before *le Bossu* attacked me. It had come from Number 18, the Vandalis' room, and I began wondering what had caused it. It had been such a peculiar noise, unlike anything that I could recall having heard before. It had sounded almost as if someone was knocking on the wall with a mallet.

Could it have been a signal of some sort? If so, it must have been intended for *le Bossu* himself, and that proved at once that I was wrong, and the three of them were in collusion. But then, if that were the case, why bother to signal, when all that was necessary was to walk into the room and talk?

After a while I gave it up: like so many other things in this extraordinary affair, there seemed to be a dozen different possibilities. Presumably, in time, we should arrive at some result, but at the moment I felt I couldn't see the forest for the trees.

The door swung open, and I looked up hoping it was John James. I was beginning to agree with him that there was but little object in remaining any longer. But it proved to be the Inspector, and with him a shrewd-looking red-haired young man with journalist written all over him, who paused the instant he saw me, and then came over and spoke.

"Good evening, Mr. Darrell," he said. "You've forgotten me: on the *Folkestone Courier*. You were good enough to give me an interview when you were playing for Middlesex in the Canterbury Cricket Week two years ago. Extraordinary affair this, isn't it?"

"Very," I agreed. "What did you find out, Inspector? You were just going to Temple Tower when you left us this morning."

"Ah! Of course," he said, "you were with Captain Drummond. Just for the moment I did not recognise you. Well, sir, you'll understand that I can't say much. Though, to tell you the truth," he added ruefully, "I haven't got much to say. I'm defeated—for the moment only, of course."

"Quite," I agreed gravely. "You found out nothing from Mr. Granger himself?"

"Practically nothing," he admitted. "It took me the best part of half an hour to force my way in. I rang the bell again and again, and nothing happened. Finally a woman came to the gate, and I told her that unless she opened it I would have it broken down: that a murder had been committed in the grounds, and that by law I must investigate. As soon as I said that she turned as white as a sheet, and opened the gate.

"'A murder!' she stammered. 'Who's been murdered?'

Now, she wasn't lying: I have enough knowledge of human nature to know that. She knew nothing about it: of that I am convinced. She shut the gate and bolted it: then she followed behind me. And when we came to the body she let out a scream and nearly fainted. I don't blame her, for the dead man was her husband. He was strangled just like the other, and he was not a pretty sight.

"However, to cut a long story short, I left her weeping and moaning and made tracks for the house and Mr. Granger. It took me the best part of another half hour to get in there: he kept peering at me through a hole in the door. Finally, he opened it, and then bolted it again as soon as I was in.

"'What do you want?' he said in a whining sort of voice.

"I told him, and I'll eat my hat if he wasn't as surprised as the woman.

"'Two,' he kept on croaking. 'Two men killed! Gaspard—and who was the other? Who was the other?'

"He clawed at my arm, as I described the other, and a look of relief came over his face.

"'That's one of them, at any rate,' he muttered.

"'Look here,' I said sternly, 'there's more in this than meets the eye, Mr. Granger. And you know more about it than you are telling me. How comes it that these two men are strangled, one inside your grounds and one just outside? Somebody must have done it: do you know who?'

"But he wouldn't say any more: Just shut up like an oyster.

"'You'll be *subpoenaed* for the inquest,' I warned him. 'And then you'll be on oath, don't forget. Someone was in your grounds last night, and that someone did the murders. Moreover, I believe you know who that someone was!'

"But he just went on muttering and mumbling to himself, and finally I left him. There wasn't anything more to be got out of him for the moment: the man seemed half crazy to me. But we'll make him speak at the inquest."

"Did you go and see Spragge?" I asked as the Inspector paused.

"I did—later," he answered. "And I did not get much out of him. He identified the body of the man in the wood as the man who had been staying with him. And all he could tell me was that yesterday, about six o'clock, a note was delivered at his farm by a small boy for the lodger—a note which threw him into a terrible state of agitation. He says he went out about eight-thirty and that is the last he's seen of him."

"Very strange," said the red-haired young man. "But good copy. Dead dog: two men strangled—one inside, one out. Very strange. I suppose you are absolutely certain it couldn't have been this man Granger himself?"

"Absolutely," said the Inspector. "He hasn't got the strength."

"Then—who did it?" demanded the journalist. "That is the point."

"Precisely," I mildly remarked, "that is the point."

"Has the doctor decided which was killed first?" asked the journalist.

"The one outside," said the Inspector. "Two or three hours before the other."

"Good!" cried the other. "Then we arrive at this conclusion, anyway."

He talked on: he was the type of man who would talk on for ever and ever, but I hardly heard what he was saying. It seemed almost impossible to realise that I could, in a sentence, explain to them the whole baffling mystery. And not for the first time did the worrying thought return to me: were we justified in withholding our information? True, I saw the difficulties that confronted us: what were we to say without incriminating ourselves? Still, the thought kept coming back, and try as I would, I could not quite pacify my conscience.

I glanced round the hall. The four golfers had risen, and I watched them idly as they reached the top of the stairs and stood for a moment laughing and talking. They moved aside to let a maid, with a can of hot water in her hand, pass them, and I remember asking myself if it were possible to imagine a more prosaic scene. The quiet English inn—the routine unvaried for years. And I remember my thoughts because of the sudden amazing change. Tranquillity, order, peace—and then, in a second, a screaming, hysterical girl standing in the open doorway of Number 18, while the hot water dripped from the overturned can into the hall below. For a second or two no one moved: the thing was so utterly unexpected as to be paralysing. The golfers, with their mouths open, stared at her dazedly: so did we. Then, simultaneously, the power of action returned to all of us. I dashed upstairs behind the Inspector and the journalist, a thousand wild thoughts in my head. But the wildest of those thoughts had not prepared me for the ghastly sight that met my eyes as we entered the room.

Hanging to one of the old oak beams was Vandali. A glance at his purple, swollen face was sufficient: the man was dead. His body sagged grotesquely, almost touching the wall that separated the room from Number 19. And with a sick sort of feeling, I realised that the strange drumming noise I had heard had been made by the poor devil's heels as he died. At his feet lay an overturned chair; evidently he had stood on it, and then kicked it away from underneath him. I heard the others talking in low tones: caught snatches of what they were saying:

"Poor devil."

"Hanged himself."

"Where is the woman?"

The disjointed phrases seemed to come from a long way off, and after a time I escaped downstairs.

Why had Vandali hanged himself? The question hammered at my brain. True, I knew nothing about the man: all that I could say was that I had seen him a couple of hours previously apparently quite happy and contented. What on earth had happened to make him commit suicide?

Then another thought struck me. When Madame Vandali left me she had gone upstairs. At the utmost, only a quarter of an hour had elapsed before I went to *le Bossu*'s room. Therefore, whatever had caused the tragedy must have taken place during that quarter of an hour, because it was impossible to think that she could have found him hanging and said nothing about it. Had they had some terrible quarrel, as a result of which she had left him and he had then committed suicide?

It seemed almost incredible that such a thing could have happened in so short a time. And yet what other conceivable solution was there? Something must have happened during that quarter of an hour to make the man kill himself, and the only person who would be able to throw any light on what that something had been was the woman.

But was she? Like a blinding flash, the thought struck me. Was she? When I had first peered up the chimney, I had stared into *le Bossu*'s eyes: the next time the opening was shut. And when I had gone into his room, it was empty. Where had he been during that fateful quarter of an hour? Did that supply the cause of the quarrel? Was it the eternal triangle once again?

I tried to fit a possible solution on those lines round the facts as I knew them. No one knew what *le Bossu* looked like: quite possibly he was a good looking, attractive man. Suppose, then, that he was an old lover of Madame Vandali, she being ignorant of the manner of man he was. Suppose he had suddenly confronted her, and she had determined at once to leave Vandali. Would that do? And honesty compelled me to admit that if it did, it was only by the barest margin. It meant that in a few minutes she had made up her mind, and left the hotel without packing, having first reduced Vandali to such a condition of hopelessness that he took his own life. Thin; altogether too thin. And yet the whole thing was so inexplicable that one could not disregard even the most wildly improbable solution.

"What on earth is all this excitement?"

I looked up to find that John James had returned and was staring up at the landing with a bewildered look on his face. I told him, and he sat down abruptly.

"Good God!" he said. "What did he do it for?"

"It is what I have been asking myself ever since it was discovered,"

I answered. "The whole thing is so utterly incredible that if I hadn't seen it with my own eyes I should hardly believe it. Well, Inspector, mysteries accumulate at Rye."

"I dunno as there's much mystery about this, sir," he remarked, crossing the hall to us. "Just a plain case of suicide. Good-evening, Sir John."

"'Evening, Inspector. Nothing to account for it?'"

"Nothing, sir. I've asked the manager, and he can't tell me anything. A charming wife, lots of money; and, apparently, not a care in the world."

And at that moment the manager himself, looking anxious and worried, came up.

"A terrible thing. Sir John," he cried. "I wouldn't have had it happen in this hotel for the world. The scandal: and you know what people are. I don't suppose I'll be able to let that room again for months."

"By the way," I remarked, "I wonder if you can tell me anything about a Mr. Thomas who was staying here. The girl in the office tells me he has just gone, and I was wondering if it was a man I met a little while ago. He had Number 19."

But he shook his head, and looked at me as if surprised that so irrelevant a detail could be introduced at such a moment.

"No, sir, I do not," he said. "I believe I saw him when he arrived, but I don't remember having seen him since. And, anyway, this dreadful affair has driven everything else out of my head."

He bustled away as the doctor came down the stairs, as if he still vainly hoped to hear something that would lessen the tragedy. And then, in a feverish attempt to restore things to their normal timetable, he pealed the dinner-gong loudly. Gradually the lounge emptied though there was only one topic of conversation to be heard on every side. And at length I was left alone with John and the doctor.

There seemed no object in staying, and yet I was loath to go. I could not help thinking that there must be some further development that Madame Vandali must return or the man who called himself Thomas. But as the time went on and nothing more happened, it seemed useless waiting any longer. And we were on the point of going when the further development occurred. Only this time it was not an hysterical chambermaid, but the Inspector, white-faced, who stood on the landing outside Number 18.

"Doctor," he called hoarsely. "For God's sake come quick."

The doctor ran up the stairs, and almost mechanically we followed him. What fresh horror had taken place in that ill-omened room? On the bed lay the motionless body of Vandali, covered with a sheet, but it was not at that we any of us looked. For the cupboard door was open and on the floor was the huddled-up body of a woman. It was Madame Vandali, and she, too, was dead.

But in this case there was no question of suicide: it was murder. The mark around her throat was plain to see: she had been strangled.

"Good God!" muttered John shakily, "this is a bit grim."

"I was going through his effects," said the Inspector, "and happened to open that door."

"Lift her out carefully," ordered the doctor. "Though it is obvious nothing can be done."

He mopped his forehead, and furiously ordered away two waiters from the door, who were looking in with wide-open mouths.

As he said, it was obvious that nothing could be done. The unfortunate woman was quite dead. Her face, too, was puffed and swollen, though not quite so badly as the man's.

"Throttled!" said the doctor shakily. "Throttled to death, poor soul."

"Yes, but who by?" wailed the manager.

The poor little man, completely unnerved by this second tragedy, was standing by the door wringing his hands. And it was left to the red-haired journalist, who had mysteriously appeared from nowhere, to supply the answer.

"Him," he said, pointing with dramatic suddenness to the bed.

We all turned and stared at him, and his ferret nose was literally twitching with excitement.

"But they were a devoted couple," stammered the manager.

Red-hair snorted contemptuously, and turned to the doctor.

"Was it you," he asked, "who examined those two men who were found dead this morning?"

"It was," said the doctor. "But what...."

"Man, don't you see?" the other almost yelled. "It is the clue: it is the answer. Who murdered those two men? Why—he did, of course."

For a moment no one spoke. I stared at John, and John stared at me: what on earth was he driving at?

"Look here," he went on excitedly, "it is clear to me. Tell me if I'm wrong. When you find three people mysteriously strangled within twenty-four hours in the same locality—what do you assume? Why—that they were all strangled by the same person."

The Inspector nodded portentously.

"That's so," he conceded.

"Very well, then," said the other. "If someone else murdered these three, why should that man go and hang himself? But supposing it was he who did it: supposing he was a murderer by instinct, and had some terrible quarrel with this woman. Possibly without even intending to, he seized her by the throat and strangled her. That accounts for his hanging himself. When he realised what he had done, half mad with remorse, he committed suicide."

The Inspector scratched his head.

"Yes—but why?" he began.

But red-hair was not to be put off.

"Find out whether this man had anything to do with Temple Tower," he cried. "I'll bet you he did."

"You win your bet," I said. "I happened to be passing Temple Tower yesterday when he and this unfortunate woman were trying to get in."

"What did I tell you?" he said triumphantly. "There's your murderer: there's the solution to the whole thing. Why he did it the Lord knows—and possibly that man Granger. And neither of them are likely to split. But he did it. Damn it! Is there any other solution? But for this quarrel here there was nothing at present to connect him with the two murders at Temple Tower. Now there is. Once a poisoner: always a poisoner. Once a strangler: always a strangler."

Once again I caught John's eye, and this time I signed to him urgently to leave the room.

"Ought I to speak?" I asked him as we went downstairs.

"How can you?" he answered. "What on earth can you say? You have got no proof. And, anyway, are you certain that that youth isn't right?"

"How can he be right?" I cried. "I heard Vandali's heels drumming against the wall before I was attacked myself."

"*Le Bossu* or no *le Bossu*," he answered obstinately, "I refuse to believe that a man can be forced to commit suicide. Come on: let's get back to Hugh's house. My head is simply buzzing."

"Where is Matthews?" I asked. "Weren't you going to pick him up?"

"He said he'd wait for me in the car," he said. "And if he wasn't there, I was to get along back."

There was no sign of him, and we started off. My brain felt as if it was going round and round in circles also: as John had said, no man can be forced to commit suicide. And yet it was not Vandali who was the murderer: of that I was convinced.

We found them all at dinner—Victor Matthews included, and they listened in silence while we told our story. And the first person to speak when we had finished was Matthews.

"I suppose," he said quietly, "that neither of you thought of asking the doctor if Vandali's neck was broken?"

We all stared at him: what was he driving at? And then he began to laugh quietly to himself as if enjoying some secret joke.

"Forgive me laughing," he said, "but it is indicative of genuine admiration. What a man! What a man!" He grew serious again. "We were wondering—all of us—how *le Bossu* was going to retrieve his error. Now we know."

"You think it was *le Bossu*?" demanded John.

"I don't think," answered the other, "I know."

Then how did he make Vandali commit suicide?"

"He didn't—for the simple reason that Vandali didn't commit suicide."

"But," spluttered John, "confound it all—he did."

"You are wrong, Sir John. Vandali was murdered: just as the others were murdered. And by that simply and kindly little act on the part of *le Bossu* he has not only removed from his path two people he wanted removed, but he has supplied the ready-made solution, so ably discovered by your journalistic friend, to account for everything."

But how do you know Vandali was murdered?" insisted John.

"Know is perhaps too strong a word," admitted Matthews. "And yet, I'm not sure that it is. Just think. If a man is hanged in the accepted sense of the word, his neck is broken, and death is instantaneous. But to obtain that result a long drop of several feet is necessary. In the case, however, of a man standing on a chair, and then kicking it away—there were one or two cases during the war of captured spies doing it—the neck is not broken. Death is not instantaneous, and is due to strangulation."

"Yes, but dash it all," objected John again, "what's that got to do with it?"

"Dry up, John," said Hugh. "I see what he is driving at."

"Strangulation, Sir John," continued Matthews. "So that, in reality, all four deaths were due to the same cause. Which puts a very different complexion on the matter, doesn't it? Our friend, by the simple process of hanging one of the dead bodies up, has made it appear as if only three were due to strangulation, and that the fourth was suicide. That being so, the solution to the whole affair would be exactly what the journalist got, and which *le Bossu* intended someone to get. I don't blame anyone for jumping to the conclusion that has been jumped to: without the inside knowledge we possess it is the conclusion we should arrive at."

"But look here, Mr. Matthews," I said, "there are still some pretty useful difficulties in the way. If we accept your theory we have also got to accept the fact that *le Bossu* walked quite openly into the Vandalis' bedroom, and strangled them one after another without a sound being heard. Further, that Madame Vandali, who must have been killed second, came into the room to find her husband hanging to the beam, and never uttered a cry. Why, she'd have screamed the place down."

Matthews smiled faintly.

"Agreed, Mr. Darrell," he said. "Put as you have done, it sounds a bit difficult. Let me, however, try and reconstruct what may have happened. While the two Vandalis were talking in the little room below, *le Bossu* was listening. Vandali goes upstairs into his room: *le Bossu* leaves Number 19, and follows him in. There he strangles him and puts the body in the cupboard. Wait"—as I again started to speak—"I can guess your objection, but let me finish first. Then he goes back to his listening-post, and shortly after Madame comes up to the room. With her he repeats the process, and having killed them both, he hangs the man on the beam, and puts the woman in the cupboard. Then once again he goes back to his room, where he finds you. Now, it's obvious he can't kill you. To do so would be to shed the light of publicity on Number 19, and the mystical Mr. Thomas. So he renders you unconscious, packs his things and departs. Moreover, Mr. Thomas will be seen no more. He has served his purpose, and he now disappears from the cast—as Mr. Thomas."

"How do you mean—as Mr. Thomas?" demanded Hugh.

Victor Matthews leaned forward impressively. Assuming that my account of what happened is correct, and substantially it must be so, there is still one grave difficulty—a difficulty which I think Mr. Darrell spotted. If a stranger walks into your room, for whatever purpose, there will be some conversation, and probably loud conversation. In Mr. Darrell's case it was a little different: he was in a room where he had no right to be, and he was taken by surprise. But with the Vandalis—especially with Madame Vandali—one would have expected a scream or some cry, at any rate. And there was nothing—no sound at all. Don't you see the almost irresistible conclusion we arrive at?"

"I'm damned if I do," said Freckles.

"Why, that *le Bossu* was not a stranger to the Vandalis, He is a man, moreover, who could walk into their room without occasioning comment on their part. Jean Picot—the chauffeur: he is *le Bossu Masque*."

He almost shouted in his excitement, and we all stared at him.

"It fits," he went on. "It must fit. He comes over as their chauffeur.

All along he has meant to get rid of them sometime or other. Having arrived he takes the first opportunity of getting the room next to them, and for the purpose he disguises himself and takes the name of Thomas. So that he has two rooms in the hotel: Jean Picot's room, and Mr. Thomas' room."

He paused and lit a cigarette, looking round the table triumphantly.

"By George! laddie," boomed Hugh, "what a brain! Picot it is, for a fiver. What shall we do? Go and push his face in? Or have a mug of port?"

Chapter 11

In Which We See a Face at the Window

The more one thought of it the more probable did it seem that Matthews was right. It accounted for so many little odd threads that had hitherto proved puzzling. Particularly the elusiveness of the so-called Mr. Thomas. It had struck me when I asked the girl in the office that she seemed very vague about him: the manager, too, in spite of the worry of the tragedy, might have been a little more helpful. But once one assumed that he and Picot were the same person, much of the difficulty disappeared. To a master of disguise, such as *le Bossu* almost certainly was, there would have been no difficulty over entering Number 19 as Mr. Thomas, and leaving it, if he so wished, as Jean Picot. His presence in that part of the hotel was easily accounted for in his role of chauffeur.

Then again the chimney-pot episode. It had seemed to me that it had caused the Vandalis so little surprise that they must be privy to it. And they probably had been, thinking it was Jean Picot who had pushed it over at Hugh. But a Jean Picot who really was their chauffeur and accomplice not a Jean Picot who was using them to his own ends entirely.

All the way through it was the same thing, and it was impossible not to feel a certain unwilling admiration for the swine. For just so long as a person was useful to him, *le Bossu* employed him. Then without the smallest compunction he murdered him. *Le Rossignol* was allowed to make his ladder, and almost put it in position on the wall. Then—death: that hideous silent death which, had it suited him, would have been my portion.

The Vandalis had been allowed to live only as long as they served his purpose. While it had seemed possible that they might get the jewels from Granger, *le Bossu* was perfectly prepared to let them try. He was, in fact, a past-master in letting the cat pull the chestnuts out of the fire for him.

It all fitted in, as Matthews said. On hearing of the plan he had forthwith driven off to Laidley Towers and obtained it, returning in time to hide in the shadow of the warehouse as we started off in the car. Then, later on, they were the lights of his car that we had seen on the main road—going and then coming back. And having drawn blank there, he had returned and tried the sea road till he found our car and removed the sparking-plugs.

"He's a blinking marvel," cried Hugh. "Equalled only by our Mr. Matthews."

Matthews waved a deprecating hand.

"My dear sir, you must not forget that I know him. But I assure you that on the score of brain I lay no claim to be in the same street as *le Bossu*. However, this time, by a combination of circumstances, I think we've got him. And our principal asset is Sir John's plan."

"You think he will still go on with it?" said John doubtfully.

"A man is not going to kill four people for nothing," answered Matthews. "And though the risk will be great, *le Bossu* is accustomed to risk. He must guess, of course, that we shall be there. That he knows about Miss Verney is, I should think, almost certain. And he will doubtless arrive at exactly the same conclusion as Sir John did—namely, that the best way of spotting the tree is for her to return to Temple Tower tomorrow, under the pretext of getting her luggage. Further, he will assume that once the tree is found we shall lose no time in searching for the entrance to the passage. And then he will rely on his own cunning. That is how I see it, gentlemen. Moreover, I see another thing, too. The inquest will be, I should imagine, the day after tomorrow. He, if it can possibly be done, would like to be clear of Temple Tower before the publicity, which is going to be given to Granger and all his doings, occurs. And so I believe *le Bossu* will be prepared to run an additional risk, if he can pull it off tomorrow night. If it was feasible he would do it tonight, but it isn't. He does not know where the tree is."

"And so, on your theory," said Hugh, "we are going to be the last bunch of pussy-cats for the monkey. Supposing we refuse to play?"

"Nothing would please him more," laughed Matthews. "Though we have the easiest method of spotting the tree, there are others. A thing like that is not going to deter *le Bossu*. And if we refuse to play we leave him a free hand. Besides, our friend is quite a good enough judge of human nature to know that you are not going to let me down. I've got to play, any way."

"My dear fellow," cried Hugh horrified, "I was only jesting. Why, great Scott! This is where the fun begins. We'll dot him one all right."

"The only point," said Freckles doubtfully, "is this. Now that we know Picot is *le Bossu*, oughtn't we to say something to the police?"

"The old, old difficulty," answered Matthews.

The difficulty which confronts us at every stage in our career. I speak as a policeman myself. We know—or we think we know: but can we prove? And at this stage of the proceedings we lay ourselves open to very grave censure for not having spoken sooner. Catch him in the act, and it becomes a very different matter. We have a definite result to show: a tangible asset. Besides"—his voice sank a little, and the dreamy look I had seen before came on his face—"he's my meat."

"Your meat he shall remain, old lad," laughed Hugh. "We'll just come along and help in the mincing."

And at that moment Pat Verney screamed. She was staring at the window, and as I swung round I had a momentary glimpse of Jean Picot's face pressed against the pane. His features were distorted with rage: his eyes were fixed on Victor Matthews. For a second I saw it, and then it seemed to me that the crack of a revolver and the sound of breaking glass were simultaneous with the lights going out. A bullet went past my head with a wicked *ping*, and a further crash of glass showed that no one was hit.

"*Le Bossu*," shouted Matthews. "After him."

"Who put out the light?" came Hugh's quiet voice.

"I did," cried Matthews. "I'm by the switch now. Somebody stay with Miss Verney: come on the rest."

"No earthly use," said Hugh. "The night is too dark. But I wish the damned fellow wouldn't break my glass. I think he was having a pot at you, Matthews."

"I'm quite certain of it," he answered.

"Good God! The door is opening," yelled Freckles.

And even as he spoke, there came a half strangled shout which turned into a hideous gurgling noise. It ceased as abruptly as it had begun, and then the door shut again.

"Lights," said Hugh curtly. "And, Peter, keep your gun handy."

But the light revealed nothing except an almost incredible sight. Victor Matthews, with his hand to his throat, and his eyes staring, was half crouching, half lying against the wall. His lips were moving, but only inarticulate sounds came from them. And on his face was a look of utter terror. Hugh sprang to the door and flung it open. The hall, which was dimly lighted, was empty, but the front door was open. And after a time he came back into the room.

"Our old pal *le Bossu* going all out," he remarked thoughtfully. "Undoubtedly a gentleman of nerve."

"Two hands—got me—by throat," gasped Matthews, and still the terror remained on his face. He was peering fearfully round the room, as if he expected *le Bossu* to materialise once more, and every now and then a long shuddering sigh shook him.

"Spot of whisky?" said Hugh. "By Gad! That's calm, you know," he went on as he crossed to the sideboard. "First of all he has a pot shot at you: and then he comes into the bally house, and says 'How d'you do?'"

"Do you require anything, sir?" Denny had quietly materialised. "I thought I heard a shot."

"Just go and say *shoo* at the front door, my trusty fellah," said Hugh. "But mind you don't get strangled or anything. If you think it is likely, call me."

"Very good, sir. Shall I lock up after that?"

"Yes—lock up. But say *shoo* two or three times, as if you meant it. And then bring some more glasses. And beer. You know," he continued as Denny left the room, "this bally fellow is growing on me. Peter—for sheer nerve—he's got old Carl Peterson beat to a frazzle."

"At any rate," said, "it has definitely settled one thing. Picot is *le Bossu*."

"That is so," he agreed. "And it seems to me that the thing to do now is to lay out our plan of campaign, provided, that is to say, Matthews is feeling fit enough."

"I'm all right now, thanks," said Matthews. "The thing was so completely unexpected that it shook me for a moment."

"I'll bet it did," said Hugh. "Deuced nasty business having a bird like that keeping his hand in on you. Did you say *shoo*, Denny?"

"Three times, sir," answered the butler, putting down the beer. "Only a cat responded to the threat."

"Good," said Hugh. "We may not cut much ice with old Picot, but with cats we're perfect devils. Now the next move, Denny, is with Mrs. Denny. Ask her to go and ferret round in Mrs. Drummond's gear and get the necessary wherewithal for Miss Verney for tonight. Miss Verney will sleep in the green room. Now, what about you, Matthews? I think you'd better stay as well. You can sleep in my dressing-room—afraid it is the only one left. And you can sleep soundly, because the only way into it is through my wife's and my room. So that if old Picot returns we can give him a thick ear between us.

"Thank you. Captain Drummond," said Matthews. "I'll accept your offer with pleasure."

He had quite recovered, and the colour had come back to his face. He now appeared almost amused at the whole thing: Hugh's very matter-of-fact conversation seemed to have pulled him together.

"Splendid. Very well then, Denny—that's all settled. Lock up everywhere, and then you can turn in. Now," he went on, as Denny left the room, "tomorrow, at crack of dawn, somewhere round about ten o'clock. Miss Verney, accompanied by Scott, will repair to Temple Tower. Having arrived there, while Miss Verney gets her kit, Scott will wander round the grounds, get the tower and the eastern turret in line and then mark the tree so that we shall know it again. That clear?"

"Absolutely," said Freckles.

"Right. Then I suggest. Miss Verney, that you should push off to bed. You must be completely exhausted. And don't feel alarmed: you're quite safe."

"I'm not a bit frightened," she answered. "And I think I will go: last night was not a particularly restful one."

"I'm for the shore, too," said John. "Any chance of that bally fellow coming back?"

"Always a chance," said Hugh. "But we'll shutter all the ground floor, and unless he's a cat-burglar as well as a strangler, he won't get in. Off you push: there will be mighty little sleep for anyone tomorrow night. How's the neck, Matthews?" he went on, when the other three had gone.

"Quite recovered. But when next I meet Picot. . . ." He paused expressively. "And that will not be till tomorrow night. Our friend, I am open to a small bet, will not be much in evidence by day."

"No," agreed Hugh. "Probably not. Well, would you like me to show you your room?"

He led the way upstairs, and I mixed myself another drink. Used as I was to Hugh's methods and moods, there was something about him tonight that I couldn't quite understand. His complete calmness and nonchalance under the most unusual circumstances I was accustomed to, and his manner, since the attack on Matthews, had been just what I should have expected. But there was an underlying something that beat me. No one else would have noticed it, but then no one else in the room knew him as I did. And when he came down the stairs again I tackled him.

He gave a lazy grin.

"It's his gall, old Peter, his gall, that tickles me to death. Plastering notices on my trees, and then doing target practice amongst the crockery. Damn the fellow, it might be his house. And then to come in and give poor old Matthews the once over."

"But why the devil didn't you go after him?" I cried.

"Nerve shaken, old boy," he said earnestly. "I assure you I was all of a tremble."

"Confound you, Hugh," I laughed, "don't talk such appalling tripe to me. There's something at the back of your ugly face."

"A desire for beer, Peter. More beer. Much more beer."

He lit a cigarette, and, with his eyes half closed, he lay back in his chair blowing smoke rings. And now I knew I was right: it was the attitude he invariably adopted when he was thinking. Absolutely motionless, save for the movement of his arm as he lifted his cigarette to his mouth, he sat there staring at the ceiling. Then, quite suddenly, he began to laugh gently to himself.

"That's it, Peter. Gall to the *n*th degree. But, by Gad! Old boy, a dangerous man to play games with—damned dangerous. I wouldn't miss tomorrow night for a thousand pounds. As Matthews says—it all fits in. As far as I can see, there isn't a flaw up to date—but what is he going to do when he finds us sitting over the entrance to the passage? It won't be too easy for the bird."

"My own impression is that he will do nothing," I said, "for the simple reason that there will be nothing to do."

"Think so?" he laughed. "Well, well—we shall see. Another pint, old boy, and then what about a little shut-eye?"

"What are you doing tomorrow?" I asked.

"This and that, Peter," he answered. "As a matter of fact, I think I shall take it easy. Do accounts, or something of that sort."

"Do accounts?" I gasped. "If you weren't so damned large, Hugh Drummond, I should welt you good and hearty."

I stood up: I was beginning to feel infernally sleepy. But when I reached the top of the stairs Hugh was still in the same attitude, with a fresh cigarette between his fingers. And from what I knew of him it was more than likely that he would remain there for hours. Something was worrying him, though for the life of me I couldn't see what. The one big problem—the identity of *le Bossu*—was solved. And the only thing that I couldn't see—as I said to Hugh—was what *le Bossu* could hope to do against five of us the following night.

I slept like a log, despite the stiffness of my neck, and arrived down to breakfast before anyone except Victor Matthews.

"*Le Bossu*'s neck treatment seems to be conducive to early rising," I said.

"Yes," he laughed. "And somebody else was up pretty early, or stayed up mighty late. Your reporter friend has spread himself."

He passed over a copy of the *Folkestone Courier*, and I glanced at it. Undoubtedly Matthews was right: Ferret-face had wallowed in it.

Amazing Crime on Romney Marsh
Incredible Triple Murder and Suicide
Mystery of the Walled House

The headlines shrieked at one, and I ran my eye down the page. It contained nothing that we did not know already, but one point became increasingly clear, as I read on. Before many hours were out, there would be hordes of people on the spot, armies of reporters. The account in the London papers was brief—just a summary of what had happened. But with the *Folkestone Courier* giving tongue as it had, the other papers would be sure to follow suit.

"Get off as soon as you can, Miss Verney," said Hugh after breakfast. "It strikes me that this road is shortly going to look like Egham on Gold Cup day."

She started off with Freckles five minutes later, and he turned to Matthews.

"What's your programme?" he asked.

"Jean Picot," answered Matthews tersely. "There is no other problem. And though I don't think there is the smallest chance of my seeing him today, there is no harm in trying. There is nothing to do until tonight, and so I shall go into Rye and nose around."

"Good," said Hugh. "As you say, it can do no harm."

And when John decided that he would go back to Laidley Towers the same arrangement as the previous day was fixed up. He would drop Matthews in Rye, and pick him up again on his return in the evening.

"That leaves only the old firm, Peter," said Hugh, as John's car disappeared through the gates. "And what does the old firm do?"

"Accounts," I grinned.

He was staring thoughtfully over the sun-baked marsh.

"Quite right," he said, "accounts. To settle accounts is always an excellent thing to do. But in view of the fact that you bore the burden and heat of the day yesterday, I would like you to take a rest today. I want you to stay here. You can knit yourself some underclothes, or indulge in any other form of dissipation you like. But stay here—and keep your eyes skinned."

"What are you going to do yourself?" I demanded.

"Settle accounts," he repeated. "Or, at any rate, do the preliminary bookwork. And if you've got no other way to occupy yourself, ponder on one thing. If you saw that plan sticking out from under the bed, why was *le Bossu* suddenly stricken with blindness?"

So that was what had been worrying him the night before. If hi words had any significance at all, he was implying that *le Bossu* had dropped the plan on purpose: that it was no accident and he had intended me to pick it up. And the notion was so completely novel that I must have stood for quite five minutes after the roar of the Bentley had died away, staring down the drive.

All of us, and most certainly I personally, had assumed that the dropping of the plan had been a slip. We had based our plan of action on that theory: we had, in military parlance, appreciated the situation from that point of view. And here was Drummond quietly suggesting to me that the whole of our foundation was faulty.

I sat down and began to weigh up the points for and against. And the more I thought of it, the more likely did it seem that he was right. *Le Bossu* had been in no hurry: he had quietly and systematically packed, taking about half an hour over it, and had then left. Was it likely that he would have dropped such a valuable asset as the plan, or, having dropped it in a distinctly conspicuous place, that he would not have seen it? Against that, why in the name of fortune should he have done it at all?

Matthews' theory that he would still carry on was based on the idea that, though he had lost the plan, he would turn his loss to good account, by letting us find the entrance for him. But it put a very different complexion on matters if he had arranged for us to have it. To make the best of a bad job was comprehensible: deliberately to make the job bad was not. And it was absurd to say that only by using Miss Verney could the location of the entrance be found. There must be other ways, even though she afforded the simplest.

The devil of it all lay in the fact that this new idea complicated things so much. While it had been left as an accident—as a slip on *le Bossu*'s part—everything had seemed plain sailing. Now that we knew who he was, it had only seemed to be a question of waiting until he walked into our hands, either in the grounds of Temple Tower, or somewhere outside. But this notion of Drummond's, if it was correct, altered the whole situation. What was at the back of *le Bossu*'s mind, that had caused him to do it? He must know that we would take advantage of the verse and would find the entrance. Then why had he done it? And the more I thought of it, the more utterly incomprehensible did it seem.

Unless—I sat up suddenly—unless the whole thing was a trap. Step by step I traced it from the hypothesis. *Le Bossu* wished to get rid of us, as he had got rid of the other four who stood in his way. He wanted to murder us, as he had murdered them. But with us he was confronted with a difficulty: he couldn't get us individually as he had got them. We were always together. So he decided to try and do us in collectively. He presents us with a definite spot to gather together at, and prepares that spot beforehand, with some infernal machine like a bomb.

I checked there: how could he find the place? He might have got into the grounds after he had left us the preceding night—waited for the first faint streaks of dawn—and found it then. But in that case why didn't he beat it while the going was good, and go straight on into the house? So that wouldn't do.

And then in a flash it came to me. The spot was not prepared, but *le Bossu* was. Once when we were bunched together there, he would steal as near as he could in the darkness, and throw a bomb amongst us, either killing or wounding the lot. Then he would go calmly along the secret passage, probably murder Granger, take the jewels and clear out. If alarm was caused by the explosion of the bomb, he would trust to luck to escape in the confusion.

Once again the incredible audacity of the man staggered me. That I had hit the only possible solution, once granted Hugh's theory was right, seemed to me obvious. There could be no other reason which would have caused him to give us a piece of information, which above all others it would seem he would have kept to himself. And the objection which might be advanced—namely, that without the plan we should not have found the spot—was easily met. True, we might not have found the exact spot, but we should have been wandering round in the locality. We had already interrupted him once, when he was killing the wretched Gaspard, and he was not going to run the risk a second time. And as the full realisation of the man's cold-blooded ferocity sank into my mind, I was inclined to agree with Hugh that compared to him, Carl Peterson had been a turtledove.

The morning wore on slowly. Midday came, and there was still no sign of Miss Verney or Scott, though an increasing number of cars had passed the gate on the way to Temple Tower. And then, at half-past twelve, the Inspector looked in, ostensibly to see Drummond, but in reality to quench his thirst.

"Reporters like flies," he said. "And there's one—probably a photographer—circling over the house in an aeroplane. Look—there he is now."

I glanced up: sure enough there was a machine passing backwards and forwards over Temple Tower,

"You've found out nothing more, I suppose?" I asked him.

"Nothing, sir," he said. "I can't say that I hold with those newspaper chaps myself, but I'm bound to admit that I think that red-haired young fellow has got it right this time. That is, as far as the actual murders are concerned. The man Vandali did them, and then hanged himself. But as to why, he doesn't know any more than I do. Tomorrow, I think, should help us a little there."

"At the inquest, you mean?" I said.

"That's right, sir—at the inquest. That man Granger will have to talk then. I've been up there this morning, but he says he is sick and can't see anyone."

"By the way," I said casually, "these Vandalis had a chauffeur, didn't they?"

He nodded, and drained his glass,

"I've examined him already," he said, "but he can't tell me anything. Speaks very little English. From what he says he has only been with them about a month, and knows nothing about them at all. Secretive sort of chap: I wouldn't be surprised if his past was a bit hectic. But as far as this show is concerned, he doesn't come into it. He has no idea whatever as to why they went to Temple Tower: didn't even know they had been there, in fact. No, sir. Granger is the man. Even though he had nothing to do with the actual murders, he knows why they were committed."

He took his leave, and I sat on thinking idly. The aeroplane had finished its manoeuvres over Temple Tower, and was making off in the direction of Lympne: presumably the photographs had been taken. And then, happening to glance at my watch, I found, to my surprise, it was one o'clock.

"Will you have lunch now, sir, or will you wait?" said Denny, coming out of the dining room. "Mr. Scott has just returned."

"Hasn't Miss Verney come?" I cried.

"She has not," said Freckles, appearing on the scene. "I did my level best to persuade her, but when Pat sticks her toes in she's like a mule."

"We'll have lunch, Denny," I said. "Now what has happened?"

"After the devil of a lot of fuss we managed to get in," he began. "And, incidentally, it's lucky we went when we did: when I left the place, ten minutes ago, a crowd of some fifty people hailed me as the murderer. However, we got in all right, and Pat went straight into the house while I oozed round the grounds. There was no difficulty whatever about spotting the tree. It is a big oak standing by itself in a bit of a clearing, and you couldn't possibly fail to get it, even at night."

"Did you find the entrance to the passage?" I asked.

"I can't say I did," he said. "To tell you the truth I wasn't quite certain which way North was. I had a vague dip, but the only thing I saw was a rabbit scrape?"

"Doesn't matter," I said. "We'll get it tonight by the Pole Star. Go on."

"Well, I sat about the grounds for over two hours, when Pat suddenly appeared. And, according to her, the bloke was entrenched in his room absolutely gnawing the blotting-paper with fright. Worse, far worse, apparently, than he's been before. Kept on saying 'He can't get in: he can't get in,' and wanting to know if they could force him to go to the inquest if he was ill. In fact, she seemed almost sorry for him, though I pointed out to her that, from what we'd heard, he must be a pretty ungodly maggot. Still, you know what women are—queer fish."

I nodded gravely.

"Is that why she is staying with him?" I asked.

"Not on your life," he said, lowering his voice mysteriously. "The old bean thinks she is well on the road to spotting some more cubby holes. Secret hiding-places," he explained kindly, as he saw my look of bewilderment, "where he has hidden the rest of the stuff. She's got one—the panel by the fireplace—already, and she strongly suspects the waste pipe in the bathroom to be another. Apparently he gave tongue like a wounded hare on hearing the water turned on, but that was probably due to fright at the thought of washing. However, she thinks, to cut the thing short, that if she does a bit of nosing about this afternoon she might find out some pretty useful information. I thought it a bit risky myself, but she said that that was what Matthews had said she ought to do. And so I pushed off, and trickled back here. Though I don't like the idea much—leaving her practically alone in a house with a bloke crazy with fear."

Undoubtedly the Toad was in an awkward position. A criminal himself, with hundreds of thousands of pounds worth of stolen stuff in his possession, he dared not avail himself of police protection. Nor was he in a position to give the police any information as to the real terror that was hanging over him—*le Bossu*—for the very good reason that, unlike us, he didn't know who *le Bossu* was. He could give no description of him. And it struck me that if ever there was an example of evil bringing its own retribution, that was it. All these years, flying from hiding-place to hiding-place, in mortal terror of an unknown man. What a life! *Le Rossignal*, at any rate, he knew by sight, but any stranger might have been *le Bossu*. And then, when at last he had got his loot over from France, to be run to earth by both of them, unable to do anything save sit and wait behind his barricades."

"I wonder if he knows about the secret passage?" I said thoughtfully.

But to that question there was no answer: all that we could arrive at was that he had said nothing about it to Miss Verney. Which, of course, proved nothing at all.

The afternoon dragged on slowly until at about seven o'clock Hugh returned, and I lost no time in putting my theory in front of him.

"I haven't said anything to Scott," I told him. "But, if your idea is right, and that plan was left there on purpose, I don't see any other solution that fits. He wants to get us bunched, and then out us."

But somewhat to my surprise Hugh would have none of it.

"Not that I put it a bit beyond him, Peter," he remarked. "If it suited his purpose, he would blow up a babies' crèche without scruple. But I cannot think that that would suit his purpose. Killing a stray individual silently is one thing: but to burst a bomb in the middle of the night is a very different affair. In all probability Temple Tower will have a certain amount of police attention tonight, and if the hell of an explosion takes place, it will be the scene of considerable activity. And there is another thing too, Peter. Supposing this entrance is all rusted over: supposing it takes a considerable time to get in? Then, according to your theory, he is going to draw the attention of everybody to the one spot which he wants to keep private."

"Well, what the devil is your idea then?" I said peevishly.

"Something far more subtle, old boy," he remarked with a grin, and from his tone of voice I knew that that was all I was going to get out of him. There are times when an oyster is chatty compared to Hugh.

"Here is John," he said, glancing out of the window. "But no Matthews. I wonder where he has strayed to."

"I left the policeman *wallah* running round in small circles in Rye," said John as he came in. "I'd fixed to meet him at a quarter to seven, and he didn't appear till ten past. From what he said he seems to have found out something completely new this afternoon. And he told me to tell you not to wait dinner for him, but that he would come up after."

"Good," said Hugh. "Then we might get down to it."

"And what have you been doing all day, old horse?" went on John chattily.

"This and that, laddie," said Hugh. "Trying to make four equal six, to be exact."

"Presumably there is some meaning in your remark," said John kindly. "But at the moment I confess it eludes me."

"And yet the fact that under certain circumstances four are as good as six will, unless I've bloomered badly, prove to be the deciding factor," laughed Hugh. "Come on, chaps: let us go and feed our faces."

CHAPTER 12

In Which We Hear the Noise of Turning Wheels

That Hugh had some theory of his own was obvious, but by what possible method of subtlety *le Bossu* hoped to outwit us defeated me. His objection to my bomb idea was sound, I realised, but there seemed equally powerful objections to the use of cunning. Boiled down to rock-bottom facts, if five of us who all knew Jean Picot by sight were sitting round the entrance of the passage, it would require the deuce of a lot of subtlety to get past us. Force would be out of the question, and so what was going to happen? And the more I thought about it, the more did I come back to my original answer to the question—nothing at all. We should spend a night of intense discomfort for no result whatever.

Dinner was over and we were sitting in the smoking-room. In half an hour it would be sufficiently dark to start, but there was still no sign of Victor Matthews. And we were just wondering when he would roll up when the telephone rang close by my chair.

"Probably him," said Hugh. "Take the call, Peter."

It was, and I told him we were all waiting.

"Good," came his voice. "Listen, Mr. Darrell; the most extraordinary development has taken place. I'm hard on *le Bossu*'s trail. I think he has lost his nerve. Will you come at once—all of you—to Tenterden to the—Oh! My God."

His voice rose to a hoarse scream, then stopped abruptly, and for a moment or two I was too stupefied to speak.

Then, "Matthews!" I shouted wildly. "Matthews! What's happened?"

But there was no answer—only silence, though again I shouted into the instrument.

"Steady, Peter," came Hugh's voice. "What is the excitement?"

"It was Matthews," I said. "He's just said he was hard on *le Bossu*'s trail, and wanted us all to go to Tenterden at once. He was just going to say the name of the hotel, when he screamed out 'Oh! my God.' Then nothing more. *Le Bossu* must have got him."

"Give me the receiver," said Hugh quietly. "I'll ring the exchange."

We waited for what seemed an eternity.

"That last call you put through to me," he said. "Where did it come from?"

Again an interminable delay, and then he turned round.

"The A. A. road box," he remarked, "on the road to Tenterden. I know it well. How very extraordinary."

"Extraordinary!" I said. "It is more than that: it is uncannily devilish."

It seemed so easy to reconstruct the scene. Matthews pausing on his way to Tenterden, believing himself hot on *le Bossu's* trail. He sees the A. A. box; decides to ring us up. And then as he stands there, unconscious of his danger, the very man he thought he was hunting steals on him from behind. The hunter hunted. And now a fifth murder to *le Bossu's* credit.

"Come on," said Hugh quietly. "This requires investigation."

We tumbled into the Bentley and started off. I could see Hugh's face silhouetted against the reflection of the headlights, and it was like an expressionless mask.

"It's simply amazing, Peter," he said suddenly. "I can't understand it. You're certain it was Matthews?"

"Of course I'm certain," I answered. "I'd know his voice anywhere."

He relapsed into silence again, and I tried to make out what was puzzling him. It seemed to me to be a development quite in keeping with the whole affair.

"Here's the telephone box," he remarked, "about fifty yards ahead."

He pulled up the car, and in the glare of lights the box stood out clearly outlined by the roadside. But of anything else there was no sign: the road was empty, there was no trace of any body.

"He would have hidden it," I said. "He wouldn't leave it where anybody passing could see it."

"No," said Hugh. "He would not. Can it be possible?" he added half to himself. He suddenly switched off the lights. "Come on—we must look. But, for God's sake, move warily. There's something here I don't understand at all."

Halfway to the box he halted, and for a time we stood in the road listening intently. Not a sound could be heard save a train in the distance, and I suggested we should go a bit closer, and begin to search.

"What I'm afraid of," said Hugh in a low voice, "is a trap. If Picot strangled Matthews, he must have heard what Matthews was saying, as he crept up to him from behind. If so, what will he assume? Why, that we shall do exactly what we have done. The flies are walking straight into the parlour, and your theory, Peter, of the bomb is quite feasible here. We must string out: I'll go first. And don't make a sound."

He faded into the darkness, and we followed at intervals. Every now and then I stopped to listen, but I heard nothing except an owl hooting mournfully in a little wood ahead of us. Suddenly I saw a light on the road some twenty yards in front; Hugh had turned his torch on to the ground at the foot of the box, and was examining it carefully. I almost called out to him: if there was any chance of a trap, he was surely asking for trouble. But after a moment or two he switched it off again, and once more I crept forward till I came to the telephone box myself. He had disappeared, and for a while I stopped there trying once more to reconstruct in my mind what had happened.

What would *le Bossu* have done with the body? Hidden it, of course, but hidden it as quickly as possible. A hedge ran behind the box, but as far as I could see there was no gap in it, and after a bit the hopeless futility of finding the body at night struck me. One might stumble on it, but the chances were all against it. And at that moment I heard Hugh's low whistle.

He was standing in the road, and I joined him.

"Look here, Peter," he said, "this is utterly futile. It's a hundred pounds to a banana skin against finding him."

"I quite agree," remarked Freckles, looming up. "I've stubbed my toe, and I don't want to play any more. The only way to spot him will be by day. Take an aeroplane and fly over the ground low, like that bloke was doing this morning at Temple Tower."

"What's that you say?" yelled Hugh. "An aeroplane over Temple Tower?"

"What under the sun is the excitement?" I cried. "I saw the fellow myself. A journalist taking photographs."

"Journalist be damned," snapped Hugh. "Why in God's name didn't you tell me that before? To the car—and leg it."

Almost speechless with amazement I followed him: what on earth was the great idea?

"The one point that was missing," said Hugh tensely, as the speedometer touched seventy. "If only you had told me, Peter! Don't you see, man, the vital significance of it? The line between the tower and eastern turret, when produced, hits the ground at one end, and the other goes into the air. Get into that line from the air and you pick up the tree. It wasn't a journalist who was in the plane: it was *le Bossu*. And *le Bossu*, whilst we have been wasting time here, has calmly entered Temple Tower on the strength of the information that we thought only we possessed. Merciful Heavens!" he suddenly added in a low voice, "and the girl is there, too."

The car roared on, whilst I cursed myself bitterly and savagely. Why had the point not struck me? I had accepted the Inspector's remark about a press photographer without thought. It had seemed quite a probable explanation, and I hadn't bothered to look any further. And now, with a sick feeling of fear, I realised the result. *Le Bossu* was loose in Temple Tower, and Pat Verney was alone and unprotected in the house. Just as Hugh has said, he had assumed we should come to Matthews' aid, and had turned that assumption to good account. Probably we had actually passed him on the road as we came, in one of the cars we had met.

"Lord! Peter," said Hugh, as I expressed my opinion of myself, "this is no time for regrets. And it wouldn't matter a tinker's curse, old man, but for the girl. But it is the one point that has been worrying me ever since *le Bossu* presented us with the plan. How was he going to find the tree without our assistance? And since it seemed an impossibility to me, I assumed he was proposing to invoke our assistance. On that assumption I mapped out his plan of campaign—a plan which I think I told you was one of subtlety."

"What was it?" I asked.

"All in good time, old boy," he said. "This is not the moment for discussing theories that have proved to be wrong. All that we have to concentrate on at the moment, is beating the gentleman. But I will say one thing: I agree with Matthews' description of him. He is a very clever and dangerous man. And I blame myself bitterly for having given way to an extremely stupid and foolish impulse."

But what that impulse was I had no time to ask, because at that moment we drew up outside Hugh's house.

"Bolsters," he said. "One apiece."

"What on earth do we want bolsters for?" cried John.

"Denny," shouted Hugh. "I want four big bolsters."

"Very good, sir," said Denny. "I will get them at once."

"If I asked for four elephants," said Hugh, "Denny would get them at once. My dear John," he remarked, "you don't suppose, do you, that our friend is going to leave the rope ladder in position on the wall? All nicely ready so that we can follow him in? He is going to get over himself, and then, with that wooden implement, remove the thing altogether, hiding it somewhere inside the wall. Moreover, he won't even go over in the same place as he went over before, so that we can dismiss the ladder as a method of entrance."

"Four bolsters, sir," said Denny at the door.

"Good," said Hugh. "Now some ropes. I want about four yards."

"Very good, sir," said Denny. "I will get it at once."

"We may not have a rope ladder," remarked Hugh, "but we'll get a damned good makeshift. Don't get fidgety, young fellah," he added to Freckles. "I know what you're thinking, but believe me these preparations are necessary. There ain't much good arriving at the wall and having to stand outside the whole night looking at it."

"I'm blaming myself over that aeroplane," said the youngster miserably. "It's I who ought to have spotted it much more than Darrell. Two or three times when I was standing by the tree I actually noticed the thing coming straight towards the house in a line with the tower. By God! if anything happens to Pat ..."

"Nothing is going to happen to Miss Verney," said Hugh quietly. "And here is Denny with the rope. Now then, a loop at one end, and we're ready. Except for one thing. Here are three whistles. Each of you take one of them, and keep them handy. And those whistles are only to be used for one purpose. If, in the darkness, *le Bossu* gets one of you, put it to your mouth and blow like hell."

"Are you going to take the car?" I asked, and he nodded.

"It will be wanted before the night is out," he said enigmatically. 'And this time we will take precautions over sparking-plugs. Now then—up and over."

And with a feeling strongly reminiscent of zero hour in France, in my chest at any rate, we followed him to the gate, carrying bolsters and the rope. But this trip there was no question of seventy miles an hour: we crept along at the car's most silent speed, with only our side-lights on. As I worked it out, *le Bossu* had about half an hour's start on us at the most, but half an hour was a terribly long time for that cold-blooded murderer to be given a free hand. And though I quite saw the necessity for silence, I chafed at the slow rate we were going.

A hundred yards from the beginning of the wall Hugh stopped. A grass track ran off the road, and he backed down it for about thirty yards till a jink in the hedge completely hid her from anyone passing. Then he padlocked both sides of the bonnet; took out the safety key, and we left her.

To make absolutely certain, we first of all searched under the bushes where the rope ladder had been left, but there was no sign of it. Hugh's forethought over the bolsters was justified. *Le Bossu*, guessing it would be somewhere near the spot at which we had previously entered, had found it and used it, and we wasted no further time. We passed up the bolsters one by one to Freckles, who was standing on Hugh's shoulders, and he wedged them in between the spikes. Then he fixed the rope, and in turn we swarmed up and down the other side. The final act had started.

The first thing to do was to locate the tree, and we crept silently forward. To keep in touch had been Hugh's order as we started, and he led us quickly through the undergrowth. Away to our right lay the house, sombre and forbidding. Two lights shone from it—one from a window at the very top, and the other from one about halfway up. At last we came to the old chapel wall, and he paused.

"Now then, Scott," he whispered, "you take the lead. And not a sound."

The tree stood, as Freckles had said, in a little clearing, and we found it without difficulty. But it was some little time before Hugh made the next move. He stood underneath it listening intently, though everything was silent, save for the faint creaking of the branches in the breeze. Once I thought I heard the crack of a twig not far off, but it was not repeated and I dismissed it as imagination. And once I could have sworn I saw a dark shadow move between two bushes a few yards away.

"For God's sake let's get on with it," muttered Freckles. "This is giving me the jumps."

"Shut up," said Hugh curtly. "Use your ears and not your mouth."

At last he seemed satisfied, and stepped out into the open. The Great Bear was easy to spot, and from it the Pole Star. Thirty long paces north—our next task—was simple, and there the answer lay.

The excitement of the thing was getting me now—what was the answer going to be? Should we find some hole open in the ground—some ancient rusted door, perhaps, through which *le Bossu* had already passed? Or should we find *le Bossu* himself still trying to force an entrance, and unable to do so single-handed?

Twenty-five: twenty-six long steps, and Hugh paused, again peering into the darkness ahead. I could hear my heart beating in the deathly stillness: even the night breeze had died away. But nothing stirred—nothing moved in front.

Twenty-eight: twenty-nine: thirty. We were there—but where was the answer? We were standing on an ordinary piece of roughish turf exactly the same as the ground we had walked over from the tree. But of any secret entrance to a passage there was no trace. In front of us were more bushes, but the actual spot where we were standing was in a little open space. And round that space we felt our way, exploring every inch of it. The result was nil: something had gone wrong. Wherever the answer lay, it wasn't there.

That the tree was the correct one Freckles was prepared to swear. That the directions had been thirty long paces north we were all prepared to swear. So it boiled down to the fact that the directions were wrong. But if they were wrong for *us*, they were also wrong for *le Bossu*. He was in the same boat as ourselves, and in that lay the only consolation.

The thing was so completely unexpected. All sorts of other difficulties we had been prepared for, but none of us had ever thought of the possibility of not finding the entrance at all. And the problem that immediately confronted us was what to do next. Somewhere within the grounds was the man we wanted; but how were we to get at him? Wait till dawn and hope for the best, or what? One thing seemed obvious: it was useless to try and look for him in the darkness. And that course being eliminated, it really seemed that there was nothing else to do but to sit tight and wait with what patience we could.

It was Hugh who was the most worried. Freckles, now that any danger to Miss Verney had gone, was quite happy: John and I were inclined to view the matter philosophically. But Hugh had worked himself into a condition of positive irritability, which was an unheard-of thing with him.

"I want that swab, Peter," he fumed, "as a cat wants milk. And what is he doing now? That is what I can't make up my mind about. Is he still here in the grounds, or has he done a bunk? Why should he stop on when he has once found out that the verse is wrong?"

"Well, my dear man," I said, "one thing is pretty obvious. If we can't find him inside the wall there is even less chance of our doing so outside. So it seems to me that we have either got to sit here and hope, or toddle back to bed."

And even as I spoke there came a most peculiar noise from the house. It sounded like the clanging of a gong, and we all sprang up and stared through the bushes. The noise went on for perhaps a quarter of a minute: then it ceased as abruptly as it had begun.

"A burglar alarm for a fiver," said Hugh. "Now, who has caused that to go off?" He was rubbing his hands together in his satisfaction. "He's inside, you fellows, he hasn't done a guy. And he is trying to get into the house. He has hit a trip wire or something of that sort. But where—damn it—where?"

Still we peered in front of us, trying impotently to see. Somewhere in that inky blackness was *le Bossu*, but he might as well have been in Timbuktu for our chances of catching him.

He can't get in through a window, anyway, "said Hugh, "short of using dynamite. If only that damned fool inside would realise that he is far safer if he lit every room in the house instead of cowering there practically in darkness. Keep your eyes skinned for the flash of a torch, or the faintest suspicion of a light."

But there was nothing: the darkness remained impenetrable, and the minutes dragged slowly on. Had *le Bossu*, alarmed by the sudden noise, given up, or was he still in front of us trying to break in? It was the uncertainty of it and the impossibility of doing anything to make sure that was so maddening. And yet we were better where we were than blundering round blindly. Suddenly Hugh gripped my arm.

"Peter," he said tensely, "look at the top room. There were three shadows there a moment ago."

I stared up at it: the light shone out undimmed. And then, there appeared for an instant the shadows of three people. Distorted into fantastic shapes, they showed up clear in the light—then they vanished again. Miss Verney and Granger—but whose was the third? Even as I asked myself the question it appeared again—grotesque and monstrous, with outstretched arms. *Le Bossu* was in the room.

"We must get in," cried Freckles in an agony. "We must. If necessary by the front door."

The boy was almost beside himself, and small blame to him. Until that moment the situation from his point of view had seemed all right: now everything was changed. If the third shadow was *le Bossu* the danger was enough to appal anyone, let alone the fiancé of the girl who was now facing him.

"Can't you fire through the window?" he muttered. "Drummond, you must do something."

"Steady, old boy," said Hugh, and though to the others his voice was quite normal, I caught the note of almost feverish anxiety in it. In fact, he told me afterwards that in the whole course of his life he had never felt so desperately afraid.

"I visualised the scene, Peter," he said to me a few days later, "as if I had been in the room myself. I could see Granger and the girl sitting there, believing themselves to be perfectly safe. And then the door slowly opening, and that great masked figure standing in silence watching them. Granger crazy mad with fear: the girl wondering desperately what to do, and where we were. She would play for time, of course, and provided Granger handed over the stuff, it was possible that *le Bossu* would spare her. That was all I cared about, naturally. Nothing else mattered. Even allowing *le Bossu* to escape altogether was infinitely better than that the slightest damage should come to her. But what to do? Peter, I damned nearly went bughouse. There was that poor devil jibbering beside us, and I knew that the most fatal thing we could do was to give away the fact that we were in the grounds."

"You see," he went on, "our only hope was to let *le Bossu* think he had the whole stage to himself. And the devil of it was that to all intents and purposes he had. He had got into the house, and we hadn't. And it was possible, I thought, that if he remained in ignorance of our presence he might not hurt the girl. Whereas, if we went and pealed on the front door bell, we gave the whole show away without doing any good. Up till then we had all of us thought that he, like ourselves, was outside. Now we knew he'd got in. How? Not by the door: not by a window. So how? It must have been by the passage.

"Gosh! Old boy, my brain was moving as the poor old thing had never creaked before. Passage, passage, passage—the word positively hammered at it. *Le Bossu* had found the entrance: we hadn't. Why? We had followed out the instructions to the letter: the same instructions that he had followed out before us. But we couldn't have done, or we should have found the entrance ourselves. What followed irresistibly? Why, that the instructions we had followed were not the same that had guided *le Bossu*. It was just about that stage of my brain storm," he added with a laugh, "that I bit young Freckles' head off, if you remember, for interrupting. Poor devil! He couldn't help it, I know, but I was absolutely keyed up. I felt I was on the right track, but what was the next step?

"If the instructions were not the same, *le Bossu* had deliberately altered them before passing the plan on to you. He had read them aright himself first: then he had cooked them for our benefit. And at that point I almost despaired. He might have written anything—the most complete rot and gibberish. Bad thing—despair, and the ray of hope came quick. Would he have dared to write rot? His object was to keep us in some safe place out of the way, while he walked in. If the verse he had invented was meaningless, it would not have produced that result. Besides, he knew that at any rate part of the verse was far from meaningless: it had led us straight to the tree. Therefore the alteration he had made was a small one—yet it was sufficient. And it was then that I made the remark that so astounded you: the solution had hit me like a kick in the stomach from a mule."

So, four days later, did Hugh fill in for my benefit the two minutes that followed the appearance of *le Bossu*'s shadow in the upper room. To us who were with him, they had seemed an eternity. He had stood there absolutely motionless, without speaking, save for one remark, when, as he said, he bit the youngster's head off. John was muttering to me that we must do something: Freckles was almost sobbing in his despair. And then, like a bolt from the blue, came Hugh's sudden remark.

"Sixty yards. Ample at night. That's it. Wait by the tree."

"What the devil are you talking about?" I cried, but he had vanished, and, a little dazedly, we walked towards the tree. I could hear him near at hand: with *le Bossu* inside the house the necessity for silence had gone. And suddenly he loomed up out of the darkness.

"I've found the entrance," he said quietly. "Our friend altered two letters in the verse before passing it on to us. S to N and U to R. Thirty long paces north took us exactly sixty long paces from the spot we wanted to find, which happens to be thirty long paces south of the tree. Come on."

At the time it had seemed to me the wildest piece of guesswork that had come right: an unworthy suspicion for which I afterwards abased myself. But the fact that it had come right was all that mattered, and a few seconds later we were standing in front of the entrance. Some bushes screened us from the house, and Hugh switched on his torch.

It consisted of a hole in the ground, from which mouldering stone steps went downwards. It had evidently been covered with boards and rubbish, because these had been removed and now lay in an untidy heap beside the edge. Rotting green fungus was growing on the sides of the steps and walls, and the spot reeked with the putrid smell of decay.

Earth was lying thick on the steps, and in the light of the torch footprints were plainly visible—footprints which went towards the house and did not return, grim proof that we were not mistaken over the shadow. Not many minutes previously *le Bossu* had passed along that passage, and with a curt warning to walk warily, Hugh led the way down the steps.

The air was dark and foetid, though the passage itself proved to be of a comfortable height to walk in. The floor was rough and uneven, and the walls consisted of crude blocks of stone, moss covered and crumbling in places.

For about twenty yards it ran in a straight line: then it jinked sharply to the left, and Hugh paused.

"Presumably," he said, "we are now under the chapel wall. And from this point the passage runs straight to the house. So we've got to carry on without a light."

He switched off his torch: undoubtedly he would have been a sitting shot for anyone lying up for us at the other end. But feeble though the glimmer had been in front, it had served its purpose: now that it was out, the darkness seemed the most intense thing I had ever known. It pressed on one till one felt it was tangible. Not one glimmer of even faint greyness, but a solid black wall closing in on one from all sides.

From my recollection of the position of the chapel wall, I estimated the distance to the house from the jink in the passage, to be about sixty yards. And I guessed that we had gone about thirty when suddenly the same noise began as we had heard in the grounds before. But this time it was much louder. It came from the house in front of us—the loud insistent clanging of a gong. I stopped instinctively: we must have run into the same alarm as *le Bossu*.

The others had halted also: I could hear John's quick breathing just in front of me. And what happened then, happened so quickly that it is hard to recall the exact sequence of events.

First there came a loud creaking noise from close by us—so loud that it quite drowned the clamour of the gong.

Then a sudden shout from Freckles—"My God! the walls are moving."

Then light—blessed light—from Hugh's torch.

Only one momentary glimpse did I get of the amazing scene before Hugh's roar of warning galvanised us all into activity.

"Back for your lives."

And just in time did we all get back. Another half second and Hugh, who was the last out, would have been caught. As Freckles had said, the walls were moving: they were closing together for a length of about ten yards in front of us. Like two gigantic millstones they approached each other until they met with a dull thud in the centre. The meaning of the line about the turning wheels was clear.

"An unpleasant death," said Hugh grimly, his torch fixed on the solid block of stone that now confronted us. "But the damned annoying thing is that we are on one side of the obstruction and *le Bossu* is on the other. He got through and we didn't. Back to the entrance: there is nothing more to be done here."

And there was nothing more to be done there either. Fifteen yards only did we go before we found that the walls had closed behind us also. We were shut in the space between them: caught like rats in a trap.

For a moment even Hugh gave way to despair and cursed wildly: then he pulled himself together.

"No good biting the bedclothes," he remarked. "Let's explore our quarters."

The exploration did not take long, and certainly did nothing to raise our spirits. There was no possible way out, until the mechanism should operate in the other direction. We could go neither forwards nor backwards. And the roof presented no hope either. It looked perfectly solid, and judging by the number of steps we had come down at the entrance there were at least four feet of earth on top of it. In fact the only ray of comfort lay in the fact that though the moving walls had completely blocked us in, there was a space between the top of them and the roof. Not large enough for one of us to crawl through, but sufficient to allow of the passage of air. There was no danger of our being suffocated. Also for the same reason our prison was not soundproof: we could shout and in due course somebody would be certain to hear us. But who? What was the good of shouting when the whole house was in the hands of *le Bossu*? He wasn't likely to let us out.

It was the thought of that that drove us nearly insane. At that very moment, whilst we stood there powerless to do anything, *le Bossu* was free to do what he liked in the stronghold itself. And Miss Verney was in his power. He had the whole night in front of him to find the stolen stuff, and then what would he do? Kill Granger for a certainty, but what about the girl? If he was the type who would kill one woman, he certainly wouldn't scruple about killing another if it served his purpose. And then, leaving us where we were, he would quietly depart having beaten us all along the line. True we did know who he was but that was very cold comfort. To devote the rest of one's life to the pursuit of Jean Picot was an inadequate return for what he had done to us, even if we ever caught him.

We didn't talk: there was nothing to say, just as there was nothing to be done. Just once Hugh put his hand on Freckles' shoulder and said "Buck up, old man: no need to despair yet." But for the rest we sat or stood in silence, each busy with his own thoughts. And after a while Hugh switched off the torch, which was beginning to run low, and black, overpowering darkness came down on us again.

Not a sound came from the house; each minute seemed like an hour as it dragged by. And at length I began to doze where I stood. Suddenly I felt Hugh's grip on my arm: a faint light was filtering over the top of the barrier between us and the house. I glanced at the luminous dial of my wrist watch; and it showed a quarter to one. For nearly two hours had we been imprisoned.

The light flickered a little, and then grew steady. Still there was no noise; only that faint illumination proved that someone was about on the other side. Then, without warning, there came the most ghastly sound I have ever listened to in my life—peal after peal of wild maniacal laughter. It rose and fell—echoing round us: then, abruptly, it ceased. And a moment or two later the light flickered again, and then went out. Darkness was on us once more: darkness and silence.

"My God!" stammered Freckles in a shaking voice, "what was that?"

My own forehead was wet with sweat, and even Hugh's iron nerve was a bit shaken. Regardless of his failing battery he had switched on his torch: even its feeble glow was welcome after that devilish laughter. Was it Granger, or was it *le Bossu*? Gone mad suddenly.... loose in the house.... And no one blamed the youngster when he suddenly hurled himself hysterically at the stone barrier and began to beat at it with his fists.

"Damn you," he screamed, "damn you—open."

And to our stupefied amazement it did. At the time—not knowing the reason—it seemed like a miracle: afterwards when we did know the reason, and the marvellous part played by that marvellous girl, it seemed no less of a miracle. But at the moment we could think of nothing save the fact that the prison door was opening. The wheels on which the walls moved creaked and groaned, until, with a thud, they came to rest in their proper place. The way to the house was free.

But not at once did Hugh move: the possibility of a trap was still there. It might have been the man whose frenzied laughter we had heard who had opened the walls. And if that was so he might be even now waiting for us out of sight, inside the house, to pot us one by one as we came out of the passage. At last he went with a rush, and from inside there came the single sharp clang of the gong. And with each of us as we dashed through the clang was repeated. But after that there was silence. No movement came from the walls: no movement came from the house. The man whose laughter we had heard was not there.

We were standing in a sort of stone basement, from which stairs led to the upper part of the house. Further delay was useless now: the time had come to meet *le Bossu* on equal terms. And so we raced up the stairs behind Hugh. A light was shining above us through an open door. And in the doorway he stopped abruptly.

"My God!" he muttered. "Look at that."

We crowded round him. It was the hall we were in, and the big chandelier in the centre was lit. Hanging from it, just as Vandali had hung from the beam in the Dolphin, was Granger. He was swinging to and fro, and as he moved the tips of his toes brushed against the carpet.

Suddenly there came footsteps on the stairs above us, and we swung round. Faltering they were, and unsteady: no man was making them. A figure in white appeared, clutching the banister: then, tottering and swaying, it came down towards us—a step at a time. It was Pat Verney, and with a great cry Freckles sprang to meet her.

But she hardly seemed to see him, as she stood staring at us with a look of frozen horror in her eyes. She just gave a little cry of: "Has he gone?" then, without another word, she pitched forward insensible.

Chapter 13

In Which the Account is Settled

And now, before I tell of the last grim fight between Hugh Drummond and *le Bossu*, I will go back a few hours, and write of what happened in Temple Tower while we lay prisoners in the passage. Not for three or four days did we hear it, and, bit by bit, we got it from Pat Verney. And because the horror of it was still on her, she got the horror of it across to us, so that I feel that I actually was present myself in that upstairs room where it happened. Wherefore I will write of it as if I had been a silent and invisible witness, and not as the teller of a secondhand tale.

At eight o'clock Pat Verney had dinner in her own room. It was served by Mrs. Gaspard, and to her dismay she discovered that the instant it was dark the servant proposed to go. Nothing, she said, would induce her to remain another night in the house, and so the girl found herself confronted with the prospect of being left alone in the house with a man who was to all intents and purposes demented with terror. For a while she hesitated: should she go too? She weighed it up in her mind, as she stood by the window staring over the grounds. Dusk was beginning to fall, and in her imagination she seemed to see phantom figures slinking through the undergrowth already. Then she took a pull at herself. Even if *le Bossu* did come, were there not five of us? And already she had discovered another of Granger's hiding places: afterwards she might discover more. She had agreed to go and sit in his room at the top of the house, after she had finished her meal, and with luck she might get him to talk.

Nine o'clock came, and she turned on her light. In half an hour or so she would go to Granger: until then she tried to concentrate on a book. From below there came no sound: Mrs. Gaspard had gone, and much as she disliked the woman it seemed as if the last link with the outside world had snapped. She and the Toad were left alone to face the unknown terrors of the night.

"Don't be an ass, Pat Verney," she told herself. "You and your unknown terrors! *Le Bossu* will probably get a thick ear, and with your share of the reward you will be in a position to tell Miss Mudge to go to blazes."

But try as she would she couldn't be altogether common sense about it. There was something in the incredible cold butchery of *le Bossu* that prevented anyone being normal about him. Supposing he did dodge us: supposing he came first—what then? Little did she think that she was actually going to get the answer to her question, poor kid.

At half-past nine she put down her book: even Granger's society seemed preferable to none at all. She opened her door; outside the house was in darkness. No lights were lit in the passage, and for a while she hesitated. No lights ever were lit in Temple Tower, but tonight she wondered whether she should turn them on. From all around her came those queer noises that occur in every house after the sun goes down, but each sudden crack of a board sounded to her like a footstep on the stairs. And at length she turned and fairly ran up to Granger's room, feeling every moment that hands might come out of the darkness and clutch her by the throat.

The Toad was seated at his desk, muttering to himself. He looked up as she entered, and it seemed to her that he looked lower and more debased than ever. Some trick of the light perhaps, or a leering expression of cunning that had for the moment replaced his chronic terror, may have caused it, but the fact remained that she very nearly returned to her room.

"Sit down. Miss Verney," he mumbled. "Sit down. Will he come tonight, do you think?"

"Will who come, Mr. Granger?" she asked.

"The other one," he said. "The one who is the devil himself."

His claw-like hands were moving like talons, and suddenly he burst into a cackle of laughter.

"He has been once. I know: I know. But the police don't. He caught the Nightingale, and he caught Gaspard: with his hands—so."

Fascinated, she watched his hands curving as if a man's throat was inside them.

"The Strangler: the Silent Strangler," he went on. "That is what we called him in the old days. And other names, too. But *le Crapeau* was his match: *le Crapeau* beat him."

She said nothing: not by the tremor of an eyelid did she give away the fact that she knew the whole story. To let him talk was her object, in the hope that he might give away the secret of his various hiding-places. And it never seemed to occur to him that to anyone who knew nothing of the story what he was saying must have appeared absolutely gibberish.

"By the old mill near Bonneval the Toad hid the stuff. Deep down under boards and sacks. He feared the police: but he feared the other one more. For to offend the other one—to play him false—meant death. Till then, no one who had done so had ever lived: but *le Crapeau* did, for he could not find *le Crapeau*."

"How do you know all this, Mr. Granger?" she said quietly.

But he didn't seem to see the relevance of the question: apparently it didn't strike him that he had given himself away utterly and completely. And after a while, as he went on chuckling and talking more to himself than to her, she began to realise that the man's brain had partially gone. Sudden flashes of suspicion pulled him up periodically in his rambling story, but only for a moment. Then he was off again in full spate, as she put it.

"Beaten them all," he kept on repeating. "*Le Crapeau* beat them all. He was clever, was the old one. And now he will beat them again. The Nightingale"—he shook with hideous, silent laughter—"the Nightingale. The Strangler got him, but he won't get the Toad. The Toad is too clever for him."

"What does the Strangler look like?" she asked.

But he took no notice of the question, hardly seemed to hear it, in fact. On and on he rambled, incoherently mixing up the past and the present, until she gave up any attempt at listening. And after a while a sense of unreality stole over her: she felt the whole thing must be a dream. This crazy man gibbering and muttering: the bright lit room, with its barred window making a black patch against the night, was a figment of imagination. And even as her eyes began to close, a sudden deafening clamour filled the room.

In a second she was wide awake. The noise was coming from a gong fastened to one of the walls. It was evidently worked by electricity, and for a time she stared at it in bewilderment. What had suddenly started it ringing? Then she looked at Granger, and it took all her strength of mind to bite back a scream. For the man's face was that of a devil. His lips were drawn back in a snarl, showing his yellow, discoloured teeth, and he was half standing, half crouching by his desk, with his eyes fixed on the gong. Then suddenly, with a grunt that was animal-like in its ferocity, he hurled himself across the room and forced home a big electric switch.

Almost immediately the gong ceased, and in its place she heard another noise, this time coming from down below. Then that ceased also and there was silence, save for Granger's wild laughter. He was dancing round the room like a madman, yelling and shouting, but after a while he calmed down a little.

"Beaten him: the old one has beaten him," he mouthed. "The wheels have turned: the Strangler is caught."

And now terror got hold of her: what did he mean? In a flash the line of the verse came back to her: *The sound of turning wheels—beware* But what was she to do? Something had happened below in the secret passage: something which filled Granger with such delight that he was almost off his head. Something, moreover, which made him think he was absolutely safe.

She forced herself to be calm. She must act, and act quickly. Granger believed that the Strangler was caught below: to her it seemed certain that it was us. And so she did the one fatal thing. Believing us to be in some deadly peril, she argued that if it had been caused by putting in the switch, it would be removed by taking it out. And so, utterly regardless of the crazy madman, she dashed to the wall and pulled it out.

For a moment or two he did not seem to realise what she had done then, with a scream of bestial fury, he hurled himself at her. Desperately she clung to the handle of the switch, whilst from below came the creaking, grinding noise once again. What had shut was now opening let her but hold it a little longer and we should be safe. Thus she argued whilst Granger clawed at her throat, mouthing foul abuse at her. Then there came one sharp clang of the gong above their heads, and silence from below. She had succeeded: we were free. Her hands relaxed weakly from the handle: she sank, half fainting, on the ground.

Standing over her, with murder in his eyes, was Granger. So great was his fury that he seemed to have forgotten the Strangler, forgotten everything save his animal fury with her. His hands shot out once more and gripped her throat—gripped it till there came a roaring in her ears. He was murdering her: would we never come? And even as she had given up hope, a shadow fell on them both, and over Granger shoulder she saw a great masked figure. *Le Bossu Masque* had arrived

"*Crapeau: Crapeau.*"

Like a whiplash, the words cut through the room, and the grip relaxed from her throat. For a moment or two the relief was so great that she could think of nothing else: then she scrambled to her feet with a feeling of sick despair. We had not come: *le Bossu* had. Opening the switch had been the worst thing she could have done.

"So, *Crapeau*, we meet again. What have you to say?"

Granger, his hands plucking feverishly at his collar, was cowering in a corner, whilst *le Bossu* stood motionless in the centre of the room.

"Doubtless a lot, *Crapeau*. But it will keep for a while. Just now I would like an explanation of that interesting mechanical device in the secret passage. Quickly, *Crapeau*: very quickly. I have an idea that before the night is out it may come in handy once again."

"Spare me," screamed Granger, dragging himself forward on his knees. "Spare me. I'll tell you everything."

"Speak!" hissed the other. "And at once."

"A stone in the floor," explained Granger in a shaking voice. "If you stand on it it rings that gong by electricity. Then that switch makes the walls close. It used to work differently, by some mechanism, but I had it altered."

"I see. So when you heard the gong ring, *Crapeau*, you knew that someone was standing on the stone. You knew that I had come for you, *Crapeau*. And so you put in the switch."

The Toad was grovelling at the other's feet in his terror.

"That is easy," continued *le Bossu*. "What is difficult is why you took it out again. Or was it the lady?"

"It was, you foul murderer," said the girl contemptuously, and *le Bossu* gave a little hissing chuckle.

"Considerate of you," he remarked. "Do you think the gong will ring again tonight or not?"

He stood there shaking with silent laughter, and she stared at him fascinated.

"Because, if it does, we know what to do," he continued, "to ensure that we shall not be interrupted. Your friends are a little foolish to pit their brains against mine. And now, *Crapeau*"—he turned once more to the cowering man—"come here."

Granger rose and slunk towards him like a beaten dog.

"To gratify my curiosity I am going to ask you a few questions, and then we will proceed to the business of the evening. Where did you hide yourself, *Crapeau*, so that even I couldn't find you?"

"In Switzerland," whined Granger.

"Switzerland!" said *le Bossu* thoughtfully. "That's where you bolted to, was it? However, it matters not. What you did in those far-off days is old and stale, and I grow weary of you. All these years you have slunk through the world, *Crapeau*, in fear of your life. Never knowing when *le Bossu Masque* would come: never knowing when his hands would steal round your throat. You hid yourself here: you barricaded yourself in thinking you would be safe. And now you see the result. Your precautions were useless: *le Bossu* has found you. The time of reckoning has come."

Clang went the gong again, and *le Bossu* turned to the girl.

"Quicker than I had expected," he murmured. "But this time the switch will remain in, young lady."

He forced it in, and, sick with apprehension she heard the gong cease abruptly and the creaking noise come from below. Then silence.

"A pretty little prison," purred *le Bossu*, "where your friends will remain until I have finished. And perhaps longer than that. It all depends—on you. Should you attempt to open the switch"—his fingers touched her throat, and she shrank back in horror—"I should have to take steps to prevent you succeeding. And then they might have to stop there for days, or even weeks. So remember. Go and sit on the other side of the room."

She stumbled over blindly: there was something immeasurably more terrifying in that soft hissing voice even than there had been in the animal fury of Granger,

"Now, *Crapeau*, to business. What have you sold in these past years? Give an account of your stewardship."

"Only enough to live on, and to buy this house," pleaded Granger. "By the blood of the Virgin, I speak the truth. The rest is all here: take it."

"I shall take exactly what I want," said *le Bossu*. "I trust for your sake that you have not sold the emeralds."

"They are here," cried Granger, fumbling with unsteady hands at the opening by the fireplace. "All of them."

Fascinated in spite of herself the girl watched *le Bossu* as he tossed them from hand to hand in lines of living green fire.

"The beauties," he whispered. "The beauties. Now, *Crapeau*—the rest. Put them on your table, and I will choose."

And then for the next hour the scene must surely have been as amazing as any ever thought of in the wildest fairy story. From different hiding-places all over the room came every conceivable form of treasure. Pearls, rubies, diamonds, exquisite miniatures, littered the desk, until the mind reeled at the value of what lay there. And all the time *le Bossu* sat motionless in his chair. Once only did he make a movement, and that was to pick up an exquisitely chased gold cup and turn it over in his hands.

"Divine work," he said thoughtfully. "A pity that it must remain."

Another hour passed in a sort of semi-stupor for her, while *le Bossu* made his choice. Each stone was carefully examined, and either returned to the table or placed carefully in one of the velvet bags he had taken from his pocket. No word was spoken, and once when Granger ventured some cringing remark he was bidden curtly to be silent. And for the second time that night the sense of unreality came over her. The great deformed figure at the desk, silent and absorbed: the fawning, obsequious Granger at his side, were just parts of some ghastly nightmare.

At length *le Bossu* rose: he had finished, and for a space he stood staring at Granger. His back was towards the girl, but in his eyes there must have been something which told the other the truth. For with a sudden frenzied cry he hurled himself on his knees and grovelled for mercy.

"Spare me," he screamed again and again. "I have given you all."

"*Crapeau*," came a terrible voice, "what was the penalty for disobeying me in the past?"

"Death," moaned the other.

"Is there any reason, *Crapeau*," went on the voice, "why you should escape that penalty?"

And then *le Bossu* paused and swung round. For the girl had seized him by the arm, and was shouting at him hysterically.

"You're not going to murder him," she cried. "It's monstrous: it's...."

The words died away on her lips, and she gave a little moaning sob of terror, and cowered back. For his eyes seemed to be glowing with some strange light, a greenish-yellow light, which bored into her brain and numbed her. Then like a flash he turned again. There came a choking squeal: then silence save for a faint hissing noise. *Le Bossu* was strangling *le Crapeau* before her eyes.

He seemed to her like some monstrous spider, who had at last got the fly in its clutches. Her brain refused to act: she could only lean against the wall moaning pitifully. And suddenly it was all over. With a thud Granger fell on the floor: the strangler's work was done. For a moment she stared at the victim's face. Then, with a little sob of utter horror, she fainted.

When she came to herself the room was empty. And it was only the heap of rejected stuff which still lay on the table that told her it had been grim reality and not some ghastly dream. *Le Bossu* had been there, he had murdered Granger and had gone. But had he? For the moment he was not in the room, but at any instant he might return and complete his work by killing her.

Now was her chance to open the switch. Shakily she got to her feet, and it was when she was halfway across the room that the crazy maniacal laughter, which we had heard in the passage, pealed through the house. For a second or two she paused, clutching the table, wondering whether the murderous fiend was even now playing with her as a cat plays with a mouse. Then, as the laughter ceased, she took a little run forward and pulled out the switch. And so did she come stumbling down the stairs to us—a girl who had reached the breaking-point.

We lifted her on to the sofa, and then Hugh spoke. His voice was perfectly normal, and in all probability the others noticed nothing. But I knew at once that he was in a condition of cold, overmastering rage. It was rare with him, very rare: only twice before, I think, had I seen him in a similar condition. And it were safer for a man to sit on an open barrel of gunpowder with a lighted match in his hand, than to come to grips with Hugh Drummond in such a mood.

"Scott," he said quietly, "you and John will remain with Miss Verney. When she has recovered sufficiently take her back to my house. Come, Peter."

Without another word he strode to the front door and I followed. It was open: *le Bossu* had left that way. And the instant he was outside he dodged into the bushes: rage or no rage his judgment was not blinded. In absolute silence he made his way through the undergrowth, and at such a speed that I, used though I was to his uncanny power of movement at night, was hard put to it to keep up with him. Only once did he pause, and that was when there came from the distance the sudden roar of a motor engine. Then we reached the wall, and swarmed over.

"Leave those things," he said shortly. "There will be a good deal to tell the police before the night is through, and our method of entry will be one of them."

The Bentley was where we had left her, and started at once. No tampering this time, and a few minutes later we spun past Hugh's house.

"Where are we bound for?" I asked.

"The Marsh," he answered. "And the proof that four can be as good as six. But, my God! Peter, we've cut it fine this time."

Through Rye, and along the straight stretch to the fork, where he turned right-handed along the sea road. We were going to the same place as the first night when we had visited Spragge's Farm. And it was not until he was getting out of the car that he spoke again.

"If by any chance he does me in, Peter," he said gravely, "shoot him as you would shoot a mad dog."

So it was here that the final battle was to come. Somewhere in the sand dunes Drummond and *le Bossu Masque* were going to meet. How Hugh knew I didn't ask: he was in no mood for idle chatter. That he did know was enough for me: that he had known all along was obvious now. And even at that moment, keyed up though I was, I couldn't help realising the torment of mind he must have gone through when, as a prisoner in the passage, he thought his plan was going to fail through no fault of his own.

Side by side we crept over the sandy hummocks. He was taking a course almost parallel with the sea, but a little inshore. And after we had gone about four hundred yards, he put out his hand as a warning. Evidently we were near the spot. In front of us lay a dune higher than the average, and up this he wormed his way on his stomach. I followed him, and then, inch by inch, I raised my head to see what was on the other side. And in that instant I understood.

Below us was the motor-boat we had found on our visit to Spragge's Farm. It had been moved from its original position, and now it lay, its bows pointing to the open sea, in a little creek. We had cut in on *le Bossu*'s line of retreat.

"We may have to wait some time," whispered Hugh in my ear. "But that is better than being too late."

And then began an eerie vigil. The ceaseless roar of the sea: the harsh call of some night bird above our heads, were the only sounds. And after a while there came that faint lessening of the darkness over Dungeness that heralded the approach of dawn. I glanced at my watch, it marked a quarter to three.

Suddenly Hugh gripped my arm.

"He is coming," he whispered.

I had heard nothing myself, but of old I knew that Drummond at night was not as other men. And then, I, too, heard the noise of a stone being dislodged. It came from inland, and I peered in the direction of the sound.

"There he is," breathed Hugh. "We will play with him a little, Peter."

And now I could see his outline plainly. He was coming along the side of the dyke towards the motor-boat. Moreover, he did not seem to be taking any precautions about moving silently: evidently he had no suspicions whatever that we were there before him. He paused by the side of the boat, and I half expected Hugh to hurl himself down the dune on to him. But he made no movement, though in the very faint light I thought I detected a grim smile on his face.

Below us, quite unconscious of his danger, *le Bossu* went on with his preparations. He was stowing some things away in the stern of the boat, and every now and then he lifted his head and listened. The possibility of pursuit was clearly in his mind, and once he paused for nearly a minute. One could just see his movements against the jet-black mirror of water: one was near enough to hear the faint hissing whistle with which he worked, like a man grooming a horse.

At length he straightened up and stepped into the boat: he was going to take off the tarpaulin that covered the engine. I glanced at Hugh: it struck me that what he had said on the drive down was true now—he was cutting it fine. Once let *le Bossu* start the engine, there was every chance in the darkness of his being able to make the sea. At any rate, the only method of stopping him would be to fire more or less blindly at the boat. But still Hugh made no movement: like a piece of carved granite he lay there staring at the boat below.

Le Bossu folded the tarpaulin, and threw it into the bows. Then he got on to the bank once more, and the rattle of a chain told us he had cast off the painter. He was ready to go. For a moment or two he stood by the side of the boat, and clear above the noise of the waves we heard him laughing. Low and triumphant, and yet with the same ring of madness in it as that wild, frenzied peal he had given at Temple Tower. Then he got back into the boat, and again I glanced at Hugh. Surely he wasn't going to wait any longer.

Crank went the starting-handle: no result. Again he tried: nothing. His laughter had ceased; and he tried once more. The engine refused to fire. And now I felt Hugh shaking silently beside me—and a dim premonition of what had happened began to dawn on me—a premonition which was confirmed a moment or two later. *Le Bossu* had switched on his torch to examine the motor. All the four sparking plugs had been removed. The meaning of Hugh's cryptic utterance about four being the equivalent of six was clear.

Out went the light, and from below us came a flood of the most frightful blasphemy. His voice was hardly above a whisper, but every word carried to our ears. Then abruptly it ceased: *le Bossu* was thinking. That he still had no inkling of our presence was obvious: he still believed himself to be alone. But alone with a useless motorboat instead of alone and well out to sea. What was he to do? He must have realised that the object of the boat was known to us; and that being the case, that we should come to it the instant we got out of the secret passage. And he must have cursed himself for not having taken more precautions to prevent us doing so. As long as he had thought that the secret of the boat was his alone, it had not mattered when we escaped: now when he knew it wasn't, everything was altered.

One thing was clear: the idea of escaping in the boat must be abandoned, at any rate, for the present. Moreover, the sooner he was away from the boat, the better for him. Feverishly he began to unpack the things he had so carefully stowed away; every second was of importance. At any moment we might be on him: from triumph he had plunged to failure. And it was then I realised that Hugh was no longer beside me: like a shadow he had vanished into the darkness. The time for play was over: the final settlement was due. I hitched myself forward a few inches, and with my revolver ready I waited. How was it going to happen?

Suddenly from about ten yards away came Hugh's clear laugh, and with a hiss like an angry snake *le Bossu* straightened up. A few seconds later came the laugh again, but from quite a different spot, and *le Bossu* spun round. Then again and again came that laugh, each time from a fresh place. Dimly I could see *le Bossu*, crouching on the bank, his head jerking round quickly at each sound: playtime evidently was not yet over. The murderous devil was to have a taste of his own medicine before the end.

"Good-evening, *Bossu*," came Hugh's drawling voice. "Your sparking-plugs are in my pocket. It was kind of you to give me the idea. Won't you come and get them?"

A snarl was the only answer.

"Five people, *Bossu*, have you murdered on this little trip. To say nothing of an attempt to brain me with a chimney-pot. I dislike people who try to brain me with chimney-pots, *Bossu*. So what are we going to do about it?"

And once again there came a snarl that was half animal in ferocity.

"I can see you quite clearly, *Bossu*," mocked Hugh. "And you can't see me. Unfortunate, isn't it? Shall I put five perfectly good bullets into your carcase, one for each person you have murdered, or would you prefer to die another way?"

There came a sudden crack from below me, and a shot went droning harmlessly over the Marsh.

"Quite the wrong direction, my friend," said Hugh easily. "Don't, I beg of you, add a harmless cow to your bag. And you haven't answered my question. Which way would you prefer to die, *Bossu*? Because you are going to—very shortly. You won't say? Then I have a suggestion to make. You shall die as you have lived—by strangling. Does that appeal to your sense of humour?"

Silence from below, and once again Hugh laughed.

"Putting on the robes of office, are you, *Bossu*? The false hump: the mask: the long black hood. I have been wondering off and on why you bothered with quite such an elaborate makeup. The mask I can understand: even the hump. But it was the hood that defeated me. Am I right in supposing that a fold of loose stuff like that round your neck, gives you a considerable advantage if your adversary tries to meet you at your own game and endeavours to strangle you? I can assure you that you needn't be afraid of giving away any of your parlour secrets: you will never need them again. You won't speak? Not very chatty tonight, are you, *Bossu*?"

It was growing lighter now, and I could plainly see the great black figure below me. He was staring around like a wild beast at bay, trying to locate Drummond, and in his right hand was an ugly-looking revolver. And knowing the nature of the brute I slipped my own gun a little further forward: it was not a moment for taking chances.

"It was clever of you to think of the aeroplane today," went on his invisible tormentor. "Indeed I don't mind admitting it was a stroke of genius. Very nearly—so very nearly—it enabled you to pull it off. In fact, *Bossu*, I quite agree with all that that dear fellow Victor Matthews said about you. But it doesn't alter my opinion that you are a nasty bit of work: so nasty, to be exact, that I grow weary of you. I would fain seek ale in my humble cottage. Throw your gun into the water, *Bossu*."

The drawling voice had ceased: the order came curt and stern. But the man below still glared savagely round him. Came a crack, and a stab of flame. Another crack from *le Bossu*, who had fired at the flash, and Hugh's mocking laugh.

"Through your hump that time, *Bossu*, and more peril to the cows from you. I am a very much better shot than you, so if you take my advice you won't go on playing at that game. I give you exactly five seconds to throw your gun into the water. The next time I fire it will be through your revolver hand."

For a moment or two *le Bossu* seemed to hesitate: then without a word he flung his revolver into the creek.

"Good!" said Hugh curtly. "Now, *Bossu*, put your hands above your head."

Again came a momentary hesitation, then his arms, grotesquely draped in the black hood, went above his head. And simultaneously

Hugh emerged from behind a sand dune twenty yards away. His gun was in his hand, and he walked slowly along the edge of the water till he reached *le Bossu*. And then for a space there was silence.

I watched fascinated: had ever day dawned on a more incredible scene? This monstrous masked devil—this murderer many times over, facing a man in whose face there was no glint of pity.

"Strictly speaking, *Bossu*, I suppose I should hand you over to the police," said Drummond quietly. "But we are not speaking strictly at the moment. And so I propose to give myself the extreme pleasure of anticipating the hangman. Do not imagine, *Bossu*, that I shall suffer in any way. I have here a witness in the shape of Mr. Darrell who will swear that you made a dastardly assault upon me, should any questions arise."

He paused: then he flung his revolver up to me.

"Right, strangler, I am ready. Do you begin, or shall I?"

And now, the necessity for concealment gone, I stood up. I was almost shaking with excitement, but neither man paid any attention to me. *Le Bossu* had dropped his arms, and was crouching a little. His body swayed slightly from side to side: his hands, with the fingers curved like steel hooks, were in front of him, stretched out towards Hugh. And suddenly, like a flash, he sprang.

Came a dull heavy thud, and a short laugh from Drummond, as *le Bossu* crashed on his back. Hugh's fist, with fourteen stone behind it, had caught him on the point of the jaw.

"Fight on, strangler," said Hugh quietly. "Fight on. There is no time limit to this round."

And then to my amazement he stepped back a pace. He was staring at *le Bossu* fixedly with an expression on his face I couldn't fathom.

"By God! Peter," he cried, "his eyes have gone green. The brute is not human."

But human or the reverse, the next instant he was fighting for his life. Snarling and panting, infuriated by the blow, *le Bossu*, for the next minute, gave Hugh all he wanted. Once he got his hands to Drummond's throat, only to have them torn away. He tried to wrap himself round Drummond: he fought like a maddened beast. And at one moment I, who knew his strength, began to feel uneasy.

But not for long: the strangler had met his match at last. Under the hood went Hugh's vicelike hands, and the snarling gave place to a hideous gurgling noise. Then that, too, ceased. And when Hugh finally relaxed his grip, it was into the boat, which he had planned to take him to safety, that *le Bossu Masque* fell dead.

"His eyes were green, Peter," Hugh said to me. He was rubbing his hands together thoughtfully. "A sort of greeny yellow."

He bent over the dead man, and ran his hands through his pockets.

"The loot," he said curtly. And then—"Greeny yellow. For a moment it shook me."

"Anyway," I remarked, "Jean Picot will strangle no more."

He stared at me thoughtfully.

"You'll blame me, Peter: you'll all of you blame me. I ought to have told you sooner. But I never thought it would be quite such touch and go as this."

He stepped into the boat, and ripped off the mask and hood from the dead man. And I gave an involuntary cry.

"You knew?" I almost shouted.

"All along," he said.

For the man who lay dead in the boat, his face still distorted in the snarl of death, was Victor Matthews.

CHAPTER 14

In Which the "Maid Of Orleans" Returns from Boulogne

"My dear people," remarked Drummond lazily, "you have every right to pelt me metaphorically with bad eggs. I abase myself: I grovel. I should have let you into the secret. My only excuse is that between you I thought you'd give it away to the swab: and in addition I believed I had the situation easily in hand."

We were all of us sprawling in easy chairs in his garden late that afternoon.

"How did you spot it?" demanded Freckles.

"I spotted it when he was telling us the tale," said Hugh. "All about the Chateau du Lac Noir, which, incidentally, I have taken the trouble to verify. It was all absolutely true. In fact, where Matthews' cleverness came in was that all the way through ninety per cent, of what he told us was the truth. But to go back to the moment when I spotted it. He reached out his left hand to pick up a glass of ale. In doing so his sleeve slipped back, and on his forearm were some most peculiar red marks. They were evidently caused recently, because in places the blood was showing purple under the skin. And I found myself wondering idly what could have caused them. I suppose suspicions like that come in a flash, and to start with it was only a suspicion. It struck me that they were exactly the sort of marks that would be caused by a dog savaging a man's arm that was protected by a sleeve. What does a fellow do, instinctively, if an animal flies at him? He flings up his left arm to protect his face, and uses his right for attack. I studied his sleeve. The cloth was not torn, but its condition was on the tired side. And from that moment I began to read everything that happened by the light of the supposition that Victor Matthews was *le Bossu Masque*. I was prepared to abandon it at any moment, but it was always present in my mind. The revolver shot through his coat, of course, was a very old trick. It might have been fired by someone else: equally well it might have been fired by himself as a blind. The first thing was to go through everything that had happened, and find out if there was any episode that ruled it out. And up to date there wasn't. The chimney-pot on my head: there was no reason why Matthews shouldn't have done it. You get the line I was going on? True, there was no proof that he had: but there was no proof that he hadn't. Therefore the chimney-pot didn't rule him out.

"Stealing John's plan. Once again there was nothing to prove that Matthews wasn't the culprit. He had plenty of time to go to Laidley Towers, steal the plan, and then be back at Spragge's Farm at the hour we saw him.

Then came number one difficulty—my sparking-plugs. True, there was time for him to have walked back to where the car was, after he had been caught by the light, whilst we were lying up. It didn't absolutely rule him out—but I didn't like it very much. And Jean Picot began to float into my mind. Where did he come in? It was him we had seen skulking by the warehouse when we started in the car. Was he in league with *le Bossu*? If so what about the Vandalis? At that time I had to leave a lot to chance, and all I had arrived at up to date was that nothing had happened which absolutely ruled him out.

"Then came the biggest poser of all. Why, in view of the fact that he had got well away from us, after the murder of Gaspard, had he deliberately delivered himself, so to speak, into our hands? Well, the answer to that, after a good deal of thought, struck me this way. We were a completely unexpected factor in his calculations. Four large men barging round for sport, were a complication he hadn't bargained for at all. He had failed to get into Temple Tower, through knowing nothing about the verse at the back of the plan. So he knew he would have to try again the following night. And he came to the instantaneous decision that if we were going to be there he would sooner have us as allies than enemies. That seemed to answer that.

"Then the Inspector arrived on the scene with the information about the Nightingale's murder. And I cast my optic on Matthews' face. There was no doubt about it: the news had upset him. He was annoyed. How did that fit in with my assumption?

"All right: at any rate, it didn't disprove it. When he murdered the Nightingale his idea was that he would be through with the whole thing that night, and since the Nightingale had served his purpose by supplying the ladder, he was a nuisance who might well be removed. If you remember, Matthews himself said all this afterwards, which was where his damned cleverness came in. It was true, and his momentary annoyance was due to the fact that, having failed to get in, the body had been found; as he said, it cut *le Bossu* short for time, meaning that it cut him himself short for time. Then along comes Miss Verney with the news about Gaspard, and he realises that both these murders, which wouldn't have mattered if he had succeeded the night before, are now going to complicate things badly. Police, reporters—the light of day on Temple Tower—altogether very awkward. How was he going to rectify it? I assure you I was as interested as he was.

Well, we know how he rectified it. The coldblooded, unscrupulous devil proceeds to murder both the Vandalis, and throws suspicion for all four murders on Vandali. Matthews was Mr. Thomas of the Dolphin. But it was there he nearly overstepped the mark. He had forgotten Jean Picot, a gentleman with whom I had a long talk yesterday afternoon.

"Jean Picot is another of these birds with a past, and Jean Picot has been serving two masters. He had been with the Vandalis as chauffeur for three years, and in his queer way was absolutely devoted to her. But as I say, he had a past, and Matthews knew that past. And so he had but little difficulty in persuading Picot to help him. And, as a matter of fact, it was Picot who actually removed the plugs from the car, acting under Matthews' orders.

"But when it came to the murder of the Vandalis, Picot stuck in his toes. He knew it was Matthews who had done it—or Thomas as he called him—but he couldn't prove it. And exactly what happened in that room we shall never know. As Mr. Thomas, Matthews had undoubtedly become acquainted with the Vandalis. And presumably he carried out that double murder in much the same method as he described it. Only he put it on Picot.

"A clever touch, that. In the first place it gave him a ready-made *Bossu* to plant on us: in the second, it would fit in with any possible attempt Picot might make to get even. In fact, I should imagine that our friend, as he sat in the dining room that evening, just before Picot's shooting practice, must have thought himself on velvet.

"He had removed four obstacles in his path, without any suspicion falling on him. The outside public thought the murderer was Vandali: we thought it was Picot. In addition to that he had all of us eating out of his hand. And at that time I thought, as I told you Peter, that his plan was one of subtlety. He had presented us with the map—incidentally, how any of you could ever have thought that was an accident I don't know. It was the one flaw in an otherwise brilliant scheme. However, he had to take a chance, and he took it.

We now know he made an alteration in the verse, but that does not affect what I believe his scheme to have been. It merely gave him an alternative line of action which, as events turned out, he availed himself of. And his scheme, I am convinced, was this. He intended to remain Victor Matthews with us to the end. With us he would have entered the grounds. No trace of *le Bossu*. With us he would have found the entrance: with us he would have forced his way into the house, and in the name of law and order compelled Granger to disgorge. And then, somehow or other, he would have given us the slip. That was his scheme, I am convinced, before I gave way to an extremely stupid impulse.

"You remember when Picot let drive through the window and Matthews turned out the lights. Well—I couldn't help it: I knew I was a fool at the time—but I just couldn't help it. The door opened slowly, didn't it?—largely because I pulled it. Then it shut, largely because I shut it. And Matthews screamed and gurgled, largely because I had my hands on his throat."

"You're the limit, Drummond," cried Freckles ecstatically.

"Far from it, young fellow," said Hugh gravely. "It was a damned silly thing to do, knowing what I did. From being absolutely confident that he had us fooled, he suddenly became suspicious. Was it Picot who had caught him by the throat, or was it not?

"However, the mischief was done, and I did my best to rectify it. I took the precaution of making him sleep in a room from which he could not get out without my knowledge, and I did my best to allay his doubts. But I know I didn't succeed. It was then he changed his plan, and took the alternative. It was then he decided to work alone to make use of what he knew was the right verse, and leave us to stew in the wrong one.

"But at once he was confronted with a difficulty. Miss Verney and Scott were going to find the tree, and under his first scheme of working with us that was good enough for him: working alone it wasn't. He had to find that tree for himself. And he thought of the aeroplane.

"Admittedly the man was a devil incarnate, but you can't deny it was a stroke of genius. Not only did it make him independent of us, but it had the secondary effect of lulling me into a fool's paradise. I did not see how he could get in without us. That he was going to have a dip at it that night I knew: I was lying up in the Marsh yesterday when he moved the motor-boat from its original position to where Peter and I found it."

"That's when you took the plugs?" I said, and he nodded.

"How was he going to get in?" he went on. "That was what seemed to me to be the essence of the whole thing. And all through yesterday I still believed that my original idea was right. Knowing nothing of the aeroplane or the change in the verse, it was impossible to allow for the alternative plan. Even when he gave his cry for help over the telephone, I still felt absolutely safe, though that little effort positively reeked of suspicion. Why an A. A. box, of all places, to ring up from? And by what possible fluke of fate could he expect us to believe *le Bossu* was waiting there for him? But once again, believing that we were indispensable to him, I saw no risk in going. In fact, to tell you the truth, so preposterous did it seem to me as a blind, that I half believed something had happened to him. That possibly he had persuaded Picot for some reason or other to go with him in the car, and that in the middle of a message to us, Picot had actually set on him. Anyway, we know he didn't, and Matthews got a start on us that, had it not been for Miss Verney, would have proved fatal. A very salutary thought, chaps: he got away with it as near as makes no odds, and but for her, he got away with it entirely.

"Anyway, that's that: only one little ceremony remains. From inquiries I made yesterday I gather that Count Vladimar still lives in the Rue Nitot in Paris. And since this property is his"—he held up the velvet bag—"I took the liberty of telling him that a charming lady, accompanied by a graceless young blighter, would wait upon him in due course to restore it, and to entertain him with an account of how it was recovered. He expressed himself as delighted, and confirmed the fact that the reward still stood. And so I have much pleasure in presenting Miss Verney with the bag of nuts, prior to consuming one or even two beakers of ale."

"But it is impossible, Captain Drummond," cried the girl, "We must share it."

"My dear soul," said Hugh, with a grin, "it's too hot to argue. Peter would only spend it in drink and riotous living, and my share would go in bailing him out. As for John, churchyards are full of Inspectors of Taxes who have died of shock on seeing his income tax cheque. They didn't know there was so much money in the world."

And so it ended—that strange affair which had started in an Apache revel nearly thirty years ago. Vengeance had come on the last two of that motor-bandit gang: vengeance had come on the mysterious being who had employed them. Whether his real name was Matthews no one will ever know. From inquiries we made, the fact emerged that there was a man of that name, whose description tallied with Matthews, employed in the Paris police round about 1900, and whose reputation was above reproach. And if they were the same it may well be that it was an extraordinary example of dual personality, a second case of Jekyll and Hyde. For without some such explanation it is well-nigh impossible to conceive how the suave, capable, courteous man we had known could turn on the sudden into a snarling brute-beast murderer.

****

The *Maid of Orleans* drew slowly into the side. Leaning over the rail was the usual row of cross Channel passengers calling out greetings to their friends on the quay. An odd Customs man or two drifted out of their respective offices: the R.A.C. representative raised entreating hands to High Heaven lest one of his charges should arrive without his *triptyque*. In fact, the usual scene on the arrival of the Boulogne boat, and mentioned only because you must end a story somewhere, and Folkestone Harbour is as good a locality as any.

Standing side by side on the quay were two men, waving their hands in that shame-faced manner which immediately descends on the male sex when it indulges in that fatuous pursuit. The targets of their innocent pastime were two women whose handkerchiefs fluttered in response from the upper deck. And since these two charming ladies have come into the matter again, it might be as well to dispose of them forthwith. They were, in short, the wives of the two men, arriving on their lawful occasions from Le Touquet, where they had played a little golf and lost some money in the casino. Which is really all that needs to be said about them, except, possibly, their first remark, chanted in unison, as the ship came to rest.

"Have you both been good while we've been away?"

"Of course," answered the two men, also in unison.

The Oriental Mind

The Oriental Mind

Hugh Drummond sat with a beer. Outside, a pea-soup fog drifted sluggishly against the club windows; inside, the most crashing bore in Europe was showing signs of vocal labour. It was therefore with feelings of considerable relief that, over the rim of his tankard, he saw Algy Longworth approaching. Anything was preferable to the bore, so he waved a large hand benignly.

'You may approach the presence, Algy,' he remarked. 'Do you feel as lousy as you look?'

'I thought I should probably find you drinking yourself to death in here,' said Algy. 'I will join you in a pink gin.'

Drummond beckoned to a passing waiter.

'And to what do we owe the pleasure of your visit?' he asked.

'Can you lunch today, old boy?'

'Who with and where?'

'Me and a wench.'

Drummond looked at him suspiciously.

'Where's the catch?' he demanded. 'If she's the goods you don't want me, and if she isn't I don't want her.'

Algy grinned.

'Not this outing, laddie. You just listen while I hand out all the dope that I know myself. Have you ever heard me mention Marjorie Porter?'

'Probably,' said Drummond resignedly. 'But don't let that deter you.'

'This morning I got a letter from her,' continued Algy. 'It was written from her home in Norfolk, and she asked me to give her lunch at the Berkeley today. She went on to say that it was urgent, and . . . wait a moment. I'll read you this bit.'

He produced a letter from his pocket.

'She says: "Haven't you got a friend who is very strong, and likes adventure? Do bring him too if you can. I really do want help."'

Algy replaced the letter, and finished his drink. 'There you are, my boy. Damsel in distress appealing for assistance. What about it?'

'So far,' said Drummond, 'you have our ear. But I'd like to get the form a bit better. Who is this Marjorie Porter?'

'A damned nice girl. Her father and mother both died when she was a kid, and since then she has lived with her uncle, one John Greston, at Macklebury Hall. He had a son, whom I never met and who died out East some months ago. There was something a bit odd, so I heard, over the matter, but I haven't seen Marjorie since then, so I really don't know the facts.'

'And this John Greston. Have you met him?'

'Once: years ago. He's a great big giant of a man, and he must be rising sixty.'

'So you've got no idea what's stung the girl?'

'Not an earthly. But I know her well enough to feel sure that she wouldn't have written what she did without good cause.'

'All right, old boy,' said Drummond. 'You can count me in. I'll be at the Berkeley at one.'

****

He was a bit late, and when he arrived Algy was already there talking to a very attractive girl. And having been duly introduced the three of them went in to lunch.

'It strikes me, my pet,' said Algy, after he had given his order, 'that you'd better begin all over again. All that Hugh knows is that you live with Uncle John in Norfolk.'

'It's really very sweet of you, Captain Drummond,' she said, 'to listen to the troubles of a complete stranger, but honestly I am most terribly worried.'

'Cough it up, Miss Porter,' said Drummond. 'If you only knew you're really doing a kindness to two great lazy brutes who are both bored stiff with life.'

'Did Algy tell you about my cousin? Uncle John's son.'

'I mentioned it,' said Algy. 'And incidentally, my dear, that was a thing I wanted to ask you. What happened?'

'What did you hear?' asked the girl.

'That he'd died somewhere out East.'

'He committed suicide, Algy,' she said quietly. 'And that was the beginning of all the trouble. Did you ever meet Jack?'

'I don't think I did.'

'He was an awfully nice creature, but terribly weak where women were concerned. He was the apple of Uncle John's eye—Aunt Mary died when he was about six, and I suppose that threw the two of them together. At any rate, they were inseparable until about a year ago, when Jack fell in love with a woman at least ten years older than himself. Which might not have been so bad if she'd been a decent sort.

'I only met her once, when he brought her down to Macklebury Hall; and what Jack saw in her was beyond my comprehension. She was a hard-bitten gold-digger of the most blatant description, and she didn't even take the trouble to be civil to him. She was good-looking in her way, and she certainly knew how to put on her clothes, but having said that you've said all. She ordered him about like a dog, but he just didn't seem to see it. He was completely infatuated.

'Uncle John, of course, was furious, and when Jack announced his intention of marrying her there was the most appalling row, which ended with Uncle John telling him straight out that if he did he'd cut him off. As you perhaps know, Algy, Uncle John is a very wealthy man, but the threat produced no effect at all on Jack. What was money compared to the woman he loved, etc.? So my uncle had a brainwave and wrote the same ultimatum to the dame. And you can take it from me that that acted quicker than a dose of dynamite. She dropped Jack like a hot potato, and left for a long trip to the East to soothe her outraged nerves.'

'How long ago was all this?' asked Algy.

'Eunice Radnor sailed just twelve months ago. Jack, despite all we could do to stop him, followed by the next boat. He was mad with his father for having written to her, and they had one row after another before he left. Which made it all the worse for Uncle John when he heard about the tragedy.

'At first the news was very skimpy; just a bald telegram announcing that Jack was dead. Then came a letter from the head of the police in Ceylon giving the details. It appeared that she had got off the boat at Colombo, and was living in an hotel there when Jack arrived a fortnight later. How he found out she was disembarking there we don't know: he may have wirelessed her boat or something. At any rate, he tracked her down and went to see her. And what happened at the interview we don't know either, of course.

'According to the hotel boys very high words were heard coming from the room, and one swore that he had heard two men's voices inside. But this she denied absolutely when questioned later. At any rate, Jack was seen to leave the hotel in a state of great agitation—the interview had taken place after dinner—and no one seems to have seen him alive again. Four days later his body was found at the foot of some cliffs a few miles from Colombo, and he had evidently been dead for some time.'

'Then he may have slipped over,' remarked Drummond.

'Just what I said to my uncle, Captain Drummond, to try and soften the blow. But I'm afraid he didn't believe it, any more than I did. What happened, I fear, is obvious. Jack tried to persuade her to change her mind, and when she wouldn't he just went out and took his own life.'

'I wonder if there *was* another man,' said Algy thoughtfully.

'More than likely, I should think,' remarked the girl. 'And several at that.'

'And it broke your uncle up?' said Drummond.

'Completely. He began to blame himself for the whole affair. Said that if he'd handled the matter differently Jack would still be alive, and all that sort of thing. And nothing that I said seemed to have the slightest effect. Then a month ago Hubert Manton suddenly appeared on the scene.'

****

'Hubert Manton is another cousin, but a distant one. And I don't think I've ever met anyone to whom I took such an instant dislike. Apparently he's been abroad all his life: in fact I, actually, had never heard of him. But Uncle John explained who he was, and raised no objections to the brute parking himself on us. He certainly raised no objections to doing so, and there he still is at Macklebury Hall. He brought a native servant with him, whom you suddenly come on unexpectedly round corners, and who terrifies the rest of the staff out of their senses. Personally, I think he is infinitely preferable to his master but that's neither here nor there. He is called Chang, and he was pathetically grateful to me the other day when I bound up a bad cut in his hand. You poor dears,' she added with an apologetic smile, 'must be wondering when I'm going to get to the point.'

'Not a bit,' cried Algy. 'Tell it your own way, my pet.'

'The first thing that happened took place two days after this Manton man arrived. I was wearing India rubber shoes, and so when I went into the library, I made no sound. And there, to my surprise, standing with his back to me, was Chang. He was holding a photograph in his hand, and studying it closely. It was a photograph of Jack.

'"Do you know that gentleman, Chang?" I said on the spur of the moment.

'He nearly dropped the frame, he was so startled: then he put it back on the table.

'"No, Missie," he said. "Chang not know gentleman."

'And at that moment Hubert Manton came in, so that he overheard Chang's reply. He said something in native dialect that I couldn't understand, and Chang slunk out of the room. Then he apologized to me for the servant being in the library at all and the matter passed off. In fact, it was such a trifling thing that I forgot all about it till a week later, when I was up for the day in London.

'I was walking along Piccadilly past the Ritz when the lights went red and the traffic stopped. And just as I got abreast of a taxi I happened to glance inside. There, to my utter amazement, I saw Hubert Manton and Eunice Radnor. They neither of them saw me, and I hurried past for fear they should. The last thing I wanted to do was to meet that woman again. But once I was out of sight I began to do some pretty hectic thinking.

'You see, Uncle John had told Hubert Manton about the tragedy, and the Radnor woman's name had been mentioned. Why, then, had he concealed the fact that he knew her? Was it because he thought it tactful not to let Uncle John know that she was back in England? Or was there some other reason? And if so, what could it possibly be?

'I puzzled and puzzled all the way back in the train, until suddenly a wild idea flashed into my mind. As I told you, I'd forgotten about Chang and the photograph: now the episode came back. Had Chang been lying when he said he didn't know Jack? For if that was the case, something very funny was in the air.'

She paused and lit a cigarette and the two men waited in silence.

'You see, Captain Drummond,' she continued, 'Chang has never been to England before this time, and the only occasion Jack ever went abroad, except to Switzerland, was the fatal trip to Ceylon. So that if Chang had recognized the photo, the only time he could have seen Jack was in Colombo. Further, Chang has been in Hubert Manton's service for years, and if Chang was in Colombo it was more than likely that his master was also. So could it be possible that Hubert Manton was lying when he said that he was in China at the time of Jack's death? Was his the other man's voice the boy thought he heard in the room? I tell you, Algy, my brain began to reel with all that it implied.

'I tried to reason myself out of it; to tell myself that I'd built up the whole thing on the supposition that Chang was lying. But all the time that other question came hammering back; why had Hubert Manton kept the fact that he knew Eunice Radnor a secret? I wondered if I should tell my uncle; drop out a remark casually at dinner that I'd seen them together in London. But some instinct warned me not to; if there was something going on, I could be of more use if I kept my knowledge to myself.

'And then began the other thing which is what finally made me write you, Algy. Even Simmonds, the butler, remarked on it to me. My uncle seems positively to dislike me near him, and what is even worse than that, he's very queer at times. I've found him muttering to himself, and he's developed a sort of strange nervous twitch in his left eye. He spends the whole of his time with Hubert Manton in his study. I've often heard them talking far into the night. And one day I tackled the Manton thing on the subject, because I think Uncle John ought to see a doctor. Would you believe it, he assured me he'd noticed nothing unusual. Why, a child could see that my uncle is not normal. So obvious is it, in fact, that for the past week I've locked my bedroom door each night. And two nights ago I was glad I'd done so.

'I'd fallen asleep when a sound woke me. The fire had died down, but there was still just enough light to see across the room. And the handle of the door was slowly turning. I watched it, fascinated, too terrified even to call out and ask who was there. Then, when whoever it was found the door locked, he gave it up and I heard footsteps going softly away down the passage. And the next morning, I wrote to you, Algy.'

And a deuced sensible thing to do, darling. What do you make of it, Hugh?'

Well, one thing sticks out a yard. Whether Miss Porter is right or wrong about Manton, something must be done about her uncle's condition. Can't you get the local pill to come and vet him?' he went on, turning to the girl. 'Ask him to lunch, so that it doesn't seem a professional visit.'

'I can try,' said the girl doubtfully. 'But I'm afraid it wouldn't do much good. All he could do would be to prescribe some medicine and Uncle John would immediately throw the bottle at his head. He loathes doctors.'

Drummond smiled.

'I see,' he remarked. 'Well, can't you go away for a time? Either your uncle's condition will improve, or he'll get so bad that he will *have* to be seen by a doctor.'

'I could do that, but I don't want to,' she said, 'I hate the thought of leaving him alone with Hubert Manton.'

'Then what do you suggest yourself, Miss Porter?'

'I was wondering, though I know it's a terrible lot to ask, if you and Algy could possibly come down and tell me what you think yourselves. You're men of the world, and you'd know far better than I whether I'm talking rot or what you think I'd better do.'

'My dear soul,' said Drummond, 'I'd be only too delighted to come down, and so I'm sure would Algy. But it's not quite so easy as that. What possible excuse have we got for suddenly appearing on the scene? I'm a complete stranger, and I gather Algy hardly knows your uncle at all.'

'I realized that difficulty, Captain Drummond, and I've thought of a way round it. Couldn't you stage a breakdown near the gate, and then walk up to the house to ask if you can use the telephone? I'll be in the hall and recognize Algy. Then if you time it for about a quarter to eight the least I can do is to ask you to stay to dinner. I know it's an awful sweat, and I'm positively ashamed at asking you to do it, but it would be such a comfort to me to have your opinion.'

'Don't you worry about that end of it, Miss Porter,' said Drummond. 'It's no sweat or bother at all. I was just wondering if we could improve on your scheme, and I don't think we can. It's simple and direct, and what could be fairer than that? Now, when do you go back?'

'This afternoon by the three-fifteen.'

'Then, since there is no good delaying, we'd better do it this evening. OK with you, Algy?'

'OK by me.'

'Then at a quarter to eight, Miss Porter, you can expect to see us on the doorstep with our tongues hanging out.'

'A nice child,' he continued to Algy, after they had put her into a taxi, 'but for the life of me I don't quite see what we're going to do about it. Even if Uncle John gets the jitters at dinner and Manton eats peas with a knife, I don't see that we're much further on. However, if it eases her mind, it gives us a nice trip into the country. Away, hellhound—you offend me. And you may call for your Uncle Hugh at four o'clock.'

****

The plan worked without a hitch. At half-past seven a car might have been seen to stop a few yards away from the entrance to Macklebury Hall—a car from which the two occupants immediately emerged to delve under the bonnet. And five minutes later, well satisfied with their handiwork, they turned into a long drive which led through an avenue of trees up to the house. On one side they passed stabling sufficient for a dozen horses; on the other a lake, complete with swans, lay placid in the still evening air. A house reminiscent of the old spacious days: too often now, alas, a drug upon the market.

Their ring was answered by the butler, over whose shoulder they could see Marjorie Porter talking to a man.

'My compliments to your master,' began Drummond gravely, 'and would you ask him . . .'

'Algy!' cried the girl incredulously. 'What on earth are you doing here?'

'Good Lord! If it isn't Marjorie.' Algy waved delightedly. 'Look, darling: the bus has died on us outside the gate. Can we ring up the local tinker, and tell him the dread news? And by the same token, meet Captain Drummond. Miss Porter.'

'Of course you can ring up, Algy. Simmonds, show Mr Longworth the telephone. And you must both stop to dinner.'

'That's very nice of you, Miss Porter,' said Drummond. 'It seems lucky that we broke down where we did.'

'And where are you making for?' asked the man.

'Oh, I forgot,' cried the girl. 'Mr Manton: Captain Drummond.'

The two men bowed slightly.

'Hunstanton,' said Drummond. 'A few days' golf seemed indicated.'

He was conscious that Manton was studying him closely; he was also conscious that there was no necessity for him to return the compliment. For Manton was an almost perfect example of a type he knew well—the hard-bitten crowd who live by their wits. And some of them are charming, and some of them are not: but all of them want watching.

'All set,' cried Algy, coming back into the hall. 'The local gear crasher is sending up a minion. I hope Mr Greston is in good form, Marjorie.'

'Not too good, I'm afraid, Algy,' she answered, 'I was talking to Mr Manton about him just before you arrived. I'm very worried. I wish I could persuade him to see a doctor.'

'At the moment, my dear Marjorie,' said Manton, 'I'm afraid you can't. You know his views on doctors generally, and though I agree that he seems a little nervous and irritable this evening, it would only make him worse if you suggested it. I'll just go along and tell him we've got guests for dinner.'

'A little nervous and irritable!' cried the girl furiously as he left the hall. 'Captain Drummond, I don't believe he wants my uncle to see a doctor.'

'Was Mr Greston worse when you got back?' asked Drummond.

'Yes. At least, I think so. There's such a queer look in his eyes.'

'I wonder,' began Drummond thoughtfully, only to break off as he saw Manton returning.

'My uncle wants me to apologize for him,' he said as he joined them, 'but he thinks he will have his dinner in his study.'

'I do hope we're not being an infernal nuisance,' remarked Drummond to the girl.

'Not a bit,' she answered. 'Have you told Simmonds?' she asked Manton.

'I have. And now what does anybody say to a drink? Sherry? Gin and French? Will you fellows help yourselves?'

'I'd rather like to wash my hands, if I may,' said Drummond. 'Messing about with a car doesn't improve them.'

'Of course. How stupid of me not to have thought. I'll show you both the way.'

****

'What do you make of it, Algy?' remarked Drummond when Manton had left them. 'Can there be anything in the girl's idea that Manton doesn't want his uncle to see a doctor?'

'Ask me another, old boy. He certainly doesn't seem to want to see us.'

'Or Manton doesn't want him to.'

'But what's the motive, Hugh? What's the great idea?'

Drummond was whistling softly under his breath. 'I'd very much like a glimpse of Mr Greston,' he said at length.

'Short of gate-crashing the study, I don't see how you're going to get one,' remarked Algy as he dried his hands. 'Incidentally, what do you think of Manton?'

'I don't,' said Drummond. 'But I'm flummoxed the same as you, Algy. What's the great idea? If it is Manton who doesn't want the old man to see a doctor or to see us, what is his object? He can't be poisoning him: the Manton breed don't murder. Or are we both barking up the wrong tree, and making a mystery where no mystery exists? Don't forget that we're basing everything on what the girl has told us. And she, bless her heart, may be exaggerating without meaning to in the least.'

I don't think she is, Hugh,' said Algy decidedly. 'I believe that there is some funny stuff going on. But what or why, has mo guessing.'

'Then what are we going to do about it? We can't make any excuse for stopping on after dinner when the car is repaired. Moreover, I don't see that we're going to find out anything more if we do. We've already vetted Manton, and we're not going to see the uncle.'

'Let's wait and see,' said Algy. 'Something may happen. And in the meantime I require alcohol.'

They went back into the hall to find Manton alone.

'I fear,' he remarked as they joined him with their drinks, 'that my dear little cousin is worrying herself unnecessarily over her uncle. I suppose you know about the tragedy of his son?'

'Yes,' said Algy. 'Very sad, wasn't it?'

'Well, there is no doubt that since then he has been a little queer and moody. Like tonight, for instance. He just felt he didn't want to meet strangers. But it's no case for a doctor. In fact, with a man of my uncle's temperament, a doctor would only make matters worse.'

'Quite,' remarked Drummond. 'Over things like that I think that a man is generally the best judge. Algy was telling me about the son while we were washing. A terrible thing. What happened to the woman?'

'I don't know at all. She must, I gather, have been a pretty poor specimen.'

'I was told her name once,' said Algy.

'Yes, I heard it too,' remarked Manton, 'but it slips my memory Careful: here's my cousin.'

The girl was coming down the stairs, and the men made way for her by the fire.

'Would you get me a glass of sherry, please, Hubert?' she said.

'With pleasure,' he answered, crossing the hall.

And as he did so, like a flash, she handed Drummond a note, with an imperative sign for him to put it in his pocket. That she was upset about something he could see, but when Manton returned with the sherry, she was talking ordinary banalities about plays. And shortly after they went in to dinner, the note still unread.

He got his chance over the fish. Algy, who had seen the whole thing, had cornered Manton; and under cover of talking to the girl Hugh read the contents.

'My bedroom door has been tampered with. The key won't turn.'

Drummond's face was quite expressionless as he continued his dinner, though his brain was working at pressure. He realized at once that that simple little statement put everything on a very different oasis. Whatever he might have thought before, by no possibility could the girl be exaggerating over such a point as that. The matter had definitely assumed a very sinister aspect.

That Hubert Manton had been monkeying with the key for purposes the reverse of honourable he dismissed as unlikely. The gentleman was certainly not a fool, and if ever a cast iron certain raspberry was assured over tricks of that sort, the present case was it. No: he felt convinced that that was not the reason. So what was it?

The native servant—did he supply the clue? Possibly: possibly not. The uncle? Again possibly: possibly not. And the more he thought about it, the more clear did it become to him that there was only one method of solving the problem—to let the problem solve itself after suitable precautions had been taken. And to do that it was essential that no suspicions should be aroused.

The first difficulty was to get a word with the girl alone. The conversation had become general, but in any case he was too far away for her to attempt to say anything at the table. And it was not until the port had circulated that the problem was solved by the sudden appearance of Chang, who whispered something to his master.

'Excuse me,' said Manton, rising. 'My uncle wishes to see me about something.'

'May Allah be praised,' said Drummond as he left the room, 'listen: there's not a moment to be lost. Can we get into your room from outside, Miss Porter?'

'Yes. If Algy gets on your shoulders he can reach the balcony outside the window.'

'Good. When you go to bed, show a light so that we shall know the room. Get undressed and go to another room. Lock yourself in. Got that?'

'Yes.'

'Algy, you have a married sister at Hunstanton who knows Miss Porter well. Ask Miss Porter to go over and stay with her tomorrow for a few days to play golf. Do it in front of Manton. Your sister is not on the 'phone, so we can't fix it tonight. All set?'

'All set.'

'And you're to accept, Miss Porter.'

'Right.'

****

'That's simply grand,' said Algy as the door opened and Manton returned. 'Mary will love to see you again, my pet. Come over tomorrow and bring your mallets. We'll have some foursomes and you sto[p] as long as you like.'

'Going on a visit, Marjorie?' remarked Manton as he sat down.

'Mr Longworth is suggesting that I should go over and stay wit[h] his married sister whom I was at school with. I'd love to Algy.'

'If only the old girl was on the 'phone we could have fixed it fo[r] you to come with us tonight,' continued Algy. 'But as it is, we'd bette[r] make it tomorrow. You don't happen to know,' he went on, turning t[o] Manton, 'if they've brought the bus up?'

'It's outside the door. Magneto trouble, I gather.'

'Then I'd better go and pay the warrior,' said Algy.

'And we had better push on,' remarked Drummond, 'or Mary wi[ll] be wondering what's become of us. A thousand thanks, Miss Porte[r], for feeding us. And we'll be seeing you tomorrow. Goodbye, Mr Man[-] ton. I hope Mr Greston will be quite recovered by the morning.'

'What's the game, Hugh?' said Algy as they spun down the drive.

'The note that girl passed me said that her door had been inte[r-]fered with and she couldn't lock it,' answered Drummond. 'I don[t] like it, Algy. So there is only one thing to do. Take her place in h[er] bedroom tonight and see if anything happens. By letting it be thoug[ht] that she is leaving tomorrow, it may precipitate matters.'

'So she wasn't exaggerating,' said Algy thoughtfully. 'I suppose i[t] safe leaving her there now.'

'I can't think that anything is likely to occur until the staff h[as] gone to bed. Have you got any rope in the car? You have? Good. The[n] we'll park the bus somewhere and go back to the house. And whe[n] the time comes, you get on to the balcony first, fix the rope, and I'[ll] swarm up.'

They had not long to wait, and luckily the night was warm. Ju[st] after eleven had struck from a church in the distance a light we[nt] on in a room on the first floor and they saw the girl framed in th[e] window. Then she withdrew and they could see her shadow as sh[e] moved about.

'Give her ten minutes,' muttered Drummond, 'and then we'll get in[.]'

But ten minutes passed; fifteen; twenty, and the light still remain[ed] on, though no longer was there any sign of her shadow.

'She can't be taking all this time,' said Drummond uneasily. 'We'll ha[ve] to chance it, Algy. Can't help it if she's not in a rig to receive visitors.'

They crossed the lawn swiftly, and Drummond hoisted Algy on [to] his back. And a moment later Algy was astride the parapet outside t[he] window.

'All right,' he whispered. 'She's gone.'

He paid out the rope and Drummond joined him.

'Why the devil did she leave the light on?' he muttered. And then he gave a sudden gasp. 'My God! Look there.'

Sticking out from the other side of her bed were her legs. She was lying on the floor in her dressing-gown, and as they dropped on their knees beside her they each gave a sigh of relief. For she was not dead, but her breathing was heavy and stertorous. And on the table beside the bed stood a tumbler of milk, half drunk.

'Drugged,' said Drummond shortly. 'Which complicates matters a little. Not knowing the house, we can't put her in another room.'

'We'd better lift her on to the bed, anyway,' remarked Algy.

'I don't think so,' said Drummond. 'If anything is going to happen that's where they would expect her to be. We'll put her in that cupboard, and then we will await developments, which are bound to occur. They can't have doped her for nothing.'

The cupboard was amply big enough, and they made her as comfortable as they could with cushions. Then, switching off the light, they took up their positions in the corner between the cupboard and the wall. And only just in time. Hardly had they got there when the door opened and someone came cautiously in.

'Missie. Missie. Wake up. Wake up.'

'Chang,' breathed Drummond.

'Missie. Wake up.'

****

The beam of a torch flashed on the bed, and they heard a little gasp of astonishment. Then it travelled round the room, pausing for a moment on the chair where her clothes were thrown. Came a chuckle, and as silently as he had come Chang withdrew, though to their surprise he did not close the door.

'We're certainly in the front row of the stalls,' muttered Drummond. 'What on earth is that peculiar noise?'

From the passage outside there came sounds as of a sack being pulled along. They came to the door and into the room. Then they heard a heave, and the creaking of the bed as something heavy was put on it. Once again came a chuckle, and the door was softly shut. Chang had departed.

'This requires investigation,' whispered Drummond, taking his own torch out of his pocket. 'My sainted aunt!' he muttered as the light picked up the bed. 'Look at that.'

Lying there, in what appeared to be a drunken stupor, was Hubert Manton.

'This, my dear old Hugh,' remarked Algy at length, 'is beyond my form. Why should Chang deposit the unconscious body of his master on Marjorie Porter's bed?'

'I'm thinking that we shall know before the night is much older,' said Drummond gravely. 'Help me to put Manton on the floor. As I said, I don't think that bed is going to be a healthy place.'

They laid him down on the floor, so that the bed came between him and the door: then they again took up their position in the corner by the cupboard. The curtains were eddying in the faint breeze; save for that the house was silent. And then suddenly a board creaked in the passage outside.

'It's coming.'

Another creak, nearer this time; then the handle was softly turned and the door began to open. Suddenly it was flung wide, and something bounded into the room. They heard a terrific thud on the bed and Drummond switched on his torch. Confronting them was a huge gaunt man holding a crowbar in his hand. His eyes were wild and staring, his face was twitching. And after blinking at the light for a second or two he twirled the crowbar round his head as if it was a walking stick and hit at the torch furiously.

Drummond side-stepped coolly; all the instincts that go to make the perfect fighting machine were alert. And there was need for them to be an immensely powerful madman is not a pleasant customer to handle.

The maniac lunged again at the darkness behind the torch, and Drummond saw his chance.

'Light, Algy,' he said quietly, and dived straight at the big man's knees, bringing him down with a crash just as Algy switched on. The crowbar flew across the floor, but the madman was not finished. He scrambled to his feet and rushed at Drummond, but at that game there could only be one result. A straight left caught him on the point of the jaw and he went down as if he had been pole-axed.

'And this is the poor devil whom Manton described as being a little nervous and irritable,' said Drummond grimly. 'Just lash his legs Algy, with our bit of rope: I'm taking no chances with that gentleman. And then we'll get on with it. It seems to me that much remains to be elucidated over this night's work.'

'And it seems to me,' remarked Algy, 'that Chang is the man to do the elucidation. What's the game, you black devil?'

****

The native was standing in the doorway staring in amazement at the bound man. Then he glided round the bed and saw Manton. And involuntarily Drummond took a step towards him. For as he looked at his master there came into his face an expression of such rage and hatred that he almost ceased to be human. But it vanished as quickly as it came, and when he turned to the two men he was once again the impassive oriental.

'Did you drug Miss Porter, Chang?' said Drummond sternly.

'No, master. Him drug Missie.' He pointed at Manton.

'And who drugged him?'

'Chang. Chang know everything. Him want big man kill Missie, so him gave big man native drug and tell him lies about Missie. Him say Missie bad woman, and big man believe because of drug.'

'But why did he want big man to kill Missie?' asked Drummond incredulously.

'Big man hang: Missie dead. Him get money.'

'And even if they hadn't hanged him they'd have put him in Broadmoor,' said Drummond to Algy. 'Go on, Chang.'

'Him meet white lady Colombo. Him knew white man in picture downstairs.'

'So the girl was right,' said Drummond. 'Did him kill white man in Ceylon?'

'Chang not know that.'

'And why didn't you tell someone about all this sooner?'

'Chang hate him. Chang want him killed. Chang love Missie. Chang see Missie not hurt. When Chang found Missie not here, Chang thought Missie in other room.'

'Truly,' said Drummond, 'the mind of an oriental is tortuous. What happened to Uncle John doesn't appear to have come into the reckoning at all. Algy, find the telephone and ring up the police. If we don't get that swine Manton fifteen years for this I'll eat my hat. My only regret is that we didn't leave him on the bed.'

ALSO FROM LEONAUR
AVAILABLE IN SOFTCOVER OR HARDCOVER WITH DUST JACKET

THE EMPIRE OF THE AIR: 1 *by George Griffiths*—*The Angel of the Revolution*—a rich brew that calls to mind Verne's tales of futuristic wars while being original, visionary, exciting and technologically prescient.

THE EMPIRE OF THE AIR: 2 *by George Griffiths*—*Olga Romanoff or, The Syren of the Skies*—the sequel to *The Angel of the Revolution*—a future Earth in which nation states are given full self determination when the Aerians, the descendants of 'The Brotherhood of Freedom,' who have policed world peace for more than a century, decide they are mature enough to have outgrown war.

THE INTERPLANETARY ADVENTURES OF DR KINNEY *by Homer Eon Flint*—*The Lord of Death, The Queen of Life, The Devolutionist & The Emancipatrix*.

ARCOT, MOREY & WADE *by John W. Campbell, Jr.*—The Complete, Classic Space Opera Series—*The Black Star Passes, Islands of Space, Invaders from the Infinite*.

CHALLENGER & COMPANY *by Arthur Conan Doyle*—The Complete Adventures of Professor Challenger and His Intrepid Team-*The Lost World, The Poison Belt, The Land of Mists, The Disintegration Machine* and *When the World Screamed*.

GARRETT P. SERVISS' SCIENCE FICTION *by Garrett P. Serviss*—Three Interplanetary Adventures including the unauthorised sequel to H. G. Wells' *War of the Worlds-Edison's Conquest of Mars, A Columbus of Space, The Moon Metal*.

JUNK DAY *by Arthur Sellings*—". . . . his finest novel was his last, Junk Day, a post-holocaust tale set in the ruins of his native London and peopled with engrossing character types . . . . perhaps grimmer than his previous work but pointedly more energetic." *The Encyclopedia of Science Fiction*

KIPLING'S SCIENCE FICTION *by Rudyard Kipling*—Science Fiction & Fantasy stories by a Master Storyteller including 'As East As A,B,C' 'With The Night Mail'.

DARKNESS AND DAWN 1—THE VACANT WORLD *by George Allen England*—A Novel of a future New York.

DARKNESS AND DAWN 2—BEYOND THE GREAT OBLIVION *by George Allen England*—The last vestiges of humanity set out across America's devastated landscape in search of their dream.

DARKNESS AND DAWN 3—THE AFTER GLOW *by George Allen England*—Somewhere near the Great Lakes, 1000 years from now. Beneath our planet's surface tribes of near human albino warriors eke out an existence in a hostile environment.

AVAILABLE ONLINE AT www.leonaur.com
AND FROM ALL GOOD BOOK STORES

ALSO FROM LEONAUR
AVAILABLE IN SOFTCOVER OR HARDCOVER WITH DUST JACKET

THE FIRST BOOK OF AYESHA by H. Rider Haggard—Contains *She & Ayesha: the Return of She.*

THE SECOND BOOK OF AYESHA by H. Rider Haggard—Contains *She and Allan & Wisdom's Daughter.*

QUATERMAIN: THE COMPLETE ADVENTURES—1 by H. Rider Haggard—Contains *King Solomon's Mines & Allan Quatermain.*

QUATERMAIN: THE COMPLETE ADVENTURES—2 by H. Rider Haggard—Contains *Allan's Wife, Maiwa's Revenge & Marie.*

QUATERMAIN: THE COMPLETE ADVENTURES—3 by H. Rider Haggard—Contains *Child of Storm & Allan and the Holy Flower.*

QUATERMAIN: THE COMPLETE ADVENTURES—4 by H. Rider Haggard—Contains *Finished & The Ivory Child.*

QUATERMAIN: THE COMPLETE ADVENTURES—5 by H. Rider Haggard—Contains *The Ancient Allan & She and Allan.*

QUATERMAIN: THE COMPLETE ADVENTURES—6 by H. Rider Haggard—Contains *Heu-Heu or, the Monster & The Treasure of the Lake.*

QUATERMAIN: THE COMPLETE ADVENTURES—7 by H. Rider Haggard—Contains *Allan and the Ice Gods, Four Short Adventures & Nada the Lily.*

TROS OF SAMOTHRACE 1: WOLVES OF THE TIBER by Talbot Mundy—B.C.--an adventurer set during the Roman invasion of Britain.

TROS OF SAMOTHRACE 2: DRAGONS OF THE NORTH by Talbot Mundy—B.C.—Caesar plots, Britons war among themselves and the Vikings are coming.

TROS OF SAMOTHRACE 3: SERPENT OF THE WAVES by Talbot Mundy—B.C.--Caesar is poised to invade Britain—only a grand strategy can foil him!.

TROS OF SAMOTHRACE 4: CITY OF THE EAGLES by Talbot Mundy—B.C.—Rome—Tros treads in the streets of his sworn enemies!.

TROS OF SAMOTHRACE 5: CLEOPATRA by Talbot Mundy—Tros and the Roman Empire turn to the Egypt of the Pharaohs.

TROS OF SAMOTHRACE 6: THE PURPLE PIRATE by Talbot Mundy—The epic saga of the ancient world—Tros of Samothrace—draws to a conclusion in this sixth—and final—volume.

AVAILABLE ONLINE AT www.leonaur.com
AND FROM ALL GOOD BOOK STORES

ALSO FROM LEONAUR
AVAILABLE IN SOFTCOVER OR HARDCOVER WITH DUST JACKET

THE PRISONER OF ZENDA & ITS SEQUEL RUPERT OF HENTZAU by Anthony Hope—Two famous novels of high adventure in one volume.

THE GLADIATORS by G. J. Whyte Melville—A Classic Novel of Ancient Rome—Three Volumes in One Special Edition.

THE COMPLETE CAPTAIN DANGEROUS by George Augustus Sala—The Adventures of a Soldier, Sailor, Merchant, Spy, Slave and Bashaw of the Grand Turk

ORTHERIS, LEAROYD & MULVANEY by Rudyard Kipling—The Complete Soldiers Three stories.

SIR NIGEL & THE WHITE COMPANY by Arthur Conan Doyle—Two Classic Novels of the 100 Years' War.

THE ILLUSTRATED & COMPLETE BRIGADIER GERARD by Arthur Conan Doyle—All 18 Stories with the Original Strand Magazine Illustrations by Wollen and Paget.

THE OHIO RIVER TRILOGY 1: BETTY ZANE by Zane Grey—The land along the Ohio River is newly settled. Indomitable men and women—Col. Zane and his family, the McCollochs, Wetzel, the "Death Wind" Indian killer, among them—have hewn a life out of the frontier wilderness.

THE OHIO RIVER TRILOGY 2: THE SPIRIT OF THE BORDER by Zane Grey—Fort Henry still stands as a bastion for the settlers on the frontier along the Ohio River. More pioneers are now moving west to carve new lives out of the wilderness.

THE OHIO RIVER TRILOGY 3: THE LAST TRAIL by Zane Grey—This final volume of Zane Grey's Ohio River Trilogy is a gripping finale to a great series—another thrilling story of life and death on the early American frontier and a classic in the tradition of Drums Along the Mohawk.

THE NAPOLEONIC NOVELS: VOLUME 1 by Erckmann-Chatrian—This book comprises two linked novels—*The Conscript & Waterloo*—about the adventures of a young conscript in the French Army. during the Napoleonic wars.

THE NAPOLEONIC NOVELS: VOLUME 2 by Erckmann-Chatrian—*The Blockade of Phalsburg & The Invasion of France in 1814*—the events portrayed in these two novels of the Napoleonic period properly fit in time between those of the first volume. They appear together here since each—unlike the other two in this series—is a stand alone work.

AVAILABLE ONLINE AT **www.leonaur.com**
AND FROM ALL GOOD BOOK STORES

ALSO FROM LEONAUR
AVAILABLE IN SOFTCOVER OR HARDCOVER WITH DUST JACKET

THE LONG PATROL *by George Berrie*—A Novel of Light Horsemen from Gallipoli to the Palestine campaign of the First World War.

NAPOLEONIC WAR STORIES *by Arthur Quiller-Couch*—Tales of soldiers, spies, battles & sieges from the Peninsular & Waterloo campaingns.

THE FIRST DETECTIVE *by Edgar Allan Poe*—The Complete Auguste Dupin Stories—The Murders in the Rue Morgue, The Mystery of Marie Rogêt & The Purloined Letter.

THE COMPLETE DR NIKOLA—MAN OF MYSTERY: 1 *by Guy Boothby*—*A Bid for Fortune* & *Dr Nikola Returns*—Guy Boothby's Dr. Nikola adventures continue to fascinate readers and enthusiasts of crime and mystery fiction because—in the manner of Raffles, the gentleman cracksman—here is character far removed from the uncompromising goodness of Holmes and Watson or the uncompromising evil of Professor Moriarty.

THE COMPLETE DR NIKOLA—MAN OF MYSTERY: 2 *by Guy Boothby*—*The Lust of Hate, Dr Nikola's Experiment* & *Farewell, Nikola*—Guy Boothby's Dr. Nikola adventures continue to fascinate readers and enthusiasts of crime and mystery fiction because—in the manner of Raffles, the gentleman cracksman—here is character far removed from the uncompromising goodness of Holmes and Watson or the uncompromising evil of Professor Moriarty.

THE CASEBOOKS OF MR J. G. REEDER: BOOK 1 *by Edgar Wallace*—*Room 13, The Mind of Mr J. G. Reeder* and *Terror Keep*—Edgar Wallace's sleuth—whose territory is the London of the 1920s—is an unlikely figure, more bank clerk than detective in appearance, ever wearing his square topped bowler, frock coat, cravat and muffler, Mr Reeder is usually inseparable from his umbrella.

THE CASEBOOKS OF MR J. G. REEDER: BOOK 2 *by Edgar Wallace*—*Red Aces, Mr J. G. Reeder Returns, The Guv'nor* and *The Man Who Passed*—Edgar Wallace's sleuth—whose territory is the London of the 1920s—is an unlikely figure, more bank clerk than detective in appearance, ever wearing his square topped bowler, frock coat, cravat and muffler, Mr Reeder is usually inseparable from his umbrella.

THE COMPLETE FOUR JUST MEN: VOLUME 1 *by Edgar Wallace*—*The Four Just Men, The Council of Justice* & *The Just Men of Cordova*—disillusioned with a world where the wicked and the abusers of power perpetually go unpunished, the Just Men set about to rectify matters according to their own standards, and retribution is dispensed on swift and deadly wings.

AVAILABLE ONLINE AT www.leonaur.com
AND FROM ALL GOOD BOOK STORES

ALSO FROM LEONAUR
AVAILABLE IN SOFTCOVER OR HARDCOVER WITH DUST JACKET

THE COMPLETE FOUR JUST MEN: VOLUME 2 *by Edgar Wallace*—*T. Law of the Four Just Men & The Three Just Men*—disillusioned with a world where th wicked and the abusers of power perpetually go unpunished, the Just Men set abou to rectify matters according to their own standards, and retribution is dispensed c swift and deadly wings.

THE COMPLETE RAFFLES: 1 *by E. W. Hornung*—*The Amateur Cracksman The Black Mask*—By turns urbane gentleman about town and accomplished crickete life is just too ordinary for Raffles and that sets him on a series of adventures that hav long been treasured as a real antidote to the 'white knights' who are the usual hero of the crime fiction of this period.

THE COMPLETE RAFFLES: 2 *by E. W. Hornung*—*A Thief in the Night & N Justice Raffles*—By turns urbane gentleman about town and accomplished crickete life is just too ordinary for Raffles and that sets him on a series of adventures that hav long been treasured as a real antidote to the 'white knights' who are the usual hero of the crime fiction of this period.

THE COLLECTED SUPERNATURAL AND WEIRD FICTION OF WILKI COLLINS: VOLUME 1 *by Wilkie Collins*—Contains one novel 'The Haunte Hotel', one novella 'Mad Monkton', three novelettes 'Mr Percy and the Prophe 'The Biter Bit' and 'The Dead Alive' and eight short stories to chill the blood.

THE COLLECTED SUPERNATURAL AND WEIRD FICTION OF WILKI COLLINS: VOLUME 2 *by Wilkie Collins*—Contains one novel 'The Two Dest nies', three novellas 'The Frozen deep', 'Sister Rose' and 'The Yellow Mask' and tw short stories to chill the blood.

THE COLLECTED SUPERNATURAL AND WEIRD FICTION OF WILKI COLLINS: VOLUME 3 *by Wilkie Collins*—Contains one novel 'Dead Secret,' tw novelettes 'Mrs Zant and the Ghost' and 'The Nun's Story of Gabriel's Marriage' an five short stories to chill the blood.

FUNNY BONES *selected by Dorothy Scarborough*—An Anthology of Humor ous Ghost Stories.

MONTEZUMA'S CASTLE AND OTHER WEIRD TALES *by Charles B. Co ry*—Cory has written a superb collection of eighteen ghostly and weird stories t chill and thrill the avid enthusiast of supernatural fiction.

SUPERNATURAL BUCHAN *by John Buchan*—Stories of Ancient Spirits, Ur canny Places & Strange Creatures.

AVAILABLE ONLINE AT www.leonaur.com
AND FROM ALL GOOD BOOK STORES